It was late afternoon ⟨...⟩n. Emma gazed in awe a⟨...⟩at came up to the edge of the railway line. Everywhere looked grey and dirty. Even the air was filled with smoke that put a haze over the city.

Eventually, the train slowed and came to a steam-escaping halt. Doors swung open and, following Tessa, Emma stepped down to the platform. She was immediately caught up in a world of whistles, escaping steam, and people. Hundreds and hundreds of people; not only passengers from the many trains that stood in lines beneath the high-domed roof, but also a great many vendors. Women and men, boys and girls, selling everything from flowers to hot pies, each seeking to out-shout the others in advertising their particular wares.

Emma was overawed by the sheer volume of people about her, but at the same time she found it incredibly exhilarating.

'Well, this is it,' Tessa declared, amused by her companion's expression. 'You've arrived in London. Now, let's go and find ourselves a bus to take us home.'

Fires Of Evening

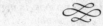

E. V. Thompson

WARNER BOOKS

A *Warner* Book

First published in Great Britain in 1998
by Little, Brown and Company

This edition published in 1999 by Warner Books

Copyright © E.V. Thompson 1998

The moral right of the author has been asserted.

A CIP catalogue record for this book
is available from the British Library.

ISBN 0 7515 2402 6

Typeset by Palimpsest Book Production Limited,
Polmont, Stirlingshire
Printed and bound in Great Britain by
Clays Ltd, St Ives plc

Warner Books
A Division of
Little, Brown and Company (UK)
Brettenham House
Lancaster Place
London WC2E 7EN

Fires Of Evening

BOOK ONE

BOOK ONE

1

'Jacob Pengelly! Do you mind explaining to me why you've brought me along this path? Don't tell me again that it's the quickest way to Josh Retallick's house, I just don't believe you!'

Emma Cotton grabbed the coat of the young man walking an arm's length ahead of her and pulled him around to face her. Hot cheeked and hands on hips, she straddled the narrow path and demanded an explanation.

To the left of them, dangerously close, the ground dropped away to the floor of a white-walled clay pit, hidden far below at the foot of a sheer, man-made cliff.

Ahead and behind the young couple, the path wound through a waist-high forest of tall, spindly ferns, interspersed here and there by islands of darker green needle-leafed gorse bushes.

'It's as quick a way as any.'

Jacob spoke without looking directly at her and Emma knew instinctively he was not telling the truth.

'. . . Anyway, how would you know whether or not it's the right way? You don't even know the way to the Gover valley. Without me you'd be hopelessly lost.'

'I may not know my way around here, but I'm not stupid,' retorted Emma. 'When we set off the sun was on our left. Now it's on our right. You're walking me around in a circle. Why?'

Jacob had the grace to look embarrassed, but he was not yet ready to explain his motives to this positive and precocious young woman.

Emma Cotton must have been about nineteen years of age and he was twenty, but she carried an air of being much more worldly than he, or any of the other girls he knew.

Actually, he knew very little about her apart from what she had told him on the way from the clay works office. She had arrived in the St Austell area only that day from a small and remote community on the edge of Cornwall's Bodmin Moor.

Her home was less than thirty miles from St Austell, yet for those who lived in either place they might have been on different planets.

'You fancy me, don't you? That's why you've brought me this way.' Emma's blunt assertion tore into his thoughts, but she had more to say. 'You've brought me this way because there's no one around and you hoped I'd let you do it to me. That is why we've come this way, isn't it?'

Jacob's mouth suddenly felt dry and he fought to control the panic he felt rising within him.

What she had just said was partly true. It had been no more than a very vague idea, put into his head by fellow clay workers. Jacob and his workmates had seen Emma arrive at the Ruddlemoor works office. They presumed, by the way she was dressed, she had come to apply for work as a bal maiden, trimming the blocks of dried clay to make them ready for shipping. It was a task that gave employment to many local girls. They greeted her with whistles and cat-calls.

When the captain of the clay works detailed Jacob to guide Emma to the home of Josh Retallick, his workmates had been forthcoming with advice about what he should do with her once they were out of sight among the clay waste tips.

Josh Retallick had once owned Ruddlemoor, but had passed it on to his grandson, Ben, about nine years before. An old man now, Josh lived with his wife Miriam in a house in the Gover valley.

Belatedly aware she was not to be employed as a bal maiden, they assumed she was going to the Gover valley to take up employment in the Retallick household. Probably as a house servant.

Suddenly, and startlingly, Emma spoke once again. 'All right then. Where shall we go to do it?'

Her words filled Jacob with dismay. Basically shy, he had little experience with girls. Finding himself in this unanticipated situation, he was forced to face the fact that this particular girl terrified him.

He wished Captain Bray had chosen someone else to guide her to the Gover valley – or that he had not allowed himself to be influenced by his workmates.

While Jacob had been changing out of the thick,

double-soled boots worn by the workers in the hot-floored clay 'dry', they had made much of the wonderful 'opportunity' that had so unexpectedly come his way.

Captain Bray had mentioned that the girl was from Bodmin Moor. As soon as the captain had left the clay dry, one of the men enviously declared that Jacob was being given 'the opportunity of a lifetime'.

Moorland girls, he informed Jacob knowingly, were totally devoid of morals. They would romp in the fern with anyone. He did not explain that the sole basis for such an observation was one of his distant cousins. A resident of Bodmin Moor, she had given birth to an illegitimate child some fifteen years before.

'What's the matter, Jacob? Has the climb up here sapped all your energy? What would your mates say if you went back and told them nothing had happened between us, after you'd brought me all the way up here? Or would you go back and lie to them? Tell them you had done it to me?'

Stung by her mockery, Jacob came close to panic. His plans had not extended beyond taking her to the Gover valley via a route where many of the young men and women from the clay works did their courting.

The route had been suggested by one of his workmates and had received enthusiastic and noisy endorsement from the others.

Jacob had thought that once it was established he had brought her along this particular path, he would not need to divulge what had – or had not – taken place. Indeed, it was possible his silence on the matter might actually add to his prestige.

He had not reckoned on finding himself in the company of a girl who was willing to take the lead in such a situation.

'Well, come on then. Do you want to or don't you?' Emma taunted him. She seemed to be enjoying his embarrassment. He could not make up his mind whether or not she was merely teasing him.

'I . . . I'd better take you to where you've got to go and get back to work.'

'You should have thought of how much of a hurry you were in before bringing me all the way up here. My legs ache. I'm going to sit down here for a while.' She promptly matched her words with the deed and sat down on the grass between the pit edge and the path.

Before Jacob could protest further, the air was rent by the strident sound of a klaxon. It came from somewhere deep in the pit alongside them.

The noise continued for perhaps twenty seconds. When it ended, Emma asked, 'What on earth was that?'

'It was the blasting warning!' There was urgency in Jacob's voice. 'It means they're going to set off explosives in the pit, down there.'

He pointed in the direction of the deep pit, the edge of which was only a few paces from where Emma was seated. 'We'd better get away – and quickly!'

Emma looked at him scornfully. 'You're making that up, Jacob. You just want to get me on my feet and moving again. Come on, admit it.'

Suddenly and unexpectedly, she smiled. 'Why did you bring me up here, Jacob, if it wasn't for what you thought you might be able to do to me? Did your mates put you up to it?'

'We don't have time to talk about that now. If they

begin blasting in the pit some of the rocks could be thrown high enough to reach us here. It's a dangerous place to be. Come on.'

'I still don't believe you – and you haven't heard the last of this. What was said about me, Jacob? What made you think it would be worth your while bringing me so far out of our way?'

Leaning back, resting her hands on the ground behind her, she said, 'And don't tell me this is the quickest way to the Retallicks' house. I really don't believe you.'

She began climbing to her feet. Suddenly, there was the sound of a violent explosion. It was so close it hurt Jacob's ear-drums and he felt the earth shudder beneath his feet.

A split second later the edge of the pit collapsed to within an arm's length of his feet. It happened without any warning. The ground simply fell away.

And Emma Cotton fell with it.

2

Jacob stumbled into the works office of the Cargloss Clay Works fighting to recover his breath. His face contorting in frustrated agony, he tried desperately hard to speak.

'The blast . . . Girl up top . . . Went over . . . edge.'

George Crow, captain of Cargloss, had been seated at a desk in the office. Making sense of Jacob's disjointed message, he leaped to his feet causing his chair to crash backwards to the floor.

'What do you mean, a girl's gone over the edge? What was she doing there in the first place? The warning was sounded. Didn't she hear it?'

'Yes, but . . . that doesn't matter. She went over the edge . . . she needs help.'

Jacob was still breathing heavily, but the words came more easily now. 'On my way in I saw the place where you were blasting. It's not sheer. It should be possible to scramble to the top . . .'

'Try that and you'll have the lot slip down and bury you and anyone who might be up there. The top of the face wasn't meant to come down. It must have been loose. The only way we might rescue anyone would be to lower a man from the top – and that'll be dangerous enough.'

A pasty-faced clerk seated at a desk had been listening to what was being said and Captain Crow turned to him now. 'Gather half a dozen men and send them up top to where the girl disappeared. They'll need to take a rope with them – but don't take all the men from one place. I'm here to keep the Cargloss works in profit, not to waste time searching for some damn-fool young woman who was somewhere she shouldn't have been.'

Rounding on Jacob once more, he asked, 'How was it you saw what happened? Where were you?'

'I'm from Ruddlemoor. I . . . I was sent to show the girl to Josh Retallick's house in the Gover valley.'

'You came round the edge of Cargloss to get there?' Captain Crow's eyebrows indicated his disbelief.

Much to Jacob's relief, he did not immediately pursue the matter. 'Go with my men. Show them exactly where the girl went over the edge. I'll go out to the pit and make certain nobody disturbs the fall from this side. If we start a slide it'll be a week before we find the girl's body and the men will be more interested in finding it than in producing clay.'

Captain Crow's callous words sent a chill of horror through Jacob. He had come to the clay works office to obtain help to rescue Emma. He had not considered the possibility that she might be dead.

He did so now with the knowledge that Captain Crow took it for granted they were seeking to recover Emma's body. He was forced to acknowledge the Cargloss captain might be proved correct.

The six Cargloss men sent to the scene of the accident seemed at first to be more optimistic than their captain. As they toiled up the steep path beside the pit they gave breathless examples of miraculous escapes by men employed in the clay works and tin mines in the area.

'Mind you, I've never heard of a woman surviving after such an accident,' said one of the men gloomily.

Despite his desperate concern for the fate of Emma, Jacob thought the positive young girl would have had her own ideas on such a prejudiced attitude.

It was with a sense of shock that he realised he too was now thinking of her in the past tense. He fervently hoped she was still alive. It was unthinkable that her life should be taken in such a way.

The hope sprang from a genuine concern for Emma. He was not optimistic that his punishment would be any more lenient in the event of her survival.

Jacob had already accepted that he would be punished. The route from Ruddlemoor to the Gover valley should not have taken Emma and him anywhere near the Cargloss clay pit. He would be called upon to explain his reason for taking her along the pit-edge path. Finding a plausible explanation was not going to be easy.

A sudden and alarming thought came to him. What if it was believed he had taken her along the remote path in order to attack her?

It was something suspected by Emma herself and there were bound to be rumours. Many would emanate from his own workmates, in the Ruddlemoor dry.

It might even be suggested he had attacked her, then

pushed her over the edge of the pit, taking advantage of the Cargloss blasting operation to cover up his crime!

'Are we nearly there?'

The question from the Cargloss man broke in upon Jacob's runaway thoughts. Looking about him, he replied, 'It's just beyond the next clump of gorse. You can see where the explosion took the ground away right up to the edge of the path.'

When they reached the spot, the youngest of the Cargloss men dropped to his stomach and eased his way to the broken rim of the pit.

He was almost close enough to look over the edge when a section of earth dropped away immediately ahead of him.

Wriggling back hastily, he exclaimed, 'That's dangerous! There seems to be an overhang just there. Anyone going over is likely to end up with a couple of tons of earth, rock and clay on top of him.'

'Perhaps one of us should go back down below to have a look,' another of the Cargloss men suggested.

Jacob looked from one speaker to the other in dismay. 'There's no time for that. If Emma's lying down there injured every minute might make the difference between life and death.'

'Half the pit face went down with her,' one of the men said callously. 'She's probably dead already. There's no sense in risking another life.'

'Then lower me down,' Jacob demanded. 'I'm not leaving here until we've found her – dead or alive.'

The men exchanged uncertain glances among themselves. Then the worker who carried the coil of rope shrugged it from his shoulder. 'If you want to risk your own neck we'll not argue with you. After all, you're the one who was with her when she fell.'

Something in the man's voice told Jacob that these men were as sceptical of the circumstances surrounding the accident as Captain Crow had been.

He realised it was no more than a foretaste of what he could expect from others.

Passing one end of the rope to Jacob, the Cargloss worker said, 'Here, tie the rope around you using your own knot. Once you're over the edge your life will depend on how good it is.'

3

Edging slowly backwards, Jacob moved closer to the rim of the great man-made chasm, each step covering less ground than the last as he neared the edge.

His legs were trembling so much it seemed they were entirely independent of the remainder of his body. Trying hard to control them, he took up the slack on the rope held tug-o'-war fashion by the six Cargloss workers.

He still had a short distance to travel when part of the ground gave way beneath him. One foot trod air and as the men holding the rope took the strain he fell to one knee.

Making a rapid decision, Jacob called, 'I'm going over the edge now. Make sure you keep a tight grip on that rope – and listen for my shout when I need you to hold fast.'

The nearest man's grunt could have meant anything. Gritting his teeth, Jacob leaned back until he was almost parallel with the ground. A moment later he was walking clumsily down the sheer, crumbling face of the clay pit.

'Hold it!' Jacob shouted the command a few moments later.

The rope tautened and his descent was brought to a halt. Now, for the first time, he looked down – and immediately wished he had not.

The floor of the clay pit appeared much farther away than he had imagined it would be. Diminished in size by distance, a group of Cargloss workers was gathered around the base of a great white pyramid of China clay and waste brought down by the explosion. The ragged peak of the pyramid, resting against the pit-face, was still some distance below him.

Jacob's stomach contracted in a sudden bout of fear. He quickly shifted his gaze from the men below him to the great pile of clay and waste sloping down from the wall of the pit.

He could see nothing of Emma. With a feeling that was close to despair, he called on the men holding the rope to begin lowering him once more.

As he approached the jumble of rock and clay, his attention was drawn to a darker patch among the white mass. He had looked at it before but had dismissed it as no more than a pocket of earth brought down from the top of the pit face.

It was, but as he drew nearer he saw something else. Even now, it took some moments for him to realise he was looking at Emma! Half covered with earth and clay, she lay in the shadow of a huge piece of rock.

'Lower me faster!'

Jacob needed to shout the command twice more before the speed of his descent increased to any extent.

'Stop!'

This time the order was obeyed more speedily. Jacob landed gently in the soft China clay dust and immediately sank ankle-deep beside Emma.

His arrival precipitated a frightening slip of earth and clay that poured down the surface of the pyramid. Reaching down hurriedly, he took a grip on her dress, fearing the whole mass of tumbled clay was about to fall, and Emma with it.

Emma showed no sign of life. Jacob's first thought was that his worst fears had been realised. Then, as he tried to pull her clear of the earth and clay that buried much of the lower half of her body, she groaned.

Frantically, still keeping a hold on her with one hand, he began scraping away the earth and clay. Another shifting of the loose ground on which he was standing brought him to a halt.

Jacob called for more rope from the men above him. When he had enough, he tied a loop about Emma's body, beneath her armpits. Satisfied she was now secure, he resumed the task of clearing the clay and rubble covering her, this time using both hands.

He had been working for some minutes when he heard Emma groan again. Looking up from his task, he saw that her eyes were open.

'My leg hurts.' She spoke in a painful whisper.

'I'll be as quick as I can, Emma. Once I've cleared all this away we'll have you out of here in no time at all. You're going to be all right.'

'What happened . . . ?'

As she spoke, she tried to ease herself into a more

comfortable position. It caused the clay beneath her to shift and she screamed in pain.

'Don't move!' Jacob was alarmed that the whole loose pyramid on which they were standing would shift and bring more of the pit-face down upon them.

Emma's face was contorted in an expression of agony, but she said, 'I'll try not to. It's just . . . it hurts so much.'

Jacob discovered there was a large piece of rock resting on one of her legs. It proved difficult to move. He succeeded eventually, but the final movement caused Emma to yell out in agony.

The piece of rock dislodged by Jacob bounced down the slope of the pyramid, causing a minor landslide, which sent the men in the pit scattering hurriedly.

'Right, now let's get you up to safety.'

'How will you do that?' An alarmed expression replaced the pain on Emma's face.

'I'll carry you. Don't worry, I'll be as gentle with you as if you were a baby.'

Jacob hoped he sounded more confident than he felt. When he had thrown off the piece of rock he had seen that the leg that had been trapped was very badly gashed just below the knee. He suspected the bone was broken, too. Getting to the top of the pit was likely to be excruciatingly painful for Emma.

His fears were quickly justified. Calling for the men above him to take up the slack on the rope, he reached down and lifted her in his arms. The action caused her such pain, she screamed once again and he felt her whole body shaking.

Calling for the men on the rope to begin pulling them up as quickly as they could, Jacob waited until the rope tautened, then, with Emma trying hard to bite back her torment, he leaned back at a frightening angle and began walking up the pit-face.

It was not an easy rescue. When they were less than halfway to the top a section of the cliff face crumbled beneath Jacob's feet and dropped away into the pit.

For a few precarious moments, the young couple swung freely in mid-air, with Jacob being battered against the cliff. Emma turned her face in to his shoulder, her arms locked tightly about his neck.

'I'm frightened, Jacob. I'm frightened . . .'

Before he could reply, there was a sudden roaring sound from below them. Glancing down, Jacob saw that the fall from the pit-face had dislodged the top section of the pyramid. Boulders and rubble were pouring helter-skelter down the slope, gathering pace and substance along the way.

The Cargloss men who had been watching the rescue from the floor of the pit were now fleeing in all directions once more.

Meanwhile, Jacob had his own problems. The men at the top of the pit had heard the sound of the landslide, and were now pulling harder than ever in a bid to bring Jacob and Emma to safety as quickly as possible.

Jacob found himself spinning dangerously at the end of the dangling rope, frequently crashing hard against the pit-face. Nevertheless, in spite of his own predicament, he did his best to protect Emma and prevent her injured leg from suffering more harm.

Not until his cries for the Cargloss men to cease hauling were heard was he able to use his feet to brace himself against the pit-face.

Shouting to the men to resume hauling them up, he

walked clumsily up the jagged pit-face. A few minutes later, with Emma still in his arms, he was hoisted to safety. As he reached the rim of the pit, she was taken from him and laid gently down on the grass beside the path.

Only now did Jacob realise the strain that had been put on his legs by the rescue ordeal. Momentarily unable to stand, he sank down beside Emma.

As two of the older men comforted her, the others congratulated Jacob. Then one of them ran off to inform the Cargloss works manager of the success of the rescue.

Before he went, Jacob told the man to send a stretcher up for Emma and have arrangements made for her to be taken immediately to the hospital in nearby St Austell.

4

Despite Jacob's protests that he should return to work at Ruddlemoor, he was persuaded to accompany Emma to the hospital. He had sustained a number of quite severe cuts and grazes to his knees, back and shoulders. There was also a cut on the back of his head.

As the young couple were on their way to St Austell hospital in a Cargloss cart, Ben Retallick, owner of the Ruddlemoor Clay Works, caught up with them. He was riding one of the fine horses from his stables.

Jacob was not overjoyed to have his employer appear on the scene. Much to his surprise, the works owner ignored him and spoke to Emma as though he knew her well.

'How are you, Emma? Are you in much pain? The Cargloss captain tells me he fears you've probably broken a leg.'

'It certainly feels like it,' Emma agreed. 'It really hurts.'

Turning his attention upon Jacob, the works owner

snapped, 'What were you doing up by the edge of the Cargloss pit in the first place? Captain Bray said your instructions were to take Miss Cotton to my grand-parents' home in the Gover valley. You shouldn't have been anywhere near Cargloss.'

Before Jacob could reply, Emma said, 'It was all my fault, Cousin Ben. It's the first time I've ever been to clay country. I asked Jacob to take me up to where I might look out and see something of what was going on.'

Jacob's surprise was not entirely due to her unexpected defence of him. She had called Ben Retallick 'cousin' – yet he and the other men in the Ruddlemoor dry had thought her to be a prospective servant . . . !

Ben was not entirely placated. Still frowning at Jacob, he said, 'Why didn't you heed the warning that Cargloss was about to begin blasting? Their captain assured me the klaxon was sounded.'

'It was,' Jacob agreed unhappily. 'But there wasn't very much time between the warning and the blasting. Far less than we give at Ruddlemoor. Besides, none of the overburden had been removed from the pit edge. There was nothing to make me think it was likely to be blasted away. I believe their explosives men made a bad mistake.'

The 'overburden' was the layer of earth and stones that covered the deposits of China clay. It was usual to remove it before an attempt was made to recover the clay, in order that there should be as little contamination as possible.

'I've heard that the safety measures at Cargloss aren't all they should be,' Ben said somewhat less aggress-ively. 'I'll have words with their owner about it – but I'm still not entirely happy that you should have been so close to Cargloss when they were blasting. However, I'm prepared to accept it wasn't entirely your fault. Besides, if what I was told at Cargloss is true, you probably saved Emma's life – and at no small risk to your own. Well done. I'll see you're rewarded. I'll ride on now and make certain a doctor is waiting for you both at the hospital.'

When Ben Retallick had ridden off, Jacob asked Emma, 'Why did you take the blame and tell Mr Retallick that going up by Cargloss was your idea?'

'Would you rather I'd said I didn't know what we were doing up there and left you to find an explanation for him?'

Jacob shook his head. 'I don't think I could have come up with one. I wasn't even sure myself why I took you there. Thanks, Emma. You've just saved my job. I . . . I'm sorry for what happened to you.'

'Well, like Ben said, you probably saved my life. I owe you more than you owe me.'

After remaining silent for some minutes, Jacob asked, 'Why didn't you tell me when we set out that you're Mr Retallick's cousin? Me and the others in the dry all thought you were going to Gover valley as a servant girl or something.'

'Is that why we went the long way round? Because you and the others believe that servant girls are easy? What did you do, toss a coin to see who'd be the one to go with me and prove what a big strong man he is?'

Emma lay on the floor of the wagon, dirty, dishevelled and with her injured left leg bound to a makeshift splint. Yet, in spite of being at such a disadvantage, she still possessed the ability to dominate Jacob with the power of her scorn.

'It wasn't like that at all,' he protested feebly. 'It was Cap'n Bray who said I was to be the one to take you to the Gover valley. Like I said, I had no idea you were Mr Retallick's cousin.'

'Don't try to convince me that taking me up there was all your own idea, Jacob. I just don't believe you. Anyway, I'm not a full cousin to Ben Retallick. His grandma and mine were sisters, so we're distant cousins, really. We've only met a few times, when he's come up to Bodmin Moor.'

'Then why were you on your way to the Gover valley?'

'I'm the youngest of six girls. Pa died some years ago and we've been finding things a bit hard lately. Ben helped us out from time to time. Last time he came visiting, he suggested I might like to come here to look after his grandparents.'

Giving Jacob an unexpected but weak smile, she added, 'So you weren't really so far wrong about me. I wouldn't be much more than a servant, working for Great Uncle Josh, and Great Aunt Miriam.'

'I could hardly have been more wrong about you,' Jacob replied, ruefully. 'I'm sorry, Emma. I really am. If I'd used a bit more common sense you wouldn't be lying here in pain, with a broken leg.'

'True,' Emma agreed with cruel honesty, 'but it wasn't entirely your fault. If I hadn't played the fool and led you on, we'd have been well past the Cargloss pit when they carried out their blasting.'

Jacob looked at her uncertainly. 'You mean . . . you wouldn't have let me do anything, anyway?'

'No, I certainly wouldn't!' Emma spoke vehemently. 'Not you, your mates, nor anyone else. Not until I've found the man I want to marry – if I ever do decide to marry. There are lots more important things in life than marriage.' She continued to glare at him.

Highly embarrassed, Jacob sought to get away from the subject of what she might or might not have done had the explosion not occurred. 'What will you do until your leg's better? You won't be able to look after Mr Retallick's grandparents now. You'll need someone to look after you.'

'I don't know.' Emma frowned. 'I haven't had time to think about it yet. Perhaps that's just as well. Anyway, we'll see what they have to say at the hospital about my leg, first of all. In the meantime, tell me something about yourself.'

Jacob thought there was very little about his life that was worth relating, and he said so. Nevertheless, by the time they entered the small Cornish town Emma knew that he was an only child and lived in Carthew, close to the Ruddlemoor Clay Works. He had worked for Ben Retallick for seven years, since he was thirteen years old. His father also worked at Ruddlemoor, as an engine man. His mother, before her marriage, had worked in an adjoining clay works, as a bal maiden.

In addition, Emma learned that none of his family had ever travelled outside Cornwall. Indeed, Jacob had never ventured farther than Bodmin, just a few miles distant from his home and work.

It was a life style repeated in many thousands of homes in and around clay country in the summer of 1913.

Jacob would have liked to learn more about Emma. However, by now they were in sight of the small St Austell hospital and Ben Retallick was hurrying to meet them. He had alerted the hospital and a doctor was waiting to receive them when they arrived.

5

The hospital doctor swiftly established that Emma had fractured a bone in her leg, halfway between ankle and knee. It would need to be placed in a plaster cast.

While she was being prepared for this, the doctor examined Jacob. He decided it was necessary to stitch a deep cut just behind Jacob's shoulder.

When Jacob left the casualty cubicle, awkwardly shrugging on his jacket, he found Ben Retallick seated in the waiting area.

'You all fixed up now, Jacob?'

'Yes thanks, Mr Retallick, but I think they're making a lot of fuss about nothing. I've had worse cuts in the works and never had to have stitches put in 'em.'

Ben smiled. 'I've heard it said that a clay man rarely goes to a hospital unless he's carried there. I'm sure the cut will heal a lot quicker because of what they've done, but you needn't hurry back to work. I'll speak to Captain Bray.'

Jacob winced inwardly. He knew that when he did return the works captain would have a great deal to say to him about losing working time as a result of taking Emma on a roundabout route to the Gover valley.

'Emma's likely to be here for some time yet,' the works owner added. 'They're making certain the bone in her leg is set correctly. There's also a nasty gash to be treated. You might as well go on home.'

'If it's all the same to you, Mr Retallick, I'd like to wait here until Emma's ready to leave.' After an initial hesitation about the propriety of questioning the works owner, Jacob asked, 'Where will she go now? I mean, she's not going to be fit enough for a while to look after Mr Josh and Mrs Retallick along in the valley.'

'She'll come and stay at Tregarrick. My wife hasn't been too well lately. Emma will be company for her.'

Jacob had seen Tregarrick – Ben Retallick's home – only from a distance. It was a large and attractive mansion situated at the entrance of the Pentewan valley, to the south of St Austell. The clay works owner had bought it shortly before marrying another of his distant cousins, a girl who had herself once worked on the clay works as a bal maiden.

He was aware of Ben's interesting background, as were all of the Ruddlemoor workers.

Ben had been born in Matabeleland, in Southern Africa. His father had been killed in a tribal uprising, and he had come to England to live with his grandparents soon after the Boer War. His accent and Southern African background had caused him many problems for a while, especially with soldiers who had served in that war. Once these had been overcome, he took over Ruddlemoor from his grandfather and quickly established himself as one of the most successful clay owners in the district.

He had also earned himself a reputation as being one of the most accessible of the employers. It was this that gave Jacob the courage to ask, 'Would I be allowed to call on Emma when she's at Tregarrick?'

If the question took Ben by surprise, he did not allow it to show. Instead, he looked at Jacob with a new interest. He saw a young man who was wearing clay-stained working clothes that had seen better days, but he was a tall, well-built and good-looking young man. It was not surprising Emma had found him attractive enough to suggest he should show her around clay country.

'Come as often as you like, Jacob. She'll no doubt quickly become bored, not being able to do more than hobble around. Being shut up in Tregarrick with a couple of old fogeys won't be Emma's idea of fun.'

In spite of his success as a clay works owner, Ben Retallick was not yet thirty years of age. Jacob thought he hardly came into the category of an 'old fogey'. Nevertheless, he murmured his thanks.

They sat in silence for a few minutes. It was broken by Ben. 'You work in the dry, don't you, Jacob?'

Jacob nodded.

'How are things there? Any problems?'

Jacob shook his head. 'None.' He was puzzled. If Ben Retallick needed to know what was happening anywhere in the Ruddlemoor works, he could ask Captain Bray. Jacob suspected the young mine owner had something else on his mind – and he was right.

'Some of the mine owners are worried about this new Union organiser. It seems he's been around the various clay works stirring up the men. Have you seen anything of him at Ruddlemoor?'

Now Jacob realised why Ben Retallick was asking him about 'problems'. The Workers' Union, representing working men throughout Britain, had recently appointed a full-time organiser, Sydney Woodhouse, to the area.

In recent months there had been an upsurge in the demand for China clay. Woodhouse was telling the men who worked in the industry that they too should be reaping the benefit of increased profits. Prompted by Woodhouse, the Union submitted a demand for an increase in the weekly wage of the clay workers. They were asking for a wage of twenty-five shillings, an increase of three shillings and sixpence on their present rate.

The demand had been rejected out of hand by the employers. The Union was currently pursuing an aggressive recruitment drive, in order that it might take effective action to back up its demands.

'He's been to Ruddlemoor,' Jacob conceded, 'but he's been to every other works in the St Austell area, too. I don't know what success he had with them, but he certainly didn't recruit anyone from the dry – at least, not on our shift.'

'Good! I have no objection to any of the men being in a Union, but not if it's one with the expressed intention of intimidating employers. We had quite enough of that sort of thing when I first came to Ruddlemoor . . . but you wouldn't know very much about that.'

It was true that Jacob had no first-hand knowledge of what had gone on in the time of which Ben Retallick was talking, but he could remember his father talking to his mother about it. For a while it had seemed the China clay industry would go under. Ben Retallick had done much to bring it to order.

It was doubtful whether he would be able to do the same again, Jacob thought. Sydney Woodhouse had mounted a persuasive and aggressive campaign on behalf of his Union and the time was ripe for action. Many of the China clay workers were deeply discontented with wages that were barely sufficient for a man to maintain a family. They were joining the Workers' Union in increasing numbers, believing this to be their only way forward.

'What do you think about this Union business, Jacob?' Ben put a direct question to the young Ruddlemoor employee.

'To be honest, I haven't thought very much about it,' Jacob replied cautiously. 'I know my pa's against it. He says if the men want to put their jobs on the line they should put their trust in a Cornishman. He believes Woodhouse has been sent here from London to further the aims of the men who pay him, not to make life easier for clay men.'

'That sounds fair, Jacob. I wish the men would listen to men like your father, but past experience of such matters tells me they won't. Anyway, enough of such talk. This is neither the time nor the place for it.'

Rising to his feet, he said, 'I'll be getting along now. I must call in at Tregarrick and tell Lily, my wife, what's happening about Emma. I'd better let my grandparents know, too. They'll still be expecting her. I'll have my carriage sent here to pick up Emma and it can take you home. I'd send my new motor car, but a chauffeur isn't starting until tomorrow and I haven't yet mastered the art of driving. You'd both likely finish up with more injuries than you have at the moment. Thanks once more for all you've done for Emma – and for telling me how things stand with the Union at Ruddlemoor. I look forward to seeing you at Tregarrick when you call on Emma.'

With this, Ben Retallick strode out of the hospital.

Behind him, Jacob thought about what had been said. He felt greatly relieved that he had not allowed himself to be persuaded to join the Workers' Union the previous day.

Woodhouse had addressed the Ruddlemoor workers as the day shift went off duty but had gained no new recruits to his Union on this occasion. Cornishmen were notoriously reluctant to be rushed into making decisions about such matters. However, they had listened to him, and much of the talk in the works today had been about what he had said to them.

The Ruddlemoor workers were more content with their lot than many of those employed elsewhere, but they too had begun to believe they had a right to a higher wage than they were being paid now.

It was Jacob's belief that men were joining the Union in sufficient numbers to cause serious trouble in clay country – and it would not be long in coming.

6

'I'm not at all certain that having Emma living at Tregarrick will be a good idea.'

Lily Retallick made the comment as she and Ben walked in the afternoon sunshine in the garden of Tregarrick. He had just returned to the house and told her what had happened and of his plans for Emma.

'Why do you say that?' Her statement surprised Ben, and he added, 'She's always been one of your favourites. "She has more life in her than the rest of the family put together" was how you once described her to me. I thought she'd be good company for you.'

'It's because she's so lively that I don't think it's such a good idea having her here,' Lily replied, only half joking. 'It's likely to remind you of the way I once was.'

'I won't have you saying such things, Lily.'

Ben brought his wife to a halt and pulled her to him. He was immediately aware, as he had been so often recently, of how thin she had become in recent months. She felt very fragile in his arms. She had been examined by a number of doctors, but none had been able to discover exactly what was wrong with her.

'We have a wonderful life here, Lily. It would be even better if we could get you back to full health once more. I thought having Emma here for a while might help.'

'You worry far too much about me, Ben. Perhaps having Emma here will take your mind off my problems – but not entirely, I hope. I like having you care.'

'I doubt if having Emma here will prevent me from worrying about you – and neither she nor anyone else will ever stop me from caring.'

'I'll settle quite happily for that – and I've no doubt Emma will liven the place up. Now, tell me more about this accident she's suffered.'

When Ben told her all he knew, Lily frowned. 'This Ruddlemoor man should never have taken her up by the Cargloss pit. The path runs so close to the edge it's dangerous even when they're not blasting.'

'You're absolutely right, but you've said yourself that Emma is a very determined young lady. If she decided that was what she wanted to do, it would take a very strong-willed young man indeed to deny her. Anyway, by risking his own life to rescue her he more than made up for any error of judgement on his part.'

Ben released Lily and they resumed their walk along the gravelled garden path.

'Who is he? Do I know him?'

'Probably. His name's Jacob Pengelly. His father also works at Ruddlemoor.'

'I remember Jacob when he was a small boy. Most days he'd be at Ruddlemoor to meet his father when he came off shift. I've met his mother too. They're a nice family.'

'I'm glad you think so.' Ben smiled at her. 'Jacob asked for permission to call on Emma while she's here. I told him he could.'

'Well! Emma hasn't exactly wasted the short time she's been in clay country!'

Lily gave her husband a questioning look. 'How do you feel about having a young Ruddlemoor worker about the place?'

Ben shrugged. 'It'll be for Emma to entertain him, not you or me.' More thoughtfully, he said, 'All the same, it might prove useful. That new Union man from London has brought trouble with him. He's spreading discontent among the men. They're demanding a pay increase and threatening strike action if it's not given to them. Matters are likely to come to a head in the very near future.'

'Well, for what it's worth, my sympathies are with the men. They're not exactly overpaid at the moment, are they?'

'No,' Ben conceded. 'And the China clay industry is doing well right now. We could no doubt afford to give them a rise, but the other owners have pointed out that we didn't ask the men to take a pay cut during these past few years when owners have been struggling to stay in business.'

'No owner has had to face the problem of bringing up a family on a guinea and sixpence a week, Ben. If we can afford the increase, why don't we give it to them?'

'Without the clay owners there would be no money at all going into homes in this area,' Ben said patiently. 'Mining has all but collapsed and China clay is all that stands between the workers' families and starvation. An extra three and sixpence a week doesn't sound much but some of the works can't afford to pay such an increase just yet. They've big debts to pay off. Yes, I know we can afford to pay what they want, but the clay owners must stick together. If I pay it, agitation will increase at all the other pits. Works will close and men and women will be put out of work. That's the harsh reality of what Woodhouse is agitating for.'

Ben made a resigned gesture. 'But that isn't what the men want to hear. They'd rather believe what Woodhouse has to say. Well, God help them. When it comes to the crunch – and sadly I believe it will – the Workers' Union won't.'

In a back room of the General Wolfe public house in St Austell, two men sat at a table. Near-empty beer glasses stood in front of them, with a great many handwritten sheets of paper scattered about. One of the men was Sydney Woodhouse, the salaried regional organiser employed by the Workers' Union.

The other man was Arthur Corran, a Union representative elected by the men of the Carne Stents China Clay Works, a comparatively small company.

Corran was looking worried. Shaking his head, he began to gather up the papers on his side of the table. 'I hope you're right, Sydney. I still believe we're taking too much of a chance by making our move so soon. We ought to have a lot more dialogue with the owners before we contemplate strike action.'

'Nonsense!' Sydney Woodhouse was remarkably cheerful. 'I've been speaking to men all around the clay country. There's not one Union man who isn't more

than ready to come out. You start the ball running at
Carne Stents and the rest will come out to support you.
Trust me.'

'There are still not as many clay men in the Union as
I would like to see. Where are we strongest?'

'We're strong everywhere – and getting stronger
every day. I've seldom met up with a more militant
bunch of men – and I've known some over the years,
I can assure you. They're ready to take whatever action
is necessary to gain a living wage – and you and your
men will have the honour of going down in history as
the brothers who spearheaded the action.'

'Well . . . I'll speak to my men. But I'd rather we
waited for another few days in order to whip up more
support.'

Arthur Corran had serious reservations about Carne
Stents being the first works in clay country to down
tools and come out on strike over the pay issue.
He was in favour of the men being paid more of
course. They deserved a sizeable pay increase. But
Woodhouse's methods were not those he would have
chosen to achieve their aims, and certainly not immediately.

'How long do you think this strike will last, once it's
begun?'

Sydney Woodhouse was well aware of his colleague's
doubts. He was contemptuous of his wavering now the
time for action was at hand, but he tried to reassure
him.

'It's difficult to say. My guess is, if we can bring all
the works in the area to a complete halt, the owners will
cave in and it'll all be over in a week.'

'I hope you're right. There are a few thousand men

working in the clay business in Cornwall. Most have families to support.'

'Of course I'm right. You worry too much, Arthur. You shouldn't. Each man who's out on strike will receive ten shillings a week. That will cut into Union funds, but it's nothing compared to what a prolonged strike would cost the owners. Mark my words, they'll see sense when clay stops leaving the works and more money is being taken from their bank accounts than is going in.'

Downing the dregs of his drink, he banged the empty glass down noisily on the table. 'It's market day. Let's get off there and see what early-shift men we can find there. We should catch a good few of them. I'm willing to bet there aren't very many of them who won't back up what I've already said to you.'

7

'There was no need for you to wait for me. You could have gone home ages ago.'

Progressing awkwardly towards him on a pair of crutches, Emma spoke grumpily. Nearby, an anxious nurse watched her progress, demanding more than once that she 'Slow down!'

'I didn't mind waiting,' Jacob replied. 'Mr Retallick is sending his carriage for you. He said it could take me home as well. It'll be a new experience for me.'

'I hope it makes up for the experience you missed up by the Cargloss pit,' Emma said spitefully.

She was not a happy person. The doctor had told her she would need to keep the plaster on for possibly as long as six weeks. The thought of having to move around for such a length of time with a heavy weight on her leg did not appeal to her.

Embarrassed by her words, Jacob glanced at the nurse before saying, 'I've already said how sorry I am about that.' He hesitated a moment before adding, 'Mr Retallick also said I could come to visit you at Tregarrick – that's if you'd like me to. I don't want to impose upon you, or Mr Retallick, but I'll be off work for a while with time on my hands.'

When she made no reply, he explained, 'They put some stitches in a cut on my back. I can't go to work until they're taken out. I'll be off work for about a fortnight, I reckon.'

Emma shrugged in a somewhat indifferent manner. 'You can come if you want to.'

Jacob decided Emma was playing up and he became unexpectedly manful. 'It's got nothing to do with what I want. I'm not coming to Tregarrick if I'm not welcome. Mr Retallick was kind enough to say I could visit you there, but I'm not going to take the risk of embarrassing him.'

Emma was startled by Jacob's unexpected show of firmness. 'You actually asked him if you could come and see me?'

'That's right.'

'Well, if you're that keen to see me again, I won't stop you.'

'That's fair enough. Now, shall we go?' He was facing a window and had seen a carriage turn into the hospital entrance.

As Jacob held the door open for her to pass through the doorway, a second nurse came hurrying to the door, a newspaper in her hand.

Speaking to Emma, she said, 'Here's the newspaper the doctor said you could have.'

'Thank you. Will you carry it for me, Jacob? I feel as clumsy as a three-legged duck trying to use these things.' She glared down at one of the crutches tucked beneath her arms. 'If I don't get the hang of them quickly I'll throw them away and hop around.'

In the carriage, after Jacob had given the driver directions to his home, Emma took the newspaper from him and began to turn the pages, apparently looking for a particular news item.

Glancing up, she saw Jacob watching her. 'Have you seen this today?'

'No, we only have the local paper at home and it's not due out for another couple of days.'

Jacob had seen that the newspaper handed to him by the nurse was a London publication.

'There's a story in it about a suffragette who's been killed. She threw herself in front of the king's horse at the races.'

'That was a stupid thing to do. Why did she do it?'

'To help the suffragette cause; to get votes – and a whole lot of other things that women should be entitled to without having to fight for them.'

'How is throwing herself in front of a racehorse going to help her, or any other woman to get the vote? I can't think of any government that would want to give the vote to women who throw themselves in front of horses. Of course, if enough of them do it there'll be no one to give the vote to!'

'She did it because she's a suffragette, that's why.'

Jacob looked puzzled and Emma said, 'I suppose you do know what a suffragette is?'

'Of course I do. She . . . she's a woman who does stupid things because she thinks the vote should be given to women, the same as to men.'

'That's only part of what it's about, Jacob. Look, we work, the same as men, don't we? And women have as much to do with bringing up the family as men do. Girls go to school and are just as clever as men – when we're given a chance to be. Why shouldn't we have as much of a say as men in managing the country?'

It was evident that Emma felt very strongly about the matter. Jacob knew almost nothing about the suffragette movement, but instead of admitting his ignorance, he asked, 'Are you a suffragette?'

'No, but I would be if I had the chance.'

Further discussion on the role of suffragettes came to an end when the elderly carriage driver called out to Jacob:

'We're just coming up to Carthew. Which is your house, son?'

Carthew was a small, scattered community, close to Ruddlemoor. The diminutive cottages were situated on either side of the road that connected St Austell with Bodmin.

Jacob pointed out a cottage in a river valley, beside the road. Its rooftop was on a level with the carriage in which they were travelling. 'You can drop me here. There's only a narrow path down to the cottage.'

'When will you come to see me at Tregarrick?'

Emma's earlier indifference about having him visit her at the home of her distant cousin seemed to have disappeared. She sounded almost eager at the prospect of seeing him again.

'Whenever you like.'

'Tomorrow?'

Jacob was taken by surprise. He had expected her to suggest a vague meeting, perhaps the following week.

The realisation that she really wanted him to call on her gave him a moment of very real pleasure. 'All right then. Tomorrow afternoon?'

'I'll see you then.'

'Jacob!'

He had started to climb out of the carriage when she called to him. Her voice was pitched low, so that her words would not reach the ears of the Tregarrick carriage driver.

When he turned, she said, equally softly, 'Remember to stick to the story of what we were doing up by the Cargloss pit. It was my idea we went that way, all right? If we both say the same thing there'll be no trouble for anyone. Try to embellish it for your friends at Ruddlemoor and there'll be an almighty row.'

For a few moments Jacob looked at her as though he was about to argue. One thing was certain, she was the bossiest young woman he had ever known. But in the matter under discussion she was holding all the trump cards.

'All right – and thanks again.'

8

Jacob stuck to Emma's version of the accident when, after his mother had ascertained he had not suffered serious injury, she questioned him about it. He later had to repeat his story when his father returned from work at Ruddlemoor.

As Emma had suggested, it was better for everyone that her version of events was believed. Nevertheless, Jacob had a problem with his conscience when he learned that blame for the accident was being laid at the door of the Cargloss works captain. He was being taken to task for not ensuring adequate time had elapsed between the sounding of the warning klaxon and actual blasting.

He eased his feeling of guilt with the knowledge that the warning time *had* been inadequate.

Attention was diverted away from this uncomfortable aspect of the accident when Jacob told his parents of Emma's kinship with Ben Retallick and informed

them he would be visiting her at Tregarrick the following day.

'Well now, there's a thing to be happening!' Eve
Pengelly exclaimed, beaming at her son. 'Fancy our
Jacob going to the home of a clay owner! You just
mind your manners while you're there, young man.'

'It's not the best of times for a clay worker to be
getting friendly with an owner,' Absalom Pengelly said
seriously. 'Things are happening in the clay industry
that I, for one, don't like. Ben Retallick's always been one
of the better clay owners as far as Ruddlemoor workers
are concerned, but there's trouble being stirred up from
outside. Ruddlemoor men aren't going to be able to step
aside from it. Before long the gulf between owners and
workers will be too wide to be bridged. The men are
already talking about "them" and "us". They won't be
as pleased as you are at knowing young Jacob's calling
on an owner.'

'I'll be calling on Emma, not on Ben Retallick,' Jacob
retorted.

Even as he spoke he was remembering the conversation with Ben Retallick when Emma's leg was
being treated. He wondered whether the Ruddlemoor
owner was hoping he would keep him informed of the
men's plans. He dismissed the idea. Had that been Ben
Retallick's idea, he would not have suggested that Jacob
stay away from work.

'You might be certain of why you're going to Tregarrick,
but there's some of the men who won't want to believe
you,' Absalom said. 'They're hell-bent on a strike right
now. This London man has convinced them they'll win
when push comes to shove. Personally, I don't think we
have a hope in hell of winning. We never have and I

doubt if we ever will. The owners have the money to hold out, we haven't. But the men will need to learn that lesson the hard way. Trouble is, when things start to go wrong they won't accept that they've gone about things the wrong way. They'll be looking for scapegoats. Make sure you're not one of them.'

'You always were one to look on the black side of things,' his wife chided. 'Be pleased that our Jacob's thought of as respectable enough to go calling at the house of a clay owner. There's many as wouldn't be.'

'I've got nothing against him going,' Absalom declared, 'I'm warning him to be careful, that's all. That Union man was around Ruddlemoor again last thing today. He's finally persuaded some of our men to join his Union. Rumour has it that half of Cargloss and most of the Carne Stents men are already members. There's trouble brewing, Eve. Serious trouble. I don't want our family caught up in it.'

The trouble forecast by Absalom Pengelly was not long in coming. It erupted the following day. Jacob was on his way to Tregarrick early in the afternoon when he met with a cyclist coming from the direction of St Austell, pedalling furiously.

Red-faced and perspiring copiously, he braked to a halt beside Jacob. 'You on your way to St Austell to join up with the Carne Stents men?'

Mystified, Jacob said, 'No. Should I be?'

'They've come out on strike and are marching into town for a meeting. Sydney Woodhouse will be there to speak to them. He's sent me to go round the rest of the works and tell all Union members. He wants them to down tools and attend the meeting. It's being held outside the market building. I'll see you there . . . Brother.'

So it had started, just as his father had feared it might. Jacob wondered what it would mean to those men who, like he and his father, had not joined the Union.

He thought about it all the way to St Austell. Here, his fears were somewhat allayed. When he heard shouting coming from the vicinity of the market building, curiosity took him in that direction.

He had expected to find the area, which was adjacent to the church and the main shopping street, crowded with clay workers. In fact, the striking workers numbered no more than thirty-five. They were heavily outnumbered by curious onlookers, with the blue uniform of a constable in evidence here and there.

Sydney Woodhouse had not yet arrived to address the striking workers and they seemed at a loss about what they should be doing now they had reached their gathering point. One or two of the men occasionally made a desultory attempt to lead a chanted recitation of their demands, but they received very little support from fellow strikers.

Occasionally, one of the strikers would recognise a fellow clay worker among the bystanders and call upon him to come and join them. When one of them beckoned to Jacob, he felt it was time he left.

Fifteen minutes later, he reached Tregarrick. Here, he met Ben Retallick riding out.

'Hello, Jacob. Emma's inside. She's fretting because she expected you earlier than this. She's not going to be a happy invalid, I'm afraid. But I'm sure she'll cheer up when she sees you. I'm just on my way to Ruddlemoor.'

Jacob had been wondering whether he should tell the Ruddlemoor owner about the Carne Stents meeting. Ben's amiable greeting dispelled any remaining doubts about where his loyalty should lie.

'I wouldn't go through town, if I was you, Mr Retallick. The Carne Stents men have come out on strike. They're holding a meeting up by the market building. I was told that Sydney Woodhouse is going there to speak to 'em.'

'Is he now? Thanks for your warning, Jacob, but I think I'd like to go and listen to what lies Woodhouse will tell the men. I might even be able to put them right about some of them.'

'I don't think that would be a good idea, Mr Retallick. The Carne Stents men have always been a bit of a peculiar bunch and they don't know you as we do.'

Ben grinned. 'Thanks again, Jacob, but I can't see them attacking me in town, in broad daylight, can you? How many are there?'

'Probably no more than thirty-five, but there are a lot of people standing around waiting to see what's going to happen. Some clay men among 'em.'

'Are the police there?'

Ben nodded.

'Then I shall be fine.'

Ben kneed his horse forward, but reined in again before he had gone more than half a dozen horses' length from the younger man.

Turning around, he called, 'Jacob! I'd rather you said nothing to Mrs Retallick about my going to this meeting. If you mention it to Emma make certain she says nothing either.'

9

❦

'But they must have said something while you were there, Jacob. Can't you remember anything at all? Is everyone in clay country likely to come out on strike? What about bal maidens? Are they being called out on strike too? Were any of them at the meeting?'

Jacob and Emma were seated in a small cosy lounge in Tregarrick. He had just told her of the meeting of striking clay workers taking place in St Austell, but she wanted to know far more about what was happening than he knew. She made it clear that she found his lack of observation exasperating. He, in his turn, was surprised by her keen interest.

'I've told you all I know. I didn't notice any bal maidens among the crowd, but I wasn't really looking for them. Anyway, I don't suppose any of them are in the Union.'

'Why not?' Emma bristled with indignation.

'I don't know. Perhaps, like me, they're not particularly interested in the Union.'

'Neither am I, but if men are members then women should be allowed to join too. They'll be affected by a strike just as much as the men.'

'I suppose they will be.' Jacob was wishing he had never mentioned anything about the meeting of the strikers to her. 'It's not something I've ever thought about.'

'That's because you're a man, Jacob Pengelly. This is a man's world. Women don't count for very much in your world, do they? They don't have the vote and when there's a strike no one stops to think of the effect it will have on them. A woman is expected to feed her family on nothing while the men all get together to pat each other on the back and brag of how loyal they're being to their principles. Boasting of how they'll have the determination to hold out for however long it takes for the owners to meet their demands. Not one of them will go home and ask his wife what she thinks he ought to do. God! If I didn't have my leg in plaster I'd go along to this meeting and stir them up with a few questions they wouldn't want to answer.'

'Then perhaps it's as well you do have a broken leg,' Jacob said unsympathetically.

'Just what do you mean by that, Jacob Pengelly?' Emma demanded.

'I mean that the men in the clay works aren't ready to accept such ideas, especially from a stranger to the area. As for these suffragette ideas of yours – you're not old enough to vote even if they decided it should be given to women. Anyway, Mr Retallick's gone to the meeting to put a few questions of his own to them –

but you're not to tell that to Mrs Retallick, she'd worry about him.'

'He's not likely to ask them any questions that will affect the women who work for him at Ruddlemoor,' retorted Emma. 'Women are no more important to the owners than they are to the Union.'

'Look, let's stop arguing about it. Neither of us can do anything to change things. It's a beautifully warm day. Why don't we go outside in the garden. It's not often I have the chance to enjoy the sunshine. I'm usually shut away in the dry at Ruddlemoor.'

Emma grumbled that she had yet to master the art of walking with the aid of crutches, but she led the way, going out through the kitchen, where the Tregarrick cook, aided by a perspiring kitchen maid, was baking cakes.

Once in the garden, they made their way along a gravel path that wound between rose bushes heavy with headily perfumed flowers. Eventually, they came to a seat, set back in a small arbour.

'This is as far as I'm going for now,' Emma declared. She sat down awkwardly, her injured leg stretched out stiffly in front of her.

Seating himself beside her, Jacob thought it was as romantic a situation as he could have wished to share with Emma. Her next words shattered the illusion.

'Do you think it's fair that women should be treated as though we're not as important as men, Jacob? As if we really don't matter very much.'

Jacob sighed. It was an expression of resignation. He had hoped they had put a discussion on the thorny subject behind them.

'Of course not. I don't really believe there are very

many men who do think that way. Where do you get these ideas from anyway? I wouldn't have thought there were many suffragettes up there on Bodmin Moor.'

'I can read, can't I? I did some cleaning work for old Mrs Dingle, in Henwood village, until she died. She used to have a London newspaper sent to her regularly. It was full of what the suffragettes are doing. But even if I hadn't read about it I'd still want to know why we are treated differently to men.'

'Because men and women *are* different, I suppose.'

'You know what I mean, Jacob. At least, I hope you do. We're living in a man's world – and it's about time things were changed.'

Jacob was saved from having to find a reply to Emma's latest statement by the sound of footsteps on the gravel path. Someone was approaching the house from the gardens. A few moments later Lily Retallick came into view. In her hand she held a large pair of scissors and a small bunch of roses.

Smiling at them, she said, 'Hello, you two. It's nice to find you out here enjoying the sunshine.' Extending a hand to Jacob, she said, 'You must be Jacob Pengelly. When we last met you were no taller than this.'

The hand holding the scissors indicated a height that reached to her thin waist.

Standing up hurriedly, Jacob shook her hand and said hesitantly, 'I hope you don't mind me visiting . . .'

'Of course not! It's nice to know Emma has someone of her own age to talk to – but don't let her get on to the subject of suffragettes, or she'll talk of nothing else. It's a subject that generates a whole lot more heat than is good for most folk. I know. The treatment of women was my mother's favourite topic, especially when I was younger. Between that and Trade Unionism there was very little else talked of in our house.'

Jacob's gaze switched to Emma, but she was staring straight ahead, expressionless.

Lily was a shrewd woman. 'Oh dear! Am I too late with my warning? Perhaps you'd both better come inside the house and have something to drink.'

'We've only just come outside,' Emma declared ungraciously.

'Then I'll have something sent out to you,' Lily said. 'You can wait here for it to come while I take Jacob off for a few minutes to help me cut some more roses. The thorns have already drawn blood.'

She held up a finger that had a small globule of blood showing at its tip. 'I thought I might find the gardener, but he's probably busy in the vegetable garden. He thinks flowers are a waste of his time and Ben's money.'

She turned to walk off with Jacob, but once he was out of earshot, Lily came back to where Emma sat stiffly upright. Speaking too quietly for her voice to carry to the waiting Jacob, she said, 'He's rather nice, Emma – and so are you. Save all this talk of suffragettes until he's got to know you a little better. It would be a pity to frighten him away.'

At first Emma was indignant at Lily's words, but the more she thought about it, the more she realised Lily was probably right. Jacob had a quiet, almost shy manner, yet once or twice he had said or done something to indicate he possessed considerable strength of character.

She also conceded that his friendship – and she assured herself this was all it was – mattered to her.

*   *   *

'It's very good of you to come calling on Emma,' Lily said to Jacob, as he cut some blooms from a rose bush farther along the path from where they had left Emma.

'It was the least I could do.' Jacob carefully handed her two blooms and reached up for a third. 'I feel guilty about her broken leg. I should have grabbed her and run the moment I heard the Cargloss warning.'

'I don't think "grabbing" Emma would be a good idea, whatever the circumstances,' Lily said. 'She's a girl with very fixed ideas of how she expects the men about her to behave.'

Jacob grinned wryly. 'I've already discovered that. I'd hardly heard of the suffragettes before I met Emma. She seems to know quite a bit about them.'

'She does,' Lily agreed. 'I dread the thought of ever having her, my mother and Ben's grandmother staying at Tregarrick at the same time. It could lead to a revolution of the country's women.'

She took another rose from Jacob. 'But she's a good girl, for all that – and a very bright one. You won't meet many like her around these parts, Jacob.'

'I've already realised that, Mrs Retallick – not that I know very many girls. But I do think Emma is very special.'

'Good for you, Jacob. You're a very discerning young man – and you've certainly met under rather unusual circumstances.'

Lily decided she liked Jacob. All she had to do now was ensure that Emma felt the same. Somehow, in spite of the abrasive front that Emma showed to the world, she did not think it was going to be so very hard.

10

‹What did you and Lily talk about?' Emma put the question to Jacob when he returned to the seat carrying two glasses of lemonade.

Handing one to Emma, he sat down beside her before replying. 'She was singing your praises. Telling me what a bright girl you are.'

'Oh? Is she trying to marry me off already? I haven't been here for a full day yet.'

Lowering his glass from his mouth, Jacob stared at Emma in disbelief. 'I think you must be the most ungrateful girl I've ever met! Someone says something nice about you and you feel you need to find a hidden meaning in their words. Why?'

When Emma did not reply immediately, Jacob said, 'Mrs Retallick likes you. She probably thinks that's a good enough reason to pay you a compliment. Don't folk behave like that up on Bodmin Moor?'

'Bodmin Moor folk are no different to those anywhere

else.' Unexpectedly, Emma smiled wryly. 'It's me who's difficult, Jacob. It's become a habit. With no father about the house for as long as I can remember, everything that needed doing about the house had to be done by one of us girls. As I was the youngest it usually meant that I was the one to do it while the others were out earning money. I made certain that everything I did was as good as any man would have done it.'

She added the rider with a fierceness that was characteristic of her.

'I learned well during the time I was at school, too. I was better than anyone else in the class, boys or girls, but no one ever praised me for it. All the teacher would say was, "What a pity all that learning is going to be wasted, Emma. Now, if you were only a boy . . ."! What I wanted to know was, why should it be wasted? If I was clever enough to do something better than anyone else, why shouldn't I be allowed to make use of it? I didn't believe it should matter whether I was a boy or girl, man or woman. How would you feel if people treated you like that?'

'Pretty much the same as you, I suspect,' Jacob admitted. 'But I can't really say. I don't think I've ever done anything better than anyone else.'

Emma looked at Jacob in thoughtful silence for a few moments. There was genuine sympathy in her expression when she said, 'Don't talk yourself down, Jacob. It took real courage to rescue me from over the edge of that clay pit the way you did. Most men I know would have been far too scared, but you weren't. I'll always admire you for that.'

As though embarrassed by her admission, she finished off her drink, put the empty glass on the seat beside her and reached out for her crutches. 'Now, help me to my feet and we'll have a look around the garden together. I've never seen a house with a garden as large as this before. Mind you, I've never been inside such a big house, either. It's got so many rooms it's possible to get lost in it. Do you know that Ben bought Tregarrick for Lily before he'd even asked her to marry him . . .'

When Ben reached St Austell, he found the striking workers and onlookers still gathered in the meeting place, in the shadow of the church.

There were more of them now and there was an air of excitement among them. The Carne Stents strikers had been joined by men from two other clay works. It would appear the dispute was escalating.

Ben realised he would be ill-advised to ride his horse through the crowd. Backing away, he turned in at the stables of the nearby White Hart hotel, handing his horse over to the hostler.

By the time he returned to the crowd they were being addressed by Sydney Woodhouse. He was warmly praising the 'courage' of the Carne Stents men for setting an example to their fellow clay workers.

Noisy applause erupted when he declared the Carne Stents strikers had spearheaded the way for other work-ers to act in support of their just pay claim. He assured them that within a matter of days every works in clay country would be idle.

When this happened, he told them, it would be the workers calling the tune, not the owners. Warming to his subject he promised them that part of the huge profit being made by the owners would soon be placed where it belonged. In the pockets of the men who earned it and not in the swollen bank accounts of greedy owners. He added, to noisy encouragement, that the owners were vampires who had been living on the blood of their workers for far too many years.

He urged the men to put their trust in the Workers' Union. To emphasise his case, he pointed out that only three years before clay workers were earning eighteen shillings a week. Thanks to Union negotiations, it was now twenty-one shillings and sixpence. He asserted that this was still not enough.

He reminded his audience that day after day ships were leaving the nearby ports of Par, Fowey and Charlestown, carrying China clay from Cornwall to the world. Vast profits were being made by the industry. The workers deserved to be given a share of these.

By now, Woodhouse's oratory was in full flow. He declared that locomotives, pulling a quarter-of-a-mile line of trucks, laden with clay, left the sidings by night and day. They were bound, he informed his listeners, for the industrial Midlands, earning more and more wealth for the already rich China clay works owners of Cornwall.

To thunderous applause, Woodhouse declared that the owners could well afford the very reasonable rise demanded by their workers. They could, he insisted, afford far more. However, unlike the owners, the men were not greedy. Twenty-five shillings would make life easier for their families and this was all they were asking.

As the latest round of cheering subsided, Ben's voice rang out unexpectedly. 'You're talking nonsense, Mr Woodhouse. Dangerous nonsense.'

There was a sudden, astonished hush. Men turned

towards Ben with a mixture of anger and disbelief. But he had not yet finished.

Addressing the Union organiser, he said, 'You're inciting men to take a course of action that can bring only distress and hardship to their families. It also threatens the very future of the industry that provides them with their living.'

Sydney Woodhouse frowned angrily at the man whose interruption had brought his fiery oratory to a halt. 'Should I know you, sir? I can't recall a meeting . . .'

'Ben Retallick, owner of Ruddlemoor.' Identifying himself, Ben forced his way towards Sydney Woodhouse and the small group of Union officials gathered about him.

As he drew nearer, a growing swell of sound rose as a result of his self-identification.

'With your permission, I would like to speak to the Carne Stents men and put the record straight.'

While Ben was approaching, Woodhouse whispered an aside to the men about him. Two of them immediately moved forward to block Ben's advance.

'This is a gathering of Union members, Mr Retallick. The owners have had an opportunity to have their say. No doubt they will again – when the men press their claim for a just living wage.'

'Are you afraid to allow any views but your own to be heard, Mr Woodhouse? Is your case so fragile?'

Ben had reached the front of the crowd now. For a moment it appeared that one of the two Union officials would use physical force to prevent him advancing any farther. However, a single look from the works owner was sufficient to make the man think again. Ben was a well-built, fit man with a tough, no-nonsense manner.

Two more officials moved forward to back their Union colleagues, but someone in the crowd called, 'Let Retallick have his say. Let's hear him make a case for not giving us what we want – if he can.'

The call was taken up by others and the men blocking Ben's path looked back at Woodhouse uncertainly.

The Trade Union organiser was reluctant to have his moment of triumph stolen by an employer, but he was sufficiently experienced to realise that refusal to allow Ben to speak was likely to be used against him in the future.

'Very well, Mr Retallick. I am sure everyone will be most interested to hear why you consider rich men cannot afford to give their workers an increase of a mere three and sixpence a week. As one of the workers just said, make a case against it – if you can!'

'I haven't come here to "make a case", Mr Woodhouse, only to point out one or two facts you seem to have overlooked.' Standing beside the Union organiser, Ben turned to address his remarks to the crowd.

'Mr Woodhouse has just claimed his Union was responsible for raising your wages to a guinea and sixpence three years ago. I'd like to point out that Ruddlemoor was paying that sum to its men ten years ago. Be that as it may, that's the wage that's being paid throughout the industry now. You're intelligent men, you don't need me to point out that we've just been through a very difficult couple of years. Yet I can't think of one clay owner who suggested pay should be cut then, even though scarcely any profit was being made by the "rich" owners of whom Mr Woodhouse was talking.'

Ben realised his words were falling upon deaf ears when someone in the crowd called, 'You're not having a bad year now, why can't you give your men an extra three and six a week? That's not much to ask.'

'A very good question,' Sydney Woodhouse agreed. 'I'd like to hear your reply, Mr Retallick. Your profits are measured in thousands of pounds. My members are asking for a mere three shillings and sixpence to improve life for their wives and children. A small enough sum, surely?'

Sydney Woodhouse smiled at Ben triumphantly.

'It's a small enough sum,' Ben conceded. 'Small enough, that is, until you cost it out, using sound accounting methods and not emotive words.'

There were derisive jeers from Ben's listeners. He held up a hand and waited until he had achieved a degree of silence. 'Let me give you an owner's figures for this small pay rise for which you're asking. Ruddlemoor pays wages to nigh on a thousand men. This "small" pay rise of which you speak would cost me almost ten thousand pounds per annum. Yes, profits are good this year – and I stress *this* year – but they're not that good.'

The sum quoted by Ben had brought gasps from his listeners. Few could take in the thought of dealing in such vast amounts of money.

Woodhouse attempted to seize back the advantage he realised he was in danger of losing.

'You're talking of great amounts of money, Mr Retallick, but you and the other owners have a very strong Association. You wouldn't lose that much. You'd simply pass on the cost of any increased expenditure to the buyers.'

'And price ourselves out of business?' Ben looked at Woodhouse contemptuously. 'There are other countries with China clay deposits. Customers buy from us not only because our quality is good but also because we are able to sell at a highly competitive price. Push the price up and they'll buy from elsewhere. If that happens your members will be spending their days sitting at home, with no money coming into the house.'

'There's not an owner in Cornwall would allow business to go elsewhere,' Woodhouse retorted, with more confidence than he felt. 'You'd compromise. Cut your profits a little. One thing's certain, you wouldn't have to manage on twenty-one and sixpence a week.'

Woodhouse's statement received noisy acclamation from his listeners and Ben knew his argument had fallen on deaf ears.

'I've told you the situation as I see it, Mr Woodhouse. I can't speak for the other owners because I haven't discussed the matter with them. However, I doubt very much whether their response will be any different to my own. Put your case again in six months' time if sales continue the way they are right now. But striking in support of your demands will achieve nothing. Indeed, it might mean that many men will find themselves permanently out of work at the end of the day.'

'Is that a threat to our Union members, Mr Retallick? I can assure you that if it is—'

'Don't try to twist my words, Mr Woodhouse. I'm not threatening anyone. I am merely trying to inject some economic sense into your argument. It's something that appears to be lamentably lacking.'

Sydney Woodhouse appealed to the crowd gathered about them. 'You've just heard from an owner who's come here in his fine clothes to tell us how poor he and the other owners are. Will you go away feeling sorry for him? Or are you going home to your wives and families and saying, "We've struck the first blow to gain a reasonable living wage"? Tell them they might have to tighten their belts for a week or two, but then they'll be able to enjoy the sort of wage that workers are being paid in other parts of this country of ours. I know what you're going to do, but why don't you tell Mr Retallick for yourselves?'

The roar of support for the Trade Union organiser frightened pigeons from the roof of the nearby market house. Apprehensive policemen standing at the edge of the crowd began pushing their way through to where Ben was standing.

'I think that gives you your answer, Mr Retallick,' Woodhouse said, triumphantly. 'By the end of the week there'll not be a works in the area still operating.'

'You'll find it easier to get the men out of work than put them back,' Ben said sadly. 'The men are listening to you now, Mr Woodhouse. I doubt if you'll still be a hero when this is all over.'

A few minutes later, surrounded by a ring of anxious policemen, Ben was escorted through the crowd of strikers, their jeers and boos ringing in his ears.

The strike of the clay workers had begun in earnest.

11

Later that same evening, Jacob was at home preparing for bed when his father returned from the Ruddlemoor China Clay Works, at the end of the late shift.

Taking off his jacket, impregnated with fine clay dust, he beat it against the wall of the house beside the back door as he might a carpet. Then, removing his clay-encrusted boots, he placed them just inside the door.

By the time he entered the house and sat down at the kitchen table, a steaming hot meal of bacon pudding was on a plate in front of him.

As he ate, Absalom Pengelly spoke to his wife and son of the events of the day. Men from four clay workings had come out in support of the Carne Stents men. However, much of the talk at Ruddlemoor had been of Ben Retallick's spirited defence of the owners' position at the gathering of striking Union members.

'Even those who are in the Union admit it took a

brave man to stand up against the strikers in their present mood,' Absalom said as he forked food in his mouth.

'Ben Retallick's never lacked courage,' his wife added. 'Do you remember the labour troubles he had when he took over Ruddlemoor ten years ago? He wasn't much older than our Jacob then, but he took on not only the men but the other owners as well. He's never been afraid of a fight.'

'That's as maybe,' Absalom agreed. 'He'll win this one eventually, but not in the short term. Many of the men at Ruddlemoor are against a strike, but we won't be able to stand back from it. Feelings are running too high in clay country. I heard that men at Carne Stents who refused to come out were stoned by the others. One of them's got a badly gashed face.'

'Well, at least you're out of it, our Jacob,' Eve said, with some relief. 'That injury of yours might turn out to be a blessing in disguise. I only wish your father could find a way to keep clear of the troubles.'

'I don't suppose you met up with Ben Retallick when you were at Tregarrick today?' Absalom put the question to his son.

'As a matter of fact I did,' Jacob said. 'He was just leaving the house as I arrived. He stopped long enough to have a brief chat with me.'

He did not add that he had been the one to tell the mine owner about the meeting of the clay workers in St Austell.

'Will you be going to the house to see this young girl again?' Eve asked.

'I doubt it,' Jacob said, disconsolately. 'She spent most of the time I was there talking about "suffragettes" and such things. She believes women should have some say on whether or not their men go out on strike.'

'Does she now?' Eve Pengelly expressed tight-lipped disapproval. 'Such ideas are best left to those who have nothing better to think about.'

'I don't know,' Absalom said, unexpectedly. 'The girl does have a point. It's the woman of the house who has to make ends meet when the money stops coming in.'

'That's all part of a wife's duty,' Eve declared firmly. 'Every woman accepts such responsibility when she marries. If that's all this young woman has to say for herself you're better off not seeing her any more.'

Jacob spent the next day at home in the small Carthew cottage, thoroughly bored. A large tree had recently been brought down behind the cottage. Jacob thought he would take the opportunity to saw it up, but the action of sawing pulled a stitch from the wound in his back and he was forced to stop. For the remainder of the day he moped about the house, his mother complaining that whenever she turned around he was there, getting in her way.

The following day began as though it might follow a similar tedious pattern, but mid-morning, when Eve Pengelly was beginning to show her irritation at having him "under her feet the whole time", they both heard the unfamiliar sound of a motor car engine.

The vehicle was coming along the road from the direction of St Austell, and it was an unusual enough occurrence for Jacob and his mother to go outside the cottage in the hope of catching a glimpse of it.

It was an impressive sight in dark red, with gleaming brass lights and a round radiator of the same metal. To

the great surprise of those watching, the vehicle drew
to a halt on the road immediately level with the cottage
and someone began waving excitedly to them from the
passenger seat.

'Jacob! I've come to fetch you, to take you to the beach.
I've got a picnic hamper for us. Come on!'

It was Emma!

Before Eve had time to remember the reservations she
had expressed about Emma's suitability as a companion
for her son, Jacob had said a hurried 'Goodbye' and
was running to the waiting motor car. He clambered
in the back with Emma, and there was a sound from
the vehicle that, Eve told her husband later, sounded
like a cow being strangled.

Then, with much waving of hands and a great deal
of crunching of gears, the motor car was turned around
and heading back the way it had come.

Eve Pengelly watched it until it disappeared from
view. She went back inside the cottage shaking her head,
muttering that she didn't know what the world was
coming to with such monstrous things being allowed
to use the roads.

'Isn't this marvellous!' Beside Jacob, Emma bounced up
and down on the seat, as excited as he had ever seen
anyone. 'The driver started work yesterday and Ben
said he could drive me to come and fetch you in the
motor car. Lily suggested we should go to the beach
for a picnic and she had some food and drink made up
for us.'

'It's great fun,' Jacob agreed uncertainly.

He did not find talking easy. The motor car was being
driven at what seemed to be rapid speed along a road

that had been furrowed by the wheels of heavily laden clay wagons.

'Where are we going?' Jacob saved the question until the car reached the smoother, hard-surfaced roads of St Austell. Here it was forced to reduce speed because of the presence of pedestrians and horse-drawn vehicles.

'I don't know,' Emma confessed. 'Lily said there was a nice beach along the valley from Tregarrick, close to the Pentewan harbour. She's told the driver to take us there.'

'That's right.' The driver had heard Jacob's question and Emma's reply. 'There's a lovely stretch of sand along there. It's called The Winnick. We used to be taken there on the clay train from St Austell for our Sunday school outing when I was a boy. We'd have a lovely time.'

Jacob knew the spot. It was a wide expanse of sand with cliffs on either hand. The river that ran beside the Pengelly cottage entered the sea here. His father had once taken Jacob there to view a ship that had run on to the rocks when trying to enter the tiny Pentewan harbour.

'I thought you were coming to visit me yesterday, Jacob. Why didn't you?' Emma put the question to him as they left St Austell behind and took the road past Tregarrick.

'There were things that needed doing at home,' Jacob said untruthfully, remembering how bored he had been.

'It had nothing to do with me saying what I thought about women not being treated fairly?'

'No.' Jacob told a second lie, but this time he qualified his reply, 'Mind you, it did get a bit boring when you wouldn't talk of anything else.'

For a moment, he thought she would be angry with him. Instead, she gave him a somewhat self-conscious smile. 'All right, I'll try not to say anything about the rights of women – for today. We'll enjoy the sand and the sea, and our picnic.'

Suddenly serious, she said, 'All the same, I want you to know what I think of the way things are, Jacob. It's something I feel very strongly about. I like you and I like being with you, but I can't change how I feel about the way women should be treated. If it makes you feel uncomfortable, I'd rather you told me. Not today, but later, when you've had time to think about it. You see, I don't want to grow too fond of you, if you really disagree with the things I believe in. I believe that men and women should be partners. Equal partners, each one as important as the other. That's the way I want it to be for me if I ever marry.'

Jacob opened his mouth to make a reply, but Emma's finger on his lips silenced him. 'No, Jacob, don't say anything now. Let's forget about everything except enjoying ourselves. Look, here's the sea! We're there!'

12

❧

The chauffeur, driving Ben Retallick's Hotchkiss motor car, returned to The Winnick at six o'clock that evening to pick up the young couple. By this time, Jacob and Emma were sunburned, tired – and very happy in each other's company.

Jacob's earlier apprehension had been proven groundless. Not once during their day on the beach had Emma mentioned either suffragettes or the rights of women. He would have been willing to share Emma's company for many more hours, had it been possible.

Emma was equally content to be with Jacob. They had enjoyed a lot of fun together. When she discovered it was impossible to walk to the edge of the sea because her crutches sank in the soft sand, he had carried her there, "piggy-back" fashion.

With a gentle tide lapping about them, he had put her down and supported her in a one-legged paddle that brought on fits of uninhibited laughter as they tried to retain their balance.

At one stage, Jacob had to leave Emma balancing precariously on one leg while he rescued one of her crutches that was in danger of being washed away. In so doing, he slipped and sat down in the water, causing even more hilarity.

When he carried her up the beach once more, Emma discovered the exertion had caused his back wound to start bleeding once again.

Her concern for him was entirely genuine. At the picnic spot she insisted he take off his shirt to allow her to examine the wound. When she was satisfied it had stopped bleeding, she washed the blood from his shirt with water heated on the luncheon basket's small spirit stove.

After enjoying the meal provided for them by Lily, they talked and walked some more, all the time learning about each other and their respective families.

By evening, each felt they had known the other for much longer than a mere four days.

Jacob walked towards the waiting motor car, carrying the luncheon basket, with Emma swinging along on her crutches beside him. The arrival of the motor car had probably been timely. A heavy bank of cloud was building up out to the south west.

A summer storm was in the offing, but it did not prevent Emma from saying, 'I have enjoyed today, Jacob. I think it's probably the happiest day I've ever known.'

'Even though you've got a broken leg?'

'Yes, even with that. How about you?'

'It's been a very happy day for me too, Emma. One I'll

always remember. I . . . I wish it didn't have to come to an end.'

'Honestly?'

He nodded.

'I'm glad, Jacob. I'm very glad we were able to have today together.'

The chauffeur brought further private conversation to an end by coming to meet them and taking the luncheon basket from Jacob.

Sitting close to each other in the back of the Hotchkiss, neither said very much on the drive to Tregarrick. All too soon, it seemed, they turned in to the drive of the big house.

As the motor car approached the house, Jacob and Emma could see Ben and Lily standing outside the front doorway. The works owner appeared agitated. He had probably only just arrived home, because Jacob could see a groom leading a saddled horse in the direction of the stables.

'Mr Retallick looks upset about something,' Jacob said, as the motor car crunched to a halt on the gravel driveway. 'I hope nothing's wrong at Ruddlemoor.'

'He's got a lot of worries at the moment,' Emma said. 'He's very unhappy about this strike. But I'm sure he won't mind if you stay and have a drink before you go home.'

'Hadn't we better wait to see if I'm asked by Mr or Mrs Retallick?'

Before Emma could reply, Ben called out to Jacob and hurried towards them, followed more slowly by Lily.

'Don't leave the car, Jacob. I'll get the driver to take you on home.'

Unable to hide her disappointment, Emma said, 'Oh!

I was hoping Jacob might be able to stay for a drink, or something, before he went.'

Struggling to get out of the car, doing her best to adjust her balance on the two crutches while Ben was talking, she had not noticed his expression.

Jacob had. Concerned, he asked, 'Is something wrong?'

Ben nodded. 'Just about every works in clay country has come out on strike today. Ruddlemoor among them. Less than fifty per cent of the men were in favour of a strike, but a large crowd of workers from other pits threatened them – and their families. There was some violence.'

Jacob had a sudden, chill premonition. 'Was my pa involved?'

'I'm afraid so, Jacob. He refused to put out the fire in the engine room and locked the door against the strikers. A rock was thrown through the window and he was badly cut about the face. I arrived just after it happened and took him to hospital. He's at home now, but there's some concern about the sight of one of his eyes. It's too early to know anything for certain just yet, but I can assure you I'll have him seen by the best eye surgeon in the country.'

Visibly shaken, Jacob looked at Emma. 'I'd better go home right away.'

'Of course, Jacob. I . . . I hope he's going to be all right. Please come and let me know as soon as you can.'

He nodded before turning back to the works owner. 'Thank you for what you did for Pa, Mr Retallick. It's sad that it's come to this. We didn't expect this sort of trouble at Ruddlemoor.'

'Tell your mother I'll see the family doesn't suffer as a result of what's happened. I'll be around to see her before long. In the meantime, you're welcome to come calling on Emma whenever you like. That way I'll know how your pa is keeping.'

Jacob climbed back inside the motor car and was driven away along the long driveway to the road. When he turned he saw Emma balancing precariously on her crutches as she waved to him. He returned the wave.

He was concerned for his father and the injury he had suffered to his eye, but Jacob suddenly felt a deep pity for Emma. She had enjoyed a very happy day. It was sad this had happened to spoil it for her.

He hoped they might be able to repeat the experience at some time in the near future. He had not known Emma for very long, yet she already meant far more to him than any other girl he had ever met.

13

When Jacob hurried inside the Carthew cottage, he found his father seated in his usual wooden armchair, beside the gleaming, black kitchen range. A lop-sided bandage was wound around his forehead, dropping down on one side to hide his left eye and ear.

A number of cuts was visible on his face and neck. One, following the line of his cheekbone, was stitched like a herring-bone, the skin painted yellow with anti-septic iodine.

'Mr Retallick's just told me what happened to you at Ruddlemoor. He sent me home in his car. How are you feeling?'

Absalom Pengelly turned his head painfully in order to look at his son. To Jacob's alarm he saw a tear trembling in the corner of the eye that could be seen.

When Absalom spoke it was with some difficulty because of the stitches in his face. 'I've been working at Ruddlemoor since I was ten years old. Thirty-five years without ever knowingly doing a bad turn to anyone. Yet they do this to me. That hurts more than any of the cuts on my face.'

The tear escaped and trickled down the side of Absalom's nose.

Jacob had never seen his father cry before. It screwed him up inside. 'None of the Ruddlemoor men would have done this to you, Pa. They wouldn't do such a thing.'

'Of course they wouldn't. That's what I've just been telling him,' Eve said. Not usually a woman who demonstrated affection for her husband in front of anyone, she now crossed to him and gingerly held his head to her. Her eyes too revealed her distress. 'Why, I swear there's not a man anywhere in clay country who doesn't have respect for Absalom Pengelly. I've heard men say as much, many a time.'

'That might have been true once, Eve, but not any more. Too many men from outside have been taken on these past few years. They don't remember the time when Cornishmen were crying out for work. The days when miners from down Camborne way would block the road outside every clay works gate, begging to be taken on for any kind of work. Producing clay's not a way of life for the likes of them. They're out to wring all they can get from it. It's them who Woodhouse appeals to. They're happy to be his bully boys.'

He spoke painfully and with difficulty.

Stroking her husband's hair, Eve said to her son, 'Jacob, you'll find a shilling in the pot on the mantel. Take a jug along to the Sawles Arms and get your pa a quart of ale. He needs something to cheer him up – and put a coat on, it's begun to rain.'

Her suggestion made Jacob realise just how concerned she was for his father. Brought up in a staunch Methodist family, she had always disapproved of the very occasional drink taken by her husband.

The Sawles Arms was frequented by many of the Ruddlemoor men and there was a momentary silence as Jacob entered the taproom. Then, just as suddenly, the room erupted in noise as men clamoured for news of the injured engine man.

Jacob thought it would have cheered his father greatly to have heard the well-wishers. Men not only from Ruddlemoor but from surrounding pits too.

If any further proof was needed of the esteem in which Absalom Pengelly was held by his fellow men, it came when the notoriously tight-fisted landlord of the Sawles Arms declined to accept Jacob's money for the quart of beer.

Back at the cottage, Absalom sipped his beer and listened as Jacob told of all the men who had asked after him and sent wishes for a speedy recovery.

'They can wish as much as they like,' Absalom declared bitterly. 'The man who put a stone through the engine-room window will find he's responsible for a lot more suffering than a few cuts. With the fire drawn, the Ruddlemoor men will still be out long after the strike is over and everyone else is back at work. They'll see their families going hungry long after others get back to normal.'

'Are you sure the engine's stopped working?'

Jacob was aware of the seriousness of the situation. Ruddlemoor was one of the deepest pits in the area. Unless the pumps were kept working it was in constant danger of flooding – especially when they experienced rain as heavy as that now falling.

'If the pickets don't let another engine man in, Ben Retallick's as likely as not to close down the works permanently. He threatened to do it the last time there was trouble. It's not as though he needs the money Ruddlemoor makes for him.'

'Surely the men must realise this for themselves, Pa?'

'Those who are foolish enough to listen to men like Woodhouse aren't yet ready to hear the truth. He's told them the strike won't last longer than a week or two. I've even heard it said he's hinting it could be over in a matter of days. Folk who believe him must have short memories – especially where Ben Retallick is concerned. The last time the men went on strike he told them they could stay out for as long as they liked. He hasn't changed. The other owners are no different. They won't be dictated to by the likes of Woodhouse. Even if Ben Retallick decides he'll carry on working Ruddlemoor, there'll be too much water in the pit for the men to go back when the others do. That means Ruddlemoor men will be taking no wages home to their wives – and they'll certainly not get any from the Workers' Union.'

'It's a good job there's no Union for their wives,' Eve said, with some feeling. 'If there was, the men might think twice before going off and doing such stupid things. I doubt if any of them went home and asked what their wives thought about them coming out on strike.'

Jacob looked at his mother quizzically. Despite the criticism she had made a couple of days before, she was echoing the words of Emma!

'Do you think Ben Retallick realises the importance of keeping the Ruddlemoor engine working, Pa?'

'I doubt if he cares either way, boy. He's rich enough to ride out a strike, however long it takes – and you can't expect him to be upset about the men having no wages. The strike is their doing, not his. He's always paid a fair wage. Most of the Ruddlemoor men are already taking home more than the twenty-five shillings Woodhouse is demanding for them. Ben Retallick might have expected to be able to rely on their loyalty.'

Jacob knew this was true. Unlike most other works, the Ruddlemoor men were paid for any overtime they put in. He also knew that a great many of them had always spoken against taking strike action. He wondered what could have happened to persuade them to change their minds.

He reached a sudden decision. 'Enjoy your ale, Pa. I'm going back up to the Sawles Arms.'

'Jacob! It's one thing for you to go there to fetch something to cheer up your pa, I don't approve of my family spending time at the Sawles Arms – or in any other public house, for that matter.'

'There are a whole lot of Ruddlemoor men in there, Ma. I think they should be told what Pa's just said. That if the pump stops they're likely to find themselves out of work for far longer than they expect.'

'Now don't you go getting yourself into any more trouble.' His mother expressed her concern for him. 'I've got both my men home sick, but at least you're still bringing in a wage. Get yourself hurt in an argument with those who don't agree with what you're saying and you can't expect Mr Retallick to carry on paying you.'

'Don't worry, Ma. I'll not be doing anything that Mr Retallick could possibly find fault with.'

14

When Jacob entered the Sawles Arms for the second time that day, it was far more crowded than on his earlier visit. He had difficulty making his way through the crowd to where the perspiring landlord was serving behind the scrubbed wooden bar.

Many of the customers were Ruddlemoor workers, although there was a fair smattering of customers from other works in the area.

Without pausing from his task of serving drinks, the landlord expressed surprise at seeing Jacob once more. 'Don't tell me your pa's drunk his ale already and is wanting more?'

'When I left him he was supping quite happily at home and he sends his thanks. No, I came here to have a word with some of the Ruddlemoor men.'

'There's no charge for talking to whoever you like – as long as you don't stop 'em from drinking. I need to take as much money as I can, while I can. Once this strike bites there'll be little money in clay country to spend on ale. It's not only clay workers who'll be hit by the walk-out – but publicans don't have a Union to give *them* hand-outs.'

'Unless the men are prepared to listen to what I have to say they'll be without money to spend on ale for far longer than they're expecting.'

'In that case, the sooner you talk to them the better. Most of those you know are over in the far corner, around the dartboard. Will you be taking a drink with you?'

Jacob was not a regular drinker, but he had occasionally visited the Sawles Arms with others from the Ruddlemoor dry. Usually it was on special occasions, such as birthdays or when a man was to be married.

'I'll have a half-pint of your small beer, please.'

Small beer was one of the weakest of the alcoholic beverages sold in the Sawles Arms and the landlord complained, 'I can see I'm not going to get rich from serving you.'

'If things go the way I hope they will, I'm going to need a clear head tonight,' Jacob retorted.

Jacob carried his beer to a corner of the crowded bar room, where a group of men was trying to play a game of darts despite the pressure of the crowd about it.

The Ruddlemoor men greeted Jacob with some surprise. One or two who had not been in the public house at the time of his earlier visit asked about his father. All agreed it had been 'a bad business'.

Once they had ascertained that Absalom was as well as might be expected, there was a certain amount of banter about Jacob's own injuries, and the manner in which they had been sustained.

One of the men of Jacob's own age suggested slyly that he couldn't imagine why it was Jacob 'hadn't rolled over the cliff with that young maid from up by Bodmin'. He added that it was well known, that Bodmin Moor girls took a powerful grip on a man when they were making love.

Jacob felt the need to defend Emma's reputation and, when the laughter had died down, he said, 'It was a good job I didn't try anything on with her. She's related to Ben Retallick.'

'Ah! That explains it then,' one of the older men said somewhat ambiguously. 'Old Josh Retallick was mining up on the moor before he came down here to take over Ruddlemoor. Half of them who live up there are related to him in one way or another, so I hear.'

'That's as may be,' Jacob said, 'but I haven't come here to talk about young girls from Bodmin Moor. I've got something of far more importance for you to think about.'

He told them of his father's warning about what would happen to the Ruddlemoor works if the engine was not kept working to operate the pumps.

After listening to him in silence, one of them asked, 'Is it really that serious?'

An older worker answered for Jacob. 'He's not exaggerating, boy. I can remember some years ago when the engine broke down for only a couple of days. Slurry settled in the level and hardened and there was nothing could be done about it. We had to dig a new level.'

The 'level' was a tunnel dug deep beneath the floor of the pit to carry the liquid mixture of clay, sand and water – or 'slurry' – from pit to works for processing.

'There'd be no work for a week or more if we had to cope with flooding in the pit at the same time. Your pa's right, Jacob. We'd really be in trouble.'

'It's all very well saying the engine should be kept running, but what can we do about it?' another clay worker asked. 'You saw what happened to Absalom when he wouldn't stop work. The Union's put pickets on the gate – and they're not Ruddlemoor men.'

Turning to one of the men who worked in the dry but on another shift, Jacob said, 'Tom, you're a Union man now, what's the purpose of a Union?'

Taken by surprise, the man to whom Jacob had put the question said, 'Why . . . to look after the interests of its members. To make certain we're paid a decent living wage and to secure our jobs, I suppose. At least, that's the reason I joined.'

'I can't see that the Union is looking after your interests if it forces engine men to draw the fires. I'd say that's putting all our livelihoods at risk. No one here will be drawing a wage until long after the men from other works have gone back to work. Not only that, if the same thing is happening elsewhere, some owners just won't be able to afford to bring their pits back to working order. They'll go under and a lot of men will be put out of work permanently. No one's going to take on a man who's out of work because he took part in a strike.'

'That's right enough.'

'What will the Union do about that?'

The men about Jacob made comments that were in general agreement with what he had been saying.

'Well then, what are we going to do about it?' Jacob asked.

The men lapsed into silence until one man asked gloomily, 'What can we do?'

'I'll tell you,' Jacob replied. 'We can go along to Ruddlemoor, light the engine fire and set the pumps working again.'

Tom, a recent recruit to the Union, was aghast. 'We can't do that. That'd be blacklegging! I'd be thrown out of the Union.'

The reaction of the men about him made him acutely aware they were not interested in his standing with the Workers' Union.

In desperation, he added, 'Anyway, even if we did go to Ruddlemoor and get past the pickets, we'd need an engine man to start the engine and work the pumps.'

'No we wouldn't,' Jacob corrected him. 'I've seen Pa do it often enough and when I was a kid he'd let me do lots of the things he had to do in the engine house. Switching things on and off. I can work most things in there almost as well as he can.'

'But . . . there's still the pickets.'

'So? They may not be Ruddlemoor men, but they're still clay workers. They'll know what we're talking about, at least. Let's go and speak to them.'

15

It was raining in earnest when Jacob and seven Ruddlemoor men left the Sawles Arms to walk to the clay works. By the time they arrived at their destination it was coming down so heavily the approach to the works was a murky rainwater lake that reflected yellow light from the open gatehouse door.

There were only two pickets inside the gatehouse. Jacob knew they would not dare attempt to physically prevent the Ruddlemoor men from carrying out their plan.

In the doorway, with the Ruddlemoor men gathered about him he announced his intention of going to the engine house.

'You'll find it pretty crowded up there,' the picket declared. 'Sydney Woodhouse and the rest of the pickets are up there too.'

'Woodhouse is here, at Ruddlemoor? What's he doing?'

'He and the others are up there talking to Mr Retallick

about the same thing you're here for, I reckon. Getting the engine working again.'

'Ben Retallick's here?' Jacob knew he shouldn't be surprised. Ben Retallick had not been afraid to take on Woodhouse at the meeting of the strikers in St Austell. However, the picket's next words came as an even greater surprise.

'No, not Ben Retallick, old Josh Retallick, Ben's grand-father.'

'Josh Retallick?! Why, he must be almost ninety by now. It can't be him.'

'It is. He arrived with Captain Bray, riding together in a pony shay. They both looked like drowned rats when they got here.'

Speaking to his companions, Jacob said, 'Come on, let's get up to the engine house and find out what's going on.'

Followed by the others, Jacob hurried to where the engine house stood close to the edge of the great pit. In daylight it was dwarfed by a giant waste heap built up over many years, but tonight the rain hid the conical white pyramid from view.

The men were guided to the engine house by the lights shining out from its windows. Jacob pushed open the door and entered the building followed by the other Ruddlemoor men.

Inside, a tall, elderly but clear-eyed man was the dominant figure in a group of men gathered in front of a cold engine. Captain Bray stood beside him. They were surrounded by some nine or ten others. One was Sydney Woodhouse.

At the sound of the door opening, Josh turned to see who had come in, but it was Woodhouse who challenged the newcomers. 'Who are you? What are you doing here?'

'We're Ruddlemoor men,' Jacob declared, 'and I don't doubt we're here for the same reason as Mr Retallick. To try to stop the works being ruined and having nigh on a thousand men being put out of work.'

'The Ruddlemoor Clay Works is closed as a result of strike action. I'm Sydney Woodhouse, Area Organiser for the Workers' Trade Union. The best thing you can do is go home and leave this to those who know how to negotiate such matters.'

'I know who you are. But your idea of negotiation seems to be limited to throwing rocks through a window and injuring an innocent man going about his business inside. I think it best if we stay around for a while.'

Sydney Woodhouse frowned. 'Who are you? Are you a Union member?'

'No, and I doubt if I ever will be now. The name's Pengelly. Jacob. I'm the son of the engine man whose sight is in danger as a result of the stone put through that window by one of your brave Union men.'

Jacob inclined his head in the direction of the broken window.

'I'm sorry about the injury to your father, of course, but there's no proof the stone was thrown by a Union man.'

Woodhouse tried hard to hide the anger he felt at Jacob's words. He was fully aware of the image he needed to portray to the Cornish members of his Union.

'I'm sorry to hear about your father, too,' Josh Retallick said. 'I remember him well from the days when I was more closely involved with Ruddlemoor – but what are you doing here tonight? I hope you're not looking for revenge for what's happened. It wouldn't help things.'

'I realise that, sir. No, my pa is worried about the fire being drawn here. He was speaking of what's likely to happen if the pumps are idle for very long. With the sort of weather we're having right now, I'd say his worries are justified.'

'No doubt about it. That's just what we've been telling Woodhouse.'

Jim Bray, Captain of the Ruddlemoor works, spoke for the first time. 'Unless the engine's set to work and the pumps operating by morning, the Ruddlemoor men will be out of work long after this strike's over. It seems everyone is aware of the seriousness of the situation except the man who's supposed to be looking after the interests of the workers. What he's doing is certainly not going to help the Ruddlemoor men.'

'Nor anyone else,' Josh Retallick endorsed the captain's words. 'But I don't doubt Mr Woodhouse realises that, now he's had time to think about it.'

The fact that a thousand men were employed at Ruddlemoor, all of them either Union members or prospective members, had not been lost upon Sydney Woodhouse. He was also aware that Josh Retallick was deliberately offering him a way out of the predicament he was in, without losing face in front of the men.

He took the proffered opportunity.

'The Workers' Union was formed to help the working man, not make his life more difficult – and I represent the Union here. I dislike intransigence almost as much as I do violence. Unlike most of the owners, I'm quite ready to listen to reasoned argument. You're a reasonable man, Mr Retallick. So am I. If all works owners were the same there would be no strike. All right, I'll allow the engine houses to remain working – but only in those pits where it can be proved that serious damage might be caused if the engine men are called out. You can set the Ruddlemoor engine to work now.'

'Good!' Suddenly brisk, Jim Bray said, 'I'll send out to find an engine man. We'll have things working again by morning.'

'We can have it working long before then,' Jacob declared. 'I came here tonight to fire up the engine – whether we had Mr Woodhouse's permission or not. I'll make a start on it right away.'

Aware of Jim Bray's doubts, he said, 'It's all right, Cap'n. I've been helping Pa here since I was old enough to walk. I can do the job as well as any engine man.'

'Go ahead, Jacob.' The authorisation came from Josh Retallick. 'The sooner the engine's running and the pumps working, the better. Cap'n Bray can bring in an engine man to check on what you've done as soon as he can find one. If he says you've got everything running all right, he might consider letting you work as an engine man until your father is well enough to take it on again.'

Delighted at Josh Retallick's faith in him, Jacob set about lighting the fire beneath the boiler and preparing to bring the engine into use.

He was almost ready to check out the pumps when the door was flung open and a very wet Ben Retallick burst in upon them.

'What the hell's going on here? Grandfather! What are you doing out on a night like this?'

'I've been out in far worse weather, Ben. As for what we're doing here . . . We're here looking after your interests. Cap'n Bray, Jacob and myself. We've all come to get the engine started again and the pumps working.'

'Never mind the pumps, or Ruddlemoor come to that. You should never have come out on a night like this. Look at you! You're soaked to the skin!'

'I'll soon get warmed through, now that young Jacob Pengelly's got the engine working again. He's a boy to watch, Ben. He's almost as good an engine man as his father. He has the interests of Ruddlemoor at heart, too.'

'Right now I'm more concerned for you than I am for the works. Come on, Grandfather. I've got my carriage outside. We'll get you home. On the way you can tell me what's been happening. I think you'd better prepare yourself for what Grandma will have to say to you about coming out in such weather, too.'

'She'll say nothing I haven't heard before, Ben – and I think you ought to express your thanks to young Jacob. He arrived at Ruddlemoor prepared to take on Woodhouse and his pickets to start the engine working again.' Turning his attention to Jacob, he said, 'I'm impressed with you, young man. My grandson will be too when he's had time to think about it. You're the sort of young man I'd have wanted working for me in the old days.'

Nodding an acknowledgement to Jacob, Ben Retallick hurried his grandfather out of the door of the engine house. Behind him, Jacob brought the pumps into use, warmed by the old man's praise.

16

⚜

Three days after the Ruddlemoor engine was brought back into operation, Josh Retallick died in the St Austell hospital. The cause of death was given as pneumonia. Had he lived another few days, he would have been eighty-nine years of age.

The morning after his night-time excursion to Ruddlemoor, Miriam had entered her husband's bedroom to find him with a raging temperature and having difficulty breathing.

The family doctor, hurriedly summoned from his house, declared the retired clay works owner was suffering the effects of a severe chill. He personally conveyed Josh to the hospital and had him admitted immediately.

During the course of the next couple of days it became increasingly evident to all his many visitors that Josh was fighting a losing battle for life.

As news spread of the seriousness of his illness, he

was visited by many of the county's dignitaries. The High Sheriff, Lord Lieutenant and civic leaders all called at the small hospital to convey their wishes for a full recovery to the doyen of clay works owners.

'I shouldn't let it go to your head,' Miriam had said to her husband as the Chairman of the County Council departed from the small private room where Josh was lying. 'It was the likes of him who would have preferred to see you hang when you were transported all those years ago.'

'It seems now as though all that happened in another lifetime, Miriam.'

Miriam was referring to the time when, as a young man, Josh too had been involved in the type of activity that eventually led to the formation of Trade Unions. Such actions had been regarded as seditious in those days.

Brought to trial, Josh had been fortunate to escape with his life. Instead, his punishment had been banishment to a penal colony. However, transportation had led to the founding of the Retallick family fortunes. Eventually granted a full pardon, he had returned home to Cornwall, accompanied by Miriam.

Josh's hand was being held by Miriam and she squeezed it affectionately. 'It was a lifetime ago, Josh, but you've achieved more than most men. It hasn't all been easy, but if I had my time over again I wouldn't miss a single one of the days we've spent together.'

'Nor me,' Josh declared breathlessly, his lungs labouring for air. He returned the pressure on her hand. 'But I fear I haven't very many days left.'

'I won't have you speaking like that,' Miriam leaned

closer to him. 'You're a fighter, Josh Retallick. You always have been.'

'It's all right, Miriam. We've had a wonderful life, you and I. Ben will take good care of you now . . .'

'Hush now, do you hear me? Save your breath and your energy. You'll be back home with me in the Gover valley before you know it.'

They were her last words to him. Josh died in his sleep only hours later, with Miriam still holding his hand.

'He was a wonderful old man,' Emma said to Jacob, brushing away her tears. 'There wasn't a man or woman up on the moor, especially around Sharptor, who didn't have cause to be grateful for what he'd done for them and for their families. You wouldn't find them listening to some Union man who was talking against Josh Retallick. They'd have run him out of Cornwall.'

She and Jacob were seated in the garden of Tregarrick. The exertions he had undertaken on behalf of Ruddlemoor had caused the wound in his back to break open yet again. This time he had needed to have it re-stitched at the hospital where Josh had died.

Jacob had been sent home with a warning. He was not to resume any form of work until it had been approved by a doctor.

He had come to Tregarrick thinking Emma might be pleased to see him, but she was not very good company today, as she had admitted to him earlier.

'How is Mr Retallick taking the death of his grandfather?' Jacob asked.

'He's angry with the Ruddlemoor men. He says if they hadn't come out on strike, his grandfather would still be alive. He's right, of course. Yet I can sympathise with the men too and their reason for taking strike action. It can't be easy bringing up a large family on the wages they're earning. After all, it's not as though Ben can't afford to pay them more.'

'That's what Woodhouse says about all the owners. I know I should agree with him, but I just don't like the man. Anyway, after what's happened to Pa, I'm angry with the Union and the men who've joined it.'

'You're almost as mixed up as I am, Jacob. My sympathies are with the men, but it's difficult for me to say what I think, living here with Ben and Lily. They're both so good to me.'

At that moment Jacob saw an old woman, dressed in black and leaning heavily on a stick, coming along the path from the direction of the house.

'There's someone coming.'

Peering past him, Emma said, 'That's Great Aunt Miriam. Ben insisted she should come and live at Tregarrick for a while. Personally, I don't think she'll ever return to the Gover valley.'

As Miriam drew closer, Jacob rose to his feet respectfully. When she was level with them, Miriam stopped and her lively, dark eyes scanned him from head to toe.

'Who are you?'

'Jacob Pengelly, Mrs Retallick. I . . . I'm very sorry about Mr Retallick.'

'There's no need to be. He led a long, full and fulfilled life and he died with nothing on his conscience. The Good Lord will find a place for him, I'm certain of that.'

Using her stick as a teacher might use a pointer, she pushed it in his direction and said, 'You're the lad who brought Emma up from the Cargloss pit.'

'That's right, ma'am.' The lively, dark eyes made him feel uncomfortable.

'Ha! I still can't understand what you were both doing up there in the first place!' Her piercing gaze had not wavered. Now she asked, 'Didn't you arrive at the Ruddlemoor engine house while Josh was there?'

'That's right, ma'am.'

'Why? What were you doing there? Were you one of the strikers?'

'No, ma'am. I intended firing-up the engine, whether Woodhouse agreed to it or not. As it happened, Mr Retallick was able to persuade him to let the engine begin working again, so there was no trouble.'

'Were you there out of concern for Ruddlemoor or because you were angry your father had been hurt by the strikers?'

Jacob found Miriam Retallick's direct questions disconcerting, but he answered her honestly. 'It was a little of both. I believe the men deserve the extra money they're asking for, but it isn't worth putting Ruddlemoor out of business for the sake of three and sixpence.'

The gaze remained fixed upon him for perhaps another half-minute. Then Miriam turned to Emma. 'I've always liked a man who didn't just talk about the things he thought were wrong but who set out to put them right. He's honest too. You could do a lot worse, Emma. A lot worse. Hang on to him.'

Leaving these words of wisdom hanging on the air behind her, Miriam Retallick resumed her walk along the garden path, leaving Emma and Jacob too embarrassed to look at each other for some minutes.

17

The funeral of Josh Retallick brought the town of St Austell to a halt. Since arriving in clay country twenty years before, he and Miriam had attended the Wesleyan chapel in the town. It was situated beside the main road that passed by Ruddlemoor and it was here that the funeral service was held.

Both Josh and Miriam were well known and respected in the town and all the local and regional newspapers had reported the death of Josh Retallick.

They also printed a summary of the adventurous life he had led since his birth on Bodmin Moor's Sharptor in the year 1824.

As a mark of respect to this remarkable son of Cornwall, the shops in the town closed for the duration of the funeral service and in the cortège were representatives of many of the great families of Cornwall.

Ben had let it be known he did not want to see any Ruddlemoor men at the funeral service. He held the striking workers responsible for his grandfather's death. Nevertheless, the Ruddlemoor men, including Jacob and his father, were among those who lined the route to the chapel.

There were many other clay workers present too and they removed their headgear and bowed their heads respectfully as the carriage carrying the coffin passed by.

All were aware that a link with Cornwall's great mining past was passing before their eyes.

Entering the chapel beside Miriam, Lily squeezed the older woman's arm. 'Grandfather Josh was a well-respected man. You must be very proud.'

'Respect is like fashion, Lily. A whimsical thing that counts for very little. I fell in love with Josh when I was eleven years old. I loved him as much on the day he died as I did all those years before. He loved me too. That meant more to both of us than the fickle regard of others.'

Swinging along behind them on her crutches, Emma heard Miriam's words. She pondered on them throughout the long eulogistic service that followed.

Early that evening a servant from Tregarrick came to the small Pengelly cottage with a message for Jacob. It was from Emma. Her family was staying at the house overnight. Emma wanted to introduce him to them.

The idea of meeting so many members of Emma's family on the day of such an important and public funeral did not appeal to Jacob at all. However, he had been trying to think of some way in which he could bring Emma to Carthew to meet his parents. She could hardly refuse if he acceded to her request now.

Despite his misgivings he was secretly pleased to have been asked. It meant Emma viewed their relationship as being something stronger than friendship.

Accepting the invitation, Jacob hurried to get ready, taking far more care with his appearance than usual. As a result he had to endure the gentle mocking of his father and the excited fussing of his mother.

Eventually, satisfied with his appearance and wearing his Sunday-best serge suit, Jacob set off. His mother's advice on how he should behave in the company of 'gentry' followed after him until he reached the road.

There were a great many people milling around in the gardens of Tregarrick, but his mother would have been disappointed had she seen them. Most were dressed no more elegantly than a Sunday congregation of the local Methodist chapel.

As he neared the house, Jacob slowed his pace uncertainly. Then he heard his name being called. Looking about him, he saw Emma making her way towards him from one of the side lawns.

Despite the crutches she was using, the two girls by her side were finding it difficult to keep up with her.

Reaching him, Emma said excitedly, 'Hello, Jacob. I'm glad you were able to come.' Indicating the two girls with a movement of her head, she said, 'These are two of my sisters. The tall one is Jane, the other one is Cissy.'

Both girls were scrutinising him with great interest and Cissy, with a boldness he found embarrassing, said, 'Well! Aren't you the lucky one, our Emma. He could carry me out of a pit any day of the week.'

Pointedly ignoring her sister, Emma said, 'I was

telling the family about you. How you rescued me from the Cargloss pit. When Lily said we'd been seeing each other quite often since then, my ma said she'd like to meet you.'

Emma was bubbling over with excitement. Jacob thought it hardly in keeping with a funeral party, but decided she must be overjoyed to have her family about her for the day.

She led him to where a number of women were seated about Miriam. Here she introduced him to her mother.

Kate Cotton was a small, washed-out woman, who had probably once been very pretty. Holding out a limp hand, she eyed Jacob speculatively.

'So you're the young man who risked his life to save our Emma. We're all very grateful to you, Mr Pengelly. She had no right to put anyone's life at risk. But she's always been far too headstrong for her own good . . .'

Kate Cotton suddenly remembered that, besides Emma, she had two more unmarried daughters living at home. Jacob might be a potential husband. She added hurriedly, '. . . Yet she's a good girl, for all that.'

Aware of the knowing grins of Cissy and Jane, she added, 'Far less trouble than some others I could mention.'

Smiling up at Jacob, she said, transparently, 'Come and sit here and tell me something about yourself and your family . . .'

For some twenty minutes Jacob underwent a searching and, at times, embarrassing interrogation by Kate Cotton and he became increasingly ill at ease.

On two occasions Emma tried to bring the questioning

to a halt, but her mother continued talking as though she had not heard her.

When succour eventually arrived, it was from an unexpected source.

Ben Retallick had joined the group a few minutes before. After listening with restrained amusement to Kate Cotton, he said to Miriam, 'Are you all right, Grandmother?'

'No, I'm not. I've had enough of folk for today. I shall go up to my room now.'

'I'll come with you,' Ben volunteered – but Miriam had other ideas.

'No you won't. This young man can walk with me and hold my arm when we reach the stairs. Come along, Jacob.'

He rose to his feet gratefully, but Miriam observed the dismay on the face of Emma. Her mother had monopolised Jacob for the whole of his visit to Tregarrick. Now Miriam was taking him off!

'Don't worry, young lady. He'll be back in a few minutes. While you're waiting, see if you can find a drink for him. All the talking he's done will have given him a thirst.'

Miriam rose to her feet and, leaning heavily on her stick, walked away from the group.

Jacob walked slowly by her side. Before they had passed beyond the hearing of the others, Miriam said loudly, 'If everyone was like Kate Cotton, all young men would need to go around carrying a pedigree in their pockets. Listening to some of the things she was asking you reminded me of the questions Josh put to a horse dealer when he bought a stallion to cover a mare I owned at the time.'

Choking on the polite reply he intended making, Jacob said, 'I don't mind. I'm sure she only has Emma's interests at heart.'

'She has Kate Cotton's interests at heart, Jacob, believe me. She married off her daughter Mabel to a butcher twice the poor girl's age. The man she really wanted to marry was a young lad who'll never be more than a cowherd on a poor moorland farm – but he wasn't good enough to suit Kate.'

When Jacob made no reply, Miriam cast a glance at him. 'What are your feelings for young Emma, Jacob?'

'I like her, Mrs Retallick. I . . . I like her very much.'

She looked at him once more. 'I suppose that would pass for enthusiasm among young people today. Anyway, it's a start . . . Help me up these steps, if you please.'

Jacob took her arm and helped her up the wide steps that led to the main entrance and into the hall beyond.

'Emma's very fond of you, I can tell you.'

'How do you know?' Jacob asked the question eagerly.

Miriam made a derisive sound. 'Young man, I've lived for almost ninety years. I can tell things about most folk that they don't know about themselves. Emma's one of them . . . Give me your arm again.'

They had reached the wide and impressive staircase that rose from the centre of the hall.

As they began to ascend the stairs, slowly, Miriam said, 'That girl's got more about her than the rest of her family put together. She thinks about things in the same way I did when I was her age. Things go deep with her. So deep you'll never realise they are there until you know her well enough. She'll never be one of those "comfortable" women, though. You won't find her sitting at home raising an endless string of children. No, nor waiting for her husband to come home so she can put a meal on the table in front of him, afraid to contradict anything he has to say. Whoever takes on young Emma isn't going to have that sort of life.'

They had reached a wide landing now and Miriam paused for a moment.

'But if a man wants a woman who'll be his strength when he needs it most, who he can turn to when he's got a serious problem and who'll be his soulmate for the whole of their lives together, then he'll thank the Good Lord if he's the one she chooses.'

Miriam began climbing the stairs once more, with Jacob's support.

Halfway along the passageway at the top of the stairs, Miriam stopped at a door and said, 'Here we are, young man. Thank you for helping me up the stairs.'

'It's been a pleasure, Mrs Retallick.' He hesitated. 'Is there anything else I can do? I mean . . . I know it must have been a very unhappy day for you. Can I ask the servants to bring you something?'

'No, but thank you for thinking of it.' Giving him one of her disconcerting looks, she added, 'I've already told you that Emma reminds me of myself when I was her age. Well, you remind me of my husband, Josh – and you'll never be paid a higher compliment by anyone. I may be the only one to see it at the moment, but the two of you are made for each other. Don't lose her, Jacob. She's a very special girl, and I believe you're a very sound young man.'

'Thank you, Mrs Retallick, but . . . you're sure there's nothing I can do for you?'

'Nothing, Jacob. Josh may be dead, but I know he can still hear me. I'll speak to him for a while, then say a prayer and get to bed. Go back downstairs now. Take Emma away from her mother and those sisters of hers. Find the right moment and tell her how you feel about her. Whatever she says to you, don't lose her, Jacob. You won't find another like her.'

Jacob thought of Miriam's words as he walked home in the dusk of that late summer day. He had not been able to follow Miriam Retallick's advice. Wherever he went with Emma, it seemed that one or other of her sisters came too.

Nevertheless, he felt he had passed Mrs Cotton's critical scrutiny and Emma seemed happy.

That would have to suffice for now.

18

The morning after the funeral, Captain Bray arrived at Tregarrick early, asking to speak to Ben.

Shown to the study, he found the works owner busy writing letters of acknowledgement to those who had sent commiserations on the death of his grandfather.

Putting down his pen, Ben raised a strained face to his works captain.

'Good morning, Jim. What can I do for you? Has there been any new development in the strike?'

Jim Bray nodded. 'Some of the Ruddlemoor men called to see me at home last night. They asked me to pass on their condolences to you.'

'A hollow sentiment in view of the incident which caused my grandfather's death.' Ben spoke bitterly. 'If they hadn't gone on strike and forced the shut-down of the engine, he would still be with us now.'

'The men feel that very deeply. Nothing's going to bring your grandfather back, of course, but they've asked me to tell you they intend returning to work later today, as a token of respect for him.'

'Well! That's unexpected, to say the least.' Ben leaned back in the chair and looked up at his works captain. 'How do you think Woodhouse will react?'

'I don't know, that's why I thought I should come and see you right away,' Jim Bray said, his concern plain to see. 'Woodhouse won't allow the men to go back to work without putting up a hell of a fight. He knows that if the Ruddlemoor men are working the strike doesn't stand a chance of succeeding. We're the biggest employer in clay country. I believe he'll go to any lengths to bring them out again. If the men are to stay in work we'll need police protection for them and their families – and you have far more influence with the police authority than me.'

'Are you convinced they'll do as they say? Go back to full working?'

Jim Bray nodded. 'All except a handful, yes.'

Ben sat deep in thought for some minutes. When he eventually raised his head once more, he said, 'I've got mixed feelings about this, Jim. The strike has to be broken, one way or another, but this is going to put Ruddlemoor right up there in the firing-line. As you say, Woodhouse must realise he needs to break us – or we'll break the Union. What's your opinion?'

'I'm a clay captain, Ben.' The Ruddlemoor captain had known Ben for long enough to call him by his first name. 'All I'm interested in is producing clay and making a profit for you. But, as you say, this strike has to be broken. I'd rather it wasn't Ruddlemoor that had to fight everyone else's battles, but if that's the way it's got to be, so be it. You bring the police in to give us protection and I'll see to it that Ruddlemoor produces clay.'

'That's all I need to hear, Jim. Get back to Ruddlemoor and be ready to take the men back on the books. I'll go into St Austell and see the police superintendent. With any luck, we'll bring this strike to an end more quickly than looked likely a couple of days ago.'

Police Superintendent Carey Pollitt gave a sympathetic hearing to Ben's request for a strong police presence at the Ruddlemoor works. He was also deeply apologetic.

'There are two hundred and fifty officers in the Cornwall constabulary, Mr Retallick. At this very moment a hundred of them are performing duties right here in the St Austell area. All are working extra hours. Every clay works has its own special problems. Reports of intimidation and actual acts of violence are being reported on an almost hourly basis – and we have to look into each one of them.'

The superintendent shrugged. 'I'll certainly give you any help I can, but I fear it may be very little more than you are receiving at present.'

'When Ruddlemoor resumes work the level of picketing is bound to escalate, with a subsequent increase in intimidation and violence. You're not telling me you'll stand by and do nothing when that happens, surely?'

'No, Mr Retallick, but until the problem actually exists I'll have difficulty convincing my chief constable of the full seriousness of the situation we are facing here. Once he does appreciate the problem, I am hoping he will put into operation a plan I have already submitted to him.'

'May I ask what it is?'

'More constables, Mr Retallick. If things become really ugly – and I am inclined to agree with you that they will – I have suggested we seek the aid of other police forces. I have already had an offer of help from the police of Devonport.'

The superintendent leaned closer to Ben. 'Another force I have in mind is the Glamorgan Constabulary. Officers there have had considerable experience in dealing with striking miners. However, this is told to you in the strictest confidence, you understand?'

Ben nodded, but said grimly, 'It will be a sad day for Cornish workers if outside help needs to be brought in to enable the men and women of the county to go about their lawful business.'

'A sad day indeed, Mr Retallick. Made all the worse by having Cornishmen inflict violence on those of their fellows who insist on exercising their right to work. As you will appreciate, my main task is to ensure the law is not broken. Open your works, Mr Retallick. That is your right. The Union's right is to picket your works and try to persuade your men to remain on strike. But such picketing must be peaceful. If it gets out of hand, I will take all steps necessary to bring it under control, even if it does mean bringing in constables from outside the county.'

Leaning back in his chair once more, the senior policeman said, 'There you have it, Mr Retallick. You and I are both faced with a difficult situation. I fear it cannot have a peaceful end – unless, of course, you and the other owners change your mind and agree to the pay rise demanded by the Workers' Union.'

'Mr Woodhouse and his Union already know that isn't possible. If prices in the clay market hold, I and the

other owners should be able to offer the men a modest
pay rise in, say, six months' time, or possibly sooner.
We can't do it immediately. We need to consolidate our
markets first.'

Superintendent Pollitt shrugged his shoulders in a
gesture of resignation. 'Yesterday Mr Woodhouse sat
in that very seat and assured me the owners could
afford to pay his men what is being demanded. He
had come here to complain about what he referred to
as the "heavy-handed tactics" adopted by my constables
at one of the other works. He declared his men were
only demanding a fair wage from owners who could
well afford to pay it to their employees. He said the
strike will continue until you and your fellow owners
give in to the men's demands. I fear this will be a long
and increasingly bitter struggle, Mr Retallick. While the
dispute is running its course, neither you nor I are going
to make any friends.'

19

Emma greeted Jacob joyfully when he found her on their favourite seat in Ben Retallick's large garden. Jacob came to Tregarrick most days now.

'I saw the doctor today. He says my leg has healed much faster than he expected. I'm to go to the hospital tomorrow and if all is well I can have the plaster cast removed. Isn't that wonderful news?'

'Great! But the plaster has only been on for a little over four weeks. That doesn't seem long enough for a broken leg to mend,' Jacob said dubiously.

'He says I'm a good healer, whatever that means.'

It was a glorious summer evening. Jacob had been on the morning shift at Ruddlemoor. He had come to visit Emma after having only a hurried meal at his home.

He was no longer employed in the dry. Instead, he had resumed work at Ruddlemoor as a trainee engine man, working with his father. Absalom had recovered from his injuries, although he still wore a patch covering his eye, and was awaiting an appointment with a specialist to learn whether the loss of sight was permanent.

Two weeks had elapsed since Ruddlemoor reopened. Pickets were always present at the works' gate. They were occasionally noisy, but no serious attempt had so far been made to prevent the men from working.

Nevertheless, there was an air of nervousness among the workforce. Whenever support for the strike showed signs of weakening, picketing action was stepped up. The last couple of days had seen a serious escalation in incidents of violence throughout clay country.

Cornwall's chief constable had kept the promise made to Ben by the St Austell superintendent and had called in help from outside police authorities.

Thirty policemen had arrived by train the previous day from the dockside town of Devonport. It was known more would soon arrive from Bristol, and there was a strong rumour of at least a hundred constables being brought in from Wales.

'What shall we do to celebrate the removal of your plaster cast?' Jacob asked.

'Will you take me to St Austell to look around the shops?' Emma asked eagerly.

Jacob looked doubtful. 'Surely you won't be able to do much walking immediately?'

'Why not? With you to help support me – if I need it – I'll be all right. I'm being taken to the St Austell hospital in Ben's motor car. Meet me there and I'll ask the driver to drop us at the shops on the way back.'

Jacob was still dubious about the plan, but he eventually agreed. Emma was so excited at the thought of being free of the heavy plaster cast and the irksome restrictions it imposed upon her, she flung her arms about Jacob and kissed him.

When she released him, an extremely flustered Jacob said, 'That . . . that's the first time you've ever kissed me.'

'So? I'm still waiting for you to kiss me!'

She had to wait for only a few more moments. Neither of them heard Lily come along the path from the house. The works owner's wife was momentarily taken aback by what she witnessed. Then, with a reminiscent smile, she backed away quietly and returned to the house.

She was in agreement with Miriam. Jacob and Emma were ideally suited. It would be nice to have wedding celebrations at Tregarrick.

When the plaster cast was removed from Emma's leg she was not as mobile as she had expected to be. Reluctantly she accepted one of the crutches she had been hoping to discard. She was to use it until she felt a walking stick would suffice.

Not being fully mobile annoyed her, but the mood passed quickly when she met up with Jacob and they began looking in the shop windows. When she had been living on the moor, the nearest town had been Liskeard, many miles away. Emma had been there on only three occasions. Shopping, even window shopping, was a new experience for her.

She was even more thrilled when Jacob bought a gilt locket and chain from one of the shops and, rather shyly, gave it to her as a present.

She insisted that he secure the chain around her neck immediately and as they made their way along the

single shopping street, she frequently put her free hand
to the gift, to make quite certain it was still there.

As they approached the market building, they heard
the noise of an excited crowd. When they drew nearer it
was evident that a meeting was being held. Jacob recognised the speaker immediately as Sydney Woodhouse.

'I don't think we want to hear what he has to say,'
Jacob declared. 'Shall we go back along the other side
of the road and look at the rest of the shops?'

'No, let's listen to him, Jacob – just for a while. I'd
like to learn what kind of a man he is.'

Emma found the appearance of Sydney Woodhouse
disappointing. A small, portly man of about forty years
of age, he was balding and had an air of weariness
about him.

He had delivered his talk from the stone surround of
a drinking fountain and was receiving loud applause
from his audience.

'It seems we've just missed what he had to say,' Jacob
said hopefully. 'Shall we go?' He felt uncomfortable in
the vicinity of so many Union men. It was possible
he would be recognised as a working clay man from
Ruddlemoor.

At that moment, Woodhouse held up his hand, calling
for silence. When the applause had died away, he said,
'Now I have a young lady who wants to say a few words
to you. She's a member of the East London Federation of
Suffragettes and her association has supported a great
many disputes involving the Trade Unions. She has
recently been in the north of England where they've
had a few problems of their own. Here she is, Miss
Tessa Wren.'

'I want to hear this,' Emma said eagerly. Taking

Jacob's arm, she leaned against him to take the weight off her aching leg.

The young woman introduced by Sydney Woodhouse was perhaps twenty-four. Wearing spectacles, there was a somewhat studious air about her, although she was by no means unattractive.

Some of the men in the crowd seemed offended that the Trade Union organiser had brought along a young woman to address them. Others questioned what she could possibly know about their problems, but the woman's voice rose above their mutterings.

'You've just listened to Mr Woodhouse telling you that things are "progressing well". Is that what you believe?'

The response to her question was minimal, with an equal number of 'Yes' and 'No' calls.

'Well, I'll tell you what I think,' the woman said. 'I believe you're losing your battle with the employers. Losing hands down – and it's entirely your own fault.'

Her words provoked an angry howl of disagreement from her listeners.

Tessa Wren allowed the response to take its course, without attempting to silence their shouted remarks. Eventually, baffled by her continuing silence, the crowd followed her example.

When she spoke again it was to repeat her accusation. 'I said it's your own fault, and that's what I mean.'

The swell of resentment rose again, but she raised her voice to shout above them. 'It's your fault because you're still playing a game. A gentleman's game – and you're not gentlemen. It's the employers who are making the rules and you're letting them do it.'

There was less anger from the crowd now. They were curious to learn what she would say next.

'The only way to get what you want – if you really want it – is to hit the employers where it hurts – and hit them hard.'

'That's easier said than done!'

'That's easy enough for you to say. How are we going to do it?'

'What do you know about it? You're not even from this part of the world.'

The shouts came thick and fast from the crowd.

'I'll tell you what I know about it – and I don't need to live in Cornwall to be able to see it for myself. I've just come from Salford, where the women working in the mills were paid far less than men who were doing the same job. Far less than you're getting – even though some were widows with families to support. In mill after mill they tried to get an increase in their pay, but no one took them seriously. Not until they got together and they all walked out, bringing every mill to a halt. That's when they won and got what they deserved – and that's the way you'll have to do it here if you're serious about getting what you're asking for. The employers stick together – so should you. Show them you mean what you say and that you don't care what you have to do to get it. None of this gentlemanly, "Never mind, we'll keep the engines running for you, sir". The engines have to be brought to a halt. Engine-house fires must be drawn. Not until you are as ruthless as the employers will you win.'

'It's all very well for you talking like that,' one of the strikers among the crowd called out. 'When this is over you can just walk away and go home. We have to stay here and pick up our way of life again.'

'Then why are you out on strike?' Tessa Wren retorted. 'Just so you can collect the Union's ten shillings a week and spend your time at home digging your garden? I thought you had called a strike in order to win a living wage. You'll not get it by doing things half-heartedly. Carry on the way you're going and in a week or two's time you'll be slinking back to work, tail between your legs, having got precisely – nothing! It's time you made up your minds whether you're free men and are going to be treated as such, or second-class men who were born to bow and scrape to your masters! I know what I'd do, but perhaps Cornish men don't have the guts of a London woman.'

Her comment brought a howl of anger from the listening men, and the sound grew.

Neither Emma nor Jacob had observed a large party of policemen assembling in a nearby side street. Emerging now, they moved out and began breaking up the crowd.

Some of the constables used unnecessarily rough methods. When the men, stirred up by Tessa Wren's scathing contempt, resisted, fighting broke out.

Jacob hastily led Emma away from the increasingly violent scene.

When they were far enough away for safety, Jacob said, 'Phew! That woman certainly stirred up the men.'

'Yes,' Emma agreed, excitedly. 'She showed them up for what they are.'

'She did it deliberately. Do you approve of that?'

'It doesn't matter whether I approve, or not. What was exciting was to see a woman able to make a crowd of men like that listen to her and get them roused up in such a manner. I thought she was magnificent!'

Jacob looked at Emma and a wave of despair swept over him. This side of her character had remained dormant during recent weeks. He had been given a strong reminder that it was still there.

Emma Cotton's boundaries extended a long way beyond a husband, children and the four walls of a small cottage.

20

Three days after the violence of the St Austell meeting, Jacob made his way to Tregarrick to visit Emma. Passing Ruddlemoor, he ignored the jeers and catcalls of pickets who had watched him leave work only a couple of hours earlier.

There were more of them out today. It was possibly coincidental, but picketing throughout clay country had been stepped up since Tessa Wren had made her speech to the strikers.

More pits had shut down too. The actual number fluctuated from day to day, but at the moment more than half had been brought to a halt by the industrial actions of their workers.

In St Austell, Jacob passed by Market House. There was no meeting here today. Only some half-dozen police constables were on duty to prevent any gathering of strikers.

At Tregarrick, Jacob was let into the house by a

servant. He met with Cissy, Emma's sister, in the hall-way. She had stayed on at the big house after the funeral to help care for Miriam until Emma's leg was fully healed.

Giving Jacob a bold, welcoming smile, she said, 'You're going to have to wait for our Emma today. She's upstairs, getting herself all made up.'

'What for?' Jacob had a moment's panic as he tried to remember whether he had arranged to take Emma out somewhere and had forgotten about it.

'Oh, it's not for you,' Cissy said, spitefully. 'We've got a suffragette coming to the house this afternoon.'

'A suffragette here – at Tregarrick?'

'That's right. She writes for various suffragette maga-zines and newspapers. She's coming here to interview Great Aunt Miriam. You'll get no sense out of our Emma until after this woman's been and gone. You might as well come out for a walk with me. I'm off to do some shopping in St Austell.'

'Won't Mrs Retallick need you here if she's getting ready to be interviewed?'

'She doesn't really need anyone to do anything for her. Anyway, she likes having our Emma around far more than she does me. You coming?'

Jacob shook his head. 'I'll wait here for Emma.'

Cissy's shrug gave no hint of her disappointment. 'You'd have a better time with me than you will with Emma today, but please yourself.'

Jacob had only a few minutes to wait for Emma. She showed no obvious signs of having gone to a great deal of trouble on behalf of the expected visitor. However, she was highly excited.

'Jacob! Guess what's happening this afternoon?'

'I know, you've got a suffragette coming to the house.'

'Who told you?' Emma pouted. 'Oh, I suppose it was Cissy.'

'That's right, but tell me about it.'

'I don't suppose I can tell you any more than Cissy already has . . . but here's Great Aunt Miriam now.'

Miriam Retallick put in an appearance at the top of the stairway. As she began to descend carefully, Jacob hurried up the stairs to her and offered her his arm.

'Thank you, young man.' Miriam took hold of his arm gratefully. When they reached the hall, she said, 'I suppose you'll be sitting in on this interview and discovering all my secrets?'

'I . . . I don't know.'

'Of course you'll be there. You've come to Tregarrick to see Emma and she wouldn't miss the opportunity of meeting a real live suffragette. Come along, give me your arm again and take me to the sitting room. On the way you can tell me what's happening with this strike . . .'

They hardly had time to seat themselves before a maid put her head in through the doorway to announce the arrival of the expected visitor as, 'The lady from the suffragettes, ma'am.'

Jacob and Emma rose to their feet. But when the maid stood back to allow the woman to enter the room, Jacob's mouth dropped open with surprise. It was Tessa Wren, the woman who had addressed the miners in St Austell a few days before!

She greeted Miriam and Emma warmly enough, but frowned when she was introduced to Jacob.

'Will he be present during the interview?' The question was asked of Miriam pleasantly enough, but no one doubted that she would rather he left the room. As though to justify her question, she added, 'I find women are far more reticent when they are interviewed in front of men.'

'Then you have only interviewed women who care what men think of them,' Miriam retorted. 'I've lost the only man whose opinion mattered to me – and I had no secrets from him. Besides, I am too old to bother about what people think of me – women or men. Jacob will stay.'

Miriam's statement brooked no argument. Jacob remained in the room.

It was not long before Jacob's presence was forgotten. Tessa Wren proved to be a skilful interviewer and gradually Miriam's remarkable story was drawn from her.

The matriarch of the Retallick family was speaking when Lily entered the room and sat down quietly without interrupting either Miriam or her interviewer.

In the living room of the quiet, Cornish manor house, a story unfolded that held the listeners spellbound. Much of Miriam's story was already known to family members, but no one had ever heard it told by Miriam.

It began with Miriam's birth in a home that was little more than a cave high on Bodmin moor. Her father was a bullying, drunken miner who had been hounded to his death by other miners after raping a young mother.

When still a young girl she had met and fallen in love with Josh. However, due in part to her father's death, she had married a Methodist preacher, even though she was carrying Josh's child – who would grow up to father Ben and his brothers.

When the preacher was instrumental in having Josh convicted of sedition and sentenced to transportation, Miriam had contrived to go with him, taking their son, Daniel.

Shipwrecked on the notorious Skeleton Coast of Africa, Miriam, Josh and Daniel had suffered great hardships during many years spent living among the tribesmen of Southern Africa.

Eventually, Josh had been pardoned by Queen Victoria. He and Miriam had then returned to Cornwall, leaving Daniel in Africa where he had been granted a vast landholding by the African ruler of Matabeleland.

Back in Cornwall, Josh and Miriam had bought the Sharptor Mine, on Bodmin Moor, where Josh had once worked. Here they spent many happy years.

After the collapse of the Cornish mining industry, Josh bought Ruddlemoor and he and Miriam moved to clay country.

Meanwhile in Africa, Daniel and his eldest son had been killed in a tribal uprising, leaving a widow and three sons to inherit his lands.

Ben, the youngest of these sons, had come to England when he was no more than nineteen years old. Eventually, he took control of Ruddlemoor, allowing Josh and Miriam to enjoy some years of happy retirement.

Miriam had been telling her story for almost two hours. During this time Ben returned to Tregarrick and slipped into the room to join the others in enthralled silence.

Eventually, Miriam brought the interview to a close in characteristic fashion. 'Well, young lady, I think I've told you enough to make an article in any newspaper or magazine, or wherever else you want to use it. Now, help me to my room, Jacob. I'll have a drink sent up and take my evening meal there. I know it's only my tongue that's been exercised, but going back over all those years has exhausted me. If you want any more, young lady, you'll need to come and see me another day. Don't bother writing, I don't reply to letters any more.'

With this she signalled to Jacob to help her to her feet. Linking arms with him she walked stiffly from the sitting room.

Miriam ascended the stairs slowly, pausing frequently to rest.

'How did your first meeting with a suffragette impress you, Jacob?' Miriam put the question to him during one of her brief rests.

'It wasn't actually the first time I'd seen her,' he said and told Miriam of the meeting in St Austell, when she had stirred up the striking clay workers.

'I wish I'd known that when we were speaking to her downstairs,' Miriam said. Then, after a few moments of reflection, she said, 'No, perhaps it's as well I didn't. She's got something about her, that one. She's not so very different to the way I was when I was a few years younger than she is now. She's a young woman with a cause. I'm not in complete disagreement with her, even though she's giving Ben and the other owners a hard time. All the same, you must try to guide young Emma away from her. If you're serious in your feelings, marry the girl as quickly as you can. If you don't, you'll lose her. Emma's a girl with a cause too, Jacob. She'll give her all to whichever one of you wins. If you love the girl, make certain it's you.'

21

'My grandmother is a truly remarkable woman,' Ben said conversationally when Miriam and Jacob had left the sitting room.

'You'll be the clay works employer,' Tessa Wren said. 'I thought you must be. I saw you enter the room, but I didn't want to interrupt Mrs Retallick.'

Ben inclined his head to her, saying, 'And you, of course, are Miss Wren. I hear you've been actively encouraging the men to extend their strike in an effort to gain their objectives.'

'They have only one "objective", Mr Retallick. A fair and reasonable wage – and I've been encouraging women as well as the men. Does that anger you?'

Tessa seemed not at all discomfited to be arguing the issue in the home of an employer.

'Anger me?' Ben did not take offence at her forth-rightness. 'No, Miss Wren, it saddens me. I am perhaps more aware than you of the need to improve the lot of our clay workers. Many owners feel the same. If prices hold, the men will get their rise in six months' time – sooner if possible, but it can't be done immediately. The clay industry has been through a very bad period. Prices have been so low that many owners have put themselves deeply in debt in order to survive. They need time to pay off those debts if they're to remain in business. They simply can't afford to raise wages for the men right now. What's more, the longer the strike lasts, the farther away a pay rise will be.'

'It's not only the men who should be given a pay rise, Mr Retallick. You employ women too, a fact that seems to have been ignored by both sides in this dispute.'

Looking around her with an expression of studied scepticism, she said, 'I can see few signs of hard times in your life style, Mr Retallick. It's a far cry from the cottages of the workers I've visited here in Cornwall.'

Lily made a disapproving sound at what she considered to be the other woman's impertinence, but it was Ben who replied.

'I'm fortunate in not needing to depend on my clay holdings for a living, Miss Wren. Most employers in the district do.'

'If you can afford it, why don't you give your workers a pay increase and set an example to the others?'

'My duty is not only to my workers . . .' With the trace of a smile, Ben added, 'And I am referring to both men and women. I also have an obligation to other owners. One employer raising wages would cause even more discontent in the industry than exists at present. I try to help my employees in other ways, as Jacob could tell you when he returns. Many workers are living in rent-free cottages, and there is no shortage of overtime working for those who need extra money.'

'No one should have to work all the hours God gives in order to earn a decent wage.'

It seemed Tessa was determined not to accept any of Ben's arguments. Lily thought it was time she brought the prickly conversation to an end.

'I think we've discussed the problems in the clay industry quite long enough for one day. It's almost time to eat. Will you stay for a meal with us, Miss Wren?'

'Thank you, no. I must write up my interview with Mrs Retallick senior and get it in the post to London. I'll have a copy of the article sent to you when the interview is published.'

Relaxing momentarily, she returned her attention to Ben. 'We may not see eye to eye on the problems of your workers, Mr Retallick, but I thank you for your courtesy. I tried to interview a Mr Robartes in Fowey yesterday to clarify some of the remarks he has made in public about the suffragette movement. He stopped short of actual violence towards me, but I had a most uncomfortable reception at his house.'

'I'll walk as far as the road with you,' Emma said, as Tessa turned to go. 'If you don't mind walking slowly.'

As the two set off along the drive from the house, Tessa asked, 'Have you always had something wrong with your leg?'

'No, I went over the cliff into a clay pit when they set off an explosion.' As they walked along, Emma described the accident and Jacob's part in her rescue.

'He doesn't impress me as a hero,' Tessa said in a dismissive manner. 'He seems far too quiet.'

'There's nothing wrong with Jacob,' Emma said defensively. 'He's got more about him than any of the others I've met.'

'What are you doing in the Retallick house?' Tessa asked suddenly. 'Do you live here?'

'For the moment. I'm a distant relative of the Retallicks – a very distant relative. I'm supposed to be a companion for Miriam, but I haven't been able to do much while my leg was in plaster, so my sister's been brought in to help too. Anyway, Great Aunt Miriam is far too independent to want anyone around her all the time.'

'I could tell that during my interview with her,' Tessa agreed. 'But she won't live for ever. What will you do when she's gone? Marry Jacob, I suppose, and settle down to a life with more kids than money coming your way?'

'That depends on how long Jacob is prepared to wait for me – or even if he wants to,' Emma said. 'I have no intention of marrying anyone just yet. There are too many things to do with my life first.'

'Oh? What sort of things?' Tessa looked at Emma with a new interest.

'The sort of thing you're doing, for one. Going around the country pointing out that women should have a say in what's going on around us. Showing we have something to offer. Take this strike, for instance. Women have their own ideas about what's going on. Yet they're expected to say nothing while husbands, fathers and brothers take decisions that will have a long-term effect on their lives and on the families most are struggling to bring up.'

'Where do you stand on this strike?' Tessa asked, frowning. 'You're living in the home of one of the most important clay works owners, yet you talk almost as though you're in sympathy with the strikers and their wives.'

'It isn't always easy,' Emma admitted, 'especially as Jacob is working in the Ruddlemoor engine house now and is determined to keep the engines running. But I've thought a lot about what's going on. I'm convinced there's a way out of it that would suit everybody. Ben has said the owners can't afford a pay rise right now, but might be able to pay it in six months' time. Couldn't the owners and the strikers come halfway to meet each other? Agree to a pay rise in, say, three months' time? That way they would both be showing goodwill and neither side could taunt the other by saying they'd won the victory.'

'You've got more than a turnip for a head, Emma. What you say is a sound common-sense solution but I doubt if you'll get either side to agree. Matters have gone too far. The men's Union needs to flex its muscles to gain new members and build up the strength it will need if it's to be a real force in the land. On the other hand, the owners believe that making concessions would be seen as weakness on their part. They're insisting the men return to work unconditionally.'

'That brings us back to what I was saying in the first place. Someone should ask the women involved what they think ought to happen.'

'They won't, of course. They never do. That's why it's been necessary to start a suffragette movement. Do you know much about it, Emma?'

'Quite a lot . . .' Emma told her companion about the woman she had worked for, in the village on the edge of Bodmin Moor.

'You should become more involved with the movement,' Tessa said, as they reached the road. 'Look, why don't we get together and talk about this some more?'

Emma was delighted. Eagerly, she asked, 'When . . . and where?'

'How about tomorrow afternoon? There's a meeting of a women's suffrage movement in Bodmin. I want to cover it for my Association's news sheet. But perhaps you have to remain here to take care of Mrs Retallick?'

'No. Cissy will do that. Miriam can't stand her, really, but she's here if anything needs to be done urgently.' Suddenly curious, she said, 'I never realised there were suffragettes here, in Cornwall.'

'There are only one or two. The women I'm meeting tomorrow are not the suffragettes you read about in the paper. They belong to the Women's Suffrage Movement. It's an organisation that's trying to improve the status of women by peaceful means. You won't find any of them chaining themselves to railings, throwing things at government ministers or anything like that.' She shrugged, dismissively. 'Doing things their way hasn't gained us anything so far, but who knows . . . ? It might, one day.'

'Perhaps you could persuade them to seek the views of women affected by the strike in clay country.'

'We can suggest it to them, Emma, but don't hold your breath while you're waiting for them to reach a decision on it. They advocate reasoned debate. That's just another excuse for doing nothing. As far as I'm concerned debate went out of the window when Boadicea set the trend with direct action.'

Tessa gave Emma a warm smile. 'Anyway, we'll have time to talk about it on the way to Bodmin tomorrow. I've hired a small governess cart for the day. But be warned, Emma. You'll know the true meaning of frustration when you meet up with the Women's Suffrage Movement.'

22

Jacob felt hurt when Emma told him she would not be seeing him the next day because she intended going to Bodmin with Tessa Wren.

'Perhaps we can meet when you get back,' he suggested.

'I doubt it, Jacob, I have no idea how long we're likely to be.'

'Well, I'll call anyway, to see if you're here.'

'I think you'll be wasting your time, but if that's what you want . . .'

Aware of his keen disappointment, Emma said, 'I'll tell you what I'll do. You've asked me many times to come to Carthew to meet your ma and pa, why don't I come over there this Sunday?'

'That'll be fine, but they'll both be at chapel in the morning.'

'I don't mind, I'll come there too. I haven't been to a chapel service since Primitive Methodists took over the running of our chapel on the moor. It will be good for my soul.'

'My ma will be very happy about that,' Jacob said. 'But I'll still come here tomorrow night, just in case you get back earlier than you expect.'

By agreeing to visit his home, Emma knew she had gone some way towards making up for his disappointment, and she made a point of being particularly attentive to him that evening. She realised that during her conversation with Tessa, she had mentioned a number of things about her relationship with Jacob she had not thought about in any detail before. Jacob would be very hurt if he knew about them.

Later that same day, a vast crowd of striking workers held a rowdy meeting outside the gates of Ruddlemoor Clay Works. The meeting coincided with the change of shift. Although the crowd allowed the men going off shift to pass through, they prevented the night shift from entering the works.

When the shift captain protested to the police they made an effort to disperse the strikers, but violent scenes ensued. There were insufficient police to make any impression on the striking men, even when reinforcements were hastily brought in.

Eventually, the police superintendent was called to the scene, but not before a number of constables had been injured. He immediately ordered the remainder to withdraw.

In a futile attempt to retain some credibility, the police set up road blocks on either side of the works. It was a belated attempt to prevent anyone, workers or pickets, approaching Ruddlemoor and provoking more violence.

At home that night, Jacob discussed the events of the day with his father.

'I think it would be best if you stayed away from Ruddlemoor tomorrow, Pa.' Jacob was concerned about the aggressive attitude his father was taking towards what was happening.

'And let those bully boys win the day? No, Jacob. I'm going in to work.'

Pointing to the still vivid herring-bone scar along the line of his jaw, he added, 'They'll see this and know what caused it. If they've got any shame, they'll let me pass and go about my business.'

'You're talking nonsense, Pa,' Jacob said. 'Things have gone beyond anyone feeling shame for what they're doing. The strikers are going all out to win. Violence is nothing out of the ordinary any more. Leave it to me to get in to Ruddlemoor – but it won't be by the front gate, I can tell you that.'

'Our Jacob's right,' his mother said. Coming from the kitchen she placed a pot of tea on the table between her two men. 'I'd prefer you both to stay at home. Mr Retallick won't expect either of you to go into work if it means risking your lives.'

Pouring the tea and placing a large cup in front of each of them, she said, 'Now, would either of you like a nice piece of potato pie? I've only just this minute taken it out of the oven.'

Jacob said he would, but Absalom said, 'No.' Then, just as she reached out to the latch of the kitchen door, he changed his mind. His change of heart caused Eve to pause and turn towards him. At that very moment there was a deafening explosion which shook the house to its foundations.

The lamp in the room where they sat flickered and almost died. At the same time, from the kitchen came the clatter of pots and pans, the sound of breaking glass and numerous items of furniture crashing against the door.

'What the—?'

Absalom pushed back his chair, but Jacob had already rushed past his mother and opened the kitchen door. A cloud of choking dust swirled inside the room, forcing Jacob back.

Picking up the lamp, he carried it to the kitchen. He was faced with a scene of utter devastation. Broken glass, crockery and pans littered the floor, furniture was thrown about the room and the back door hung at an acute angle, secured by a single hinge.

Outside, neighbours from nearby houses in the valley could be heard calling to find out what had happened and whether anyone had been hurt.

'Oh, my dear soul!' Eve said from the doorway. 'What's happened? Was there something on the fire?'

'No,' Absalom replied grimly. 'This is nothing to do with your fire, Eve. This was caused by dynamite – and I think I know where it came from. Jacob was telling me that Ben Retallick spoke of someone breaking into the dynamite store of a pit up at Greensplatt last night. This is the outcome.'

'It's a warning, Pa. A serious one. They're telling us to stop working the Ruddlemoor engine.'

Some of their neighbours had reached the cottage now. One man said he'd sent one of his sons off on a pushbike to report the explosion to the police at St Austell. Another son had been despatched to inform Captain Bray.

Meanwhile, women were expressing concern and sympathy to Eve. Totally bemused, she was suffering the effects of delayed shock, bemoaning the fate of the pie she 'hadn't taken out of the oven more than a minute or two'.

Outside the house, the men were agreeing it might have been much worse. The single stick of dynamite – and there was unanimous agreement this was what had caused the explosion – had apparently been placed in a bucket outside the back door.

'I reckon it was a warning to you, Absalom,' one of the neighbours said. 'There are only four men still working at Ruddlemoor. You and Jacob are half of them.'

'It'll take more than this to stop me working,' Absalom declared fiercely. 'But I'll never forgive whoever did this to our house. They came close to killing Eve. She'd just reached out for the latch on the kitchen door. Had the door been open, or if she'd gone through to the kitchen, she'd have been caught in the blast.'

Despite his earlier bravado, Absalom began to shake at the thought of what might have happened to his wife.

The next half-hour was hectic for the Pengelly family. Policemen hurried to the cottage from St Austell and more came from a nearby clay works. Then four more arrived in a light carriage, driven by Superintendent Pollitt. Captain Bray also appeared on the scene. He informed Absalom he had telephoned Ben Retallick to tell him what had happened.

Minutes later the works owner himself arrived in his motor car. With him was Emma! The moment the vehicle stopped she jumped from it and limped down the path to the cottage, stumbling dangerously in the darkness before she reached the area lit by the cottage lamps and the lanterns carried by those from nearby cottages.

Emma looked about her anxiously until she saw Jacob. Hurrying to him, she cried, 'Jacob! Are you all right?'

'I'm fine. We all are. It's only the kitchen that's a bit of a mess. That and the back bedroom window.'

'Thank God!' Suddenly and impulsively, Emma put her arms about Jacob and hugged him. 'I've been so worried about you on the way here. The telephone call only said that someone had set off some dynamite, damaging your house. They didn't say whether anyone had been hurt.'

Over Emma's head, Jacob saw his mother come from the cottage. Glass-filled dustpan in hand, she viewed the scene with a greater disbelief than she had displayed when she had first looked upon her wrecked kitchen.

Disentangling himself from Emma's embrace, Jacob was unable to prevent her from clutching his hand. Leading her to the kitchen door, he said, 'Ma . . . this is Emma.'

'And who else would I have thought it was?' Eve asked. 'I'm pleased to meet you, girl, but I would have wished it to be in more pleasant circumstances.'

One hand went up to her hair and, for the first time that evening, she gave some indication of the deep emotion she had been trying very hard to control. Her voice threatened to break as she said, 'It's some mess in there. Most of my crockery's smashed to smithereens . . . Absalom and me have been collecting it over all the years we've been married.'

'Let me give you a hand to clear it up,' Emma said, sympathetically. Taking the filled dustpan from Eve's unsteady hand, she asked Jacob, 'Where do I put this?'

Jacob recovered the rubbish bin, which had been blown some distance from the house by the explosion. It was distorted by the force of the blast, and there was no lid for it, but it would do.

Ben Retallick had come down the path, treading more cautiously than Emma. After talking to the men, he entered the kitchen, causing Eve to become flustered once again.

He surveyed the scene in grim silence, then Emma said, 'There's a whole lot of damage, Ben. Most of Mrs Pengelly's crockery's been smashed to smithereens, as well as a couple of chairs . . . the lamp . . . lots of things.'

'I'm very sorry about this, Mrs Pengelly,' Ben said. 'There's very little I can do about the distress it must have caused you, but I'll see you don't suffer financially for your family's loyalty to Ruddlemoor. Have Jacob make out a list of the damage caused – a full list. I'll see that everything's replaced. Everything.'

'Thank you, Mr Retallick. I thank the good Lord that no one was injured, but . . . who would have done such a thing?'

'I don't know,' Ben said grimly. 'But I sincerely hope the police will find out.'

'Whoever it was isn't going to frighten me away from the Ruddlemoor engine house,' Absalom declared fiercely.

He had come to stand in the doorway and had heard much of the conversation. 'As long as the police will see me through the picket line I'll keep the engine running for you.'

'No you won't, Absalom. I'm deeply appreciative of your loyalty and determination, but I'm not putting lives at risk for the sake of a principle. The Union wants

Ruddlemoor closed down. Very well, I'll close down. The works will remain closed for as long as the Union maintains this strike. It won't affect you, Absalom, or Jacob – or any of the other workers who have stayed out of the Union. I'll continue to pay you as though you were all still working. But those Ruddlemoor workers who are Union men and on strike will need to manage on whatever the Union cares to give them. They've wanted a war. Very well, they have it now.'

The Ruddlemoor engine man looked less than happy and Ben asked, 'What's the matter, Absalom? Doesn't that suit you?'

'You've always been more than generous, Mr Retallick, but . . . well, work to me has always been far more than a matter of just drawing my pay every month. I enjoy what I do. I know that old engine as well as I know my own family. I understand every creak and groan it makes. It breaks my heart to think of it being shut down. Of having no pumps to keep the pit clear . . .'

Ben rested a hand on Absalom's shoulder in a gesture of sympathy. 'That's the way my grandfather would have felt, too, but don't worry. Think of your engine as enjoying a well-earned rest. You'll have it working as soon as all this foolishness is over – and a lot sooner than the production men are back at work. In the meantime, I'll go up to Ruddlemoor myself and secure the engine house. I'll make certain no one gets inside to cause mischief. Now, where's Emma? I expect she'll be with Jacob, somewhere. It's time I got her home again. I doubt if you'll have a great deal of sleep tonight, Absalom. When you've finished clearing up you'll probably have the police poking around for half the night.'

23

⚜

Handling the pony and governess cart with character-istic confidence, Tessa arrived on time at Tregarrick to collect Emma.

On the way to Bodmin, Emma told her companion of the happenings at Carthew during the previous evening, adding, 'It caused an awful mess. Just about every piece of crockery Jacob's mother owned was smashed to smithereens.'

'Well, at least no one was hurt,' Tessa said. 'And if Ruddlemoor engine's been shut down then whoever did it has achieved his purpose. The other works will follow suit now. Something like this had to be done before that came to pass.'

'You approve of what was done?' Emma looked at Tessa in disbelief.

'As I said, no one was hurt and the men have achieved what they set out to do. By this time tomorrow the strike will be total and the source of the conflict between those who are working and those who aren't will have been removed. If you're asking whether I approve of what's been done to achieve this then, as a committed suffragette, the answer has to be yes. You know about the campaign being waged by suffragettes, Emma. It was decided some time ago that everything possible would be done to further our cause, no matter what it entailed. It's much the same with the Union. They've tried talking to the employers, tried reasoning with them, but they've got nowhere at all. It's time to use strength.'

Emma pondered for some time on what had been said. Tessa was an educated woman and had seen far more of life than Emma, yet Emma disagreed with her thinking.

After considerable hesitation, she said so. 'I don't think the two things are the same at all. There are two sides to the clay workers' demand for more pay. The men – and the women too – should be paid more. No one is really arguing about that, but you've heard what Ben has to say about it. The employers can't afford it right now.'

'So they say,' Tessa interrupted. 'I suppose it depends whether or not you believe them.'

Ignoring her companion's sardonic comment, Emma continued, 'The argument for women claiming equal rights with men is different. We take an equal part in life, we should be given the right to help shape that life. There is no logical argument against that.'

Unexpectedly, Tessa grinned at her. 'Now you're talking like a suffragette, Emma – and you're quite right. The argument for women's suffrage is irrefutable. It's a cause we must fight – and we have to win. The problem is that the Union feels just as strongly about its cause, too.'

The day spent at the meeting of the Women's Suffrage Movement was as boring as had been forecast by Tessa. Speaker after speaker took the platform in monotonous repetition.

Each espoused the cause of universal suffrage and quoted many instances of blatant prejudice and unfair treatment of women.

Each agreed it was time such discrimination was brought to an end. Yet, beyond writing letters to prominent people, including Members of Parliament and holding meetings such as the one they were attending, none of the speakers could offer a solution to their frustrating situation.

In a whispered aside, Tessa said, 'This is just another good cause to most of them, Emma. They look upon it as no different to helping the poor; stopping cruelty to children and animals, or demanding that criminals receive their just deserts. When they leave here they'll go home and spend the remainder of the evening slavishly sorting out the problems of home, husband and children.'

Despite airing such criticism, Tessa wrote copious notes for her Association's news sheet. Then, to Emma's surprise, her companion was called upon to address the meeting on the activities of the suffragette movement in London.

Emma found Tessa's talk spellbinding, her message in marked contrast to those who had gone before. She preached action and defiance, urging the Bodmin women to allow no law made by men to stand in the way of their ultimate goal.

She reminded them that the aim was equal status for women. She further reminded them that as things stood at the moment, women had no more rights than convicts, or imbeciles. If the women in the audience really believed in what every speaker had declared was their aim, they would need to fight for it. Fight to win.

This, she declared, was the only path to true achievement.

When Tessa ended, Emma applauded her speech wildly. The number of disapproving glances cast in her direction quickly made her aware that her enthusiasm was not shared by the others at the meeting.

The chairwoman's acknowledgement echoed their coolness by saying that while Miss Wren's talk was of great interest to all their members, it did not necessarily represent the views of the meeting.

She added, disparagingly, that the London suffragettes involved in the campaigns in the cities of Britain did not always understand the ways of their country cousins.

When the prolonged applause died away, the chairwoman declared firmly that while both women's movements were pursuing the same aim, each had opted to take a very different route.

On the way back to St Austell from Bodmin that evening, the two women discussed what had been said and Emma was asked her opinion of the meeting.

'I found your talk very exciting,' Emma said. 'As for the others . . . I think my grandmother could have summed it up very well. One of her favourite sayings was, "Enough hot air to fill an oven, but nothing in there cooking." That's what I thought about it, too.'

Tessa chuckled. 'I like that saying, Emma. I must use it in an article, or perhaps a talk, sometime.'

They chattered about the meeting for a while longer until Emma asked, 'How do you see your own future, Tessa?'

The question took Tessa by surprise. 'Why . . . I'll just carry on campaigning until we get the vote, I suppose – and we will get it, one day.'

'I'm sure we will – so what will you do then?'

'I don't think I've ever looked that far ahead, Emma. I've never looked beyond winning the cause. I don't know, it depends how old I am, I suppose. I'll probably get married – if I can find a man who'll treat me as an equal human being and not as one of his possessions.'

'So you don't actually dislike all men?'

'Good Lord, no!' Tessa smiled at Emma. 'Indeed, I find some men very attractive indeed – but they're usually the wrong ones. Your Ben Retallick, for instance.'

'Ben?' Emma was shocked. 'But . . . he's married, and when you met you spent all your time arguing with each other.'

'That's what I said. I fall for the wrong men. Perhaps it's my instinct telling me I don't really want a permanent relationship. As for arguing . . . I wouldn't expect to agree with everything the man of my choice said or did, any more than I would want him to agree with me all the time. Don't you ever argue with Jacob?'

'Not much. At least, not yet.'

Even as she spoke, Emma was thinking of the first time she and Jacob had met. While not exactly arguing, they were certainly not in harmony with each other.

'You will,' Tessa said confidently. 'The test will be whether you're still together afterwards.'

24

The day Emma spent with Jacob and his parents came
very close to disaster even before they had said more
than a few words to each other.

Because there was still not a great deal of strength
in Emma's injured leg, she was brought direct to the
Carthew chapel by Ben's motor car, driven by his chauffeur.

Her arrival caused a stir among the chapel-goers. It
was resented by those of the striking Union men who
recognised the vehicle as belonging to the owner of the
Ruddlemoor works.

However, Jacob's obvious delight when he handed
her out of the vehicle ensured that Emma was hardly
aware of anyone else about them.

She was greeted warmly enough too by Eve and
Absalom Pengelly. Jacob's mother had been particularly
impressed by the manner in which Emma had pitched in to
help after the explosion at the Pengellys' Carthew cottage.

They filed in to the chapel now, taking their places in a long pew. Emma was seated between Jacob and his mother and the service went well enough – at first.

Emma had a strong, clear voice and proved to be unexpectedly familiar with the Methodist hymnal. She had no problems with the order of the service, either, but then the Methodist circuit minister climbed up the steps to the pulpit.

Looking out over his large congregation, he announced his intention of basing his sermon on St Paul's first letter to the Corinthians, Chapter fourteen, verses thirty-four and thirty-five.

The announcement caused a minor stir among members of the congregation who were particularly well versed in the Bible, but the choice meant nothing to Emma or to Jacob.

Then the minister quoted the verses in question, in order that there should be no doubt among his listeners.

'". . . Let your women keep silence in the churches; for it is not permitted for them to speak; but they are commanded to be under obedience, as also saith the law . . ."'

Jacob felt Emma's body stiffen on the pew beside him. He reached down hastily and grasped her hand, but the minister had quoted only one of the two verses on which his sermon was to be based. He now completed the reading.

'"And if they will learn anything, let them ask their husbands at home: for it is a shame for women to speak in the church . . ."'

Jacob tightened his grip on Emma's hand, as though afraid she might leap to her feet and contest the words written by the apostle almost two thousand years before.

Emma turned her head to look at him and he could see she was having difficulty controlling her fury.

Worse was to come.

There had recently been an increase in the use of women preachers among the smaller and more radical Methodist groups. Although this had actually led to an increase in the size of their congregations the minister of the small Carthew chapel did not agree with such active participation on the part of women. He delivered a sermon stating the reasons why he believed women should not be allowed to preach in churches and chapels.

Seated very close to Emma and still holding her hand, Jacob was aware she was practically bouncing in her seat with suppressed fury.

His response was to grip her hand even tighter. Eventually, she leaned towards him and whispered hoarsely, 'You're hurting my fingers!'

He released her hand with a murmured apology but redoubled his concern.

The fact that they had been holding hands was not lost upon Eve Pengelly. She frowned her disapproval. Such gestures of affection between a young couple were out of place in a chapel.

Much to Jacob's relief, the minister brought his sermon to a close soon afterwards.

By the time the service came to an end, Emma's anger had simmered down somewhat.

Leaving the chapel, they walked to the Pengelly cottage slowly, in order not to put too much strain on Emma's leg. They were about halfway there when

Eve said suddenly, 'I thought the minister gave a very strong sermon today.'

Emma made a peculiar noise in her throat and Eve said, 'Didn't you think so, Emma?'

Jacob's face contorted in a fearful expression and he hoped desperately that Emma would absorb the question and make an innocuous, if untruthful reply.

He should have known better. 'No, I don't, Mrs Pengelly. In fact, I think it was a biased and insulting sermon from a man who should be preaching tolerance and understanding. What's wrong with women preaching in chapels?'

'I'm sure he said only what he thought was right, dear,' Eve said, in a placatory voice.

'I doubt whether he'd put very much thought into what he was saying,' Emma retorted heatedly. 'He probably went through the Bible to find something that fitted in with what he wanted to say. He was certainly not following the teachings of John Wesley. He encouraged women to stand up and express their love for the Lord. Is the minister we heard today telling us that he's right and Wesley was wrong? If he is, then he shouldn't be preaching in a Wesleyan chapel.'

'I don't suppose that was what he meant at all. It was just the way he put it. Mind you, there are too many women in the world today who seem to have forgotten the place in life that the good Lord intended for them.'

Jacob exchanged a glance with his father and agonised, waiting for Emma's wrath to erupt.

It never came. Emma's initial inclination was to meet Eve Pengelly head-on, but she had seen the expression on Jacob's face. She was aware that the success of her visit to Carthew to meet his parents was important to him.

Making a remarkable effort, she managed to say, 'I'm quite sure you're right, Mrs Pengelly.'

As they filed down the path that led from the road to the Pengelly cottage, Jacob managed to find Emma's hand once more and he gave it a grateful squeeze. He knew what it had cost her not to take his mother to task for her remark about women 'knowing their place'.

The remainder of the day passed quite pleasantly, although Jacob was constantly aware that one wrong remark from his mother or from Emma was all it would take to upset the other.

However, when Ben Retallick's motor car arrived to take Emma back to Tregarrick, the farewells on both sides seemed warm and genuine enough.

When she had gone, Jacob was eager to ask his mother what she had thought of Emma.

'Well, she's got spirit,' Eve said. 'I'll say that for her. She's not afraid of hard work, either. She proved that the other night. Mind you, she's got one or two ideas in her head that I don't agree with – but then, so have you. Besides, she's still young. She has time to learn.'

Later that night, in the privacy of their bedroom, Absalom asked Eve the same question, adding, 'I'm rather taken with the girl. I think she'd make a good wife for our Jacob.'

'Perhaps,' Eve said, enigmatically.

'Well, she's certainly bright enough,' Absalom said.

'Maybe that's the trouble,' Eve replied. 'She's too bright. I can't see her settling down to life as the wife of a Ruddlemoor engine man.'

25

❧

As summer became autumn, there was a brief lull
in violence throughout clay country. The strikers had
taken a stranglehold on the situation. Not a single works
was producing clay, yet there was no sign of the owners
giving in to the strikers' demands.

There was an air of unreality about the strike now.
It was as though each side was waiting for an outside
body to break the deadlock.

There had been no recent negotiations and even the
local newspapers seemed to have lost interest in the
ongoing dispute.

Meanwhile, families of the striking miners were desperately short of money. The ten shillings a week paid
by the Union to its members did not go far. For families
of non-members or of men who had not been in the
Union for the qualifying period, things were far worse.
Ben Retallick was the only employer paying wages to
non-Union men forced out of work by their colleagues.

Aware that the problems of daily living were undermining his Union's support, Sydney Woodhouse organised a march through clay country. Two thousand men and a great many women converged on St Austell where they held a long and rowdy meeting.

Emboldened, perhaps, by this tangible evidence of support, the speakers called on the strikers to begin picketing the houses of the clay owners in a bid to persuade them to concede to the demands of their workers.

When the listening police superintendent intervened to tell them such talk was inflammatory, he was booed to silence by the strikers.

Things began to look ugly and the waiting constables moved in to protect their senior officer. As they passed through the crowd a series of brawls broke out between the policemen and the crowd. As a result, a number of men were dragged from the crowd and handcuffed.

Although heavily outnumbered, there were enough constables to maintain control of the situation. As they retreated with their prisoners to the nearby police station, the policemen were able to beat off strikers who pursued them in an attempt to rescue their colleagues.

Frustrated, the strikers moved off, heading back to clay country. Here they attacked many of the more accessible works with stones, breaking a number of windows.

The time had arrived for sterner measures to be taken against the striking miners. Superintendent Pollitt of St Austell put in a telephone call to the chief constable at the Bodmin police headquarters.

The following day one hundred members of the Glamorgan Constabulary arrived at St Austell railway station. With them they brought their bicycles – and riot shields.

The Welsh policemen had recently been engaged in quelling rioters in the coal mines of their native land. During this action they had gained a reputation for using heavy-handed tactics. Sydney Woodhouse's strike of clay workers was heading for a violent showdown.

During the twelve hours prior to the reinforcements' arrival, there had been intense activity in clay country in an effort to find accommodation for the policemen.

A ridiculously anomalous situation immediately arose. Clay workers involved in the strike, desperately short of money, took in some of the Glamorgan constables as paying lodgers! Others were put up in village halls.

Six constables found comfortable lodgings in Tregarrick.

For a few weeks the Glamorgan policemen patrolled the clay country on their bicycles, familiarising themselves with the geography of the area.

Their presence was deeply resented by the striking clay workers. Soon the tracks upon which the policemen regularly rode were liberally sprinkled with tacks. The result was that the Glamorgan policemen spent a great deal of time mending punctures. Tempers became ragged. This, in turn, resulted in rough handling for any strikers with whom they came into contact.

The resentment between the Welsh policemen and the strikers deepened. There had been no major incident between them yet, but both sides were aware that it was only a matter of time.

The situation in many of the strikers' households too had become increasingly desperate. As a result, women began playing an increasing role in picketing and their voices were heard more frequently at the meetings.

However, they were not urging their men to return to work. Their calls were for the employers to concede to their demands and give them a living wage, so bringing the long-running strike to an end.

One evening, Emma was brought to the Pengelly cottage in Ben Retallick's motor car. While the vehicle remained on the road with its engine running, Emma hurried to the cottage to find Jacob.

She told him there was to be an open-air strike meeting in the clay village of Bugle, some two miles away. Tessa Wren was to be one of the speakers. Emma wanted to hear her. She hoped Jacob would accompany her.

Her leg was healing well, but she still suffered with a slight limp. Because of this she had been able to persuade Ben's chauffeur to take both her and Jacob to the edge of Bugle village, before returning to Tregarrick.

Jacob wanted to be with Emma, but he was uncertain about attending the meeting. However, Emma was able, without too much difficulty, to persuade him to go with her.

She insisted it would be exciting to hear Tessa speaking again. In addition, the Methodist minister who had preached that women should be seen but not heard was known to sympathise with the strikers. He was likely to be at the meeting. Emma said she would enjoy seeing his face when Tessa was making one of her forthright speeches.

Eve Pengelly was not in the house, having gone to sit with a neighbour who was believed to be dying. As a consequence, she was not available to give her views on Jacob attending a strike meeting.

Absalom was. In common with Jacob, he felt uneasy

about the matter but felt he could not forbid him to go. However, as Jacob put on his coat while Emma hurried back to the car, he said, 'Be careful while you're there, boy. Things are simmering right now. It will take very little to bring matters to the boil and spill over. When that happens, a great many people are going to get scalded.'

The meeting was better attended than either Jacob or Emma had anticipated. There must have been at least two thousand people present.

Ominously, the entire contingent of the Glamorgan Constabulary was also here, gathered to one side of the meeting place.

It was almost dusk and lanterns were already lit about the place. A few lamps were also carried by those who had come to listen.

The meeting was taking place on waste ground, close to a local China clay pit. The 'stage' from which the speakers would address the strikers was a heap of overburden, one of many dotted about the area. Jacob and Emma chose another from which to listen to the proceedings. They joined about a dozen or so young men and women who were already there.

The sheer size of the crowd promoted a sense of excited anticipation. When Sydney Woodhouse climbed on to the earthern stage, he received a cheer that startled a flock of starlings settled for the night in a copse a quarter of a mile away.

Woodhouse made a surprisingly mild speech. He told his listeners the owners had proposed that a ballot be held among the striking workers. It had been suggested it would give the workers an opportunity to say whether or not they were prepared to return to work – but Woodhouse made it clear that, if they did, it would be for the pay they had been receiving when the strike was called.

Woodhouse told his audience it was an employers' ploy. The strike had now lasted for more than two months. 'Yes,' he declared, 'the clay workers are becoming desperate – but so too are the owners. They are anxious to have the men back in work. They're losing money, and this hurts them every bit as much as it hurts a clay worker. I have told them – and I was speaking for you – I have told them we will remain on strike until men start dropping from starvation. We will remain out until the clay owners reach in their bulging pockets and pay each man a measly couple of shillings extra each week. Brothers, stay united – WE WILL WIN!'

By the time the enthusiastic applause had died down, Tessa Wren was on the platform. She began her talk on a slightly puzzling theme by asking the strikers to think of the hardships being suffered by their families as a result of the strike.

'I have heard a great deal of talk from both sides about what the men are hoping for from this strike, but very little has been said about the very real suffering of their families. Neither side has asked the wives and mothers of this community what they want – but I have! Would you like to know what they have said to me? Would you?'

There was a somewhat bemused roar of affirmation from the crowd.

'Then I'll tell you – but it's not an answer the clay owners will want to hear. The women of this community tell me they stand one hundred per cent behind their men – and they will not change their attitude if this strike lasts for a year!'

The statement brought a great cheer from her listeners, but Tessa had not finished. 'Your women and your families have suffered greatly as a result of this strike. They are still suffering. Nevertheless, they are determined that they – and you – should battle on to the bitter end. They – yes, and their children too – are prepared to starve with their men until the owners give you, and them, what is your right. Your due . . .'

Another roar of approval rose from the throats of the men and women in the crowd. They were excited, but by no means out of hand. Nevertheless, the Glamorgan police decided it was time to bring the meeting to a halt.

Swiftly forming a line, they prepared to sweep the crowd before them. Before they did so, the inspector in charge decided he would first clear the mound upon which Jacob, Emma and some other young people were standing and sitting.

But rather than explaining to the young people what they required them to do, the Welsh constables climbed to the top of the mound and began roughly pushing off those positioned there.

When someone protested, albeit mildly, one of the constables drew his truncheon and, without warning, struck the young Cornishman on the head, sending him tumbling down the steep earth bank.

As though this was a signal, the other constables also drew their truncheons and began wielding them to considerable effect. Many of the crowd could see what was going on and they began to protest.

This was the moment when the remainder of the

Glamorgan constables drew their truncheons and began beating the crowd ahead of them, irrespective of whether they were attacking men or women.

On the raised mound of overburden, one of the constables pushed Emma and she tumbled down the bank. Jacob remonstrated with the policeman and his protest brought him a blow from the truncheon on the side of his head.

Jacob fought back instinctively and knocked the constable off the mound before a blow from one of his colleague's truncheons sent him reeling.

The constable pursued him, truncheon flailing and Jacob fell from the mound to the ground.

Other constables attacked him here and Jacob tried in vain to ward off their blows.

The last thing he heard before he lapsed into unconsciousness was Emma screaming his name and calling for the Welsh police constables to leave him alone . . .

26

Still dazed, Jacob was thrust inside a police wagon with perhaps a dozen men. It was dark, but the moaning told him there were others more seriously hurt than he appeared to be.

His head throbbed from the blows he had received and he was aware he had been beaten about the arms and shoulders, but although he had an egg-sized lump on the side of his head, his exploring fingers discovered no blood.

At the police station it was a battered group of men that was unloaded from the wagon, but Jacob was more concerned for Emma, especially when one of his companions told him a number of young women had also been arrested. They had been placed in another police wagon that had not yet reached the police station.

Once inside the building, each man was required to give his name and address, then a constable informed the sergeant on duty the offence the man was alleged to have committed.

Most of the prisoners protested that the constables were telling out-and-out lies about them. If the sergeant reacted at all, it was to suggest that the complainant 'Tell the magistrate in the morning.' It dashed Jacob's hope that he would be released quickly and allowed to go home.

When it was his turn to give his name and address, one of the Glamorgan constables stepped forward to say that Jacob had refused to move on when requested to do so and had then assaulted him without provocation.

The story was such a fabrication that Jacob also protested, but with no more result than any of the other Cornishmen.

From the charge office, Jacob was led away to the cells. Here he was thrust into a small cell that had been designed to hold one person but which he found himself sharing with seven companions.

He had been in the cell for about half an hour when one of the inmates, standing by the small grille set in the door, called on his companions to be quiet.

When they stopped talking they could hear the shrill voices of women raised in protest.

Elbowing his way to the door, Jacob called through the grille, 'Emma? Emma, are you there?'

He needed to repeat his call a number of times before her shouted reply came back to him.

'I'm here, Jacob. Are you all right?'

'I'm fine – how about you?'

'Better now I know you weren't badly injured. I was scared when I saw how they were beating you. Angry too.'

'She wasn't a bit frightened,' the voice of another woman shouted above the din of the cells. 'The reason she's in here is because she set about the bastards who were giving you a beating. She's not scared of anyone, if you ask me.'

'Are you sure you're all right, Emma? They didn't hurt you?'

'Not unless she's shocked by having a hand shoved up inside her skirt,' another voice called out. 'And they did that to most of us.'

'Jed? Jed, are you there? Can you hear me?'

Another voice, shouting urgently, broke in on Jacob's conversation with Emma. For a few minutes it was impossible to make sense of anything that was being called from one cell to another as men and women tried to locate friends or relatives.

The turmoil was brought to a halt by a police sergeant, who threatened to come around and shut the hatches in each door if the noise did not die down immediately. The cells were packed and hot, with what little air there was coming via the small grilles opening to the passageway. The prisoners would suffer severely in the stifling heat if the grilles were closed, and a reluctant silence fell upon the cells.

The following morning men and women prisoners were conveyed separately to the magistrates court, escorted by large numbers of Glamorgan constables.

Here, while he was waiting in a large holding cell, Jacob was visited by a solicitor who told him he had been instructed to defend both Jacob and Emma.

He took up little of Jacob's time, merely asking him to relate his version of the evening's events. Then he asked a few questions and nodded, apparently satisfied.

'It's more or less the same as Miss Cotton told me,'

he said. 'Don't worry, Jacob. I don't think you're going to go to prison. At least, not this time.'

When the solicitor had gone, Jacob did not know whether to feel optimistic or apprehensive about the possible outcome of his court appearance.

The courtroom was crowded with spectators when Jacob was led up from the cells. He glanced around quickly, and was relieved to identify neither of his parents among the crowd.

To his surprise, Emma was brought up to stand beside him in the dock. She looked tired and dishevelled but she managed a smile for him.

When they had confirmed their names, the solicitor said he was acting on behalf of both the accused who would be pleading 'Not guilty' of the charges of assault on the police.

When the solicitor sat down, the prosecuting police inspector outlined the case for the prosecution before a Glamorgan constable was called to give evidence.

The court was entertained to a fictitious account of how he had been 'deliberately and savagely' set upon by the two defendants without the slightest provocation. His story left Emma fidgeting with indignation as she stood alongside Jacob in the dock.

Without batting an eyelid, the constable also declared Jacob was one of a group of men who had started the trouble that had erupted at the meeting.

To the surprise of the court, the solicitor said he had no questions to ask the policeman, although he wished to reserve the right to recall him after other witnesses had been questioned.

When the constable had left the witness box, the solicitor said, 'Your worship, I would like my clients to

take the witness stand and give the court a true version
of what happened.'

'Very well,' the magistrate said, seemingly not in the
least surprised that there should be two versions of the
same incident. He nodded his head to a court official
and Jacob was the first to take the witness stand.

He told the magistrate of the unprovoked attack upon
Emma and his concern for the leg that had only recently
healed.

At this juncture his solicitor intervened and said to
Jacob, 'Miss Cotton's leg had been broken as a result
of an incident where she went over the edge of a clay
pit, I believe?'

'Yes, sir,' Jacob replied, wondering exactly what this
had to do with the charge he was facing.

'Is it also true to say that you went over the edge of
the cliff at considerable risk to your own life, rescued
Miss Cotton and carried her to safety?'

'I brought her up, yes—'

'Thank you, Mr Pengelly. Will you continue your
evidence for his worship.' But as the solicitor sat down,
he said, loudly, 'Hardly the behaviour of a hooligan,
I think.'

Now Jacob told of how he protested to the policeman about the way he had treated Emma and was
promptly struck with a truncheon and knocked to the
ground, to be set upon by other policemen and knocked
unconscious.

'Mr Pengelly, did you go to the meeting with the
intention of causing trouble?' his solicitor asked.

'No, sir, why should I?'

'Why should you, indeed, but you are a striker, are
you not?'

'No. I was still working the engine at Ruddlemoor until a bomb was set off behind our house. Then Mr Retallick said I and my pa should stop working. I've never been on strike. Neither has my pa.'

'Thank you, Mr Pengelly.'

When the solicitor sat down, Jacob was asked a few innocuous questions by the Cornish police inspector. Although he was conducting the prosecution, the police-man did not seem to have his heart on the duty he was performing.

When he said he had no further questions, the defend-ing solicitor said, 'Now, your worship, I would like to call Miss Cotton to the witness box.'

Emma told a similar story to Jacob – but she put it far more forcefully, adding, 'If I hadn't gone to help Jacob, I swear they'd have killed him. They didn't stop even when they'd knocked him unconscious. I wasn't the only one who saw what was going on. I wouldn't be surprised if half of those in court today are here only because they tried to stop the Glamorgan constables beating up Jacob. There was no trouble at all at the meeting until they started it.'

Once again the police inspector's questioning was less than wholehearted.

When it was over, the defending solicitor addressed the magistrate. 'I have a list of some thirty witnesses, your worship. All tell the same story as that just given to you by Miss Cotton. I might add, that after speaking with all those involved, I feel so strongly about this matter that I am prepared to offer my services to the remainder of the defendants free of charge. Would the court like me to begin calling my witnesses, your wor-ship? I have no wish to waste the time of this court.'

'I don't think that will be necessary, Mr Mutton.'

Ignoring the clerk who was trying to attract his attention, the magistrate said, 'I am not satisfied that we have heard an accurate description of events from the officer concerned. I find both defendants Not Guilty. You may leave the court Mr Pengelly and Miss Cotton.'

There was an outbreak of hastily stifled cheering from the public seats as Emma and Jacob stepped down from the dock and were hurried from the courtroom.

They would later learn that of the twenty-three arrests made at the Bugle meeting, only five would be found guilty.

For now, they were both delighted to have been freed.

27

Ben Retallick was waiting for the young couple outside the court. After expressing satisfaction that the charges against them had been dismissed, he said, 'You spoke well in court, Jacob. I thought you put your case clearly and honestly. It seemed the magistrate thought so too. I'm very relieved you were both acquitted.'

Jacob gave his employer a wry grin. 'I doubt if my ma's going to see it the same way, Mr Retallick. She'll no doubt say I shouldn't have got myself in trouble in the first place.'

'You can tell her I'll be along to see her and your father later,' Ben said. 'But there are still some questions that need to be answered.'

He now turned his attention to Emma, showing her less understanding than had the magistrate.

'What on earth were you doing at Bugle in the first place? I would have thought a strike meeting was the last place you wanted to be. I wasn't too happy with the way you gave evidence, either. If Jacob hadn't already explained what had gone on you'd probably be on your way to prison right now. You did nothing to help yourself.'

'Tessa Wren was speaking at the meeting. I wanted to hear what she was going to say. I asked Jacob to come with me, to keep me company. As for the way I spoke in court . . . I shouldn't have needed to have to defend my actions. I'd done nothing wrong. If anyone is to blame for what happened then it's the Glamorgan police. They were looking for trouble and they were the ones who started it.'

'I'm not arguing about that. Word is going around this morning that more than sixty Cornish men – and women too – were injured at the meeting. That isn't right and I'll say so, in the right places at the right time.'

'If you don't, I will,' Emma said fiercely. 'They're brutes! The constables staying at Tregarrick had better stay out of my way if they know what's good for them.'

'I've already asked the superintendent to move them elsewhere right away,' Ben said. 'Even if you didn't make life difficult for them, Grandmother Miriam would. She says they should never have been brought to Cornwall. Her argument is that Welsh constables have no idea of Cornish ways. But, that apart, what are we going to do about you, Emma?'

'What do you mean, what are you going to do about me?' Emma asked aggressively.

'To keep you out of trouble for a while, that's what I mean. I think it would be best if you returned to Bodmin Moor until things return to normal in clay country.'

Emma tried to hide the dismay she felt at his words.

'Why? Why am I to be punished for the actions of the Glamorgan constables, Ben? That isn't fair.'

'There's no question of you being punished, Emma. It's just . . . oh, I don't know! You seem to be able to find trouble without really trying. First your leg. Now this. It will only be until this strike is over. When you come back to Tregarrick we can begin all over again.'

Jacob was upset by Ben's words and he realised Emma was too.

They continued walking for some minutes. Then, stopping suddenly, Emma said, 'No, Ben, I won't go back to the moor.'

Taken by surprise, he said, 'I'm sorry, Emma, but there's really no alternative. Right now your presence is somewhat of an embarrassment. I realise it's not entirely your fault, but your arrest is bound to make headlines in the local newspapers, especially as your address will be given as Tregarrick. But it will only be until this trouble comes to an end, I promise you.'

Emma shook her head emphatically. 'However you care to put it, I'm being punished for what's happened. As I was found not guilty, I don't think that's right. I realise I'm an embarrassment to you, so I'll move out of Tregarrick – but I'm not going back to Bodmin Moor.'

'You can come to live at Carthew. I'll speak to my ma,' Jacob spoke in sudden desperation, worried that he might lose her.

Emma put a hand on his arm, sympathetically. 'That wouldn't work either, Jacob. I have no intention of staying away from strike meetings and your ma and pa wouldn't approve.'

'They'll be all right once I have a chance of talking to them.'

'No, Jacob.' Emma spoke to him fondly. 'It just wouldn't work. I know that. So do you, really.'

'Look here, Emma, let's not do anything in haste.' Ben was alarmed at the manner in which matters were unfolding. 'Let me discuss this with Lily. There must be some way to resolve everything.' Ben feared he might have been too dogmatic about Emma's conduct.

'No, Ben, you're quite right. My living at Tregarrick is difficult for you. It is for me too. I'm beginning to feel very strongly about this strike. I believe the workers have right on their side. I have always thought so, really, but I can't express my true feelings while I'm living at Tregarrick.'

'Grandmother Miriam is going to be very, very disappointed, Emma. She's been looking forward to the day when you would be fit enough to take care of her.'

Emma shook her head. 'She'll understand better than anyone else. She thinks the world of you, Ben, but she doesn't agree with you about this strike. I'll miss you and Lily, though. You've both been very kind to me.'

'But . . . you won't be leaving Tregarrick just yet?' Jacob was dismayed by this sudden and unexpected turn of events. He had thought . . . had hoped that he and Emma had an unspoken understanding. That they would continue to see each other and, in due course, announce their engagement.

'Yes, Jacob, I'll be leaving today.'

'There's no need for such undue haste,' Ben said, really concerned now. 'If you seriously want to leave Tregarrick and don't intend going home, we'll find somewhere else for you to stay.'

'I already have somewhere,' Emma said unexpectedly. 'Tessa has suggested I should stay with her. She's in

Bodmin now. She realises how difficult it is for me, living at Tregarrick.'

'But . . . will we still be able to see each other?' Jacob was shattered by Emma's unexpected announcement. It was almost as if the whole matter had been pre-planned and was merely waiting for a catalyst like the events of the previous evening to set it in motion.

Emma squeezed his arm painfully. 'I certainly hope so, Jacob. I would be very unhappy if I thought otherwise.'

Watching the young couple, Ben realised that Emma had somehow grown in confidence overnight. The thought had occurred to Ben earlier when he had witnessed her self-assured demeanour in the courtroom.

He still believed that Emma and Jacob had something special together. However, he feared that Emma intended travelling through life at a faster pace than did Jacob.

28

Jacob stood at the Carthew roadside until Ben Retallick's motor car had passed from view, with Emma waving continuously from the back seat.

The clay works owner had offered to accompany Jacob to the cottage and explain to his parents what had happened at the Bugle strike meeting, but Jacob had declined the offer. He preferred to face his parents' wrath alone. He felt certain Ben would have put the blame on Emma for taking him to the meeting in the first place. He did not want this.

His mother had come from the house when she heard Ben's car. After hugging Jacob, greatly relieved to have him home, she touched the bruises on his 'poor face'. Then, putting all sympathy to one side, she gave full vent to her feelings about his arrest and appearance in court.

It seemed she and Absalom had been told the previous night by a neighbour that Jacob was among those arrested during the disturbances at the meeting of the Bugle strikers.

Absalom had walked to the St Austell police station late

at night, only to learn Jacob had been taken to Bodmin and would be appearing in court the following day.

Early the next morning Ben had called at the cottage. He informed Absalom and Eve that he had instructed a solicitor to act on behalf of the young couple and was going to the court hearing himself.

He refused a request from Eve that he should take her and Absalom with him to the court. The reason he gave was that she would be very distressed should the magistrate find Jacob guilty and send him to prison.

The very thought of such an eventuality was sufficient to send Eve into near-hysterics once the works owner had left.

Now, her relief at having Jacob safely home turned to anger and she castigated him for getting himself arrested in the first place.

As they walked to the cottage, she told him how ashamed she was. 'I don't know if we'll ever be able to live this down!' she declared. 'I'll never be able to hold my head up in front of the neighbours again.'

'It's not as bad as all that, Ma,' Jacob assured her. 'I wasn't the only one arrested, you know – and I was found not guilty. That means even the magistrate realised I'd done nothing wrong – and neither had I. It was the Glamorgan constables who started the trouble. They were out to arrest as many as they could and make up charges against them afterwards.'

'That's your story, young man. The police don't arrest people for nothing.'

'Cornish police might not, the Glamorgans do. You ask anyone who was there. I wouldn't be surprised if the magistrate doesn't find everyone not guilty. He certainly should.'

'I don't know what your father was doing letting you go out like that. I would have stopped you had I not been sitting up with poor Peggy Williams, God rest her soul. As if I hadn't enough to cope with having her pass away while I was with her, I come home to find you've gone off to some rowdy strike meeting and got yourself arrested!'

As they passed in through the doorway of the cottage, Eve was still telling Jacob what she thought. 'Mind you, I blame that Emma Cotton just as much as you. She has ideas that have no place in a young girl's head. I don't know what Mr Retallick thinks he's doing, letting her go off like that. He should know better, him being an owner. What are people going to say about him now, letting one of his young relatives behave in such a manner and getting herself arrested?'

'I was hoping you were going to be relieved that I was found not guilty, Ma. It means that Emma and I did nothing. That's why the magistrate let us go.'

'Well, you would say that, wouldn't you. Others will say there's no smoke without fire. I can tell you, I'll give that young Emma a piece of my mind when I see her.'

'Ma, I don't give a damn what people say or think . . .' Jacob was tired, hungry, unhappy and exasperated with his mother's nagging as they entered the kitchen where his father was seated at the table.

'That's quite enough of such language from you, Jacob – and don't let me hear you talk to your mother in that way. She's been awake for most of the night worrying about you.'

'About me or about what the neighbours are going to think? She should stop keeping on about them and just be thankful I'm here and not as badly hurt as I might well have been. After the Glamorgan police knocked me unconscious I was locked up and spent the night in a cell so crowded there was hardly room to sit down. Then I had to go to court this morning and defend myself when I'd done nothing. Now I've come home to be told off for something I've not done! As for Emma . . . the only reason she was arrested was because she tried to stop the policemen giving me a vicious beating.'

Unrelenting, Eve said, 'Well, don't expect me to thank her when I next see her. If it hadn't been for that girl you wouldn't have been there in the first place.'

'There's just no winning with you, is there?' Jacob felt mentally and physically exhausted and close to defeat. 'Anyway, you won't have to say anything to her. In fact, I doubt if you'll ever see her again. Mr Retallick was no more understanding than you, so she's leaving Tregarrick.'

Jacob had taken off his coat when he entered the kitchen. Now he put it on again. He felt he could take no more of his mother's nagging.

'Where are you going?' Eve demanded.

'Out. I need some fresh air – and a bit of peace and quiet. I've had enough of people in the last twenty-four hours.'

'Now, Jacob, your ma never intended driving you out. She's been worried about you, that's all.'

'Of course I've been worried. What mother wouldn't be when her son doesn't come home and she hears that he's been arrested. As for young Emma Cotton, you're better off without her, if you ask me. She's trouble, that girl.'

'Then you're going to have to learn to live with trouble. I'm going to Tregarrick right now to try to catch Emma before she leaves. If I do, I intend asking her to marry me. It's what I should have done the moment she said she was going to leave Tregarrick.'

*   *   *

Jacob arrived at Tregarrick only to discover, to his utter despair, that Emma had already gone.

Ben Retallick was not in the house, but Jacob was invited in by Lily. As they sat in the comfortable lounge, Lily told him that within minutes of Emma's return to the house, Tessa had arrived. She had heard of Emma's acquittal and arrived in a motor car driven by a friend, to learn the details of Emma's court appearance.

After a brief conversation with the London suffragette, Emma had packed her things and the pair had gone away together shortly afterwards.

'Do you have an address for Tessa?' Jacob asked despondently. On the way from Carthew he had carefully rehearsed what he would say to Emma. He had not anticipated she would have left so promptly.

'No, Jacob. I asked for one, but Miss Wren said she would be moving to another address in a few days' time. She said she might even be returning to London.'

The news alarmed Jacob. 'But . . . what will Emma do if she does?'

'I'm not certain. I gained the impression Tessa was expecting Emma to go with her.'

'To London?' In Jacob's mind, London was as remote as Africa.

Lily gave him an understanding smile. 'It's really no more than a train ride away, Jacob. Anyway, we have the telephone and I intend making some enquiries. As soon as I hear something I'll let you know and send you her address.'

Jacob was passing through the hall with Lily when he heard his name being called. He looked up to see Miriam coming down the stairs on the arm of Cissy.

'What are you doing here, young man? Why aren't you with Emma, making certain she doesn't get herself into any more trouble?

'All right, girl, you can let go of my arm now. I'm not going to fall over now we're off the stairs.' Speaking to Cissy, irritably, she added, 'Run off and find something useful to do – you too, Lily. Jacob, take me for a walk in the garden. That's the only place I can go these days without having folk fussing over me all the time.'

Having summarily dismissed Cissy and Lily, Miriam took Jacob's arm as they left the hallway and made their way down the steps outside the front door.

Instead of releasing his arm as she had Cissy's when the need for support was gone, Miriam retained her grip on him.

'Now, don't walk so fast, young man. Unlike a dog, I no longer need to be exercised every day.'

Jacob dutifully slowed his pace. When it was more to her liking, she said, 'Now, what's going on between you and young Emma?'

'I wish I knew, Mrs Retallick. You know about us being arrested last night, and going to court this morning, of course?'

'No one's told me the full story. Ben hasn't been near me and Lily's told me only fragments. As for Emma . . . she was in such a hurry to leave the house, she hardly had time to say "Goodbye", let alone tell me what's going on. Here, this is my favourite seat. Sit down and tell me what happened last night and why Emma's left Tregarrick in such a hurry.'

They sat on a garden seat that Jacob had often shared with Emma. Here, he told Miriam all that had occurred, from the time he and Emma had arrived at the meeting of strikers until they parted that morning.

'It's even worse than I thought,' Miriam said. 'Ben should have known better than to take Emma to task before he knew the full story of what had happened. What do you intend doing about having Emma go off like this?'

'I'm not sure there's anything I can do now,' Jacob replied. 'I came across here hoping to catch her before she left Tregarrick, but I was too late.' Hesitantly, he added, 'I intended asking Emma to marry me. If she'd said yes, I'd have known what to do. As it is . . .' his voice trailed off miserably.

'She's not ready for marriage yet, I can tell you that,' Miriam said positively. 'Emma needs to see something of life and the world before she settles down – and she's none the worse for that. Accept what she wants to do and let her do it – but don't let her disappear out of your life. If one day she decides to marry you, you'll know she's doing it because she wants to, not because it seems more exciting than the life most girls are leading. Do you know where she is right now?'

Jacob shook his head. 'All I know is that she's with Tessa Wren somewhere – Bodmin, probably. Young Mrs Retallick doesn't have her address, either.'

'Well, when this Miss Wren interviewed me she mentioned a suffragette newspaper called *The Courier*, and we have the miracle of the telephone now. If I can get someone to teach me how to use it or make a call for me, I should be able to learn something. Come back and see me in a few days' time, Jacob. I should have an address for you by then. This ridiculous strike is making life difficult for everyone, but we'll make certain it doesn't destroy the future for you and Emma.'

29

Jacob returned to Tregarrick six days after his conversation with Miriam, only to discover the Retallick matriarch was not at home.

Cissy was the only one of the family in the house. She told Jacob that, as it was a fine day, Ben and Lily had taken Miriam in the motor car to see a sick friend who lived some miles away.

Curious about the reason for his visit, she asked, 'Why do you want to speak to Miriam?'

Jacob had no intention of telling Cissy anything that had passed between Miriam Retallick and himself. 'It was just something she wanted to speak to me about, that's all.'

'Well, as there's no one else at home, would you like a cup of tea? I can have one made and sent out to the garden for us.'

'No thanks, I'd better be getting along.'

Cissy gave him a sly glance. 'That's a pity. I thought

you might want to sit with me and hear the news about our Emma.'

'What news?' Jacob's interest returned immediately.

'Like I said, it's a pity you don't have time to sit in the garden with me and hear what it is.'

'Don't play silly games with me, Cissy. If you know something just tell me.'

'Why should I? One minute you're in a hurry, then suddenly you're not any more.'

'All right, I'll have some tea with you – but tell me now what it is you know.'

'Why? A few more minutes isn't going to make any difference. If you go and sit at the table on the side lawn I'll go and see about the tea. Would you like some biscuits with it, or a piece of cake?'

Seated at the outside table, Jacob waited with increasing impatience for Cissy's return. He knew she was being deliberately tardy in order to tantalise.

She came from the house about ten minutes later, accompanied by a maid who was carrying a tray on which there were cakes and tea.

After placing the tray upon the table, the maid left, leaving Cissy to pour the tea.

She waited for him to broach the subject of Emma, but he managed to remain silent. Eventually, she said, 'What do you think about the news of our Emma?'

'I haven't had any news of Emma. That's what I've come here for.'

'You mean she hasn't told you?' Cissy feigned exaggerated shock.

'Told me what?' Jacob's patience finally ran out. 'Come on, Cissy. Stop playing games with me. What news is there of Emma?'

'About her going to London, you mean? I thought you'd have been the first one she would tell.'

Jacob was stunned. 'You mean . . . Emma really is going to London? You sure you haven't got it wrong, Cissy? That it's not just Tessa Wren who's going there?'

'I haven't got anything wrong,' said Cissy maliciously. 'It's you who's got it wrong. She's not going, she's already gone. She and Tessa. They went yesterday.'

Jacob walked home to the Carthew cottage in a state of deep melancholy. Life had taken on a whole new meaning for him during the few months he had known Emma. Now she was gone. Out of Cornwall and out of his life – and she had left without telling him of her plans. If, indeed, she had made any.

When he arrived home his mother, with silent disapproval, pointed to a letter, which had arrived for him while he was out. She knew, as he did, that it must have been written by Emma.

Jacob carried it to his room before opening it with some apprehension. Penned in haste, it was nevertheless a long letter. Emma had written it shortly before she was due to leave Bodmin with Tessa to catch a train bound for London.

As he read it, Jacob became increasingly despondent. Emma seemed to be in a state of confusion about her future. Nevertheless, she was quite obviously very excited to be going to London to become involved with the suffragette movement she had admired for so long.

There was much in the letter about the woman with whom she was travelling to London. Too much. Tessa was going to teach her to write shorthand and how to use a typewriter. She had also promised to teach her to drive, to find accommodation, and gain employment in the offices of the East London Federation of Suffragettes, at the heart of the militant suffragette movement.

There was a strong thread of regret running through Emma's letter, too. She admitted that her strong feelings for Jacob had almost caused her to refuse all that had been offered by Tessa.

Emma assured Jacob she was anxious not to lose touch and promised to write to him often from London. She hoped he would not think too badly of her for going off and leaving in such a manner and that he would reply to her letters.

Emma declared that going to London offered her an opportunity to make her way in a world she could only read about if she remained in Cornwall.

The letter ended by thanking him for the many hours she had enjoyed in his company. She made him a promise that he would be in her thoughts far more often than he would ever know.

Folding the letter, Jacob put it in his pocket and went downstairs.

Both his parents were in the kitchen and Eve greeted him with a hostile glare.

'Is Emma so ashamed of showing her face here now that she needs to write letters instead of coming to call? And there's no need for you to look at me like that. I know it must be from her. Who else would write to you?' She sniffed contemptuously. 'I suppose it's something to know the girl's capable of feeling shame.'

Jacob turned his back on his mother and walked out of the house without saying a word.

When he had gone, Absalom said, 'You shouldn't have spoken to the boy like that, Eve.'

'Oh? And why not? Somebody has to. He's not been the same since he met up with that girl.'

'Perhaps it's you who hasn't been the same since he met her, Eve.'

'What's that supposed to mean?' Eve asked indignantly. 'I'm sure she's been made as welcome in this house as she would have been in the home of any other young man she set her cap at.'

'These are difficult times, Eve. This strike's got everyone saying and doing things they wouldn't normally do. I only hope this ballot they're talking about will see the men voting to return to work. Things are getting desperate for many of them.'

'Don't I know it,' Eve declared, pushing thoughts of Emma to the back of her mind for the moment. 'Thanks to Ben Retallick there's more money coming into this house than any other in clay country. But half of it goes straight out again in loans to those who are in desperate straits. I doubt if we'll see a quarter of it back again. Even if the men were to get their pay rise and go back to work tomorrow, it will be years before they make up what they've already lost.'

30

⚜

Jacob wandered about aimlessly for more than an hour before a damp, grey mist moved down from the high ground above Carthew, drawing the day to a premature close.

He was not dressed for damp weather, but he did not feel like returning home. His mother's continuing criticism of Emma would lead to an argument – and Jacob did not feel like arguing with anyone right now.

He decided he would pay a rare visit to the Sawles Arms.

He hoped he might find some Ruddlemoor colleagues in there, but he was disappointed. There was none of the noise and bustle he had found on his previous visits. The only customers were four old men. Seated around a table in a corner, they were engaged in a serious game of dominoes.

'Well, what's this . . . a customer?' The landlord was leaning, arms folded, on the bar. 'What can I get for you, young Pengelly? A half-pint of small beer, is it?'

'No, I think I'll have a pint of your best beer, please.'

'Well! Things are looking up.' The landlord looked suddenly suspicious. 'I suppose you've got money to pay for it? I'm giving no credit, strike or no strike.'

'I've got the money. Now, do I get a beer or must I find somewhere else to buy a drink?'

'Coming up, young sir, I'm sure. It's been so long since I had someone come in and order a pint it took me by surprise – and by the look of you it seems someone's taken you by surprise.'

Jacob's hand went up to his bruised face. 'I was at the meeting in Bugle the other night when the Glamorgan constables decided to show everyone how tough they are.'

'They certainly did that all right. I had Sydney Woodhouse in here that night. His face was worse than yours. The friends he had with him were no better. I had more blood than beer on the floor that night.' In an automatic gesture, the landlord rubbed a damp grey cloth over the otherwise clean bar counter. 'Mind you, if Woodhouse and his friends do half of what they were threatening in here, there's not going to be a single clay works capable of opening up when this strike ends. To give Woodhouse his due, he'd left by the time ale had started to loosen the tongues of the men who came in with him. They weren't from these parts, so I don't know what the strike has to do with them, but they certainly spoke as though they intended making it their business. They reckoned it was time something was done to make the owners really sit up and take notice. They were talking of using explosives to blow up the engine houses, no less.'

Alarmed, Jacob realised that these men had probably been involved in the explosion that damaged the Pengelly cottage. 'Are you quite certain of this? They actually spoke of blowing up engine houses?'

'As sure as we're standing here talking.'

'You didn't hear them mention any works in particular?'

The landlord shook his head. 'Matter of fact, I think they caught on that I was a bit too interested in what they were saying. They lowered their voices and I couldn't make head nor tail of anything after that.'

The cloth went into action once more before being thrown casually into a bowl of water beneath the bar.

'Woodhouse and his mates were the last real customers I've had 'til you came in tonight.' He nodded in the direction of the four men playing dominoes. 'They come in here, order a half-pint each, and make it last all night. It doesn't pay me for the lamp oil I'm burning. Still, we've got to be thankful for small mercies, I suppose.'

The landlord had given Jacob a lot to think about so, as soon as he could, Jacob carried his drink to a table in a corner away from both the landlord and the domino-playing customers. He needed to be alone to think.

First, he took out Emma's letter and read it once more. Had she still been at Tregarrick, he could have passed on the landlord's information. But she was not. It would need to be done another way. One thing was certain. Ben Retallick ought to be told. A strike against the owners was one thing. Destroying machinery that would have a long-term effect on an individual clay works was something very different – and the Ruddlemoor Clay Works was a prime target.

The engine houses of the various works would need to be put under guard immediately if lasting damage was not to be done to the clay industry – and to any possible chance the workers had of gaining their objective.

To the delight of the landlord, it took Jacob two more pints of ale before he made up his mind. It was late but not excessively so and his information was important. He would go to speak to Ben Retallick tonight.

Jacob estimated that if he walked briskly, he would arrive at Tregarrick before eleven o'clock that night. He revised the time it would take when he realised he was not walking quite as steadily as usual.

He was unused to drinking more than the occasional half-pint of small beer. Tonight's quaffing of three pints of ale was the greatest amount he had ever drunk at one time.

His route passed along the road beside his home. He had almost reached the path that dropped down to the cottage when he detected the dim glow of a lighted pipe among the trees to one side of the road.

He recognised the tobacco smoked by his father.

'Is that you, Pa?'

'It is. I thought I'd wait here and have a chat to you before you went indoors.'

'I'm not going in just yet.'

Absalom had come from the shadows now. Sniffing the air, he asked sharply, 'Have you been drinking?'

'Yes – and I think it's a lucky chance that I have.' Controlling his slightly slurred speech very carefully, he repeated what the landlord of the Sawles Arms had told him, adding, 'I've thought about it and decided it's important enough to go and tell Ben Retallick right away.'

'I wouldn't argue with that – but I wish you'd come by such tidings somewhere other than the Sawles Arms.'

'Where it came from doesn't matter,' Jacob retorted more boldly than was usual when he was speaking to his father. 'What does is that something's done about it before serious damage is caused.'

'I'm not arguing that, boy. All I'm saying is that whatever's gone wrong in your life, you'll not find a cure for it in a public house.'

'At least I can sit there in peace, without having to listen to Ma carrying on about Emma all the time. I meant what I said, Pa. I was going to ask Emma to marry me. I still will, if she ever comes back here.'

'I know that, boy. So does your ma. The trouble is, she realises she'll be losing you when you marry. In her eyes there's not a girl in this world who's good enough for you. I like young Emma. I'd be delighted to have her for my daughter-in-law, but you've got to admit she probably wouldn't be any mother's first choice as a wife for her only son. She's got a mite too much spirit for comfort.'

Despite the resentment he was feeling towards his mother, and the seriousness of the errand he was on, Jacob realised the truth of what his father was saying. He smiled sadly. 'Well, Emma's gone now, Pa. Ma has nothing at all to worry about until she comes back – and she will, one day, I hope.'

'I've no doubt she will. But make sure your ma has nothing to worry about where your drinking is concerned, either. Now, you'd better be on your way if you're to catch Ben Retallick before he goes to bed. I'll speak to your ma and tell her what you're doing. I'll see that she goes to bed and doesn't smell the beer on your breath when you get in. Off you go now, boy – and good luck to you.'

31

There was still a number of lights on in Tregarrick when Jacob arrived. Most were on the first floor and in the attic rooms where the servants had their bedrooms.

He had no hesitation in ringing the bell, aware it sounded at the rear of the house and would be heard only by the servants.

It was a couple of minutes before he heard bolts being drawn. Then a servant opened the door to enquire what Jacob wanted.

'I'd like to speak to Mr Retallick.'

The servant recognised Jacob from his visits to the house to see Emma and knew he was not a 'gentleman'.

'Do you realise the time? Mr Retallick's preparing for bed. Can't you come back in the morning?'

'I wouldn't be here if it wasn't urgent. Will you tell him I'm here, please?'

'Oh, very well. Come and wait in the hall.'

The servant left Jacob standing in the large hallway and a short while afterwards Ben appeared.

'Hello, Jacob, this is a surprise. Do you have some news of Emma? You know she's in London, of course?'

'Yes, I've had a letter from her – but that's not why I'm here.'

Ben realised Jacob would not have come to Tregarrick at this time of night had it not been on a serious matter. 'You'd better come to my study and tell me what this visit is about.'

In the panelled, book-lined room, Jacob repeated what the landlord of the Sawles Arms had told him and Ben began pacing the study floor.

'You obviously believe this to be true or you wouldn't be here. You don't think this landlord is exaggerating, do you?'

'No, not after the explosion at the back of our house. A couple of dozen sticks were taken during the break-in at the Greensplatt works. The one that exploded at our house is the only one that's been used so far. The others could cause a whole lot of damage.'

'You're right, Jacob. I'm grateful to you for coming to tell me. I'll phone Superintendent Pollitt at St Austell, then I'll run you home in the Hotchkiss.'

'There's no need for that,' Jacob said hastily. 'I'd rather walk. I'm in no hurry to get home.'

Ben gave him a searching look. 'Well, at least stay for a drink. Here . . .'

While he was speaking he poured a very large brandy and handed it to Jacob. 'Be drinking this while I make my call. It won't take long – and I won't implicate you.'

Jacob had never tasted brandy before. He found it

heady stuff. Even the fumes from the pot-bellied glass were sufficient to make his eyes water, but he enjoyed the fiery sensation of the brandy as it went down.

Ben was not gone very long, but by the time he returned to the study, there was very little brandy remaining in Jacob's glass. Ben poured some more for him, ignoring Jacob's feeble protest. Then he poured a drink for himself.

'Superintendent Pollitt took your news very seriously. He's going to send constables to every engine house in clay country. There'll be a permanent police guard on them from now on.'

'Good! Good!' Jacob's head seemed to be nodding far more vigorously than he intended. He did not trust himself to say more.

'You said you've had a letter from Emma?' Ben was not unaware of the effect the brandy was having upon Jacob. 'Is all well with her?'

'Yes.' The head began nodding again. 'The letter came today, but she wrote it before she left . . . for London.' The last two words seemed to run together.

'Emma's going to London came as a great surprise to all of us. I've written to tell her mother what's happened. No doubt she'll blame me for allowing her to go.'

'There's not much you could have done to stop her once she'd made up her mind. Not much anyone could do,' he added morosely.

'You're very fond of her, aren't you, Jacob?'

The nodding began again, but Jacob thought he brought it under control much more quickly this time.

'We all thought she was fond enough of you not to want to go away.'

'She says she needs to do something with her life

before settling down,' Jacob declared. 'I can't blame her. I just hope she'll be happy, that's all.'

'You're a good man, Jacob . . . Are you quite certain you won't let me take you home?'

'Quite sure.' Jacob downed the remainder of the brandy and said breathlessly, 'I must go now. Thank you for the drinks.' He stood up somewhat unsteadily, supporting himself with one hand on the arm of the chair.

'Thank you for coming to let me know what you heard. You've probably prevented a great deal of damage being caused to Ruddlemoor and the other works.'

Outside, the cool night air caused Jacob's head to swim alarmingly for a few moments. He moved away from the house as quickly as he was able, aiming himself at a tree growing at the side of the driveway.

Reaching it, he leaned against it gratefully, unaware of the figure that had detached itself from the shadows beside the house and followed him.

'Hello, Jacob. What are you doing at Tregarrick at this time of night? Did you think Emma might have changed her mind and returned?'

'My coming here's got nothing to do . . . with Emma.'

Cissy moved closer to him. Close enough to smell the brandy fumes on his breath. 'Jacob Pengelly! I do believe you're drunk!'

'I . . . I'm nothing of the sort. Just had a drink . . . with Mr Retallick . . . that's all.'

'You've had a few more than one if I'm any judge. Come on, let's see how well you can walk.' She took his arm and Jacob reluctantly abandoned the comforting support of the tree.

By concentrating very hard, he managed the first half-dozen paces adequately. Then, for some inexplicable reason, his legs began to rebel. His brain was directing them to go straight ahead, but they tilted him towards Cissy.

She supported him as best she could for a few moments, but she was a slightly built girl and was forced to bring him to an unsteady halt.

'You are, Jacob. You're too drunk to see a hole in a ladder.'

This time he did not argue with her.

'You can't walk home like this, that's for certain. You'd end up in a ditch or, even worse, in the river.'

The narrow, fast-flowing St Austell river ran beside the road for much of the way to Carthew. The life of more than one drunken clay worker had come to an end in its clay-stained waters.

They began walking across the grass, heading back in the general direction of the house and its outbuildings.

'Where we going?' His tongue was no more obedient than his legs now. 'Got to get home.'

'You'll go home – but not until you can walk in the same direction you're looking.'

A few minutes later they reached the darker shadow of some outbuildings. Keeping a hold on him with one hand, Cissy fumbled for a latch with the other.

When the door swung open, Jacob smelled the sweet, fresh aroma of hay.

'Why . . . we going in here?' He wished he could focus his mind on what was happening.

'Just come inside and sit down for a little while.'

He knew he should be on his way home now, but he could not bring himself to argue with her.

'Here we are, sit down now.' It was not a suggestion but a command. Cissy emphasised it by pushing him.

He landed awkwardly in the hay, with much of Cissy's body beneath his, her arms about him. Before he could struggle free, her mouth was on his and her body was pressed hard against him.

He knew he should break free, but the closeness of her had aroused his own body. Cissy felt it and pulled him closer.

'No, Cissy!'

It was the last vestige of a drunken man's resistance. A moment later he felt her hand unfastening his belt. Then her hand slipped inside his trousers and she took hold of him.

He groaned, but now it had nothing to do with the amount he had drunk. What was happening to him seemed as though it was happening to someone else.

Cissy was vigorously pursuing her advances now. He did very little to help, but nothing to stop her. It was the first time he had made love and the amount of drink he had consumed helped the feeling of unreality.

He moaned and Cissy pleaded, 'No, Jacob . . . don't stop now. Don't stop!'

But it was all over for him. Moments later, Cissy wriggled free and pushed him away.

Sitting up, she rearranged her clothing and said, 'You'd better go now.' There was little of her earlier solicitude in the statement.

Still befuddled, Jacob climbed unsteadily to his feet and fastened his trousers.

Only now did his brain begin to register what had happened between them.

'Why, Cissy? How . . . ?'

'Oh, come on, Jacob. Don't tell me you've never done it with our Emma. I don't believe you.'

While he had been making love to Cissy, he had not thought once of Emma. He did so now.

'I feel sick.'

'Well don't throw up in here,' Cissy said hurriedly and unfeelingly. Climbing to her feet she propelled him to the door. Opening it, she bustled him unceremoniously outside.

'You're sober enough to make it home now, Jacob Pengelly. If you want to do that again, come here and call for me – but make sure you're sober next time.'

With this parting shot, she disappeared in the darkness, heading for the house.

She left Jacob staring after her in a state of bewildered unhappiness. Moments later he gave way to the heaving of his stomach and was violently sick.

32

❦

It began to rain soon after Jacob left Tregarrick. A steady, penetrating downpour that chilled him to the bone.

The combination of rain and a long walk meant that before he was halfway home he had sobered sufficiently for the full import of what he had done with Cissy to sink into his conscience.

His reaction was to stop at the side of the road and be sick once again.

When he felt better, he trudged on dejectedly. One thing was certain, he could not contemplate marriage with Emma now. It would have been bad enough had he made love to anyone else – but to Cissy of all people. Emma's sister! He would never forgive himself, he could hardly expect Emma to do so. Miserably, he admitted to himself that he did not even like Cissy very much.

When Jacob reached home he was fully sober. He entered the cottage quietly in order not to wake his parents. He did not think he could face his mother in his present state.

The rain had become quite heavy towards the end of his journey home and water dripped from his clothes as he walked about the cottage. He took most of them off in the kitchen, hanging them over the string line that stretched the length of the mantelshelf. Then he went upstairs to bed.

Tortured by the events of the evening, Jacob was convinced he would lie awake for the remainder of the night. However, he fell asleep the moment his head touched the pillow.

It seemed he had slept for no more than a few minutes before he was being shaken awake by his mother.

'Go away! I've been up half the night. Let me sleep.' Jacob pulled the bedclothes over his head in a bid to ignore her.

'I know all about you being out. Your clothes are still soaking wet, so I know you can't have been in long – but Mr Retallick is here. You need to get up right away.'

Memories of what had occurred the previous night flooded back to haunt Jacob. He sat up, trying to gather his sleep-numbed wits.

Cissy must have said something to Ben Retallick! He wondered what the works owner would have to say about what had happened? Would he insist that Jacob marry Cissy? Would he dismiss him from his employment?

'I've put clean clothes on the chair. Hurry up now and don't keep Mr Retallick waiting; he's a busy man. By the look of him I'd say whatever he's come here for is mighty important.'

Jacob tried to hurry, but his hands were so unsteady he had difficulty tying the laces on his Sunday-best boots. When he had finally accomplished the task, he took a deep breath of air into his lungs and groaned.

'Oh God! Why has this had to happen to me?'

He whispered the words to his reflection in the mirror as he put a brush through his hair, then turned away and made his way downstairs.

When he reached the kitchen, he found Ben Retallick inspecting the repairs that had been made to the explosives-damaged door.

'I'm sorry to get you up so early, Jacob, but I need to speak to you urgently. Shall we step outside for a while?'

Jacob nodded, not looking at his father or mother. He wondered whether Ben Retallick had said anything to them.

Outside the cottage, Ben said, 'Let's walk up to the car.'

When they had passed beyond the hearing of those in the house, Ben said, 'It's to do with what happened last night, Jacob.'

'Yes . . . I thought it must be.'

The dejected tone in Jacob's voice caused Ben to turn and look at him curiously before speaking again. 'I've had Superintendent Pollitt on the telephone to me this morning . . .'

Jacob looked at Ben in alarm. Surely Cissy had not made a complaint to the police about him? What if she had said he had forced her?

But Ben was still talking. '. . . The men who were overheard in the Sawles Arms seem to have wasted no time. The superintendent sent constables to every engine house immediately after we spoke. An hour later, a number of men attacked the engine house at the Halviggan works. A constable was shot in the leg and the men ran off, leaving a couple of sticks of dynamite behind.'

The full impact of Ben's news was lost on Jacob for the moment. His visit had nothing to do with what had happened between Cissy and him! The relief was so overwhelming he could have laughed out loud.

Controlling the impulse, he said, 'This is why you've come to see me?'

Ben gave him a puzzled look. 'Of course. Why else?'

'I'm sorry, I'm not properly awake yet.'

'No, of course not – and I think I might have been a little heavy-handed with the brandy – but to get back to my reason for coming here. Superintendent Pollitt wants to know where my information about these men came from. I won't give him your name, of course, but I want you to tell me everything you know.'

Jacob repeated all that the landlord of the Sawles Arms had told him.

Ben contemplated Jacob's information, then said, 'Superintendent Pollitt is determined to find these men, Jacob. I'll suggest he sends someone to speak to the landlord. I'll get him to say they want to trace the men who were seen going into the Sawles Arms with Woodhouse on the night of the trouble at Bugle. The chances are he'll repeat what he overheard. He'll certainly be able to give the police a description of the men.'

'I hope the police find them quickly. If they don't, some-one's likely to be killed.' Jacob had recovered his composure fully now.

'Hopefully, your information will help prevent that. It certainly saved the Halviggan engine house.'

Suddenly, Ben gave Jacob a brief smile. 'I'm sorry to have woken you. I really should have insisted upon driving you home last night. You obviously never reached home before the rain began. Please call in at Tregarrick when you're near. Grandmother Retallick has taken quite a fancy to you. She'd love to see you again. No doubt Cissy would appreciate the company of someone nearer her own age, too.'

Ben saw Jacob's unguarded change of expression and misinterpreted it. 'I know she's not Emma, but she does her best. She's not a bad girl, really.'

33

The shooting of a Cornish police constable had a salutary effect upon the striking clay workers, even though his wound was not a particularly serious one.

It was at first believed that the perpetrator must have been one of the men from 'up-country', who had done much to stir up trouble during the strike. Then a young man was arrested for the offence – and it was revealed he was a striker who lived in the clay country.

As a result of this latest incident, so much pressure was applied to Sydney Woodhouse that he reluctantly agreed to hold a ballot among the striking workers.

The issue put to the men was quite straightforward. Should they continue the crippling strike in the hope of gaining a minimum wage of twenty-five shillings or did they wish to return to work at their old rate of twenty-one shillings and sixpence?

Woodhouse had vigorously opposed such a ballot until now. He was fully aware that after almost two months without a living wage and with no prospect of a settlement in sight, the suffering workers would most likely vote overwhelmingly in favour of cutting their losses and returning to work.

He need not have worried. To the surprise of both Union and owners, the vote was four to one in favour of continuing the strike.

In the event, the ballot proved to be no more than a final gesture of defiance on the part of the strikers.

Even as the ballot was being held, one of the owners reopened his works, protected by a very strong contingent of constables.

For a few more weeks many strikers held out in the vain hope that the result of the ballot might have weakened the resolve of the works owners. But their optimism was misplaced. The owners did not budge from their hard line. They made it clear the men could return whenever they wished – but on the owners' terms and at the original rate of pay.

Gradually, the remaining strikers were forced to face the realisation that they they were not going to win the day. The strike crumbled and clay workers began to trickle back to work.

As hungry families saw food coming in to the houses of their working neighbours, the trickle became a flood. Woodhouse was forced to concede that the strike of clay workers had failed in its objective.

The workers had lost a great deal of money and gained nothing at all.

The Union had suffered a humiliating defeat – but at least it had the consolation of an increase in membership of some four thousand men in clay country.

* * *

As Absalom had predicted to Jacob, a great many clay workers were unable to resume work immediately. At Ruddlemoor, as at many other pits, it was necessary to first pump out the water that had accumulated in the pit bottom.

A great many mining experts had to be called in to either clear the existing drifts or dig new tunnels to bring in the clay. Not until the strike had been over for three weeks was China clay produced once more at the Ruddlemoor works.

Jacob was working again now. He had not been to Tregarrick since the night he met up with Cissy.

Whenever the mine owner saw him at the works, he suggested Jacob pay them a visit. But Jacob was reluctant to meet Cissy again. In fact, much to his relief, the memory of the night-time incident in the Tregarrick stable had begun to dim with the passing of time.

Then, one evening early in 1914, Jacob came off late shift at the engine house – and found Cissy waiting for him outside the gate of the Ruddlemoor works.

She came out of the shadows of the trees beside the gate. It gave him a shock when he recognised her in the pale yellow light from the gatehouse.

'Hello, Jacob. I thought you'd come calling on me at Tregarrick long before this. Ben said he's told you more than once that you're welcome at any time.'

'I . . . I've been very busy helping to get things working properly after the strike.'

He was glad the darkness hid his cheeks. They felt as though they were on fire.

'You don't work for twenty-four hours a day, Jacob. I find it very hurtful that you haven't at least tried to see me, after what we did together that night. You did enjoy it, didn't you?'

'I . . . I don't remember very much about it. I'd had a lot to drink.'

'But you do remember what happened?'

'Of course,' he replied miserably.

'Well, that's something. At least there'll be no argument when I tell you what it is I've come here to say.'

'Tell me what?'

As he asked the question, Jacob felt he was standing on the edge of a deep abyss.

Cissy's next words pushed him over the edge. 'I'm expecting a baby.'

Jacob felt his knees go suddenly weak. 'You . . . but . . . are you sure? It hasn't been very long . . .'

'It's been quite long enough for me to know what's happening inside me. More to the point . . . what are you going to do about it?'

'What do you want me to do?'

'I shouldn't have to spell that out to you, Jacob Pengelly. You'll need to marry me, that's what!'

'But . . . I don't love you.'

'You should have thought about that before you did what you did. Anyway, love me or not, you've got me pregnant. Now you're going to marry me.'

'Have you told anyone else?'

'Not yet, but it's not the sort of thing that can be kept secret for very long, is it?'

There was a long silence between them as they walked along the road together. Then, in a voice that gave some indication of the abject misery he felt, Jacob said, 'All right then, but . . . what do we do now?'

Unable to fully disguise the elation she felt, Cissy

said, 'The first thing you do is come to Tregarrick to see me. We can go for walks and . . . things. Let people see us together. That's what's expected of couples who are going to be married. When do you finish working late shift?'

'Tomorrow. I'm on early shift all next week.'

'Then come to Tregarrick to see me on Monday. We can have a walk around St Austell. Look in the shops for things we're going to need when we set up home.'

'All right,' he agreed reluctantly.

'Good!'

After a further few moments of silence, Cissy said, 'You can do it to me again now, if you like. Seeing as how we're going to be married and I'm pregnant anyway, it's not going to make any difference.'

'I don't think I could,' Jacob said honestly. 'I've got to get used to the idea of getting married first.'

'Please yourself,' Cissy said testily, successfully hiding her disappointment. 'But don't forget, I'll see you at Tregarrick on Monday. We'll talk about the wedding then.'

34

'Who is this Cissy you're going to Tregarrick to see – and why haven't I heard of her before?'

'You have heard of her, Ma. She's Emma's sister. She stayed on at Tregarrick after the funeral to help old Mrs Retallick when Emma broke her leg.'

'Well, if she's anything like her sister, you just watch your step, young man. Don't let her lead you into any more trouble.'

Miserably, Jacob thought he could hardly be in more trouble than he was at the moment, but he said only, 'She's nothing like Emma, Ma. I can promise you that.'

It was shortly after four o'clock when Jacob reached Tregarrick. It was a sunny day and warm, although there was a stiff breeze. Cissy, Lily and Miriam were having tea in a conservatory attached to the house and Jacob was invited to join them there.

'Well! You're quite a stranger at Tregarrick these

days,' Miriam said in her usual forthright manner. 'What's brought you here today?'

Uncomfortable at not being able to tell the full truth to the shrewd old lady, he replied lamely, 'I met Cissy the other day. I promised her I'd come calling.'

Expressionless, Miriam's gaze went from Jacob to Cissy and back again. 'I see. Well, it's nice to have you here. Now, which cake would you like? Being a true Cornishman you'll no doubt choose a saffron bun. That's what I would have had when I was your age. These days I find them too indigestible for my palate.'

Miriam dominated the conversation for three-quarters of an hour. In sharp contrast, Lily said hardly anything at all. Jacob thought she looked unwell.

Meanwhile, Cissy's impatience grew more and more transparent. Eventually she said to Jacob, 'You promised to come to St Austell with me to look around the shops, remember? If we don't hurry they'll all be shut.'

'Yes, of course. I suppose we'd better go,' Jacob spoke unenthusiastically.

'I hope you have no money in your pocket or she'll spend every penny of it for you. No more idea of thrift than a cuckoo has Cissy. I pity the man she marries. He'll need to work day and night to keep up with her wants.'

Jacob knew his cheeks had turned scarlet at the mention of marriage. He hoped no one else had noticed.

As he left the conservatory with Cissy, Miriam called after him, 'You come and see me when you return, Jacob, you hear? I want you to tell me what's happening at Ruddlemoor now the men are back. Oh, and I've a letter from Emma somewhere. I expect you'd like to read it.'

'You don't have to take any notice of her,' Cissy said dismissively, as they walked away from the house. 'She's a demanding old woman, but she'll have forgotten all about what she's said by the time we get back from St Austell.'

'I like her,' Jacob declared. 'I don't mind talking to her.'

'Will you tell her we're going to be married?' Cissy demanded.

'Not until I've told my ma and pa.'

'And when will that be?'

'When I'm good and ready.'

'You'd better not leave it too long,' Cissy said. 'Once it begins to show there's going to be a right old scandal. I want us to be properly married before that happens.'

For Jacob, it was the beginning of a miserable evening. It seemed that every shop they looked in sold something that Cissy felt was indispensable for the home they would be setting up together. Miriam's assessment of her was proving uncomfortably accurate.

As the gap widened between what he would be able to afford and what Cissy thought essential, Jacob protested that he would never have the money to satisfy her needs.

'Then you'll just have to earn more,' she said callously. 'Once you've told everyone about us getting married you can speak to Ben about getting a better job in Ruddlemoor. He'll find you one, he likes you. He might even make you a shift captain! I wouldn't mind being a shift captain's wife.'

Jacob said less and less as Cissy prattled on about their proposed marriage and the life they would lead afterwards. He did not want even to think about married life with Cissy. But there was no way out of it. He could not, and would not, deny what had happened between them. He must suffer the consequences of his own drunken stupidity.

By the time they returned to Tregarrick, Cissy was sulking because Jacob had refused to go with her to the stables where she had taken him on his previous visit.

She declared she had no wish to accompany him to Miriam's room to listen to them talking about Emma. Before leaving him at the door, she threatened that if he did not speak to his parents about their intended wedding within a fortnight, she would tell Lily and Ben she was pregnant and that Jacob was to blame.

When he entered Miriam's room, the old lady looked behind him and raised her eyebrows when he closed the door. 'Didn't Cissy want to come with you?'

'I think walking around St Austell has tired her out.'

'I wouldn't be surprised,' Miriam said enigmatically. 'Now, where's that letter from Emma . . . ?'

The letter said very little about Emma's life in London, but he winced when he read that Emma hoped he was well and still visiting Tregarrick.

After returning the letter to Miriam, the conversation turned to the night he and Emma were arrested by the Glamorgan police.

Miriam shook her head sadly. 'They made a grave mistake bringing in policemen from outside Cornwall to deal with the strikers. They've done far more damage than good, I can tell you that.' Suddenly and unexpectedly, she asked, 'Have you heard from Emma since she went away?'

Jacob had, in fact, received two letters from her.

Because of his reluctant commitment to Cissy, he had not known how to reply and they remained unanswered.

He nodded. 'She seems to be enjoying London.'

'No doubt she will – for a while. Sooner or later she'll want to return. Will you still be waiting for her?'

'I . . . I don't know.'

'You're not a happy man, Jacob. Is there anything I can do for you?'

'I'm all right,' he lied. 'I wish Emma had never gone to London, though. A lot of things might have been different had she stayed.'

'What sort of things?'

He shrugged, 'Oh, just things.'

He looked at the large marble clock standing on the mantelshelf in her room. 'I'd better be going now. I'm on early shift tomorrow.'

When he had gone, Miriam sat for a long time, thinking quietly. She genuinely liked Jacob. Something was troubling him, of this she was certain. She was equally confident that Cissy was at the root of it.

Jacob would have been very surprised to know that Miriam Retallick had a very shrewd idea of the nature of his problem. Nevertheless, there were some aspects of the affair she found puzzling.

Acting on a sudden impulse, she rose from her chair, walked to a corner of the room and tugged on a bell-pull.

When a servant girl appeared, she asked, 'Is Mr Retallick back in the house yet?'

'Yes, ma'am. He came in some time ago. He's in the study now.'

'Good. Take me downstairs to him, I wish to use the telephone.'

The telephone was sited in Ben's study.

'Now, ma'am?' The servant girl wondered whether she should do as she was told or go and tell her master. 'It's getting late . . . Mrs Retallick's already gone to bed.'

'Then we'll need to go down the stairs quietly, won't we? It's Mr Retallick I wish to speak to. Come along now. If you stand there dithering it will be later still . . .'

35

As the deadline set by Cissy neared, Jacob became increasingly apprehensive. He knew he would need to say something to his parents very soon, but he kept putting off the dreaded moment.

Jacob told himself he was awaiting the right occasion. In truth, he knew this was not so. He did not want to talk about it, any more than he wanted to marry Cissy.

When the fourteenth day arrived, his mother told him he was going about the house as though he expected a ghost to jump out at him from every corner.

When she asked what was wrong with him Jacob knew he would probably never have a better opportunity to break his news to her.

Instead, he declared nothing was wrong and went out for a walk. He went northwards, in the opposite direction to Tregarrick.

Returning to the Carthew cottage some two hours

later, he hesitated outside for a while, filled with apprehension. He wondered whether Cissy had carried out her threat to tell Ben Retallick that she was expecting his baby.

He decided she could not have done so, otherwise the mine owner would have sent someone here to find him or, more likely, sought Jacob out himself.

His mother was in the kitchen, cleaning up before going to bed. No one had called at the house. It seemed the secret had held for another day, at least.

Two weeks later Jacob was still waiting for the shockwaves from Cissy's threatened revelation to reach out and envelop him. By now he was thoroughly puzzled. She had not attempted to contact him. Yet Cissy was not a young woman to make idle threats over such an important issue as this.

The following night, as Jacob arrived at the engine house to take over his duties, the shift captain put his head around the door.

'Jacob, you're wanted at Mr Retallick's house. He's sent his car for you.'

Jacob felt his stomach contract violently in sudden fear. 'But . . . I can't go. I've just come in to take over the night shift in here.'

'The late-shift man's going to have to work on until you come back, or until I can get someone else in to take your place. That depends how long you're going to be.'

Trying desperately to put off the anticipated confrontation, Jacob said, 'Why does he want me?'

'I don't know. Perhaps he's going to make you shift captain in my place,' he said sarcastically. 'The only way you'll find out is to go to Tregarrick and see him. Hurry up, now. If you value your job you don't keep an owner waiting.'

All the lights were on at Tregarrick and it seemed no one anticipated going to bed just yet.

Jacob entered the house tremulously, wondering what form Ben Retallick's anger would take. He was met in the hall by a servant who informed him that Ben was taking an important telephone call in his study. She had orders to take him to 'Mrs Retallick, Senior', who was waiting for him in the lounge.

The very fact that Miriam Retallick was downstairs at this time of night and not in her room seemed to Jacob an indication of how seriously the family was viewing the situation. He found difficulty controlling his quaking when he entered the lounge.

Miriam Retallick was seated in a large and comfortable armchair close to the fireplace, a drink on a small table beside her.

Much to his relief, she did not immediately take him to task. Instead, she said, 'Hello, Jacob. We've got a nasty mess on our hands. Ben's speaking on the telephone right now trying to sort something out, although what he can do, I don't know.'

Jacob was not quite certain how Ben Retallick would be able to 'sort something out', but he agreed with Miriam that it was indeed a 'right mess'.

Miriam appeared mildly surprised and said, 'Who told you about it?' Before he could think of a reply to the bewildering question, she answered it herself. 'I suppose it was the chauffeur. I don't know how servants get their news so quickly. I used to think they listened at keyholes, but it can't be that. Yet they very often know what's going on before the family does.'

By now, Jacob was thoroughly confused. He was about to seek clarification from Miriam when Ben Retallick entered the room. He looked strained and drawn.

'Hello, Jacob, thanks for coming here. We've got a problem. I only learned about it late this evening when I arrived home and took a telephone call from Tessa Wren – but I suppose that was better than reading about it in the London papers.'

Jacob was more bemused than ever now. What could a London paper possibly have to do with his responsibility for Cissy's pregnancy?

'I blame this Wren woman,' Ben continued. 'It was her firing Emma up about suffragettes that started it all. I should never have allowed her to go off to London.'

'Emma? I'm sorry . . . I don't understand.'

'Oh! I'm sorry, Jacob. I thought my grandmother would have told you all about it.'

'You said you already knew.' Miriam gave Jacob an accusing look.

'I must have been thinking of something else,' Jacob said hurriedly. 'What's happened to Emma?'

'She's been arrested again,' Ben said. 'I'm afraid I can't see her getting away with it this time.'

'What's she done?' Jacob momentarily forgot his own troubles.

'As far as I can gather, she was with a party of suffragettes who tried to stop King George's car as he was driving into Buckingham Palace. They wanted to present him with a petition about women having the right to vote, I believe. When she was arrested she assaulted a police inspector. She's been taken to a police station with a whole lot of others. I've been on the telephone to London, speaking to solicitors and anyone else I think might be able to help. I'm still waiting for a return telephone call to tell me the exact charges Emma is facing.'

Jacob was as concerned as Ben about Emma, but there was another matter still hanging over his head that needed to be cleared up.

'What about . . . Cissy?'

'That little minx!' Miriam said with considerable feeling. 'It should be her locked up in prison, not her sister.'

'I doubt if you'll be seeing anything more of Cissy,' Ben said. 'She's gone home to her mother, on Bodmin Moor.'

'But not for long,' Miriam added. 'There's no harm in telling Jacob, Ben. In fact, I believe he's entitled to know the truth about the girl. Had it not been sorted out as early as this, he might even have been suspected of some responsibility for what's happened.'

'Of course,' her grandson agreed. Turning to Jacob, he explained, 'Cissy got herself pregnant by one of those policemen we had staying at Tregarrick.'

Hardly able to believe what he was hearing, Jacob made some rapid mental calculations. The policemen had left Tregarrick quite a while before Cissy had taken him to the stables on that drunken night, but she must have already suspected that she was pregnant . . . !

'How did you learn about it?' Jacob asked. He wanted to believe what Ben Retallick was saying, yet was fearful there might still be a chance he would be held responsible for her condition.

At that moment a servant hurried in to say, 'The telephone is ringing in your study, sir.'

Ben hurried from the lounge and Miriam said, 'I told him about Cissy, Jacob. You see, from my room upstairs I have a marvellous view of a great deal of the grounds about the house. I would see Cissy and this particular policeman meet up in the garden where they thought no one could see them. As time passed – and it was a very short while – his manner towards her became disgracefully familiar. When they met, they would always head towards the old stables, a place where even the most sensible of girls might get herself into trouble – and Cissy most certainly does not come into that category.'

Miriam paused to drink from the glass on the table beside her. When she had replaced it once more, she said, 'Cissy was extremely upset when the policemen were ordered from the house by Ben. I think she already had a suspicion she was pregnant. As time went by, I suspected it also.'

Miriam gave him a sharp look that made him feel uncomfortable even while he was finding it hard to hide his elation.

'After we had our little chat the last time you were here, I spoke to one of the servant girls and had her take me to the telephone. On the way I persuaded her to tell me the name of the constable Cissy had been seeing. Oh yes, all the servants knew about it. Well, I spoke to the man's inspector who had been in charge of him while the police were in Cornwall and had him order the man in question to telephone me here.'

Miriam smiled benignly at Jacob. 'As a result of my conversation with him, he travelled here to see me a couple of days afterwards and agreed that he and Cissy would marry. She has now returned to her home on Bodmin Moor to arrange it all.'

Jacob felt that Miriam must be aware of the sheer joy that was bubbling over inside him.

He was even more certain when Miriam added, 'Before she went, I asked her if there was any message she would like me to pass on to you, as you had been particularly kind to her. I'm afraid she suggested you should go to a place where you might have the devil for company. She has always been a most ungrateful girl, Jacob.'

Convinced now that Miriam had a very shrewd idea of what had occurred between himself and Cissy, he said, 'You are a remarkable person, Mrs Retallick.'

'No, Jacob, but I've lived for a very long time. There's not much in human relationships that can surprise me now.'

At that moment Ben hurried back in to the room. 'That was the solicitor I hired to defend Emma. He rang to say she's due in court tomorrow, but the case will probably be put back for a day as she's being defended. She's being charged with causing a breach of the peace, obstruction, assault on police – and there's the matter of her threatening the safety of King George and Queen Mary.'

Jacob paled. It all sounded very serious. 'What do you think will happen to her, Mr Retallick?'

'According to the solicitor she will be sent to prison, possibly to serve quite a lengthy sentence.'

Ben made a frustrated gesture, then said, 'Am I right in thinking you are still very fond of Emma, Jacob?'

Jacob nodded vigorously. With the threat of marriage

to Cissy lifted, he could openly express his feelings for Emma once more.

'Good. I'll have you taken home now. Be ready to be picked up again at dawn. Wear your Sunday best – and bring clothes for a stay away from home.'

'Where are we going?'

It was an unnecessary question. He knew the answer, even before it was given to him by Ben Retallick.

'We're going to London, Jacob. We're going to see what we can do for Emma – if we're not too late.'

BOOK TWO

BOOK TWO

1

Emma gazed out of the window as the train gathered speed, the carriages passing through the black smoke that poured from the funnel of the engine. The railway line curved away from Bodmin Road station, along the side of a steep hill above a heavily wooded valley.

Leaning back on the seat, she closed her eyes and thought of how much her life had changed in the course of a few days.

Emma was leaving Cornwall with mixed feelings. Considerable excitement at leaving the county for the first time, of course. It was to be the beginning of a great new adventure.

She was exchanging the fields, moors, cliffs and sea for the crowded and bustling capital city of England. Tessa had described it to her in terms that excited her just to think about it.

Yet Emma was aware that she was also leaving much behind that mattered to her. In particular, she would miss Jacob. She had realised, somewhat belatedly, she was going to miss him a great deal.

'What are you thinking about? Would you like to change your mind? Get off at the next station and return home?'

Emma opened her eyes and smiled at Tessa. 'I've no intention of changing my mind. All the same, there are some things I wish I might have brought along with me.'

'Would Jacob be one of them?'

Emma nodded.

'Write to him from London. If he feels the same way about you, it might be possible to persuade him to come there too, although for a while you'll be kept busy learning how things work in the office.' She paused, then added, 'Mind you, there are a great many nice men in London . . . Manny, for instance.'

Tessa smiled as she mentioned the name and Emma asked, 'Who's Manny?'

'Manny Hirsch is a wrestler. A huge man – and somewhat simple. Some of the women from the suffragette office were able to help his family some time ago. Manny's so grateful he's appointed himself as bodyguard to any of the suffragettes who he feels to be in need of protection. He's a poppet, really – and very, very useful at times. There's not a man in the whole East End of London who would dare to cross him.'

'He sounds useful,' Emma agreed. 'But tell me about the office, and what I'll be doing there.'

'Well, the office is in Dalston Lane, just off Kingsland Road, close to Hoxton and at the heart of the East End of London. It's a working-class area and the "East Enders" are good people, you'll like them. There's a flat above the office. It's where I live – where you'll live too, unless you feel you'd rather find somewhere else.'

Emma shook her head and waited for her companion to continue.

'Sylvia – Sylvia Pankhurst – used to stay at the flat sometimes, when the police were looking for her, but since she's been subject to the Cat and Mouse Act she needs someone to look after her full-time whenever she's out of prison. She now stays with a couple in Old Ford Road, not very far away.'

Emma knew from reading the papers that the Cat and Mouse Act was a law brought in by the government to thwart the suffragette hunger-strikers. There had been universal outrage at the brutality associated with forced feeding in prison and in order to overcome this, hunger-strikers were now released when they became weak and ill. As soon as the authorities felt they were fit to continue their sentences they were re-arrested and returned to prison. In this way, a relatively short sentence could be extended over a period of a year, or more.

Emma brought her thoughts back to Tessa, who was still talking.

'. . . As you know, Sylvia is the leader of our particular movement, the East London Federation of Suffragettes. At the moment we are associated with the Women's Social and Political Union, which is run by Christabel, Sylvia's sister, and their mother, the famous Emmeline. We take our lead from them, but I don't think we will for long.'

'Why not?'

'Sylvia doesn't always see eye to eye with her mother and sister. There are an increasing number of differences between them. For one thing, Emmeline frowns upon Sylvia's association with the Labour movement. She's not happy either with the support given to us by the dockers and other workers in the East End. I think the truth is that she doesn't really like men. Perhaps even more serious, there's a basic difference in their idea of women's suffrage. Emmeline believes it should be restricted to women of a certain class. So too does Christabel. Sylvia, on the other hand, wants the vote given to every woman – and to every man.'

Emma was thrilled to be talking about all the women who had been her heroines for so long, and who she had been hoping to meet. But she found the thought of dissension among them quite distressing.

She was thoughtful for a long time before saying, 'I think I might like Sylvia more than any of the others.'

'I'm quite certain you will. She'll like you too. I wouldn't be taking you to London if I thought it would be otherwise.'

'I'm glad you asked me to come with you – and that I'm going to work for Sylvia. I couldn't pretend to dislike men. I think too much of Jacob.'

After hesitating for a few moments, Emma asked, 'Do you have anyone special in your life?'

Tessa smiled rather sadly. 'Not at the moment. There have been one or two in the past I thought were special, but you'll soon learn that where most men are concerned, "Women's rights" don't extend beyond the right to allow him – and only him – into your bedroom without demanding that he marry you first.'

The two young women chatted happily on the long journey to London and Emma learned a great deal of what she might expect there.

It seemed to her that suffragettes took part in many marches and rallies. In recent months the dockers who lived close to the Dalston Lane office had taken it upon themselves to escort the women on their marches. This gave them much needed protection against their opponents and rowdies – and, on occasion, against the police too.

It was late afternoon when their train reached London. Emma gazed in awe at the row upon row of houses that came up to the edge of the railway line. Everywhere looked grey and dirty. Even the air was filled with smoke that put a haze over the city.

Eventually, the train slowed and came to a steam-escaping halt. Doors swung open and, following Tessa, Emma stepped down to the platform. She was immediately caught up in a world of whistles, escaping steam, and people. Hundreds and hundreds of people; not only passengers from the many trains that stood in lines beneath the high-domed roof, but also a great many vendors. Women and men, boys and girls, selling everything from flowers to hot pies, each seeking to out-shout the others in advertising their particular wares.

Emma was overawed by the sheer volume of people about her, but at the same time she found it incredibly exhilarating.

'Well, this is it,' Tessa declared, amused by her companion's expression. 'You've arrived in London. Now, let's go and find ourselves a bus to take us home.'

2

When the bus on which the two women were travelling reached Dalston Lane, they were little more than a stone's throw from Bow. Here the bells whose sound bestowed upon a Londoner the right to call him- or herself a 'cockney' were situated. Only those born within their range were true cockneys, but in this part of the city, Londoners often asserted that the sound carried to an improbable distance in order to claim this coveted birthright.

As the bus slowed, Emma thought that everyone in London must be in this one thoroughfare today. The street was lined on either side with stalls selling a wide variety of commodities. Although it was wider than any road Emma had seen in Cornwall, it seemed a miracle that vehicles could make any progress through the throng.

It was noisy, too. Costermongers attempted to shout details of their wares above the hubbub of the crowd and the impatient honking of motor horns added to the din.

Eventually, Tessa told Emma it was time to gather their luggage from beneath the stairs of the vehicle. They were approaching the combined office and flat that would be her home for the foreseeable future.

When the bus jerked to a juddering halt, the two women stepped to the ground and pushed their way through a good-natured crowd. As they passed along, a number of stall holders called out greetings to Tessa.

Emma found their accent much harsher than that she was used to in Cornwall, but there could be no doubting the warmth of their greetings. Most also had a warm smile for Emma.

Suddenly, a broad-shouldered giant of a man with close-cropped hair loomed in front of them and relieved them of their suitcases without saying a word.

Emma was reluctant to release the hold she had on her belongings until Tessa said, 'Emma, this is Manny Hirsch. I told you about him on the way here, remember? Manny, this is Emma Cotton. She's just travelled up from Cornwall with me to join our Association.'

Manny smiled at Emma, displaying numerous gaps in the teeth he exposed. Delighted that Tessa had spoken of him, he said, 'Pleased to meet you, Miss Cotton. You'll be seeing a lot of me while you're up 'ere. Anyfing you need, you just ask Manny. I'll see it's done for you.'

When Manny spoke he treated 'th' as though it was an 'f' and 'h' would appear to have been a letter that had been dropped from the English language. But his good humour was infectious and Emma took an instant liking to him.

'Thank you, Manny. I'll remember that.'

Soon they came to a small shop, over the front of which was painted, in gold letters, EAST LONDON FEDERATION OF SUFFRAGETTES.

Giving Emma a fleeting, reassuring smile, Tessa pushed open the door and walked inside.

It was now quite late in the day, but when Emma entered behind Tessa, she found herself in a bustling office. Girls and women sat at various desks and tables. All were occupied in writing, typing, working duplicating machines or talking loudly on telephones. The result was a high level of noise and activity.

Despite the throng of efficiency, an animated crowd quickly gathered about Tessa and Emma. All the women seemed to want to talk at the same time.

Manny clearly found such feminine numbers overwhelming. Depositing the suitcases beside a door at the rear of the office, he made a hurried exit.

The reason for the frenzied activity was soon made clear. The weekly newspaper was due on the newsstands by morning. However, Sylvia Pankhurst had been re-arrested only that day, while addressing a meeting in nearby Victoria Park.

A number of dockers sympathetic to the suffragette movement had been present at the meeting. Sylvia Pankhurst was a favourite with them and her arrest had sparked off a near-riot. Many more arrests were made than had been planned, making it likely that Sylvia Pankhurst would now face additional charges of inciting a riot.

The women in the office were working hard to change the front page of the newspaper in order to include the news of the day's happenings before distribution of the paper began during the night.

When Tessa was made aware of the situation, she immediately said, 'Emma and I will put our things upstairs in the flat, then come down and help.'

When the office staff protested that the two women must be tired after having just completed such a long journey, Tessa said, 'Nonsense! Travelling on a train gave us a very enjoyable rest. After sitting down for so long I'll be delighted to get on my feet and do something active. What do you say, Emma?'

Although she was feeling tired, Emma nodded her agreement and said, 'You'll need to tell me what to do, but I'd love to help.'

'That's what I thought. Now, let's get these bags upstairs and freshen up a little, then we'll be ready for work.'

The flat above the office was small but neat. The sitting room overlooked the busy street at the front of the premises, but from the window of what would be her bedroom, Emma looked out on a tiny yard at the rear of the building.

Beyond the yard were the backs of a row of dingy terraced houses, each with a paved garden area no larger than the living room of a small Cornish cottage.

It was a far cry from the spacious and luxurious room that had been hers at Tregarrick, but Emma felt she would enjoy living here in London's East End.

When the two women were ready, they returned downstairs. Tessa immediately took a telephone call and Emma turned to one of the women operating a copy machine.

'What can I do?'

'First of all, how about making a cup of tea for everyone?' the girl said. She could have been no older than Emma, but pinned to the front of her blouse was a 'Holloway Badge'. An enamelled purple, white and green prison arrow mounted on a silver portcullis, it signified that she had served a term of imprisonment in Holloway Prison because of her activities in support of the suffragette movement.

'You'll find everything you need in the scullery – back there.'

The young woman inclined her head towards a door at the rear of the office. All the while she was talking she continued to turn the handle of a duplicating machine, her hands black with duplicating ink.

While Emma was away making the tea, an older woman who had been introduced to Emma as Constance Leigh spoke of her to Tessa.

'She seems nice enough, Tessa, but she's very much a country girl. How do you think she'll stand up to the rigours of city life?'

'Emma will be all right,' Tessa said reassuringly. 'She's been interested in the suffragette movement for a very long time and has a remarkably strong character. While I was addressing a strike meeting in Cornwall she got herself arrested for trying to stop some policemen from giving her boyfriend a beating. She succeeded, too. Then, after spending a night in cells, she was acquitted the next day in a magistrates court. She'll be a very useful member of the society in a week or two.'

Constance Leigh seemed satisfied, but she voiced a warning. 'She can't expect such leniency from the London magistrates. They've been handing out maximum sentences to us recently. I think they've probably been given orders from the Home Office to attempt to put a stop to our activities once and for all.'

Emma returned with tea for everyone and the women in the office took their cups from her gratefully, one of them declaring it 'a life-saver'.

Shortly afterwards, Emma took over the operation of one of the duplicating machines. The woman who had been using it departed saying she needed to go home and put her young family to bed.

Emma was at first nervous of accepting the responsibility of producing pages for the newspaper, but she gained confidence quickly and was soon enjoying turning out page after page.

The newspaper was not completed until after midnight. Now the women were faced with the problem of distribution. More than fifty of the newspaper bundles were destined for England's major cities.

Having missed the overnight trains on which they were usually despatched, they would need to be put on the first available trains. Most would then reach their destination that same day.

On the other hand, those distributed for London readers would be expected to be on the newsstands at dawn, at the same time as the nation's daily newspapers.

'How are we going to get them out in time?' asked a tired, harassed and ink-stained suffragette who had been preparing copy for printing.

'I'll take them in the car,' Tessa declared confidently. 'Emma can come with me. We'll take turns driving.'

Alarmed at Tessa's statement, Emma said, 'But . . . I can't drive.'

'Oh! I forgot that.' Suddenly, Tessa brightened. 'Never mind. You can learn on the way around. Come along. We'll get the car out and we'll all help to load it up.'

3

The motor car, a smart-looking Sunbeam, was garaged beneath the arches of a railway line in a nearby street, no more than five minutes' walk away. It had been given to the suffragettes by a wealthy woman supporter only three months before.

Along the way, Tessa and Emma passed a number of vagrants in various states of intoxication. Some were seated on the pavement with their backs against a house or shop wall. A few lay in filthy gutters. Empty pockets hanging outside their garments were evidence of the enterprise of earlier passers-by. None of the men gave the two women any trouble.

In the railway arch garage, Emma sat in the driving seat, adjusting various levers on the steering wheel, as instructed by Tessa, who was finding it hard work to crank the vehicle's starting handle.

Suddenly, the Sunbeam's engine exploded into stuttering mobility, the whole vehicle vibrating with new-found mechanical life.

'What do I do now?' Emma cried out in alarm.

'Nothing. Just leave everything as it is.' After securing the starting handle, Tessa leaped into the driving seat hastily vacated by Emma.

Moments later they were rumbling along the uneven streets of East London, the engine taking on a business-like rhythm as Tessa made adjustments to the levers.

For the next few night hours, as the city's traffic thinned dramatically, they drove through the streets of London, dropping off bundles of the suffragette newspaper at various places.

Eventually, when there was virtually no other traffic on the roads and only the occasional sweeper to be seen on the main city streets, Tessa brought the Sunbeam to an unexpected halt.

'I've had enough of driving for tonight. You can have a go now, Emma.'

'Me?' Emma's startled reply was a combination of alarm and consternation. 'But . . . I told you, I don't know how to drive!'

'We all have to start somewhere,' Tessa declared firmly. 'Here . . . !

She put the vehicle into neutral and climbed from the driving seat. Then she walked around the car, waited for Emma to move over to the seat she had vacated, and climbed in beside her.

Emma's heart beat frantically as, following Tessa's instructions, the Sunbeam set off jerkily along the road. It took a surprisingly short amount of time before Emma had mastered the basic elements of driving and soon she was actually beginning to enjoy herself.

They had turned on to the Embankment, heading northwards, alongside the Thames, when suddenly a dog ran from the darkness to one side of the vehicle, barking excitedly at the noisy motor car. Fearing she was about to run over the dog, Emma swung the wheel and the Sunbeam mounted the nearside pavement. Tessa shouted urgently for her to 'Brake!' In the ensuing panic Emma stalled the engine and the motor car came to rest only inches from a lamppost.

For a few moments, Emma sat in the driving seat, shaking, but Tessa said reassuringly, 'You reacted wonderfully, Emma! Had it been me I would have probably run over the dog. Shoo! Go away, you beast.' Her last words were directed at the dog, which was still barking at the vehicle, alternately advancing and retreating.

'You'd better take over now,' Emma said, still shaken.

'Nonsense. You're doing very well. I'll start it up and back it away from the lamppost and you can take over again. You're going to make a fine driver, Emma.'

Tessa swung the handle a number of times, but the vehicle was reluctant to start. Suddenly, a policeman stepped inside the circle of pale yellow light cast by the gas lamp with which they had almost collided.

'Are you ladies having trouble?' A man of about thirty years of age, he addressed his words to Emma.

Before Emma could reply, Tessa said quickly, 'Yes, officer. I was driving along the road when a dog ran out in front of us. I swerved to miss it and ended up here, on the pavement. I only just managed to stop before I hit the lamppost. Now I can't start the damn thing again.'

Emma was puzzled. She could not understand why Tessa should lie.

The constable was puzzled too. Looking from Tessa

to Emma and back again, he said, 'It's your friend who's sitting in the driving seat now . . .'

'Well, I couldn't very well ask her to crank the starting handle for me, could I. She's operating the throttle and the choke whenever I ask her. But now you're here, perhaps you could turn the starting handle. I'm sure you're much stronger than I am.'

'Before I do that, perhaps you'll tell me what you're doing out at this time of the morning? Then I'd like to take a look at your driving licence, if you don't mind.'

Emma realised now why Tessa had lied about who had been driving. She had no licence to drive a motor car.

Tessa walked to the rear door of the car and surreptitiously winked at Emma as she reached for her handbag, which was on the back seat.

'We've been out delivering a news sheet . . .' Rummaging in her handbag as she was speaking, Tessa found what she was seeking. 'Ah! Here's my driving licence.' Pulling it out, she handed it to the constable.

Holding the licence, the young constable walked to the gas lamp and opened it.

Reading the name, he looked up sharply. 'You're Miss Theresa Wren?'

'That's right. I gather you've heard of me.'

The constable nodded. 'Indeed I have, Miss Wren – and very recently too. In fact, when I left Cannon Row police station after my meal, not half an hour ago, I was shown a photograph of you. I'm afraid it's my duty to arrest you and ask you to accompany me to the police station.'

'Arrest me?' Tessa's astonishment was not feigned.

'What for? I've done nothing for which I should be arrested. At least, not recently.'

'It's no good telling that to me, Miss Wren. There's an arrest warrant out for you. My duty is to take you in. I believe you wrote an article for a suffragette newspaper that's published today. Is it the *Rapier*? No, the *Courier*. No doubt that's what you've both been delivering. Anyway, it seems your article is considered to be inciting violence?'

Enlightenment dawned on Tessa. 'An article in the *Courier*, you say?' Then, surprisingly meekly, she added, 'Well, you must carry out your duty, of course, but you can quote me as replying that I intend lodging an official complaint against the policeman who obtained the arrest warrant.'

'That's your right, Miss Wren,' the constable said, unable to hide his relief that he had arrested a prominent suffragette without the violence that frequently accompanied such an occurrence. 'I'm glad you're behaving so sensibly about it.'

'Don't be so damned condescending!' Tessa snapped unexpectedly. 'But since I'm being so "sensible" about being arrested, perhaps you'll be the same and tell me what we're going to do with my motor car. I don't intend to leave it here on the pavement until you decide to release me from custody.'

'Does your friend drive?' the constable asked hopefully.

'No she doesn't.'

'Neither do I, so perhaps you'll continue your co-operation and drive us all to the police station. When we get there I'll make arrangements to have the vehicle cared for until it can be collected by one of your friends.'

'Very well – but driving there is your idea, not mine. I shall expect to be reimbursed for the cost of the petrol I use on the journey. Now, shall we go? Both Emma and I have had a very busy twenty-four hours. We'd like to get this over with as quickly as possible.'

4

Emma was concerned for her friend, but Tessa seemed remarkably relaxed about the predicament she was in.

It proved difficult to talk in the presence of the constable. However, when they arrived at Cannon Row the two women were able to converse in a whisper while the constable was explaining the circumstances of the arrest to a desk sergeant.

'Don't worry, Emma, they have no case against me. I can't explain why right now, but get back to Dalston Lane as soon as you can. When the women arrive for work in the morning have someone get in touch with Keir Hardie. He'll know what to do. Tell him . . .'

She was unable to say any more. The desk sergeant, a giant of a man, with a paunch that threatened to break free of his tunic, glowered at them and ordered Tessa to remain silent.

Turning his attention to Emma, he said, 'Unless you

want to be arrested too you'd better go home. Give your name and address to the constable first. We may want to speak to you later.'

Standing her ground, Emma demanded, 'What's going to happen to Tessa?'

'That's none of your business. You're not involved in it right now. If you want things to remain that way you'll leave quietly.'

'How do I get back to Dalston Lane?' Emma persisted. 'It's my first day in London and I have no money with me . . .'

'Give her a pound note from my purse,' Tessa said. The sergeant coloured up angrily. He was not used to being told what to do by his prisoners. Certainly not by a suffragette woman.

'You heard what she said,' Tessa continued. 'She's new to London. Refuse to give her my money and you'll be throwing a young girl from the country out on the streets of London. You'll be called upon to answer for it, I can promise you that.'

'Not to you I won't,' the sergeant declared. Pointing to the door, he instructed the young constable, 'Escort her outside. If she argues, arrest her.'

Emma hesitated. Her natural inclination was to argue with the sergeant, but Tessa said, 'Go, Emma. Stay on the main road and ask your way of the first person you meet, even if it's only a road sweeper. You'll find him far more helpful than any policeman. You know what to do when you get back to the office.'

Emma shook off the constable's hand, which he had placed on her arm, and left the police charge-office with him, passing through the two pairs of double doors to the street.

On the steps outside she stopped, wondering whether to begin walking to the left or to the right.

'Do you really not know which way to go?'

'Don't worry, I'll do as Tessa suggested. I'll ask someone.'

'There's no need. If you go along there a little way and walk along the main road, you'll come to Charing Cross railway station. You can catch a bus to Dalston from there.' He pointed to the left. 'There's an all-night service which will take you all the way.'

'I'll need to know which way to walk. I don't have any money on me.'

Reaching inside his pocket, the constable pulled out a couple of silver coins. Holding them out to her, he said, 'Here's two shillings. I don't know how much the night fare is but this should be plenty enough.'

Taken by surprise by his generous offer, Emma said, 'I . . . I can't accept it. How would I get it back to you?'

'You'll find a way.'

When she still hesitated, he said, 'Look, if you don't catch the bus, you'll need to walk and it's a long way to Dalston. I'm from the country too – and I have a sister who's about the same age as you. I'd hate to think of her walking across London at night on her own. Besides, it's your friend who's been arrested. You've done nothing wrong, as far as I'm aware.'

'Thank you.' Emma took the money with a sense of relief. She had been apprehensive at the thought of walking the streets of London in the dark, not knowing anything about the great city. 'What's your name?'

'George Fry. Constable number four eight five . . .'

Further conversation was brought to an abrupt halt by

the sergeant's voice. He bellowed from the charge-office for Constable Fry to return inside the police station – 'Immediately!'

Clutching the two shilling coins loaned to her by the unexpectedly friendly constable, Emma made her way to the main road and the bus stop.

Although Emma reached the office before dawn, it was nine o'clock before anyone else put in an appearance. Then three of the women who worked in the office arrived together.

By now the exciting events of the previous day and night were catching up with Emma. She felt drained of energy and the women expressed concern for her.

However, when she passed on news of what had happened to Tessa, they realised they had another crisis on their hands. Soon the telephone lines from the office were humming.

Not half an hour later, when the office was as crowded as it had been when Emma and Tessa had arrived the previous day, there was the persistent and triumphant sound of a motor-car horn from the street outside. Moments later Tessa entered the office.

Smiling broadly, she was immediately surrounded by the surprised East London suffragettes.

Emma was overjoyed to see her friend, yet completely baffled by her unexpected arrival. For a wild moment she wondered whether she might have made a daring escape from the police station!

'Emma told us you'd been arrested!' One of the women cast an accusing glance at Emma.

'And so I was. They charged me with "incitement", claiming the front page of the *Courier* was "calculated to inflame the passions of certain sections of the public". I think that's a fairly accurate quote of what the sergeant in Cannon Row police station said.'

Now the other women in the office were as baffled as Emma by Tessa's unexpected release.

'There was nothing on the first page that was remotely seditious,' one of them pointed out. 'We were merely reporting the re-arrest of Sylvia and pointing out the iniquities of the Cat and Mouse Act.'

'That's perfectly true,' Tessa agreed. 'As the police themselves discovered when they came to look through a copy of the *Courier* they found in the car.'

As she was speaking, Tessa's gaze had been circling the women in the office. It finally settled on a drab, thin woman who was employed as an office cleaner. Holding a broom, the woman stood at the rear of the office, apart from the others.

Resuming her explanation, Tessa said, 'However, when the police swore out a warrant for my arrest as editor of the *Courier*, it seemed they had no knowledge that we had changed the lead story. They were in possession of a copy of the original front page. The one you'd prepared before hearing of Sylvia's arrest.'

'How did they get hold of that . . . ?'

The speaker fell silent as she realised the implications of her own words.

'I thought about that myself, while I was in the police cell,' Tessa replied. 'It had to be someone who had access to the *Courier* in its various stages, yet who must have left the office before the change had been decided upon. I'm afraid one name in particular sprang to mind immediately.'

The others, except for Emma, realised immediately the identity of the person suspected by Tessa. They all looked towards the woman who cleaned the offices of the East London Federation of Suffragettes.

5

'You're the only one who always leaves the office by four o'clock each day, Agnes. You need to prepare an evening meal for your sick mother, your husband and your family – or so you tell us. Do your duties also include a visit to Dalston Lane police station on your way home?'

Tessa put her question to the office cleaner quietly, while the other women looked on in silence.

It seemed to Emma the woman was about to deny any knowledge of what Tessa was talking about and would brazen it out. Instead, she dropped her broom to the floor and made a desperate dash for the door.

She was prevented from reaching it by one of the women who moved to stand with her back against the door.

Frustrated in her escape, Agnes stopped. Her shoulders sagged and to Emma it seemed she had suddenly shrunk in stature.

'I'm sorry, Miss Wren. I really am. I didn't want to do it . . .'

'Then why did you? After everything we've done for you here.' Tessa's tone was one of sorrow rather than anger.

'I know!' the unhappy woman wailed. 'If it wasn't for you, I'd be on the streets now – or in the nick, likely as not.'

'Then . . . why?'

Tessa was genuinely puzzled. The East London Federation of Suffragettes had helped Agnes when her husband was out of work and her children hungry. At that time Agnes had been so desperate, she was ready to go and sell herself to the seamen who came into London docks from every port in the world.

Thanks to the rapport the suffragettes had built up with the dockers, Tessa had been able to secure work for Agnes's husband, Charlie, at the docks. She also took on Agnes as a cleaner in the Dalston Lane office.

Agnes began crying noisily. 'It was the police. They caught Charlie with some fruit he'd nicked from one of the boats. It wasn't much, just something for each of the kids. Everyone does it. But . . . he's been in trouble before and spent a year inside. They – the police – said I was to let 'em know what was happening in here. Get copies of the paper for 'em before it was out on the streets, that sort of thing. If I did, they'd see to it that Charlie didn't go down this time.'

'You ought to know they can't keep promises like that, Agnes. When was Charlie arrested?'

'A month ago,' Agnes replied tearfully.

'And he's still being held?' Tessa was startled.

'No. They let him out on bail.'

'If they haven't charged him and taken him to court yet, I doubt if they will.' Tessa looked suspiciously at Agnes. 'But you probably know this already. How much have they paid you to spy on us, Agnes?'

Agnes's instinct was to deny receiving any money for what she had done, but she changed her mind when she saw Tessa's expression. 'Not much. A few bob, that's all.'

Tessa looked around the room at the other women. 'It seems we've had a Judas in our midst for some time.'

'Can I still keep me job 'ere, Miss Wren? I won't do anything like this again, honest I won't.'

Tessa shook her head, sadly. 'No, Agnes. I've suspected for some time that someone in the office has been passing on information to the police. Too often we've arrived somewhere to find them waiting for us. It all falls into place now.'

Turning to another of the women in the office, she said, 'Give Agnes what she's owed, Rose, then send her packing.'

'What about my kids – and my sick mother? Let me stay on, Miss Wren. I won't do nothing like this again, not never, I won't.'

'Yes you would, Agnes. Not only that, money has disappeared from my desk too on occasion. You were the most likely suspect, but I always gave you the benefit of the doubt. I shouldn't have. I should have dismissed you right away. It would have saved the East London Federation of Suffragettes a great deal of distress.'

Agnes said no more until a tight-lipped Rose had handed over the wages due to her. She reached the door before turning to launch a vitriolic attack on the occupants of the office.

'I didn't really want your rotten job, anyway. I'm glad I'm going – and I'm not sorry for what I did. You're all a lot of frustrated old spinsters. The only reason you want the vote is so you can put one over on the men. You don't really care about any of us who live here in the East End. We wouldn't get a say in anything if you got what you wanted. It's only your posh women who live up west who'd become important – and don't tell me I'm wrong, because I've read the letter sent to Sylvia Pankhurst by her precious mother. Good riddance to you all, I say.' Spitting out her final farewell, Agnes fled from the office, slamming the door behind her.

The ringing of a telephone broke the silence that held for some moments after Agnes's dramatic departure. As sound erupted around her, Tessa said, 'Well! It seems we've nursed in our bosom not only a police informer but a viper.'

'Is what she said about the letter from Emmeline Pankhurst to her daughter true?' Emma asked.

'Quite true,' Tessa replied honestly. 'Although neither Sylvia nor any of us here agrees with what was in the letter. We always have – and always will – campaign for the vote to be given to every woman in the land.'

'How can you possibly all work together when you don't agree among yourselves – especially about something as important as this?' Emma was perplexed. Back home in Cornwall, before meeting Tessa, she had not been aware of any differences among the suffragettes. She had believed them all to be working towards the achievement of a single goal.

'We can't,' Tessa was disarmingly honest. 'The East London Federation of Suffragettes and Emmeline Pankhurst's Women's Social and Political Union are uneasy comrades in arms. Our differences have become more apparent recently. Sooner or later there's going to have to be a break.'

She looked about her. The women had resumed their various tasks but all were listening to her conversation with Emma with considerable interest. 'It's something we've discussed frequently, but we've all tried to fool ourselves that the break would never be necessary. I know all the members of the Pankhurst family. I had hoped that Emmeline, Christabel and Sylvia would have met up and settled their differences by the time I returned from Cornwall. Unfortunately, Sylvia's been taken back to prison again, Emmeline's out of the country somewhere and Christabel is living in Paris. They're farther apart than ever – in every sense of the word!'

'Well, thank goodness you're back with us again,' one of the women in the office said. 'We're all happy to be passing responsibility for the office back where it should be – either with you or with Sylvia.'

'Not today, you won't,' Tessa said positively. 'Emma and I haven't had a wink of sleep since leaving Cornwall yesterday morning. You'll find us upstairs if we're needed – but it had better be for something important if you do disturb us.'

To Emma she said, 'Go upstairs and put the kettle on. I'll be there in a few minutes, after I've had a quick check through this morning's mail.'

Emma left the office and Tessa was looking through the mail when the woman who had been in charge of the office in her absence said, 'How did Emma come through her first brush with the London police?'

'Very well indeed,' Tessa replied. 'For a while I feared

she would get arrested herself – as she did when I was talking to the strikers in Cornwall. She's going to be all right, believe me. I'd like to see her learn to drive as soon as possible though. She'd be very useful as our regular driver.'

She gave a secret smile as she remembered the incident that had led to their arrest. 'Mind you, she'll need some tuition. She'll also need to obtain a licence. Remind me to do something about that when I am in the office tomorrow.'

Stifling a yawn, she pushed a letter across the desk, away from her. 'That's it, I've had enough for today. No doubt there will be a great many new problems to tackle tomorrow. Until then, I'm going to bed.'

6

The next few weeks were busy ones for Emma, but she settled very well in London's East End. She soon found herself in full agreement with Tessa. Those who lived here were warm and friendly and the suffragettes did a great many things to help those in need – especially the children. They even ran a nursery to take care of the children of those women who needed to work and had no one else to turn to.

Emma was gradually accepted by the women who worked in the office, although they maintained a certain subtle reserve with her.

There was good reason for their initial caution with newcomers. Every one of the women had spent time in prison for the cause in which they had a passionate belief, and many would return to prison again. Yet it was not an experience anyone in a sane state of mind would invite.

The women remembered all too well the pain and

humiliation of forced feeding and the suffering they had experienced at the hands of police and prison authorities.

They trusted no one who had not undergone similar experiences fully. This did not mean that Emma was excluded from their activities or that she had not had the occasional brush with the law, but she had somehow managed to avoid arrest since her arrival in London.

Tessa kept her word to Emma about having her taught to drive. She brought in a suffragette named Vera Holme, who had occasionally been the driver for most of the Pankhurst family when they were neither abroad nor in prison.

Vera was one of the more colourful members of the movement and had herself spent time in prison for a variety of offences. She had chained herself to railings in Downing Street and, a skilled horsewoman, she had on one occasion used a horse as a charger, snatching the reins of a mounted policeman and galloping off with both horse and hapless rider. It took three policemen to arrest her and her crime on this occasion was defined in the magistrates court as an "Assault on a policeman".

During her time as a suffragette driver, Vera had made herself familiar with the workings of the motor cars she drove. She taught Emma much about the mechanics of the Sunbeam used by the East London office staff.

Vera was generally recognised by the others as one of the 'wilder' members of the organisation, and one day early in 1914 she took Emma as a companion on one of her not infrequent attacks on the establishment. It quickly became clear to Emma why she had earned such a reputation.

On this occasion Vera did not use the suffragettes' motor car. Instead she and Emma rode in a bus to the City of London. The staid financial centre of much of the world's banking activities, The City was inhabited by men who wore bowler hats, black coats and pin-striped trousers.

Arriving close to their destination, the two women alighted and caught another bus which would take them through the heart of The City, passing the Bank of England along the way.

They climbed the stairs to the upper deck, which was open to the elements. Here Vera revealed for the first time the purpose of their foray into the staid world of The City.

A chill wind was blowing, with a hint of rain in the air, and the upper deck was sparsely occupied, which suited Vera's purpose well. As they passed along a street with banks and offices on either side, she reached in a deep pocket and drew forth a home-made catapult fitted with strong rubber thongs.

Smiling at Emma's expression of astonishment, Vera said, 'I have older brothers. I was making these by the time I was six years old. Don't you have brothers?'

Emma shook her head. 'I have five sisters. They tried to teach me how to make dresses and sew on buttons. I was never very good at such things.'

Vera pulled a face. 'Shame! By not having brothers you missed out on a great deal of fun.' As she spoke she produced a hand-sized draw-string bag from the pocket that had housed the catapult. Loosening the string, she took out a bright silver steel ball-bearing the size of a child's marble. Placing it in the square of leather linking the two lengths of catapult rubber, she took aim in the style of an archer, stretching the rubber to almost arm's length.

When she released it, the ball-bearing sped unerringly towards a first-floor window on the near side of the road.

By the time the glass shattered, another ball-bearing was fitted to the catapult. This one went to the offside of the busy thoroughfare, the aim equally unerring.

Giving Emma a wry grin, Vera said, 'I've had plenty of practice.'

The catapult cannonade continued for much of the length of the street, during which distance only two of Vera's ball-bearing missiles failed to hit and break a window.

There was a brief, uncomfortable moment for Emma when a large single pane window broke with such a loud noise that the half-dozen fellow passengers turned in their seats to establish the source of the noise. Quite unperturbed, Vera dropped the catapult in her lap until they turned away once more.

There was another awkward moment when the bus halted to allow a bowler-hatted passenger to board. He came up the stairs and seemed about to take a seat across the aisle from the two woman. Instead, he shivered and returned down the stairs to take a warmer seat in the enclosed lower deck.

When the bus reached the end of the street, Vera calmly returned the ball-bearings and catapult to her pockets and stood up.

'Come along, Emma, we have some letters to post.'

When they alighted from the vehicle, Vera pulled a wad of stamped and addressed envelopes from another pocket. Dropping them in a nearby post box, she said to

Emma, 'They're addressed to the occupiers of the offices whose windows we've just broken.'

Emma was somewhat confused. 'Why? I don't understand . . .'

'I've sent them each a note to tell them their windows have been broken by a suffragette. I've explained that it's part of our campaign against the male-dominated establishment, and repeated our demands that we be given the vote. After all, there's no sense in smashing windows if no one knows who's doing it or why.'

Vera grinned suddenly. 'Mind you, it's great fun. Would you like us to catch a bus back along the road so you can have a go?'

Uncertain whether or not the other woman was serious, Emma said hurriedly, 'No thanks. I've never used a catapult. You'll need to teach me.'

'There's no time like the present. We'll catch a bus to Victoria Park. There's lots of space there. We'll find a few stones of the right size to use as ammunition. Ball-bearings cost money, so I save them for special occasions.'

Talking as though she was discussing ordinary, everyday events, Vera continued, 'Have I ever told you of the time Sylvia, Tessa and I took part in a demonstration at the last election? We had a wonderful time. I took my catapult along and used it to fire at a line of policemen who were linking arms to keep us out of the hall where the sitting MP was speaking. I scored hits on at least five helmets and knocked off two, despite their chin straps. It was more fun than shooting at toy ducks in a fairground, I can tell you!'

7

For some time Emma had been aware of an air of excitement in the Dalston Lane office. She guessed a demonstration of some type was being planned, but made no attempt to question any of the others about it.

Despite her work for them, Emma was still treated with a certain reserve by the other women. She found it hurtful and frequently brought up the matter in her conversations with Tessa.

The older woman explained the situation with great patience.

'They've fought together, been arrested together, and gone to prison together. Each of them is absolutely certain of the trust she can put in the others. You are still comparatively new to them, Emma. They like you and are happy to be working with you – but you're not one of them yet. You of all people should understand the way they feel. Isn't it the way Cornish men and women feel about strangers?'

Emma conceded this was so, but added, 'It's not quite the same, Tessa. I came to London with you because I feel so strongly about what you are all doing. I want to feel I'm an accepted part of the movement. I'm quite prepared to take the same risks as everyone else.'

The two women were in the small flat above the office, at the end of another long working day. It was publication day for the weekly suffragette newspaper once again, and Emma had spent many hours driving the Sunbeam, delivering the newspapers with the aid of a couple of the office suffragettes.

Her pleasure at being able to drive around the London streets grew with each passing day, but it was tiring. Motorised traffic was on the increase, with little or no fall in the number of horse-drawn vehicles on the roads.

Tessa appeared to be deep in thought. Suddenly, she said, 'You realise we're planning something fairly spectacular, don't you, Emma?'

'I'd need to be blind, deaf and stupid not to! But if no one wants to tell me what it is, I suppose I'll just have to accept it.'

Despite her words, Emma had to try hard not to keep an element of bitterness from her voice. It was hurtful to know she was not fully trusted by the other women after working so many long hours, day and night, on behalf of the organisation.

'You mustn't feel upset,' Tessa said sympathetically. 'They've learned the hard way that they shouldn't trust anyone who hasn't been to prison for her beliefs. Being put away isn't an experience anyone enjoys and they try to avoid it if they can. When they're committed to prison, many will show their defiance of the authorities by refusing to eat. In the past it's meant they were force fed. It's a horrible experience for any woman. I've heard it compared with being raped. A violation of both mind and body. Yet the women will refuse to change their stand if they are sent to prison again. Such things build a bond between them as nothing else can, I can assure you of that. I hope it's something you'll never have to experience – but knowing you as I do, I think you probably will. When you have, you'll be one of them. You'll understand then why others aren't.'

Emma did not fully comprehend Tessa's explanation, but she accepted it. 'Will I be included in this . . . whatever it is that's being planned?'

Tessa frowned. 'It wasn't my intention to have you actively involved. You're very useful to us as a driver now. I thought we'd keep you in reserve in one of the back streets with the car, ready to take anyone who is badly injured to hospital.'

Emma's stomach contracted in a moment of fear as she wondered what proposed action would result in casualties, but she said, 'I'd much rather be part of whatever it is that's going on. Vera can stay with the car. She won't mind, she's taken part in more demonstrations than most of you.'

Tessa still seemed undecided. 'Well . . . only if you're quite sure . . .'

'Look, I didn't come all this way from Cornwall to hide in some back street while the rest of you risk health and freedom for a cause I believe in just as much as you do.'

'All right.' Tessa made up her mind and smiled understandingly at Emma. 'I know just how you feel. I was the same when I came here and Sylvia felt I wasn't

ready to take part in planned demonstrations. You'd
better come down to the office for the meeting we're
holding tomorrow evening. I'll tell the others you're
coming with us. You'll need to be there when we
discuss tactics.'

'Thanks, Tessa – but I still don't know what we're
supposed to be doing!'

Emma hoped it would be nothing too violent. During
the first months of 1914, the campaign of the suffragettes
had escalated considerably. Paintings had been slashed,
buildings burned and sports fixtures disrupted.

The highlight of the previous year of protest had been
an incident that sent shockwaves of horror around the
world. Emily Wilding Davison had died beneath the
hooves of the king's horse, Anmer. She had run on to
the track in front of the animal at a crowded Epsom
race-meeting, during the running of the Derby.

It had been an individual act of sacrifice, but the
movement was determined it would not be a vain one.

Tessa's explanation of what was being planned left
Emma speechless. 'There's going to be a huge rally. It
will end – so everyone thinks – with speeches in the
Albert Hall. Most of those at the rally will certainly
attend the meeting there, but some of us have made
further plans. The king and queen are due to attend
a performance at the opera that night. We're going to
print a whole lot of leaflets, setting out the aims of our
movement. As no one in government seems to take any
notice of us, we're going to try to give the leaflets to the
king when he returns to Buckingham Palace. It should
cause quite a stir!'

8

The briefing meeting in the Dalston Lane office proved more eventful than any of the women present could possibly have anticipated.

It was dark outside, but the market was still busy, the wide variety of lamps hanging above the stalls softening the poverty lines etching the faces of many of the shoppers.

One of the costermongers had a perforated metal drum mounted on wheels. It housed a coke fire on which the vendor was cooking chestnuts. He had placed it on the roadway, across the pavement from the entrance to the suffragette premises, and the tantalising aroma of roasting chestnuts pervaded the office where the women were gathered.

The office was packed to capacity with far more women present than Emma had ever seen there before. Many were strangers to her. Tessa was outlining the plan of campaign to alert King George V to their cause.

It was a simple and flexible plan; however, it was full of ifs and buts.

The main objective was to bring their leaflet to the attention of the sovereign. As well as outlining the aims of the suffragette movement, it called his attention to the tens of thousands of his subjects – men and women – who had signed a petition calling for women's suffrage.

Tessa was showing a copy of the leaflet to the assembled women when, without any warning, there came the startling crash of breaking glass. The women closest to the door scattered as half a brick and sharp-edged fragments of glass landed among them.

The large pane of glass that had comprised the top half of the door lay scattered on the floor.

Emma was one of those close to the door. Wrenching it open, she ran outside to the street, closely followed by a couple of the women.

The chestnut seller pointed in the direction of Kingsland Road. 'They ran off that way. Two young nobs, they looked like. Not from around 'ere, either of 'em, I'd say.'

As Emma looked in the direction he had pointed, she saw what appeared to be some form of commotion and noticed a crowd gathering.

As she watched, the crowd parted and the giant figure of Manny came into view. Accompanying him, albeit reluctantly, were two young men.

One, red-faced and seemingly having difficulty breathing, was being held in a headlock beneath Manny's left arm. The other, his feet touching the ground only at every third or fourth step, might have been dangling in a hangman's noose so tight was the grip the London wrestler had upon his shirt and coat collar.

'Gawd! Rather them than me,' the chestnut vendor commented. 'They're lucky he didn't tear 'em limb from limb. Do you want me to send for the coppers to come and take them two off, missus?'

He addressed his question to Tessa, who had come from the office and was inspecting the damaged door.

Glancing up at the approaching trio, she replied, 'What for? So they can give them a pat on the back and let them go? No, I've a much better idea. These will be the two young men who've smashed windows in four East London suffragette offices in the last week. That's why I asked Manny to keep an eye on our place. I think it's high time they were taught a lesson they won't forget in a hurry.'

Manny reached them, a wide grin revealing his hit-and-miss teeth. ''Ere you are, Miss Tessa. What shall I do wiv 'em?'

'Bring them inside, Manny. I'm looking forward to talking to them.'

The angry suffragettes parted ranks to let Manny and his prisoners through, followed inside the office by Tessa and Emma. Then the other women filed back through the glass-strewn doorway.

Inside, two women were being treated for facial cuts.

'Are you all right?' Tessa paused to ask anxiously after them.

The woman who was treating their wounds looked up. 'They'll be all right. Not much more than scratches, really . . . But it's no thanks to these two.' She inclined her head in the direction of the two young men, who had been released by Manny and made to sit in chairs, uncomfortably aware of Manny's glowering presence.

'Why did you break the glass in our door? What have

we done to upset you?' Tessa asked the question of the two young men.

For a moment it seemed the men would deny all knowledge of the attack. Then one of them shrugged. 'Why not? Isn't it what you do if you don't agree with something or someone?'

As some of the women murmured angrily, Tessa said, 'No, we are seeking to right a blatant wrong. We've tried for many years to do it by reasoned argument, but no one will listen.'

The man shrugged again. 'That's your way of looking at it. A whole lot of people don't agree.'

'We know. That's the reason so many of us have been to prison for the things we do in support of our aims. What do you think we ought to do with you?'

'Please yourself.' The way in which the young man licked his suddenly dry lips belied his outward show of indifference.

'It's not as though this is the first suffragette office you've attacked, is it,' continued Tessa. 'If you went before a magistrate he'd take all the other offences into account. What would the sentence be, do you think? A month? Three?'

'Are you going to call the police?' It was the first time the second young man had spoken. He possessed none of the bravado shown by his companion. He looked scared.

'No, I don't think we'll call in the police,' Tessa replied. 'At least, not if you can pay for the damage you've caused to our office – and to the other offices.'

'We haven't got that sort of money on us,' the first young man said.

'But do you agree we can take what you have?'

The shrug came once more. 'Go ahead.'

'First, let's have your names.'

They were less forthcoming with this information, but one carried identification in his wallet and when this was revealed the other gave his name.

The wallets also yielded a combined total of two pounds and seven shillings.

'That isn't going to pay for five windows,' Tessa said, in disgust. 'We're going to have to think of something else.'

The young man who was inclined to shrug said, 'Well, that's all we've got.'

'Oh, I don't know, we should be able to raise a little more money. Manny, how much do you think we'd get for the suit he's wearing if we were to take it down to Uncle's?'

To Emma, Tessa explained, 'Uncle's is the pawnshop down the road.'

The two young men looked at Tessa in disbelief, but Manny said seriously, 'I reckon we might get five bob from it – and the same for the other one.'

Tessa nodded acknowledgement. 'And their shoes? They look quite smart. How much would we get for them?'

Manny shook his head. 'Three bob for both pairs – maybe three and six. There's not much call for second-hand shoes.'

'What are you talking about?' the more confident of the two young men demanded. 'We're wearing them.'

'Not any more. Take them off,' Tessa retorted firmly.

Now both men paled and the previously self-assured one said incredulously, 'You're not serious?'

'I've never been more serious,' Tessa said. 'Manny, you hold them while we remove their suits and shoes.'

The giant wrestler had been as uncertain as the two young men about the sincerity of Tessa's intentions, but now he moved to obey her without question.

'It's all right . . . I'll do it myself,' the quieter of the two young men said hurriedly, and immediately he began matching actions to words.

'How about you?' Tessa demanded of the other man.

Scarlet cheeked, he replied hoarsely, 'I . . . I can't, I . . . I'm not wearing any underpants.'

'Then for your sake I hope you're wearing a long shirt,' Tessa replied unsympathetically. 'Are you going to remove your suit and shoes – or shall we?'

Carefully avoiding looking up at any of the women, the young man removed his shoes, his jacket and, finally, his trousers, trying unsuccessfully to ignore the amused chuckles of the suffragettes.

When the two men stood in the centre of the office floor wearing only socks, shirts and, in one instance, a pair of pants, Tessa picked up the clothes they had so reluctantly discarded and threw them to the East End wrestler. 'Here, Manny. Take them along to Uncle's. These two are leaving now.'

'But . . . we can't go out on the streets like this!'

'No? Manny, how much do you think we would get for their shirts . . .'

The two young men fled from the office and the progress of their flight along Dalston Lane could be judged by the laughter of the costermongers and their customers.

Behind them, in the office of the East London Federation of Suffragettes, many of the women were helpless with laughter at the wickedly humorous example of Tessa's 'justice'.

For Emma, her most amusing memory was of the young man who was not wearing underpants. Before fleeing from the office, he had reached between his legs to gather the tail of his shirt in a vain bid to cover his nakedness, before dashing after his companion.

The serious business of the evening had been temporarily put to one side by the suffragettes, but there would be little humour when they carried out their planned sortie against His Majesty King George V, King of the United Kingdom, Emperor of India and Defender of the Faith.

9

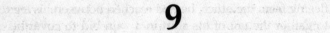

The day of the suffragette rally dawned crisp and cold in London. A vague hint of fog hung over the winding course of the River Thames and added a romantic, ethereal haze to the skyline of England's capital city.

The women began gathering early at the Dalston Lane office. The small premises were already crowded by the time the lamplighters began walking the streets, using their long, hooked poles to extinguish gently hissing gas lamps.

All the women were dressed in a similar style. Dresses of white or cream, with cardigans, coats and hats of green or purple.

The combination of colours was that which the movement had taken as its own. 'Purple for freedom and dignity; white for purity in private and public life; and green, the colour of hope', as one of the Association's members had once explained to Emma.

An air of subdued excitement enveloped the office,

but the women did not talk of their plans for the end of the day: they all knew some of their number might be on their way to prison while others headed homewards from the rally to their families.

Women from various offices in East London were to meet in Victoria Park, a popular venue for such rallies. Here they would be joined by a great many dockers and representatives of Union and Labour movements.

In Victoria Park they would form up before marching through the streets of East London, en route to Trafalgar Square. Here they would become part of a vast assembly attended by representatives of Suffragette and Trade Union organisations from all parts of Britain.

More than ten thousand women and Trade Unionists were expected to be present. Far too many for the police to consider any action against those attending the meeting who might be wanted by them for offences committed in the name of suffragism.

From Trafalgar Square, the demonstrators intended marching to the Albert Hall. Here they would listen to speeches from many suffragette leaders, including Sylvia Pankhurst.

Recently released under the auspices of the Cat and Mouse Act, she was recovering from yet another hunger-strike whilst in prison.

The publicised events of the day went almost exactly as planned, and those gathered in Victoria Park sent up a huge cheer when Sylvia Pankhurst appeared. In a typically dramatic fashion, she arrived borne on a litter, carried on the shoulders of four burly men and escorted by a number of London dockers.

The women set off from the park carrying flags and banners and preceded by a uniformed band. It was a distance of about four miles to the heart of London from their starting point, but crowds lining the route provided encouragement to sustain them along the way.

Most of the watching crowd were sympathetic to the women's cause, but there were a few boos and catcalls. However, when these occurred, they were immediately drowned out by the heightened cheering of those about them.

Before reaching Trafalgar Square the women from Victoria Park met up with a march from north London, headed by another band. For some minutes there was a certain amount of confusion as the columns merged and the conductors of both bands argued about which of them would head the long procession and which would take up position at the rear.

There was more disarray when the by now sizeable procession reached Trafalgar Square. The square appeared to be already packed to capacity. Yet somehow, with considerable good humour, room was found for more.

The speeches here were given by local leaders of the Union and Suffragette movements. Higher ranking leaders would have their say when, later in the day, they faced a capacity audience of some eight thousand assembled in the Albert Hall.

One of the speakers in Trafalgar Square was Tessa. She received enthusiastic applause when she told her listeners of the fight that had been put up by the Cornish clay workers and their wives in their unsuccessful battle to gain a decent living wage.

Emma was taken aback when Tessa called her by name and told of how she had been arrested during a meeting in support of the strikers. She was even more embarrassed when two of the dockers insisted upon raising her on their shoulders to acknowledge the applause of the crowd.

The speeches went on until late afternoon. Everyone was greatly relieved when the order came to move off once more, this time heading for the Albert Hall, where it took more than an hour for everyone to take their place.

Once the doors had been closed the speeches began. That evening Emma listened to some of the finest orators in the land putting the case for women's suffrage and workers' rights.

She was utterly spellbound by the proceedings. Not until the applause for the last speaker of the evening was dying down did she remember, with a sudden thrill of fear, what was in store for her and the other members of the Dalston Lane branch of the East London Federation of Suffragettes.

10

Darkness had fallen outside the Albert Hall by the time the thousands of suffragettes, Trade Union members and Labour supporters left the huge building.

Hundreds crowded the pavements, waiting to catch omnibuses to their respective destinations. Those with trains to catch to the suburbs or farther afield walked into the heart of the city, to main-line stations. All were in high spirits.

It had been a successful and morale-boosting day. To crown their success, Sylvia Pankhurst had been spirited away from the Albert Hall by her supporters, eluding police who had intended to re-arrest her.

The police were aware she was being borne on a litter largely for effect, and they quite logically believed that if she was fit enough to stand before her vast audience and give a stirring speech, she was fit enough to be returned to prison.

'How many of us are involved in what's going to

happen tonight?' Emma asked, hoping her voice would betray none of the apprehensive excitement she felt about the events that were soon to unfold.

'Twenty-two,' Tessa replied. 'And don't forget, if you get away or are hurt, make for Caxton Street. Vera will be waiting there with the Sunbeam.'

Emma looked about her. They were walking along Constitution Hill now, approaching Buckingham Palace – and there were considerably more than twenty-two suffragettes walking in front and behind them.

When Emma pointed this out, Tessa explained, 'Many of the women are heading for Charing Cross station. Others, from the country, will spend the night in London. They're no doubt heading for the palace gates, hoping to catch a glimpse of the king or queen, or some other member of the royal family. It will be something to tell their friends when they return home.'

When Emma frowned, Tessa elaborated, 'We're none of us anti-royalist, you know – or anti anything else, come to that. It's just that we believe passionately that our cause is a just one.'

'I wasn't thinking about that,' Emma said. 'But aren't they likely to get involved with what we're going to do if they're outside the palace?'

'A few will,' Tessa admitted. 'Most will scuttle to safety when trouble starts. Sadly, the majority of our supporters are only fair-weather suffragettes. They pay their dues and want their friends to consider them very daring. But they don't want to involve themselves in any activity that might land them in trouble.'

She shrugged. 'Never mind, their very presence outside the palace will help confuse the police once our demonstration begins.'

Tessa suddenly slowed her pace. 'Talking of policemen . . . isn't that the constable who arrested me when
we were delivering the *Courier*, the first night you were
in London?'

They were walking alongside the high wall of
Buckingham Palace gardens now, approaching the railings
at the front of the building. Constable George Fry
was standing with another policeman on the edge of
the wide pavement, watching the suffragettes as they
walked past.

His glance touched on Tessa and Emma and passed
on. Then quickly returned to them.

'He's recognised us!' Emma said in a hoarse whisper.
'What do we do?'

'Nothing,' Tessa replied immediately. 'Just leave me
to do the talking.'

'Hello, ladies!' George Fry touched fingertips to his
helmet in a polite salute. 'What are you doing in this
part of London tonight?'

Although he addressed the question to both of them,
his gaze rested upon Emma.

'We're on our way from a rally at the Albert Hall,'
Tessa replied. 'Like a great many other women, we
thought we'd come past the palace in the hope of
catching a glimpse of the king. Don't forget, Emma's
from Cornwall; they don't have many chances to see
the king there.'

'Then your luck's in,' the young constable said. 'King
George and Queen Mary have spent the evening at
the opera. They're due back at the palace in a few
minutes' time.'

Not very far away a very large policeman wearing the
uniform of an inspector was glaring in their direction.

Catching the attention of Constable Fry, he beckoned him imperiously.

'I have to go now,' George Fry said. 'I hope you get a good view of the king.'

When he had gone, Emma found she was shaking. It was part excitement and part fear. 'Do you think he suspected anything?' she asked her companion.

Tessa shook her head. 'No, he was far too friendly – but I'm concerned about the inspector he's talking to right now. I've seen him on many occasions when we've demonstrated in this part of London. We're well known to him. He could make things difficult. Go and tell all the others you can find to spread out as much as they can, but they're to remain close to the gates. If we all run at the king's car from different directions as it's about to enter the palace, one or two of us might be able to get close.'

When Constable Fry reached the man who had summoned him, Inspector Tremlett snapped, 'What do you mean by engaging suffragettes in conversation? Who are they?'

'One is Theresa Wren. She's very active in the Suffragette movement. I arrested her a while ago. The other's Emma Cotton. She's a new girl who only came up to London from Cornwall a few months ago. I asked them what they are doing here at this time of night.'

'Oh! And what answer did they give you?'

'They're on their way home from the Albert Hall after the big suffragette rally that's been going on there. Miss Wren said Miss Cotton is hoping to catch a glimpse of the king.'

'Do you believe her?' As he asked the question,

Inspector Tremlett was looking uneasily at the increasing number of purple, white and green-clad women in the large crowd gathered outside the palace gates.

'I'm not certain, sir,' George Fry replied cautiously. 'I can quite believe the younger girl might be eager to catch a glimpse of the king and queen. She's fairly new to the city and I don't think there's any real harm in her. I'm not so sure about Miss Wren. She's a personal friend of the Pankhursts and has been arrested many times for her activities.'

'I don't like the way things are shaping up here,' Inspector Tremlett said. 'There are far too many suffragettes in this crowd. Go across to the police box and call the station. Tell them I want every available constable sent here as quickly as they can be found. I want support from the mounted branch too. Hurry, Constable! I think we've got trouble on our hands.'

When Tessa saw George Fry hurrying towards the blue-painted police box she correctly guessed the reason for his haste. Inspector Tremlett had been in the Metropolitan Police force for many years. He was experienced in dealing with suffragettes. He must have realised that some form of demonstration was about to take place and had called for reinforcements.

She looked down the long, straight and well-lit length of the Mall despairingly. The success or failure of the demonstration she had planned now depended on who would reach the palace first. His Majesty the King or Inspector Tremlett's police reinforcements . . .

11

Well to the fore of the crowd at the palace gates, Emma was looking to where Tessa was holding a conversation with a couple of suffragettes from another area. Suddenly a surge of excitement swept through the crowd. It was as nothing compared to Emma's own feeling of sick excitement. It caused her stomach to contract painfully.

She knew even before switching her gaze to the Mall that the royal motor car had come into view.

As the black and gold gates of Buckingham Palace swung open, the crowd surged forward, those at the rear seeking a better viewpoint from which to see the royal couple enter the palace grounds in their motor car.

The royal Daimler slowed to round the white marble Queen Victoria memorial and it was just possible to glimpse King George V, seated with his queen inside the enclosed passenger compartment. The car neared

the palace gates and the king raised his hand to wave
to his cheering subjects.

At that moment, suffragettes from the Dalston Lane
office made their move. Either they ducked beneath
the extended arms of the policemen forming a barrier
between the king and the crowd or they simply darted
between them.

Running to the gate, the women blocked the path of
the royal car. Fearing a mass suicide on a scale that
would make the sacrifice of Emily Davison pale into
insignificance, the chauffeur braked hard, throwing his
royal passengers off balance.

Emma had been seconds slower going into action than
the others, but it proved to her advantage.

The constable standing in front of her ran forward to
help his colleagues in their bid to drag the suffragettes
clear of the open palace gates.

Clutching a wad of the leaflets printed at the Dalston
Lane office, Emma darted forward unhindered.

Climbing on to the running board of the royal vehicle,
she threw the leaflets inside the car.

Unfamiliar with royal vehicles, Emma had hoped
they would land in a royal lap. Unfortunately for her
plan, she discovered only at the last moment that there
was a glass partition between the royal couple and
their driver. The leaflets fell inside the driver's compartment.

However, Emma's actions had not gone unnoticed.
For the whole of her life she would carry the memory
of the expression of fury on the face of King George V
and Queen Mary's amused indignation.

A moment later she was pulled forcefully from the
car. At the same time, sufficient space had been cleared

in the gateway to allow the Daimler to enter the palace yard.

As the gates swung shut behind it, all mayhem broke loose outside as police reinforcements arrived at the run. They were accompanied by a half-dozen mounted policemen swinging long wooden batons.

Suffragettes who had hesitated to do anything that might embarrass the king and queen had no such scruples about attacking the police.

At the same time, some of the onlookers, outraged at the actions of the Dalston Lane suffragettes, joined in the escalating battle on the side of the police, and batons and fists flew freely.

Emma found herself held very tightly from behind. Whoever was holding her had one hand cupped firmly around one of her breasts. His other arm encircled her body and was squeezing her so tightly she found it difficult to breathe.

Bringing up one of her feet, she kicked back and, when she made contact, scraped her shoe down the length of his shin.

The grip on her relaxed momentarily and she broke free. Turning around, she saw she had been in the grip of the police inspector who had been talking to Police Constable George Fry.

The inspector reached forward now, grabbing her arm between shoulder and elbow in a painful hold. His grip hurt so much she instinctively struck at him with her fist, the blow catching him in the face.

Before she could repeat the blow, someone grabbed her free arm and pulled her away. Then she was pushed in the thick of the largely hostile crowd.

For the next few minutes, Emma was shoved back

and forth, alternately manhandled by policemen and many of the men in the crowd.

She fought back wildly as hands gripped, squeezed and were thrust roughly and crudely inside her clothing.

She was sobbing with anger and frustration when those about her were pushed violently aside. A hand gripped her arm and pulled her clear of her tormentors.

Her rescuer was Constable George Fry. Red-faced and hot as a result of his exertions, he said angrily, 'I can't condone what you and the other suffragettes did, but that's no excuse for liberties being taken with you.'

Still so furious she could hardly speak coherently, Emma said, 'So? Are you going to arrest them for what they were doing to me?'

'You're the one being arrested, young lady!'

The voice was that of Inspector Tremlett. When Emma turned to look at him she could see a swelling beneath his left eye, where she had struck him.

'Don't you dare complain about anything that's happened to you!' the big inspector said. 'You've brought it upon yourself – you more than most of your friends. You just come with me, you'll not do anything like this again, I promise you.'

The inspector gripped Emma by the shoulder roughly and tried to pull her towards him, but George Fry did not relinquish the hold he already had upon her.

'I'm sorry, sir, but I've just arrested her for obstruction and – causing a breach of the peace. I was about to take her to Cannon Row.'

For a few moments it seemed Inspector Tremlett

might dispute whose prisoner Emma was. Then, reluctantly relinquishing the hold he had upon her, he said, 'Is that so? Well, when you get her to Cannon Row, tell the station sergeant I'll be in later to add "assault on the police" to the charge sheet. You'll be taught a lesson you won't forget in a hurry, young lady – although "lady" is hardly the right word for a trollop like you.'

Glaring at Constable Fry, he said, 'This is the woman you told me was an inexperienced young girl up from Cornwall. I'll have something to say on your annual report about your inability to judge character.'

Gingerly touching the rapid swelling beneath his eye, he said, 'Take her off before I find something else to charge her with.'

As the inspector hurried off to the scene of yet another disturbance, George Fry said to Emma, 'You seem to have upset Inspector Tremlett. Don't take it to heart. He's furious because it's been rumoured that he's about to be promoted, but after what's happened here tonight he'll be lucky if he's not forced to resign.'

More in control of herself now, Emma asked, 'What's going to happen to me now?'

'I'll take you to Cannon Row police station and you'll be charged with your friends. If it wasn't for the fact that Inspector Tremlett is involved, I might have been able to let you slip away before we reached the station. There's no possibility of that now.'

'I don't want any favours from you – or from anyone else,' Emma retorted. Regretting her outburst almost as soon as it had occurred, she added, 'But thank you anyway.'

As they walked along together, George Fry asked, 'Is

there anyone you'd like me to contact on your behalf, to tell where you are?'

'No!'

It came out quickly. Too quickly, thought George Fry.

Emma thought so too. 'I knew what I was getting into when I became a suffragette. What I do is of no concern to anyone else.'

'Do you realise what prison is like, Emma? And that's where you'll be going, for sure.'

It was the first time he had used her first name, but she was more concerned with what he had said.

'Do you really think I'll be sent to prison? I didn't harm the king, or the queen. That was never my intention.'

'It doesn't matter what you intended doing. What you actually did was quite serious enough. That, and the assault upon Inspector Tremlett.'

Despite the seriousness of her situation, George Fry suddenly chuckled. 'He's going to have a wonderful black eye by the time he gets to court in the morning. It'll be a long time before he lives down the fact that it was given to him by a suffragette only half his size.'

'How long do you think I'll have to spend in prison?'

He shrugged. 'That's difficult to say. It depends a great deal on which magistrate is sitting on the bench. If it's your first time you might get away with a three-month sentence – but only if it's your lucky day. Otherwise you could end up with being put away for a year.'

Despite her apparent bravado, Emma was dismayed at the thought of spending a whole year in prison.

There was something else niggling away at the back of her mind. What if the court discovered she had once been arrested for assaulting a policeman in Cornwall? Would it matter that she had been found not guilty on that occasion?

'Here's one of your friends,' her captor's voice broke in upon her thoughts. 'It would appear she still feels she has a war to fight.'

Looking behind her, Emma saw one of the Dalston Lane suffragettes. Resisting fiercely, the woman was being dragged along the road between a sergeant and a constable.

'You chose an easy arrest, Constable Fry,' the sergeant said when he and his struggling prisoner drew level with the others. 'Has she been arrested for stopping the king's car too?'

'And for assaulting Inspector Tremlett,' George Fry added. He sounded almost proud of her.

'Is that so?' The sergeant gave her a look that contained an element of admiration – and possibly sympathy too. 'No doubt we'll all be regaled with a vivid description of the good inspector's suffering in the magistrates court tomorrow. You chose the wrong man to assault, young lady. A very unforgiving man is our Inspector Tremlett. All right, Constable Fry, we'll handcuff her to this one. Perhaps she'll help calm her down a bit.'

'There's no need for that,' Emma's captor protested. 'She's causing no trouble now.'

'Maybe not,' the sergeant agreed, 'but one of them's just escaped from Constable Williams. We'll take no chances – not with a woman who's to appear in court for assaulting Inspector Tremlett. Handcuff them together.'

12

There was no sleep for any of the women imprisoned in the crowded cells of Cannon Row police station that night. In all, thirty-four suffragettes had been arrested during the demonstration outside the gates of Buckingham Palace. The police station had not been designed to hold such numbers.

The women spent the night talking, singing and shouting responses to the hundred or so supporters who maintained a noisy vigil outside the police station.

Emma found herself regarded as the heroine of the palace demonstration. Many of those in the cells had witnessed her dash to the royal Daimler and seen her fling the bundle of leaflets inside the vehicle. She had been the only one to succeed in reaching the car.

Some of the women had also witnessed the blow she had delivered to the face of Inspector Tremlett. Many of the suffragettes had suffered humiliating manhandling by the senior policeman on more than one occasion, and so her actions were heartily endorsed by all of them. It was generally agreed that the inspector was personally responsible for much of the rough treatment meted out to the demonstrators that evening.

Emma had succeeded in doing what most of the women would like to have done.

When the night shift went off duty, the morning shift charge-office sergeant came to the cells to tell the women in what order they would be conveyed to the magistrates court for their cases to be heard.

When the 'briefing' came to an end, Emma's name had not been called. She said, 'What about me . . . Emma Cotton? You've forgotten to call my name.'

'I've forgotten nothing,' the sergeant said. 'You've got a solicitor representing you. He's just telephoned to say he'll most probably be entering a Not Guilty plea to the charges against you. Because of that, you've been put to the bottom of the court list. If your friends get up to their usual tricks in the courtroom, it's likely you'll still be waiting for your case to be heard when tomorrow comes.'

'What do you mean, I've got a solicitor representing me?' Emma demanded. 'Who is he? More to the point, who's appointed him on my behalf? I certainly haven't asked for anyone.'

'Don't look a gift horse in the mouth, Emma,' one of the other women said. 'You've probably got an admirer out there somewhere. Someone who saw what went on and wants to help. It occasionally happens. An onlooker did it for me once. If you've got a good solicitor representing you he might get a month or two knocked off your sentence. With the charges they're throwing at you that's not to be dismissed lightly. I wish someone had done the same on my behalf.'

* * *

After the sergeant had gone, Emma realised that Tessa's name had not been called. She had seen little of her after the trouble had begun the night before, but had assumed she had been arrested and lodged in one of the other cells.

When she mentioned it to another of the suffragettes, she was told Tessa was believed to have been hurt by a truncheon wielded by a late-arriving mounted policeman. Someone else thought she had seen her being helped away from the scene of the disturbance by a couple of other women.

Emma remained alone in the police cells until the early evening. Then eight of the arrested suffragettes were returned from the magistrates court, there being no time left for their cases to be heard that day.

Every one of the women arraigned before the stipendiary magistrate had refused to give her name and had pleaded 'Not Guilty' to the charges she faced, no matter how clear cut the evidence against her. The suffragettes had been arraigned before the court having been allocated numbers.

Few, if any, of the women expected to be acquitted. It was merely another form of protest, aimed at disrupting the functions of the court and tying up a great many policemen who were called to give evidence against them.

The women reported that the magistrate on duty had been handing out harsh sentences to the women.

One of them who had previous convictions said, 'I'm bound to get six months, at least.' Then, philosophically, she added, 'Never mind. Thanks to the Cat and Mouse

Act I'll be out again in a week or so. I'll be slimmer but just as determined.'

A court wardress who had escorted the prisoners back to the police station from the court was bringing another prisoner to the cell and heard her words.

Chuckling maliciously, she said, 'You've got a nasty surprise waiting for you in Holloway, dearie. The Home Secretary has just announced in Parliament that's he's suspending the Cat and Mouse Act for new prisoners. It seems too many of your lot have disappeared when they've been let out of prison. Forced feeding's back in again – at the discretion of the governor. Far from slimming down, you'll come out of prison as fat as a Christmas goose!'

The wardress went away chuckling, leaving the women in the cells to ponder her disturbing news.

Soon afterwards, due to the smaller number of prisoners now accommodated in the police station, the suffragettes were afforded the comparative comfort of being placed no more than two to a cell.

Emma was missing Tessa's cheerful companionship and the woman with whom she was sharing a cell did not help her mood.

Daphne Grantham was indignant about being locked up in a cell for a second night. She also complained bitterly that the Dalston Lane suffragettes had duped the others who had gathered outside the gates of Buckingham Palace. She declared that most, like herself, had sought no more than a glimpse of the reigning monarch.

In Daphne Grantham's view the demonstration had been ill conceived and poorly executed.

After listening to this complaint for the fourth or fifth

time, Emma said, 'It was never intended that anyone other than the suffragettes from the Dalston Lane office should become involved.'

'It was impossible not to become involved once the police began flailing about with their truncheons. Anyone wearing suffragette colours became an immediate target.'

'Isn't that what happens at most suffragette demonstrations?' asked Emma.

'Certainly not! At least, not in Oxfordshire. My father is a deputy lieutenant – and my husband Master of the West Oxfordshire Hunt. Our police show us some respect when we hold meetings. I can see things are very different here. I lay the blame fairly and squarely upon Sylvia Pankhurst. She should never have brought working-class women into the movement. How can you expect the police to show respect to women who swear like their menfolk, dress like slatterns and who are . . . well . . . no better than one expects such women to be?'

Emma tried not to allow the irritation she felt with this arrogant woman to show. 'Aren't the East End women fighting for the vote too?'

'Oh, I'm not saying it should not be granted to them one day, but they can't expect to be given such a privilege immediately. After all, few of the men in their part of London are entitled to the vote.'

Without waiting for a reply, Daphne Grantham continued, 'No, dear Emmeline – Sylvia's mother – is quite right to raise doubts about the course Sylvia and her followers are taking. The government will never agree to our demands if it means the election of members of parliament will be influenced by those who know nothing at all about politics.'

Still trying hard to keep her temper with this bigoted woman, Emma replied, 'Is it so much worse than having a government that is totally ignorant of the sad lives led by the majority of those it governs? With members of parliament elected only by a selected few?'

'Ah! But the selected few fully understand the problems facing the country as a whole, Emma. Indeed, the problems of the world. Just look at the wonderful Empire they have acquired for us.'

'If things are going so well, perhaps we are wrong to want to change things by fighting for votes for women,' Emma said innocently.

'Now you are being silly,' Daphne said disapprovingly. 'I am not suggesting that matters might not be improved. But I believe you have only recently joined our movement? One could not expect you to understand the complexity of the problem in such a short time.'

Seated on the hard wooden-plank bench that comprised one of the two beds in the narrow cell, Daphne sighed, 'This is terribly tiresome. I do hope my husband does something to secure my release very quickly.'

For perhaps another hour, Emma and her cell companion spoke of matters less controversial than their differing views on suffragism. Then they heard the sound of heavy footsteps in the corridor outside the cell door.

A few moments later the small inspection panel was slid to one side and a policeman peered through the aperture.

'I'm glad to see you looking so comfortable in there, ladies, but there are some gentlemen waiting upstairs to speak to one of you – and they've brought the divisional commander along with them.'

A key turned in the lock and the door swung open.

Triumphantly, Daphne said to Emma, 'I told you my husband would be here soon! He has a great many influential friends. I'm quite sure you won't find it too difficult settling down for the night, dear. I don't suppose you have known many of the luxuries of life.'

As Daphne moved towards the door, the constable blocked her path. 'I'm sorry, ma'am, I'm afraid the visitors are not here to see you. They've come to speak to Miss Cotton. Would you care to come with me, miss . . .'

13

Commander Harold Trethewey was waiting in the interview room, which was situated to one side of the charge-office. With him were Ben, Jacob and a solicitor.

Brought face to face with the two men from St Austell so unexpectedly, Emma came close to tears. Controlling the unexpected emotion with difficulty, she hugged Ben warmly. Then, more shyly, repeated the embrace with Jacob.

Still choked with emotion, she stood back and looked at them both. She suddenly felt grubby and unkempt and could not trust herself to speak.

The silence was broken by Divisional Commander Trethewey. His name had already given Emma a clue to the reason for his presence with Ben and Jacob in the Cannon Street interview room. The senior policeman was a Cornishman.

In fact, Harold Trethewey was the son of a China clay works owner. Ben had met him on a number of occasions when the policeman had spent holidays in Cornwall with his family.

'So you're the wild young Cornishwoman who gave a black eye to one of my inspectors!' The commander had difficulty keeping a smile from his face.

'After the liberties he was taking with me he's lucky I never kicked him where it would really have hurt—'

Emma's indignant reply was hurriedly brought to a halt by Horace Oliver, the solicitor. Clearing his throat noisily, he said quickly, 'For the time being, I think the less you say about what happened outside Buckingham Palace, the better it will be. We'll have a chat about it a little later, Miss Cotton.'

Although the solicitor's remarks were not directed at him, Commander Trethewey acknowledged them with a nod and said to Ben, 'I'll see you when you're ready to leave, Ben. In the meantime, as I'm here I might as well have a look around the station and frighten the life out of everyone. I wish you well in court tomorrow, Miss Cotton. I haven't checked which magistrate is on duty, but there are one or two who are more sympathetic to the suffragette cause than the magistrate who was on the bench today. I hope your case comes before one of them.'

When he had left the room, Emma spoke her first words to Ben and Jacob. 'What are you doing here? How did you know—'

'Tessa Wren telephoned to say you'd been arrested on various charges. She seemed to think the consequences were likely to be quite serious for you. I thought the best thing I could do was to arrange for a solicitor to represent you in court. Then I decided to come here myself and I brought Jacob along with me.'

'Why did Tessa telephone you? I've never suggested that you were responsible for me.'

'Her motives don't matter – anyway, I'm glad she did. I would have been very upset had I not learned about your trouble until I read of it in a newspaper.'

'There was no need for you to know anything about it at any time.'

'I think you should be grateful to Tessa, Emma,' Jacob said. 'She seems to have your welfare at heart – even though you'd never have been in this mess in the first place if it hadn't been for her.'

'I believe she was heavily involved in the disturbance outside the palace too,' Ben said. 'She said she'd been hurt by a policeman's truncheon, although I don't know any of the details.'

'Well there was no need to let you know – and I don't need anyone to defend me in court.'

'I think you should consider the possible consequences of the trouble you are in right now, Miss Cotton,' the solicitor said firmly. 'From the enquiries I have made, the charges you are facing are rather more serious than those of your companions. You could be sent to prison for quite a long time. I might add that legal representation has been welcomed on many occasions by your fellow suffragettes. Languishing in prison for longer than is absolutely necessary does nothing to help the cause you support, I can assure you.'

Aware of Emma's uncertainty, Ben said, 'Mr Oliver and I will leave you for a few minutes, Emma. You can discuss things with Jacob – but you won't have very long. Commander Trethewey is doing me a favour but we mustn't abuse his goodwill. I'll come back for

Jacob soon and see if you would like to talk to Mr Oliver then.'

Ben and the solicitor stood up from the table around which they were all seated and left the room.

When they had gone, there was silence in the interview room for a few, long moments. Then Emma said, 'Why didn't you reply to any of my letters, Jacob?'

'I'm sorry.' Looking across the table at her, Jacob felt pity for her well up inside him. Wearing a crumpled dress and with her hair more untidy than he had ever seen it before, she looked frighteningly vulnerable.

He also felt uncomfortably guilty about what had happened between Cissy and him. 'I meant to write, but . . .' He shrugged apologetically.

'Well, after I left Cornwall in such a hurry, I can't really blame you for not replying, but there just wasn't time to explain my reasons properly to you. I realised how much it would hurt you, but if I hadn't gone so quickly, Ben would have sent for my ma. She'd have tried to stop me coming to London, I know she would.'

'She'd have been right to, wouldn't she? If you'd stayed in Cornwall you wouldn't be facing the prospect of going to prison.'

'I wouldn't be faced with the prospect of anything,' Emma declared fiercely. 'I'd have spent the rest of my life regretting the things I'd never done and never would do. Wondering what I might have done had I come here with Tessa. You may not agree with what I'm doing, Jacob, but I'm doing something I want to do. Something worthwhile. I can't say I'm looking forward to going to prison. I'm not. But it's for a cause I really believe in. I believe in it more than anything else I've ever done.'

'Then you must accept the help of the solicitor if you

want to be out there working for them. You can't do much to help when you're in prison.'

Summoning up his courage, Jacob said, 'If you'd stayed in Cornwall I was going to ask you to marry me, Emma. I still want you to.'

Emma sat looking down at the stained table top in front of her for a long time. Just as Jacob thought it was going to be up to him to break the lengthening silence, she replied to his heartfelt admission.

'I realised that was the way things were going, Jacob. If you'd asked me before I came away I'd have said "Yes". Then we'd both have ended up regretting it. I'm not ready to settle down just yet.'

'I'll wait for you if you'll come back to Cornwall when all this is over and done with,' Jacob pleaded with her.

'"All this", as you call it won't be over and done with until we've got what we're fighting for, Jacob. Until women are given the vote and treated the way we should be.'

There was another uncomfortable silence, broken this time by Jacob.

'Is there anyone else in your life, Emma?'

'No, of course not!' The question took her by surprise.

'No one you've met since you came to London?'

'I think the only man I've spoken to is the policeman who arrested Tessa on the first night I was in London. He loaned me some money to get home that night. When I paid the money back I left it in an envelope here in the police station. I never saw him again until I was arrested myself last night – oh yes, and there's Manny.'

Despite her predicament, she forced a smile. 'Manny's a bald-headed wrestler who likes to feel he's the protector of all the East London suffragettes.'

Looking across the table at Jacob, Emma suddenly felt deeply sorry for him. He had wanted to marry her and she had left him, and Cornwall, without a word of explanation. She realised she had hurt him very much.

Reaching out, she took his hand in hers. 'I think more of you than of anyone else I know, Jacob. Probably more than anyone I'll ever know. I think of you often. Of you and me together. Many times I've wished I was more like the other girls around St Austell. Girls who'd be happy to find a man like you to settle down and raise a family with. It's something I want to happen to me too – one day. But not just yet. I need to feel I've done something with my life first.'

With an effort, Jacob managed a sad smile. 'I suppose if you were the same as everyone else I wouldn't have fallen in love with you in the first place.'

'That's the first time you've ever said you loved me, Jacob.' There were tears in Emma's eyes now as she stood up to lean across the table and kiss him. Trying to make light of the moment, she added, 'There can't be many girls who've had their man tell them for the first time he loves them when they're under arrest in a police station.'

'Probably not, but the important thing now is to see if we can do something about getting you free. Will you let the solicitor defend you?'

Emma sat down again. 'I don't think there's anything that you or anyone else can do to help me now, Jacob. Our demonstration was aimed at the king. Even some of the other suffragettes have found it hard to forgive that. All right. I'll let the solicitor defend me. But I don't think there's any doubt that I'll go to prison. The only question is – for how long?'

14

Emma was committed to prison for one month. Fortunately, the magistrate who sentenced her was sympathetic to the suffragette movement, but, as Emma had predicted, the fact that His Majesty the King had been involved could not be overlooked.

The sentence would have been longer had her solicitor not managed to convince the magistrate that she was not guilty of intentionally injuring Inspector Tremlett.

Pointing to Tremlett as he stood in the witness box after giving his evidence against Emma, Mr Oliver ridiculed the fact that a young woman had been brought to court charged with assaulting a policeman the size of Inspector Tremlett.

He asked the magistrate if anyone could seriously believe she was capable of walking up to an experienced policeman who stood head and shoulders taller than herself and delivering a blow of sufficient violence to black his eye?

The charge, he insisted, was preposterous! It should never have been brought to court.

The solicitor suggested that in the heat of the moment and in the poor light, Inspector Tremlett had only thought the blow had been delivered by his client.

Fortunately for Emma, the magistrate chose to accept her solicitor's version of events.

Jacob and Ben were in court throughout the hearing. They were both satisfied that the solicitor had done his best on Emma's behalf. Nevertheless, Jacob winced when the magistrate announced that she would go to prison for one month.

After the hearing was over they sought permission to speak to Emma in the court cells before she was conveyed to Holloway Prison. However, without the presence of the helpful divisional police commander to back up their request, permission was refused.

They had to be content with the defiant wave a pale-faced Emma gave to them as she was hustled from the dock and back down the stairs to the cells.

'I suppose there's nothing else we can do now but go back home to Cornwall without Emma,' a thoroughly despondent Jacob said.

'We'll go back in due course,' Ben said. 'Before we do I intend having a few words with a certain Tessa Wren. You go on back to the hotel. We'll need to remain there for another night. I'll see you back there later.'

Ben travelled in a motor taxi-cab from the magistrates court to the Dalston Lane office of the East London Federation of Suffragettes, the address Emma had used on the letters she had written to her family.

This was a London Ben had not seen before. He was

taken aback by the number of people thronging the busy East End market on both sides of the road.

There was a remarkable variety of items displayed for sale on the various stalls he passed on his way from the taxi-cab to the office.

One displayed a wider variety of fish than he had ever seen in Cornwall. On the same stall, shiny, live eels writhed, snake-like, in a flat, wooden-sided tray containing others entwined together in a knot that would have stretched the imagination of the most experienced seaman.

Another stall offered cheap crockery at bargain prices. The costermonger owner declaring loudly and persuasively that he would bankrupt himself were he to offer them for sale at such prices on a regular basis.

There were clothes, new and second-hand. Nearby, a cobbler hammered leather soles on a pair of old boots, using a multi-footed iron last. While he worked, the owner of the footwear sat barefooted on a low stool, waiting for the repair to be completed.

Farther along the road, men and women eating whelks and winkles from tiny shallow dishes stood chatting around a stall. On the same stall, among the heaped molluscs, a dismembered pig's head stared out across a pile of bony boiled 'trotters' which were offered for sale at a halfpenny each.

There was much to be seen, but for Ben, the memory he would always carry with him of Dalston Lane was one of noise. The hubbub of the crowds, overlaid with the spiel of the costermongers as they vied with each other for the few pence that was all most of the market-goers had to spend.

The suffragette office too was filled with chatter. The sound faltered and died away as Ben entered.

'Can I help you?' One of the women confronted Ben as he looked around him.

'I'm looking for Tessa Wren.'

A quick glance had been sufficient to discover she was not present.

'Why do you want her? Are you police?'

Ben could sense the hostility of every woman in the room behind the question.

'No. I'm Ben Retallick, a relative of Emma Cotton. I've just come from the magistrates court.'

The sudden easing of tension was almost a physical phenomenon. Sound erupted once more and the woman who had been the first to speak to him asked eagerly, 'What happened to her? Was she found Guilty? How long did she get?'

'She was acquitted on the charge of assaulting the police inspector . . .'

Ben was forced to cease speaking until the cheering died away, '. . . but she was found guilty on the other charges. She's been sentenced to a month in prison.'

The glances exchanged by the other women expressed genuine sympathy. Every one of them had suffered the rigours of life inside His Majesty's prison at Holloway.

'Now, can you tell me where I might find Tessa?'

Ben's request was again met with a distinctly guarded response.

'She's not well enough to see anyone, at the moment . . .'

'Oh yes she is!'

Tessa had come down the stairs from the flat, unnoticed. She stood in the doorway now, looking pale, an expression of pain on her face. Her left arm was strapped firmly across her chest.

'You shouldn't be up and about,' the woman who had declared she was unavailable chided. 'The doctor said you were to rest.'

Turning to Ben, the woman explained, 'Her collarbone was broken by a police truncheon.'

'I was resting, until you all gave such a cheer I almost fell off the couch. I thought the government must have announced we had been given the vote, at the very least.'

Giving Ben a wan smile, she said, 'Hello, Mr Retallick. Have you managed to see Emma?'

'Yes, I and Jacob. Her solicitor succeeded in having the assault charge thrown out but, thanks to your influence, she's got a month in prison to look forward to.'

Tessa winced, but Ben was not certain whether it was due to the pain of her injury or a reaction to news of Emma's sentence.

'She'll not be alone in Holloway. Most of the suffragettes convicted yesterday received sentences of six months. They'll be joining more than sixty others who are already in there. But you'd better come upstairs. We'll have a talk about things there.'

'There's nothing to talk about. When Emma is released from prison I intend to arrange for her to return home to Cornwall. It's where she belongs.'

'Emma might have something to say about your plans for her,' Tessa said softly, 'so I think you'd better come upstairs and have a chat about it.'

Turning, she made her way up the steep stairway to the small flat. After a moment's hesitation, Ben followed her.

In the tiny living room, she motioned Ben to a

wooden-armed chair. She perched herself on the edge
of the settee.

Ben was the first to speak. 'I hope that after a month
in prison Emma will have come to her senses and want
to return home.' Finding Tessa's quiet self-assurance
disconcerting, he spoke more belligerently than he had
intended.

'After a month in Holloway she'll almost certainly have
a different outlook on a great many things. Whether it
will make her change her mind about our campaign
is another matter. I fear women view suffragism rather
more seriously than do most men.'

Ben made no reply. He was trying very hard not to
enter into an acrimonious argument with her.

Still speaking deceptively quietly, Tessa said, 'I didn't
kidnap Emma and bring her to London, Mr Retallick.
Indeed, she had many reasons to remain in Cornwall.'

Easing her injured arm to a more comfortable position, she continued, 'Jacob was the strongest reason of
all. Emma is very fond of him. She found leaving him
behind very difficult. It was a sacrifice she made because
she believes in women's suffrage. It's a belief she held
long before she and I met at your home. Like many of
the women you have just met in the office downstairs,
she regards it as a cause worth fighting for. We have
all made sacrifices, Mr Retallick. Many far greater than
those of I – or Emma. Despite this, I doubt if you would
find one woman who would not be prepared to make
the same sacrifices again, and again, and again. Treating
women as a sub-species is an injustice. It's a wrong that
must be righted.'

'I've never doubted the justice of your cause, Miss
Wren, but I do question the methods you are employing

to achieve what you want. I would rather Emma wasn't mixed up in an organisation that actively encourages law-breaking.'

'Are you quite certain it's only Emma you are thinking of, Mr Retallick? Or does her involvement with the Suffragette movement embarrass you?'

Tessa's gentle questioning would not have been out of place had she been inviting him to choose between two varieties of sandwich.

'My sole concern is for Emma,' Ben retorted. 'She's family, and I'm extremely fond of her.'

'I'm fond of her too,' Tessa said, 'so I'm pleased we can agree on something.'

When Ben looked sceptical, Tessa added, 'Believe me, Mr Retallick, if I thought Emma really wanted to return to Cornwall, marry Jacob and settle down happily, I would do my damnedest to persuade her to do just that.'

Catching the fleeting expression of disbelief that passed across Ben's face, she said, 'I'm not opposed to marriage, Mr Retallick. One day I hope I too might marry, but it will need to be a true partnership – and that's what Emma is seeking too. We have spoken of it often. I think she might achieve what she wants with Jacob – but not yet.'

Adjusting the position of her injured arm once more, she said, 'I certainly don't dislike men, Mr Retallick. But I am utterly opposed to those who look upon women as mere chattels, affording us a status something akin to that of the family dog.'

A fleeting smile crossed Ben's face. 'I can't imagine anyone daring to suggest you belong in a kennel, Miss Wren.'

'Should I be pleased to know that?' Realising she had taken him too seriously, Tessa grimaced. 'Unfortunately, there are very many men who would disagree with you – including the majority of those in government.'

'I can do little to change that,' Ben said, 'but I'm glad we've had our talk today. I still can't agree with all your organisation is doing, but I'm a little easier in my mind about Emma – but only a little. Will you let me know when she's released from prison? Perhaps she might feel differently about returning to Cornwall then. In the meantime, if you think of anything I might be able to do for her, please call me on the telephone.'

'Of course. I'll let you know any news I receive about her. No doubt some of the suffragettes released in the next few weeks will have met her inside Holloway.'

'I'd be grateful for any news. If she really doesn't want to return to Cornwall it's probable that I, or Jacob, will come to London to see her.'

'You'd be very welcome to stay here in the flat if you do – but only if you stop calling me Miss Wren. My name is Tessa.'

'Thank you.' Ben was fully aware that the discussion between them had gone very much her way. 'Since we're being terribly civilised, perhaps you should call me Ben.'

'I will and I look forward to our next meeting . . . Ben.'

When he had left the suffragette office and Tessa had returned to the flat she sat down and found herself thinking of Ben Retallick in a way she had not thought of any man for a very long time . . .

15

✦

There were no windows in the black Maria taking
Emma to prison from the magistrates court, and no
other prisoners. The vehicle was uncomfortable and
Emma seemed to be travelling for a long time. Then
after a brief stop, it began to move forward once more,
this time very slowly.

From the sounds outside the enclosed prison van,
she guessed she was being driven through the gates
of Holloway Prison.

When the door at the rear of the vehicle was opened,
Emma saw her assumption had been correct. The police
vehicle was in a small yard enclosed by walls so high she
could not see the top of them from her seat in the van.

A heavily built woman had opened the door. She
wore a blue uniform with a wide leather belt, to which
was attached a large, steel ring on which jangled a
number of heavy keys.

'Come on you, out you get. The maid's waiting to

run you a nice hot bath and lay out your new outfit for you.'

Behind her another uniformed woman of identical build and wearing a similar uniform sniggered.

'The only problem is that the water's cold and the outfit's all one size and decorated with arrows.'

'Well, there's no one who matters who's likely to see what she's wearing, is there?' the second wardress said, equally cheerfully. 'I mean, she won't be hobnobbing with the king again in a hurry, will she?'

The tone of her voice suddenly underwent a change, and she barked at Emma, 'Come on, move yourself! Get out of there before I come in and drag you out.'

Emma was certain the woman would not hesitate to carry out her threat, and she wasted no time in vacating the prison van. But when she held out her wrists in the hope of having her handcuffs removed, the wardresses ignored her.

The handcuffs were not taken off Emma's wrists until she and the two wardresses entered the main prison building and a number of iron grille doors had been locked behind them.

Now, for almost an hour, Emma was subjected to a degrading prison admittance routine, which, she realised, was deliberately calculated to break her spirit. After she had answered detailed questions about her personal life, her head was examined for lice, and she was made to undress and forced beneath a cold shower. This done, she was given a medical examination that involved a crude search of the orifices of her body.

Finally, Emma was issued with an ill-fitting prison dress and led away to a cell. This would be her 'home' for a month. It contained a wooden bed screwed to the wall and a slop bucket. There was also a shelf screwed to the tiled wall, on which were soap and a towel, but the cell contained no mirror.

'Here you are, dearie,' the escorting wardress said, maliciously. 'This is home sweet home. I hope you enjoy your own company, because it's all you're going to get. The governor's orders are that you're to be kept in "solitary" while you're here.'

Left alone in the tiny cell, Emma felt a moment of panic. How could she possibly endure such a claustrophobic existence for four weeks?

Then her determination returned. Many others, Tessa among them, had endured far more than this in the cause of suffragism. Nothing she had been told could have prepared her for the realities with which she was now faced, but she had always known the path she had chosen to take would one day lead her to a prison cell.

Emma had no intention of languishing here until her release. She had long ago decided upon the course of action she would take when committed to prison. Now was the time to put it into practice . . .

It was not difficult to refuse the first meal brought to her cell. It was an evil-smelling mess of virtually unidentifiable vegetables, submerged beneath a sludge-like gravy containing barely edible lumps of gristly meat.

The wardress who collected her untouched plate seemed unperturbed by Emma's lack of appetite. 'You may turn your nose up at prison food now, dearie, but after a couple of days you'll look upon meal times as the highlight of your day. Taste like caviar, this will – and I'll be the best friend you've ever had, just for bringing it to you each day.'

Not until Emma had refused meals for three days was there the faintest hint of concern. She was visited by a senior wardress who arrived flanked by two junior members of her staff. One was the wardress who had so inaccurately predicted that Emma would soon lose her aversion to prison food.

The senior wardress spoke to Emma as though she were a naughty child who had refused to eat her greens. She demanded to know 'the meaning of all this nonsense'.

Not allowing herself to be intimidated by the manner of the older woman, Emma said firmly that she was not indulging in 'nonsense', but she had no intention of taking any food until she was released from prison.

'That game has been tried too often, young lady,' the senior wardress declared. 'You'll not gain your release that way. You'll be force fed with all that entails and still have to serve out your full sentence. I suggest that when we've gone, you think about it very carefully. Very carefully indeed.'

After a further day of fasting, the senior wardress visited Emma's cell again, this time accompanied by the Holloway prison governor.

A surprisingly mild-mannered ex-naval man, the governor seemed more hurt than angry that Emma would wish to cause he and his staff inconvenience by refusing to eat the food prepared by her fellow inmates.

When Emma repeated what she had already told the senior wardress, he sounded even more regretful.

'I'm afraid that if you persist in such foolish behaviour I will have no option but to order that you be force fed,

Miss Cotton. I do hope it will not come to that, it is a most unpleasant and distressing experience for everyone involved. I urge you to reconsider your misguided decision.'

'I'm taking no food until I am released from prison,' Emma declared doggedly.

When the governor and wardresses had gone, Emma lay down on her bunk. Being forced to stand during the visit of the governor, together with all the talking that had gone on, had left her feeling light-headed.

She hoped she would be able to maintain her resolve. Actually, it was not too difficult now. Her earlier longing for food had disappeared. Nevertheless, she felt increasingly weak and was having difficulty in marshalling her thoughts.

Suddenly, she had an overpowering longing to be with Jacob. She wondered what he was doing at this moment.

Just thinking about him caused tears to spring to her eyes. She brushed them away angrily. The lack of food must be weakening her. She had never felt like this before.

16

Emma was given one further day to reconsider her decision to refuse to eat, but she was determined not to change her mind.

Early the following morning she was lying on her bed in a semi-comatose state when she thought she heard voices in the corridor outside her cell. At first she thought it must be more of the hallucinations she had been having intermittently over the previous twenty-four hours. At one time during the night, she had thought Jacob was in the cell with her. She had even reached out to touch him.

Another time, she was convinced she could hear the voice of Great Aunt Miriam offering her words of encouragement.

But Emma was not hallucinating this morning. A key grated in the steel lock, the door was thrown open and suddenly the cell was filled with people.

She counted three . . . no, four wardresses. There

were also two men and one of them began speaking to her.

'We are doctors . . .'

Emma struggled to sit up. The movement set her head swimming. Before she could recover she was seized by the wardresses.

Despite her frantic struggles they held her arms and legs in a firm grip. Then one of the men took hold of her head, at the same time explaining, 'As you have refused to eat, the governor has ordered that you be force fed. I suggest you don't struggle. If you do you will only make things much worse for yourself.'

While the first doctor maintained a painful grip on Emma's head, his colleague began to feed a rubber tube coated with Vaseline up one of her nostrils and into her throat. It was extremely painful but Emma was given no respite. As the tube was forced farther down her throat she choked and gagged, but her resistance was futile against those who restrained her.

The days of fasting had taken their toll on her strength and eventually she could fight no longer. When the doctor considered the tube was far enough into her stomach, he attached a funnel to the end of it.

This done, he began pouring liquid down the tube from an enamel jug.

Emma gagged and choked on the mixture. It tasted like a vile combination of meat soup and lime cordial. She was in actual physical pain and having considerable difficulty in breathing. Just when she felt she could take no more and was trying unsuccessfully to scream, the doctor ceased pouring from the jug.

'That should do.' Lowering the jug to the floor, the

doctor removed the tube, using no more finesse than he had shown in inserting it.

'We'll be seeing you later today, and again tomorrow, young lady,' he said, at the same time nodding his head to his helpers.

Emma was released and her six torturers filed from the cell.

They had hardly closed the door before Emma turned on her side and was violently sick. Her stomach hurt, so too did her nose and throat. She retched painfully until she was convinced she had brought up everything that had been poured inside her stomach.

Sinking back on the hard wooden bed she fought for breath. She felt as though her whole being had been violated. Then, exhausted, she gave way to tears until she slipped away into a sleep that was close to unconsciousness.

She was woken roughly by a wardress. In her hand the woman held a mop. A bucket, half filled with water, was on the floor at her feet.

'Here! Clean up your mess. No one else is going to do it – and be quick about it.'

Somehow, Emma succeeded in doing as she was told. When the task was completed and the wardress gone, she sank back on the bed.

For each of the following three days the primitive, twice daily, force-feeding ritual was repeated, but by now time no longer meant anything to Emma.

Then, one morning she was woken and saw two wardresses and one of the prison doctors standing by her narrow wooden bed.

'Come on, stir yourself,' one of the wardresses said. 'You're being moved to the prison hospital.'

Emma sat upright, but when she tried to stand her legs were too weak and rubbery to support her.

'Don't exaggerate your weakness. It will get you nowhere. Nobody's going to carry you.'

Despite the callous statement, one of the wardresses had to support her on the way to the prison hospital.

For four more days Emma was force fed. On each occasion she reacted in the same way as she had on the first.

By now, she was too weak to put up more than a token resistance against the prison officials, no matter what they did to her.

Then she received an unexpected visit from an anxious prison governor. He was accompanied by one of the doctors who had been force feeding her since her refusal to eat.

'Miss Cotton, the doctor tells me you are being a very silly girl and are still refusing to eat. Do you realise you are probably doing permanent damage to your body by acting in such an irresponsible way?'

When she did not reply, he said, 'Your friends and relatives are very concerned about you. I have had a number of telephone calls from Cornwall and only this morning I received another from a police commander here in London. I wish I could have told them all was well with you.'

'So what did you tell them? That four of your sadistic wardresses hold me down twice a day while he . . .' Weakly she indicated the doctor. '. . . and the other one force a hosepipe up my nose and down my throat?'

Anger and the effort of talking left her breathless, but she had lost none of her defiance. 'The next time they telephone you can tell them something else. I'm not only refusing to eat. From today I'm not drinking, either.'

'That would be even more foolish, Miss Cotton,' the doctor said. 'Take that course and you will do very serious harm to yourself.'

'What do you care?' Emma retorted, trying to ignore the exhaustion that was rapidly overtaking anger. 'Don't try to pretend you care what happens to me. No one who treats another human being the way you have treated me can possibly give a damn about anyone.'

In spite of her resolve, tears sprang to Emma's eyes and this seemed to genuinely upset the prison governor. Resting a hand somewhat self-consciously on her head, he spoke almost apologetically. 'You are behaving extremely unreasonably, Miss Cotton, but no one wishes to see you cause unnecessary harm to yourself. We'll leave you for now. When we've gone, think of what has been said to you – and of the friends who are so concerned about your health. Give up this stupidity.'

'Do you think women should be given the vote?' Emma asked unexpectedly.

Taken aback, the governor said, 'My views on the matter are irrelevant. However, harming yourself in this manner serves no purpose whatsoever.'

Trying desperately hard to control her ragged breathing, Emma said, 'I don't think Emily Davison would have agreed with you. Her death brought our cause to the attention of the nation.'

'She was a very stupid and misguided woman who lost your cause a great deal of public sympathy by her action.'

A feeling of desperate tiredness had returned to

Emma. Nevertheless, mustering as much spirit as she could, she said, 'Emily Davison had a first-class honours degree from Oxford. She was hardly a stupid woman. She believed such a sacrifice was necessary. So do I.'

Choosing not to follow the path of such a discussion, the governor said, 'I suggest you put such thoughts out of your head and consider what I said to you earlier, Miss Cotton.'

With this, he walked from the ward, followed by the others.

Outside the door of the prison hospital, he spoke to the doctor. 'She is a very stubborn girl! Just how serious is her condition, doctor?'

The doctor shook his head in concern. 'If she continues to refuse food and carries out her threat to stop taking water, her condition will deteriorate rapidly. I consider her life will be seriously at risk within forty-eight hours.'

'Very well. Force feed her again in the morning. If she doesn't keep it down I'll order her release in the evening. The last thing the Home Secretary wants is to have one of these women die in custody.'

17

Jacob arrived at the Dalston Lane office during the early evening of the second day after Emma's release from prison.

Tessa, her arm no longer in a sling, was standing beside one of the desks. She had been discussing an article for the suffragette newspaper with one of the editorial staff. She seemed surprised, yet genuinely pleased to see him.

Hurrying across the office, she gripped his arm affectionately with her free hand.

'Jacob, what a delightful surprise! Emma is going to be so pleased to have you here. You're just the tonic she needs right now.' Releasing his arm, she said, 'You do know she's very ill? I telephoned to Ben . . .'

Jacob nodded, hiding his surprise at her use of Ben Retallick's first name. 'He told me. He'd have come himself but his wife is very ill too. He suggested I should come right away and he paid my fare. Not that he needed to, I'd have come anyway.'

'I don't doubt it.' She paused. 'Before we go upstairs I must warn you that she's not looking her best. Expect to be shocked by her appearance. She's lost a lot of weight and is still very weak. But she's better than she was when they released her from prison. With you here she'll improve faster than ever, I've no doubt. How long can you stay?'

'As long as I need to.'

'As long as you need to for what, Jacob? To persuade her to return to Cornwall with you?'

'It's what I'd like her to do. Mr Retallick would too, I know.'

'Why? Because you believe she'll marry you and settle down to raise a family?'

'Is there anything so very wrong in that?'

'Nothing at all – if that is what she wants.' Tessa looked at Jacob sympathetically. 'But in spite of all she's been through these last couple of weeks I don't think our Emma is ready for marriage just yet. One day she will be and I have no doubt it's you she'll choose, but it won't be for a while, Jacob. She's angry with the way she's been treated in prison. Very angry. She's not prepared to give up the fight and allow the powers that be think they've beaten her. But what am I doing keeping you down here. We'll have plenty of time to talk about all sorts of things. For now she'll be very happy to have you here. I know she will.'

Tessa led the way into one of the two small bedrooms where Emma was lying in a narrow bed, looking out at the small patch of dull grey sky visible above the roof of the house backing on to the office premises.

She turned her head wearily, but when she saw Jacob her eyes opened wide in an expression of delight. It would have satisfied even the most despondent suitor.

'Jacob! Why didn't you tell me you were coming? I look awful!'

Suddenly she held out her arms to him. When he went to her she hugged him – then suddenly burst into tears.

'It's all right, Emma. It's all right. Don't cry.' Embarrassed, he turned to see how Tessa was reacting to Emma's tears, but she had quietly left the bedroom.

'I'm sorry, Jacob, it's just . . . Oh, I'm so damned weak I can't control my emotions and . . . and you don't know how much I've been longing to have you with me.'

She pulled him to her once more and he felt sobs racking her whole body.

It was some time before she regained her composure. Longer still before she released her hold on him.

Trying hard to regain control of her voice, she said, 'I . . . I'm all right now. But what are you doing here? How did you know I was out of prison? How is everyone? Ben? Lily? Great Aunt Miriam?'

'Which question would you like me to answer first?' Jacob sat on the edge of the bed and smiled down at her. He was delighted with the welcome she had given to him. He had been half afraid she would not want to see him. But he was alarmed at her gaunt and weak appearance. She looked even worse than Lily Retallick.

'Tessa phoned Ben Retallick. He came to see her after you'd been sentenced and she promised to let him know when you were released. He said I could take time off work to come here to be with you if I was needed.'

'I'd love to have been a fly on the wall to listen to the conversation between them when he was here.'

'It was quite civilised, I believe, although they agreed to differ on a great many subjects. He said Tessa was as genuinely concerned for you as we were.'

'Tessa's been marvellous since I was released.' Emma reached out and took his hand. 'I'm glad I was able to speak to you before I went to prison. Knowing someone cared what was happening to me was very important when I was in Holloway.'

'Was it very bad?'

After a moment, Emma nodded. 'But I don't want to talk about it now. How is everyone in Cornwall?'

Understanding her wish to change the subject, Jacob said, 'Ben Retallick is fine, and old Mrs Retallick is likely to go on for another hundred years. My ma is as busy as ever, but we're both worried about Pa. He's never really recovered from what happened to him during the strike. He gets so down sometimes it brings Ma close to tears.'

'You haven't mentioned Lily,' Emma said shrewdly. 'How is she?'

Jacob shrugged uncomfortably. He had not wanted to mention Lily right away. Emma had enough problems of her own, but he had never been very good at evading the truth. 'She's not very well. That's really why Ben Retallick didn't come to London with me. The doctors say she has a serious lung problem.'

'That's awful! Poor Lily. Her brother died of lung disease when he was quite young, did you know? Poor Ben too – but perhaps the doctors will be able to do something for her.'

'When I left they were talking of taking her to

Switzerland. There are supposed to be some very good clinics there.'

'Ben will spare no money if there's the faintest chance of finding a cure. I hope he'll succeed. Lily is a wonderful person . . .' Jacob thought she was about to become emotional again as she added, 'I miss her too.'

'Then why don't you come back to Cornwall and stay at Tregarrick until you're better and it's decided what's going to happen to her?'

Jacob spoke eagerly, but when Emma's lips tightened into a thin line, he added hurriedly, 'I'm talking of when you're feeling a bit better, of course. You couldn't possibly travel right away.'

'Is this why you've come to London, Jacob? Because Ben's told you to try to persuade me to return with you to Cornwall.'

'I've come here because I was told you were ill – and so you are. I want to be near you.'

She squeezed his hand apologetically. 'I'm sorry. That was unfair of me.'

Jacob shook his head. 'No it wasn't. If I thought I could persuade you to come back to Cornwall I'd use every argument I could muster to get you there.'

'Do I really mean that much to you, Jacob?'

'Yes.'

Jacob shrugged. 'I only wish I'd realised it before you left.'

An unwanted memory of Cissy crept into his thoughts and he added, vehemently, 'If I had, a whole lot of things would have been different and you and I would probably be planning our wedding now.'

'Yes, I'm sure we would.' She squeezed his hand painfully tightly. 'We'd have been happy together too, but for the rest of my days I'd have been wondering what I might have done with my life. What I'm doing now is important to me, Jacob. Very important. One day we're going to achieve everything we're fighting for right now. I know we are. When we do, I'll be happy to settle down – and I don't think I'll ever find anyone I want to be with as much as I want to be with you.'

When he made no immediate reply, she released his hand. 'Of course, I can't expect you to wait for me forever. If you ever find someone else . . .'

'I won't,' he said fiercely. 'You're not the easiest woman to understand, Emma Cotton, but I don't want to try to understand anyone else.'

When Tessa peered into the room a few minutes later, she tiptoed away again, very quickly.

Returning to the office, she wondered whether the Federation had just lost one of its most promising new members.

18

Before coming to London, Jacob had given little real thought to the length of time he might need to stay in the capital. Once he realised it was likely to be longer than either he or Ben had anticipated, he felt he ought to speak to his employer. Using the suffragette office telephone, he called Ben.

When Jacob had given Ben the details of Emma's condition, Ben told him to remain in London for as long as he felt his presence was beneficial to Emma's recovery. He also urged Jacob to work hard on persuading her to return to Cornwall.

When Jacob asked after Lily, Ben said a place had been found for her in a Swiss clinic. She would be going as soon as travel arrangements could be made. Certainly within the next few weeks.

As an afterthought, Ben suggested that Jacob ask Emma if she would accompany Lily to Switzerland and remain with her for a while. It would serve a double purpose. Taking Emma away from London and providing company for Lily when Ben needed to return to England.

As he spoke, Ben's enthusiasm for the idea grew and he transmitted some of his excitement to Jacob.

When he came off the telephone, Jacob put the idea to Emma. Initially, she did not share his enthusiasm for the idea. She had no intention of leaving London and the work she was doing here.

Tessa was in the flat while they were talking about Ben's suggestion. She chose the opportunity to drop her own bombshell into the conversation.

'Actually, if you were to go to Switzerland with Lily, it would suit me very well, Emma.'

Smiling at Emma's surprise, she explained, 'I've actually been wondering how to tell you. Sylvia Pankhurst intends travelling to Paris to meet with her sister Christabel, to discuss the split that has developed between Sylvia and the rest of the Pankhurst family. As you know, the police are seeking to arrest Sylvia again. She's got to keep out of their way, and has asked me to go to Paris with her and help her to evade arrest. Once there, I'd like to stay on for a while.'

'When do you think you might be going?'

'Until today there was no firm date, but Sylvia telephoned me only half an hour ago. She suggests we leave tomorrow.'

Emma gasped. 'So soon! How long do you think you'll be away?'

'I don't know. Now the two sisters have agreed to part company there will be a great many things to be discussed. I'll keep in touch with you by telephone. If I haven't returned by the time you go to Switzerland with Lily, I'll meet the train as you pass through Paris. Actually, you'll no doubt need to change trains and spend the night there. I could arrange a hotel for Mr and Mrs Retallick. I would like to do that for them.'

Emma was thoughtful for a while, then she said, 'Do you really think I should go to Switzerland with Lily?'

'Of course! There are few activities planned for the next month or two. Things should have sorted themselves out by then. You can come back here and help us plan our midsummer campaign!'

Looking at Jacob, Emma said, 'No doubt you agree with Tessa?'

'Only if I can't persuade you to return to Cornwall with me.'

'We've already had that discussion, Jacob. The answer is – you can't.'

She hesitated for only a few minutes more. 'All right, tell Ben I'll go to Switzerland with Lily. When I'm a little stronger I'll telephone him and talk about the arrangements we'll need to make.'

Sylvia Pankhurst came to Dalston Lane the following morning to collect her travelling companion for the journey to Paris.

Dressed in black, with a widow's veil to hide her face, the famous suffragette caused great excitement in the office. It seemed everyone had something they wished to say to her.

There was wholehearted and unanimous support for Sylvia's leadership of the East London Federation. Her followers would back her in the policy dispute with the much larger Women's Social and Political Union, controlled by her mother and sister.

Shortly before her departure, Sylvia Pankhurst climbed the stairs to the small flat to wish Emma well in her fight to regain health. She personally presented Emma with the much-coveted Holloway Badge, in recognition of Emma's recent ordeal in the notorious women's prison.

The suffragette leader was herself still looking pale and frail as a result of her latest sojourn inside Holloway. However, she assured Emma the weakness and debility she was experiencing would soon pass and she would regain full fitness again.

Eyeing Jacob, she added, 'I've no doubt your return to health will be hastened by having this young man dance attendance upon you.'

Extending a hand to Jacob, she said, 'Tessa has told me a great deal about you, and of your continuing support for Emma. It's always a pleasure to meet with an enlightened young man. Unfortunately, there are still far too few of you.'

Returning her attention to Emma, she said, 'Tessa also tells me you will be going to Switzerland for a while with a sick relative. I hope she makes a full recovery. I recently received an invitation to visit the headquarters of a suffragette movement in Geneva. I have every intention of accepting the invitation sometime this summer. Make certain you remain in touch with Tessa. I will get your address from her and come and see you while I am there.'

With this promise she returned downstairs. After a warm, but hurried farewell to Emma, Tessa went too.

19

That evening Jacob left the flat to buy some provisions in the Dalston Lane market.

Although it was dark, the market was as busy as ever, but he took little notice of what was going on about him. He had a great deal to think about.

He was relieved that Emma had agreed to accompany Lily to Switzerland, even though it meant she would be farther away than ever when he returned to Cornwall. Once away from London she would be out of danger of becoming involved in activities that could result in a return to prison – at least for the foreseeable future. This would be a great relief to everyone who cared about her. He would do his best in the next few days to build up her strength and ensure she was fit enough to travel when the time came.

Having spent very little time outside the small flat since his arrival in London, Jacob did not think it possible that anyone other than the suffragettes who worked in the office would know him. It came as a shock when he stopped to buy some fruit and the stall-holder asked, 'Aren't you up here to visit that young Cornish suffragette girl? The one who's just been on hunger-strike in Holloway?'

'That's right.' Jacob's bemused expression was an indication of his surprise. 'How do you know?'

The costermonger grinned. 'Well, for a start, there's not too many around here with an accent like yours. Secondly, there ain't much goes on in Dalston that we don't know about. How is the girl?'

'Very weak. I thought I'd come out and buy a few things to help get her strength back. How much are those bananas . . . ?'

'For her? Nothing, guv'nor, and 'ere are a few apples and oranges to go with 'em. Give 'em to her with our love. I hope she's soon feeling better. She's got guts, that one. She gave King George quite a fright according to the papers. I don't wish him no harm – any more than she did – but it won't hurt him to know that some of us can say something more than "Yes, Your Majesty" or "No, Your Majesty" and tug our forelock to him.'

The market stallholder grinned again as he added, 'I bet it gave him one hell of a fright when she jumped up on the running board of his car. Good job it wasn't the old king, though. With her looks he'd have had her inside the palace in no time. Had an eye for a pretty girl did old King Edward, God rest his soul.'

Jacob encountered similar tangible expressions of sympathy for Emma from many of the stall-holders, his accent linking him with her immediately. None quite matched the warm generosity of the fruit seller, but by the time he completed his shopping he had spent very little.

Returning to the office with heavily laden bags, he was passing a narrow alleyway when, without warning, he was surrounded by half a dozen scruffily dressed young men. Before he could resist they had bundled him inside the alleyway, where the only light came from the gas lamps in Dalston Lane itself.

By pushing one of the men aside, Jacob was able to back into a narrow doorway. It offered scant protection from an all-out assault, but it meant he could not be attacked from behind and the young men would find it more difficult to hit him from either side.

'What do you want?'

Jacob realised as soon as the words were uttered that it was a foolish question.

'We'll have those bags you're carrying for a start. Then you can cough up with whatever you've got in your pockets. You must be loaded to be buying as much as you've got there.'

'Most of it was given to me,' Jacob said. 'It's for someone who's sick.'

'If she's sick she won't feel much like eating,' the apparent leader of the gang retorted as he edged warily closer. 'And if you haven't had to pay for anything then you'll no doubt have most of your money left. Hand it over.'

'No.'

His point blank refusal took the gang leader aback, but only for a moment. A movement of his head was sufficient for the others to move in on Jacob.

Before a single blow was struck, there was a roar of 'Oi!' from the entrance of the alleyway.

The big voice came from an even larger man. Well over six feet tall, he had shoulders that seemed to fill half the width of the alleyway.

'What the bleedin' 'ell do you think you're up to?'

Jacob's would-be assailants turned to face the newcomer and their leader said, 'It's nothing for you to get involved with, Manny. We're just doing a little "business" with this geezer, that's all.'

'Oh yeah? Well, I'll decide what I'm going to be involved with, not you, Alfie March. You so much as lay a finger on this young gent and I'll become so involved you'll think you've stepped into the ring to take me on for the championship.'

'We don't want no trouble with you, Manny, you know that. What's this geezer to you, anyway? He ain't one of us.'

'I says he is. He's come up to London all the way from Cornwall to be with that young suffragette who's just come out of clink after starvin' 'erself nearly to death. And anyone who's a friend of a suffragette is a friend of mine.'

'Of course!' one of the gang exclaimed. 'They got up a collection for your sister when she had an accident, didn't they? One of 'em looked after her little girl, too, until your sister was better.'

'That's right, and my sister's not the only one they've 'elped, neither. Suffragettes are good news for the East End. Set on them or their friends and you'll find you've not only taken on me but three-quarters of the dockers who live around 'ere.'

'Well, we wasn't to know who he was,' the gang leader said sulkily.

'You do now, so look at 'im and remember 'im, same

as I'll remember all of you. If any 'arm comes to 'im while 'e's around 'ere I'll come looking for you – every one of you. When I catch up with you you'll wish you'd never been born. Now scarper, before I change my mind and teach you a lesson anyway.'

The half-dozen scruffy men backed off from Jacob and moved towards the entrance to the alleyway, their gazes averted as they edged past Manny.

'They're a lot of bleedin' no-gooders,' Jacob's rescuer declared scornfully. 'There's not one of 'em who's ever done an honest day's work in 'is life. I'm almost sorry they went off so quiet.'

He spoke as the last of the would-be robbers disappeared from view.

Greatly relieved, Jacob said, 'You've saved me from a beating – or worse – and I've no doubt they'd have taken everything of value I have on me. I'm very grateful to you – but how do you know me? I can't remember us meeting before.'

'We 'aven't,' Manny agreed. 'But I've seen you around and everyone in the market knows who you are.'

He extended a large hand towards Jacob. 'I'm Manny Hirsch.'

'Jacob Pengelly. I'm very glad to know you. You mentioned a ring just now, are you a boxer?'

'No. I tried that once, but I wasn't fast enough. I'm a wrestler. Champion of all London. One day it'll be of all England too, if I can get the present champion to take me on. Right now 'e don't seem too keen.'

'Of course! I remember now. Emma has told me about you.'

Admiring the man's build as they stepped from the alleyway into the gas-lit street, Jacob was not surprised that opponents were reluctant to take him on.

'The young Cornish girl . . . 'ow is she? Is she going to be all right?'

'I think so,' Jacob replied. 'I'm hoping that some of the food I have here will persuade her to eat more than she is at the moment.'

'She's a plucky girl,' Manny declared. 'They all are. All of us who live around 'ere think the world of 'em. I can tell you, the coppers don't dare come around Dalston to arrest a suffragette.'

Suddenly serious, he added, 'But you watch your step while you're 'ere. You'd 'ave been in real trouble if I 'adn't seen that lot bundling you down the alley. Come on, I'll walk back to the office with you . . .'

20

When he returned to the flat above the suffragette office, Jacob related his adventure to Emma.

After expressing her concern at his narrow escape, she said, 'No one will dare to touch you now they know you're under Manny's protection. He's probably the toughest man in the whole of London. We're lucky that he's taken the East London suffragettes under his wing. We couldn't have a more useful ally. He's right about the dockers too, but I believe the police would rather tackle twenty dockers than take on Manny.'

Jacob saw nothing more of the East End criminal gang after that single encounter, but he often met up with Manny when he went out shopping, and the big man would occasionally walk around the market with him.

Manny was also among the first to greet Emma when she felt well enough to leave the flat and accompany Jacob on a shopping expedition. After giving her a huge hug, he admired the Holloway Badge she proudly displayed.

'Now don't you let them coppers catch up with you again. If you want to go off and do anything like that again, you let me know. I'll come with you and it'll take a whole army of coppers to nick you – I promise you that.'

As Emma continued to improve, she and Jacob gradually went farther afield. On more than one occasion they would glimpse Manny following them at a discreet distance.

After one such outing to Victoria Park, they returned to the flat when it was already dark to find the telephone in the office ringing. Emma was feeling very weary after their walk and Jacob took the call. It was Ben Retallick.

A date had been fixed for Lily to be admitted to the Swiss clinic. Ben would be passing through London with her in five days' time. He asked if Emma could be ready to travel on with them.

It was with mixed feelings that Jacob broke the news to Emma. He would be relieved to know she was not running the risk of arrest, imprisonment and forced feeding, but he wanted her to be with him. These last few weeks had been very happy ones, for both of them. He was loath to have them come to an end.

The telephone call seemed to affect Emma greatly too and she was also more tired than she had admitted to Jacob. She was lying down in her bedroom and gave him only a vague acknowledgement when he looked in to ask if she was ready for the supper he was preparing.

She had still not emerged when the meal was ready. As he had done on many occasions during the early days of her release, he put it on a tray and carried it to the bedroom for her.

Sitting up in her bed, Emma said, 'This is very kind of you, Jacob. I really don't feel like getting up again tonight – but where's yours?'

'It's in the kitchen,' he replied.

'Bring it in here. There's no sense in both of us eating alone. We can chat while we eat.'

In spite of her suggestion, when Jacob brought his meal to the bedroom he sat eating it perched on the edge of the only chair and there was very little conversation between them.

Somehow, being together like this in her bedroom brought it home to them both, as never before, that they were alone together in the flat.

Eventually, in order to break the increasingly embarrassing silence, Emma asked, 'Did Ben give you any details about the journey to Switzerland?'

'No. As I said, he's going to ring you again, probably tomorrow. He did say you'd see a marked deterioration in Lily's condition when you meet her.'

She rested her knife and fork upon her plate for a moment and shook her head sympathetically. 'It's very, very sad. If ever a married couple had so much of everything, it's Ben and Lily. Yet here they are in a situation that no amount of money can do anything about.'

'You never know,' Jacob said with more optimism than he really felt. 'The doctors in Switzerland might be able to find a cure for her.'

Emma shook her head. 'I know Ben's desperately hoping so, but I believe it's more a final desperate bid to ease her pain than any real expectation that she'll get better.'

'Don't say that,' Jacob said unhappily. 'They've both been very good to me – to both of us. I hate to think there's no hope for her.'

'So do I.' Bitterly, she added, 'It makes you realise just how fragile we are. There must be so many things she has wanted to do and never will now. I remember the woman I worked for at Henwood telling me once that I should pack all I could into life, while I could, because our time here is much shorter than we realise.'

There was silence in the room for a long while as they both thought their own thoughts.

It was broken by Emma. 'Does it embarrass you that there's just the two of us here in the flat together?'

'No,' he lied. 'But I'm not at all sure your ma would approve.'

Emma shrugged. 'That would be nothing new. Approval of me has never come easy to Ma. All the same, I don't like to have you waiting on me all the time. When we've finished eating, I'll get out of bed and clear up.'

'No you won't,' Jacob declared firmly. 'You've done more today than at any time since you came out of prison. You'll lie there and rest while I wash up. When I've finished I'll bring you in a hot drink and you can settle down for the night. You've got to be fit when Ben arrives to take you to Switzerland.'

Smiling at him, Emma said, 'Have I ever told you that you're probably the nicest person I've ever met, Jacob Pengelly?'

'No, but I don't mind you saying so – especially if you really mean it.'

'I do. Go and finish your chores, then bring me that hot drink you promised. Make it a hot milk, that's just what I fancy right now.'

When Jacob returned with the drink about half an hour later, the light in Emma's room was out. Thinking she must be asleep, he turned around and was tiptoeing out again, but then her voice came to him.

'Where are you going, Jacob?'

'I'm sorry. The light was out so I thought you must be asleep. Shall I put it on again?'

'No. Can you see to put the milk on my bedside table?'

'Just about . . .'

'Then put it down and give me a goodnight kiss.'

The bedside table was barely discernible. Jacob put the glass down very carefully before making his way to the bed.

Emma's arms reached out for him and and pulled him to her for the kiss she had asked for.

When they broke off in order to breathe, she maintained her grip on him.

Softly, in the darkness, she asked, 'Are you going to miss me when I've gone away?'

'Very much,' he replied honestly. 'More than I ever have before.'

'I'm going to miss you too, Jacob. I'll miss you very much indeed.'

'Then why don't you come back to Cornwall with me?'

'You know the answer to that, as I've told you many times. Besides, you know I've promised to go to Switzerland with Lily. You wouldn't want me to break that promise, would you?'

When he failed to reply, she said softly, 'But . . . that doesn't mean I don't want you. I feel as though every part of my body is aching for you.'

There was a long silence as Jacob tried to digest what she had just said to him.

Emma's next words left him in no doubt at all.

'Come into bed with me, Jacob. We'll each be going our different ways again very soon. Don't let's waste a single minute of the time we have left together.'

When he still hesitated, she said, 'You wanted me once, remember? When you took me up by the Cargloss clay pit? Have you forgotten?'

'I've forgotten nothing we've ever done together.'

'Neither have I. Give me some more memories to take away with me, Jacob. Please . . .'

A few minutes later, Jacob slid beneath the bed-clothes into the bed beside her. For a very long time all thoughts of parting were pushed to the back of both their minds.

21

For five days and nights Emma and Jacob lived as man and wife in the small flat above the Dalston Lane office.

The workers in the ground-floor office were aware of the change in their relationship. Although not all of them approved, they kept their opinions to themselves. No hint of criticism was levelled at the patently happy young couple.

Yet, much as both Emma and Jacob wished this happy state of affairs might continue, they could not slow the passing of time. Indeed, it seemed to Jacob that the five days and nights passed more quickly than any period of his life.

On the final day they both completed their packing in unhappy silence, aware that life would never again be the same for either of them.

Jacob was taking Emma to Paddington railway station to meet the train bringing Lily and Ben from Cornwall.

Emma would then travel with the Retallicks across London to Victoria, where they were booked on a train for Newhaven. From here they would sail on a cross-channel ferry, bound for the French port of Dieppe.

Jacob would remain at Paddington and catch a train that would take him back to Cornwall.

Their packing completed, Emma and Jacob looked about them at the small flat that had been their home for such a short but very happy time. They both wished to imprint it upon their minds.

Their eyes met and the embarrassment they had both been feeling fell away immediately. They held each other in a fierce embrace that failed to squeeze out the misery they were both feeling.

When Jacob released her, he said shakily, 'I'm going to miss you so much, Emma.'

'I'll miss you too.'

Burying her face in the front of his jacket, she said in a muffled voice, 'Do you think you'll be able to wait for me, Jacob? No matter how long it takes?'

'You know I will, but how about you? You're the one who's leading an exciting life and travelling to interesting places.'

Looking up at him, she said, 'Do you really need to ask? You know I will.'

'Then we'll be together again one day. I only hope it won't be too long.'

After they had kissed, Emma said, 'We'd better go now. The taxi driver will be outside and getting impatient.'

Jacob carried their suitcases down the narrow, steep stairs and discovered that all work had ceased in the office.

They were also informed that the taxi had been cancelled. They were to be driven to Paddington station by Vera Holme in the suffragette Sunbeam.

Manny Hirsch was in the office, looking ill at ease in the company of so many women. 'I'm here to carry your suitcases to the car,' he explained to Emma, 'on account of you not being well for so long.'

Jacob could have coped with the two suitcases with no trouble at all, but he knew Manny would be very hurt if he was not allowed to help.

It was an emotional farewell, with many small gifts heaped upon Emma. But the happy mood underwent a sudden and dramatic change when Jacob and Emma had taken only one step outside the office, the women crowding the doorway behind them.

Unnoticed by anyone in the office, two black Marias had pulled up in the roadway beyond the stalls. Now a great many policemen jumped from them, led by an inspector. Pushing their way through the throng of market shoppers, they headed for the office.

Addressing the suffragettes, the inspector shouted, 'All of you, back inside. I have a warrant to search these premises. I have reason to believe Sylvia Pankhurst is hiding here.'

He waved the document in the air as he spoke.

As the policemen tried to push Jacob and Emma back through the office door with the others, Jacob stood his ground. 'Just a minute . . . We have someone to meet. Trains to catch . . .'

'Then you'll need to catch another one. You're not going anywhere just yet.'

The policeman who had spoken tried to push Jacob back inside the office. When he continued to resist, the constable drew his truncheon and raised it as though to strike.

Before the truncheon fell, Jacob was pushed aside and Manny stood in his place. Reaching out, the giant wrestler took a firm grip on the front of the policeman's tunic. Lifting him clear of the ground he threw him backwards, bowling over two policemen who were standing behind him.

Seeing what had happened, the inspector charged forward, still waving his search warrant. He was grabbed and lifted high in the air by Manny.

Police, suffragettes and bystanders watched in breathless awe as the inspector was held at arm's length above the wrestler's head for a few seconds. Then, with a gigantic heave, he was thrown, arms flailing, to land on a nearby fish stall.

The stall was sent crashing on its side. Fish, inspector and wriggling eels fell to the ground together, while winkles and whelks scattered like marbles over the road and pavement.

Two more policemen rushed at Manny. One was promptly sent staggering backwards, choking as the result of a forearm blow to his throat. The other was seized by his truncheon arm and spun around. He too landed among the fish, cannoning into the inspector who was trying to regain his feet.

There was a confusing mêlée taking place outside the suffragette office now. Fish were everywhere and children dashed here and there snatching them up to take home, at the same time filling their pockets with winkles.

The costermongers turned on the police now, pelting them with anything that came to hand. Potatoes were much in evidence, but the missiles also included apples, turnips – and fish.

It was not long before the beleaguered policemen began an ignominious retreat to their two vehicles. As they went, the inspector, nursing an injured arm, shouted out furiously, 'You've gone too far this time, Manny Hirsch. There'll be a warrant out for your arrest by this evening. I'll see you're put away, even if I have to arm my constables with iron bars to arrest you . . .'

He ducked as a conger eel flailed through the air towards him. Still nursing his arm, he ran for the nearest police vehicle and scrambled inside.

To the cheers of the East Enders, the policemen drove off as eggs, tomatoes and an assortment of missiles splattered against the dark sides of the black Marias.

Vera Holme was cheering too, until, breaking off, she said, 'We'd better go, or we're going to be late.'

'I'll come with you,' Manny said, 'just in case the coppers try to stop you again.'

'I think they've gone back to the police station to lick their wounds,' Emma said, 'but you'd better come along while we think of what we're to do with you, Manny. You'll need to lie low for a long time – and you're too big to walk the streets unnoticed.'

A smile suddenly split her face. 'But I'd go to prison myself if I could only see that inspector flying through the air and landing on that fish stall once more!'

22

Despite the disruption caused to their schedule by the abortive police raid, the party from Dalston Lane reached Paddington station in time to see the arrival of the train on which Ben and Lily were passengers.

On the way, Vera had said she would wait at the station to convey Emma, Ben and Lily to Victoria railway station and see them safely on to their Newhaven train.

Ben and Lily stepped from the train and as porters helped to unload their luggage, Emma hurried forward to meet them, with Jacob following after.

He noticed with great sadness how frail and ill Lily looked. He hoped the Swiss doctors might be able to do something to help her, but feared it might need more than medicine to bring her back to health.

Ben was showing the strain of his concern for Lily, but he greeted Jacob warmly. Introduced to Manny, he said, 'I'm very pleased to meet you. Jacob told me on the telephone how you stepped in to prevent him from being robbed.'

'He's done it yet again,' Jacob said. 'Had it not been for Manny, Emma and I wouldn't be here now.'

As the luggage was being loaded into the suffragettes' Sunbeam, Jacob told Ben of the battle that had taken place at Dalston Lane. When he repeated the threat issued by the inspector to the wrestler, Ben was genuinely concerned.

'What will you do, Manny? If the inspector has suffered injury you might go to prison for a long time.'

Shrugging, Manny tried unsuccessfully to appear nonchalant. 'They 'ave to arrest me first. I know the East End better than they do.'

'Do you have a family, Manny?'

'Only my sister. I live with 'er and 'er husband.'

'How about work?'

Puzzled by Ben's questions, Manny replied, 'I work in the docks when they take on men, but there aren't many ships in at the moment. Most of the dockers are laid off.'

'I have an idea that will get you out of London for a while. I'm going to be away from England for some time, leaving my grandmother in my house in Cornwall. She could do with a strong, reliable man like you about the place. If I gave you the fare you could travel to Cornwall today, with Jacob. What do you say?'

'Go to Cornwall?' Manny looked at Ben as though he had suggested he should travel to the moon. 'I've never been any farther from home than Barking – and then I got lost!'

'You could have the flat that was occupied by a groom who has just left me,' Ben continued. 'It has two very nice rooms over the stables – and Jacob would be around to see that you settle in all right, wouldn't you, Jacob?'

'Of course. It would be great to have him around. You'd enjoy it there, Manny.'

'It would certainly be better than staying here in London, risking arrest and imprisonment every time you went outside your sister's house,' Ben urged.

Manny was not a quick-thinking man. Perplexed, he looked from Ben to Jacob. He still had not made up his mind when Emma called that the car was loaded with their luggage and Vera was ready to go.

When Jacob told her of the offer Ben had made to Manny, Emma exclaimed, 'What a wonderful idea! Great Aunt Miriam would just love having you around, Manny. It would settle my mind too – and Ben's. He must be very worried about his grandmother being there without Lily or anyone really reliable to look after her. I hope you've said you'll take up his offer?'

Her words helped Manny to make up his mind. 'All right then. I'll go. But I'll need to get a few things from my sister's place first.'

'Splendid!' Ben slapped Manny on his broad back. 'Here, let me give you money for a taxi to take you to collect what you need. But make it quick, in case the police get that warrant out for you. Bring your stuff back here. Meanwhile Jacob will get your ticket and wait for you. Here, off you go.'

He handed a number of banknotes to Manny before turning to Emma. 'We must go too. We haven't a great deal of time to spare.'

'I'll just say goodbye to Jacob.'

Looking from one to the other, Ben said, 'Of course.' Holding out a hand to Jacob, he said, 'Goodbye, Jacob.

I don't know when I'll be back at Ruddlemoor. I doubt if it will be for a week or so.'

When the two men had shaken hands, Ben said to Emma, 'I'll be waiting with Lily, in the car.'

As he walked away, Emma and Jacob looked at each other unhappily for some moments. She was the first to break the silence.

'I've got to go now.' Somehow Emma seemed to Jacob to grow smaller and she appeared to be terribly vulnerable as she stood before him.

'Yes. Emma . . . I want you to know these last few days have been the best of my life. I wish they could have lasted for ever.'

'That's the way I feel too,' she gave a miserable half-shrug. 'But I'm not just playing a game, Jacob. I joined Tessa and the others to help right a great injustice. It's still there.'

'I know. It's something that needs to be put right. When it is I'll be waiting for you. You can be sure of that.'

'I hope so, Jacob. I hope so with all my heart.'

Emma hugged him with such passion that, in the car, Ben and Lily both watched with raised eyebrows. Then Emma ran to the Sunbeam.

Jacob waved until the motor car disappeared from view in the traffic beyond the incline that led away from the railway station. Then he turned his attention to Manny . . .

23

❧

Tessa was waiting at the Gare du Nord in Paris when the train steamed in from Dieppe. She greeted Emma affectionately and Lily only marginally less so.

For Ben there was a warm handshake.

'You're looking tired, Emma. You too, Lily.'

In truth, Tessa was being kind to Lily. She looked very ill indeed. To Ben she said, 'Which hotel are you staying in while you're in Paris? Emma didn't know when she telephoned to say you were coming.'

'The Hotel Crillon. I've booked in for a few days. I thought Lily would need a break in the journey.'

Tessa's expression was one of sympathetic understanding. 'You've chosen a very comfortable hotel. I doubt if there's a better one in Paris. The food is superb – or so I am told. I am afraid I can't possibly afford to eat there.'

'Then you will have to come there as our guest, won't she, Lily?'

'Of course . . . but for the moment all I want to do is sleep. I'm afraid I'm not used to all this travelling. I feel utterly exhausted.'

'Then we'll concentrate on getting you to the hotel,' declared Tessa. Come, there are taxis over here . . .'

The journey to the hotel was taken in a motor taxi-cab. The driver manoeuvred the vehicle through the traffic as though it were a mechanised charger and he was on a mission to force every other vehicle off the streets.

All the time he was driving, he was talking in rapid French, occasionally gesticulating to other motorists, whom he seemed convinced were on the road for no other purpose than to offend him.

In spite of her weariness, Emma found the Frenchman's attitude to his fellow drivers highly amusing.

Lily was absolutely exhausted after her two days of travelling and had her eyes closed for most of the journey through Paris.

'What's the driver saying?' Emma asked Tessa, as they swerved around yet another slower moving driver. 'Is he swearing at them?'

'No, nothing like that at all,' an amused Tessa explained. 'He's pointing out the sights of Paris to you!'

Twenty minutes after leaving the railway station, they arrived at the Hotel Crillon. It was situated on one side of a gigantic open square and Emma looked about her in awe.

'This hotel is absolutely wonderful. I never knew such places existed!' As they entered, she looked up to where a magnificent chandelier hung from a beautifully painted ceiling. 'This must be what heaven looks like!'

'I don't know about that,' Tessa declared, impressed

despite her contempt for ostentation. 'But you should all be comfortable. Some of Christabel Pankhurst's friends stay here when they're in Paris.'

Moments later, when their luggage had been removed from the French taxi-cab by an army of porters, they were conducted to their rooms by a fussy little hotel manager, his pin-stripe trousers and dark coat immaculate.

Once in the suite of rooms Ben had booked for them, the observant Frenchman suggested that 'M' sieur might wish a doctor to be called to attend Madame Retallick?'

Lily declared she did not need a doctor – only a bed.

When she had gone to her bedroom, Ben explained to the manager that they were on their way to take Lily to a clinic in Switzerland.

The manager was duly sympathetic. 'Then I will ensure that madame is not disturbed.' After a moment's hesitation, he asked, 'I trust you will not consider me impertinent if I enquire the name of the doctor who will be treating madame?'

'She is to stay at the clinic of Dr Bertauld,' Ben replied.

'Ah! Madame could not be in more competent hands. Many guests have passed through the Hotel Crillon on their way to Dr Bertauld's clinic. Always I have welcomed them back here on their way home – fully cured. I look forward to having the same pleasure for Madame – and I trust it will not be too far in the future.'

Bowing, he said, 'I will leave you now. If there is anything you require, anything at all, I and my staff are at your disposal.'

Clapping his hands in an imperious manner, the manager mustered his porters and drove them before him from the room.

When he had gone, Ben went in to Lily's bedroom and unpacked her night-clothes from the baggage while she spent a while in the en suite bathroom.

When she was eventually settled in bed, Lily asked, drowsily, 'What are you going to do now, Ben?'

'I should really go to the railway station and make arrangements for our onward journey. But that can wait until tomorrow. I'll stay here with you for a while.'

'There's no need for you to do that, Ben. Take advantage of having Tessa here. She knows Paris. Let her take you to the station. I doubt if Emma will want to go. She's almost as tired as I am.'

Ben's uncertainly showed and Lily said, 'Go on, Ben – and there's no need to hurry back. Let Tessa show you something of Paris.'

She held out a hand to him and he took it.

'You spend so much time helping others. Me, most of all. But also Emma, her family, your grandmother, the Ruddlemoor workers. It's time you relaxed and enjoyed life a little more.'

'I'm quite happy with what I do, Lily. Nothing pleases me more than being able to help you.'

'I know, Ben – and I love you for it, but . . . Oh, I'm such a trial for you. I wish I wasn't.'

She was close to tears and Ben leaned over and kissed her. 'We'll have no more of such talk. We're on our way to Switzerland to find a cure for you, remember?'

She nodded.

'Now you must go to sleep. You'll feel better in the morning after you've rested.'

She nodded once more. 'You will go to the station?'

'Yes, if you insist.'

'Don't hurry back, Ben. Stop somewhere and have a drink. You need to relax.'

Returning to the others, Ben told them of his intention to go to the station to make arrangements for their onward journey to Switzerland. He asked Emma if she would like to accompany him. She declined, saying she did not have the energy to travel any more. She would stay in the suite looking out of the large window at the lights of Paris for a while before going to bed herself.

'I'll take you to the station,' Tessa said to Ben. 'You're going to be here for a while, so Emma and I can go out to see Paris another day. Perhaps we can arrange for a carriage and take Lily too?'

'She would like that,' Ben said gratefully. 'And I thank you for your offer of coming with me to the station. Actually, I was rather counting on it! I don't doubt things will go far more smoothly with your help.'

When they entered the foyer of the hotel, the helpful manager hurried up to them.

'Mr Retallick! Is there something wrong? Something you need, perhaps?'

'No, there's nothing wrong, thank you. It's just that I need to go to the station to arrange for a compartment when we travel on to Switzerland. Preferably a sleeper, so my wife can rest.'

'But there is no need for you to do this yourself. This is the Hotel Crillon! Tell me exactly what it is you require. I will send an assistant manager to do this for you immediately.'

In a matter of minutes, the efficient hotel manager had

everything under control and was explaining the needs of 'M'sieur Retallick' to a young assistant manager who was dressed almost as elegantly as himself.

'Well, that was easy,' Ben said to Tessa. 'But I confess to a feeling of disappointment. I was quite looking forward to seeing something more of Paris.'

'There's absolutely no reason why you can't,' Tessa said. 'Lily and Emma are where they want to be. Why don't I show you around for an hour or so? It's an experience you shouldn't miss. Paris comes to life after dark. It's when you realise what a truly magical city it really is.'

Ben opened his mouth to decline her offer. Then he remembered what Lily had said to him.

'It sounds a wonderful idea. All right, I'm entirely in your hands. Where are you going to take me?'

24

Outside the hotel a warm wind was blowing and Ben breathed it in contentedly. 'Do we need to catch a taxi?'

Tessa looked at him in amusement. 'Only the very rich travel in taxis in Paris. Anyway, you must have had enough of being cooped up in trains, boats and taxis. We'll walk. That way you'll feel something of the real Paris.'

Unselfconsciously taking hold of his arm, she said, 'I love it here. I should really have gone back to London days ago, but I don't want to leave.'

'What is it about Paris that you find so special?'

'Everything!' Tessa said expansively. 'The people . . . the cafés . . . the river . . . the wonderful buildings – oh, the whole feel of the place. It's somehow so . . . alive!'

Ben smiled benevolently at her. 'It's a long time since I heard someone express such enthusiasm. Perhaps I should have discovered Paris years ago.'

'Of course you should! Everyone should discover Paris as early as possible. Then they could plan to spend as much of their life here as they possibly can.'

'Where are you going to take me to experience some of this magic that's quite obviously rubbed off on you?'

While they were talking they had crossed the square in front of the hotel and now had a park on their left and a bridge ahead of them.

Instead of crossing the bridge as he had been expecting, she led him down a wide flight of steps to one side of it. At the foot of the steps was the river with a wide, paved walk on either side.

'*This* is the true heart of Paris,' Tessa said. Without apparently being aware of it, she leaned against him for a moment. 'The River Seine.'

Although it was a dark, starless night, there were many well-lit boats using the river and gas-lights were generously spaced along the high wall that reached from the river path to the road above them.

Nevertheless, there were many dark corners and niches along the wall. Most of these were occupied by courting couples who were seemingly oblivious to all except each other.

When Ben commented upon them, Tessa smiled. 'Haven't you heard, Ben? Paris is a city for lovers. Anyway, those I've seen so far are showing great restraint. You should see what they get up to on the *left* bank!'

'Isn't that where you're staying?'

'That's right. In a tiny apartment that's quite different to the Hotel Crillon. There are no lifts or restaurants and my "apartment" is a small room off the first-floor landing. There's a permanent aroma of cooked cabbage which comes from one of the other rooms – I've never been able to discover which one. But it's clean, cheap, fairly quiet and everyone is very friendly.'

'You're staying there on your own?'

'Of course.' Tessa looked at Ben sharply. 'Did you think I might be sharing it with someone? A man, perhaps?'

'I hadn't really thought about it until just then – and it's really none of my business anyway.'

Freeing the arm which had been linked with his, she said, 'That's right, it isn't.'

There was indignation in her reply, but it was driven away by Ben's next question.

'Would you like me to book you in at the Hotel Crillon for a few days, so you can be close to Emma?'

The question took Tessa by surprise. It was a few moments before she shook her head and said, 'Thanks all the same, but if I spent a few nights in such luxury I wouldn't want to return to the left bank. As it is I'm enjoying life there – and it's remarkably cheap.'

Ben was not particularly surprised that Tessa should have refused his offer. He said, 'How far away is this simple paradise of yours?'

They were approaching another of the many bridges that lined the banks of the River Seine and Tessa waved vaguely in the direction of the far bank. 'Over there.'

'Couldn't we go somewhere close to where you live for a snack and a drink?'

She looked at him in disbelief. 'You're staying at the Hotel Crillon! Why should you want to go to a left bank café to eat and drink?'

'Why not? You obviously enjoy it there. You might find I will too.'

After a moment's hesitation, Tessa shrugged. 'All

right.' Changing direction, she began climbing the steps
to the nearby bridge and he fell into step beside her.

When they reached the bridge, Tessa paused to gaze
down at a boatload of men. They appeared to be cele-
brating. Shouting to Tessa, they waved drunkenly.

'You seem to have scored a hit with them,' Ben said
as they resumed their walk.

'Should I be thrilled about that?' Tessa asked belligerently. 'They'd have been just as enthusiastic had I
been eighty years old and as wrinkled as a prune. They
were drunken men on a night out and I was wearing a
skirt. Not very flattering, is it?'

Ben looked at Tessa with a wry smile. 'There are times
when I find you incredibly pragmatic, Tessa.'

'Thank you, Ben. Less generous people have called it
cynicism.'

'I know you're utterly dedicated to the suffragette
cause, but what will you all do when you've won –
and I'm convinced you will win, one day?'

Tessa gave his question serious thought. 'I don't
know. It doesn't seem important, somehow. It's the
cause that really matters.'

'I can't agree with that point of view. You've all
worked very hard to achieve the thing you believe in.
You must hope for some personal gain from it.'

'Well, we'll wait until that happy day arrives and
decide what to do then.'

They had left the grand buildings behind them now
and were in an area of narrow streets in which there
seemed to be a disproportionate number of cafés, each
with customers seated at tables outside on the pavement. It was a warm night. Despite threatening dark
clouds that obscured moon and stars, it was not raining

and there seemed to be a happy atmosphere everywhere.

'Is there anywhere in particular you would like to go?' Tessa asked him.

'I'm leaving that entirely up to you. If it's a place you like then I've no doubt I will too.'

'Fine. I'll take you to Henri's.'

25

Tessa walked Ben through more of the left bank streets of Paris, until they eventually arrived at a small, back-street café which, like all the others, had tables and chairs outside on the pavement.

The owner, a diminutive, balding Frenchman, greeted Tessa as though she was one of his most intimate friends.

Because he was with her, Ben also received special attention from the effusive proprietor and his cheerful French staff.

As Ben sat at a table with Tessa, two Cognacs and two coffees on the table in front of them, Ben picked up his glass. Sipping the fiery drink, again he asked about her future once the aims of the suffragette movement had been met.

'I honestly don't know, any more than I know the future of the movement as a whole. I haven't dared think that far ahead. But I'm a good journalist. Hopefully I'll be employed by a newspaper – perhaps right here in Paris. I'd like that.'

Tessa did not feel at ease being questioned about her hopes and aspirations. Looking over the rim of her glass, she asked Ben, 'How about yourself? You must be a very rich man now. Do you have any ambitions left?'

'Not really. I have my clay works and various family interests in Africa. To be honest, just recently I haven't looked far beyond trying to find a cure for Lily.'

'Of course you haven't.' Tessa spoke sympathetically. 'It must be a great worry for you.'

'It is, especially when I remember her as she once was. She was very much like Emma, you know.'

Tessa smiled. 'Emma's a quite exceptional girl. She's very fond of Jacob, but it would be a dreadful mistake for her to contemplate marrying him just yet. Her dedication to the Federation is far too strong.'

'I know. I think Jacob does too. I only hope he'll wait for her. Those two are just made for each other. My grandmother thinks so too – and she's a very good judge of such matters.'

'Well, those who are truly right for each other usually get together sooner or later. At least, so everyone tells me.'

Ben felt there was a hidden meaning in her words. He wondered if there was someone special in her life, but he did not yet know her well enough to ask.

'Will you have another drink?' Tessa asked.

They had been drinking while they talked and Ben had not realised his glass was almost empty.

'Yes, but let me get this one. I'd also like to buy you a meal. Do you know somewhere we could go?'

'Of course – right here.'

When he looked somewhat dubious, she said, 'You won't find better food than that cooked by Henri's wife

– and at a fraction of the cost of the more fashionable Paris restaurants. What do you fancy?'

By the time Henri had produced a menu and they had chosen their food, two more extremely generous drinks had arrived – courtesy of the proprietor – and Ben was feeling more light-headed than he was accustomed to.

The café food was as good as Tessa had promised – and it arrived supplemented by a bottle of wine recommended by Henri.

The meal was followed by yet another Cognac – 'On the house'. As they drank, Henri joined them and told them stories in very bad English about some of his favourite customers, many of whom Tessa appeared to know.

When Ben eventually looked at his pocket-watch, he saw it was after one o'clock in the morning! He declared it was time he returned to the hotel. But first he would see Tessa safely home to her own accommodation. She would not hear of it.

'No, Ben. Not on your first night in Paris. You're a stranger here. I'll see you home.'

After some argument, Ben agreed – but only on condition that she caught a taxi from the Hotel Crillon, paid for by him.

Ben was presented with a ridiculously small bill by Henri, but was then required to kiss farewell to the proprietor's many friends and relatives who seemed to be occupying most of the seats in the café.

Among them was Henri's wife. A small, red-cheeked and shy sparrow of a woman, she was brought from the kitchen in order to meet 'Tessa's man from England'.

Ben left the café cocooned in a warm glow. He had thought it very late, yet it seemed that the rest of Paris had no inclination to sleep just yet.

It was necessary to walk back to one of the bridges across the river before they were able to find a taxi. Then, seated close together in the cramped interior of the vehicle, Tessa provided Ben with a running commentary on the buildings they passed on the way to the hotel.

When they arrived, Ben suggested Tessa should come inside for a drink.

Laughingly, she replied that Ben had probably had enough drinks for one night, adding, 'Perhaps we'll do it again tomorrow.'

Realising her invitation might be misconstrued, she added quickly, 'Better still, why don't we make it at a time when Lily and Emma are able to join us?'

'I'd like that,' he agreed. 'But tonight has been special. I've enjoyed your company, Tessa. You've helped me forget my worries for a while.'

'I'm glad about that, Ben.' She meant it.

'Will I . . . will we be seeing you tomorrow?'

'If you want to.'

'Of course I do. Have lunch with us. Afterwards perhaps we can all go on a ride together. You can show us some of the sights of Paris. Then you and Emma could go off somewhere. She'd like Henri's café.'

Tessa gave Ben an enigmatic smile. 'Henri and his café will remain a secret that only you and I will share, Ben. I'll take Emma somewhere else. Somewhere that she'll enjoy.'

It was only after the taxi carrying Tessa had left the hotel and as he was walking inside that Ben wondered why Henri's café should be a secret shared only by Tessa and himself.

He decided he would not dwell on the matter. At least, not tonight.

26

Ben and Lily saw a great deal of Tessa during the four days and five nights they spent in Paris. On two of the days Lily summoned up sufficient strength to go on sight-seeing tours of the great European city.

However, on each occasion the excursion used up what little reserves of strength she possessed. By evening she was too tired even to eat in the hotel restaurant. Her meals were sent up to the suite. Ben ate with her, leaving Emma free to go off with her friend.

During the afternoon of their final full day in Paris, Ben, Lily and Emma were seated in the hotel suite and Tessa was with them. They had not gone out. Lily was conserving her fragile strength for whatever the next day might bring.

When Tessa asked the others what plans they had made for that evening, Lily replied that she intended going to bed early, but insisted Ben should go out with the others.

When he protested that he would not leave her alone in the hotel, Emma said, 'I don't feel I can take another late night, either.'

Grimacing apologetically at Tessa, she added, 'I know it's a foolish thing to say after all this time, but I don't think I've fully recovered from my time in Holloway.'

'It's not foolish at all,' Tessa replied. 'I took a lot longer to recover after *my* first hunger-strike. It was months before I was really well.'

'I'm not at all certain I should be surrounding myself with so many "gaolbirds",' an amused Lily declared. 'But if Emma doesn't feel like going out, perhaps you could put up with Ben's company for another evening, Tessa? I've felt very guilty about keeping him shut up in the hotel for so long while we've been here.'

'That's most unfair of you,' Ben protested. 'She could hardly refuse now you've put the question point-blank to her.'

'Why should I want to refuse?' Tessa asked. 'In fact, I was going to suggest that Ben should call in to see Henri before leaving Paris.

'Henri is the proprietor of the café where I took Ben the other night,' she explained to Lily. 'He thinks Ben is very distinguished and ever since I told him that Ben was born in Matabeleland he's been pleading for me to take him back there. It seems Henri's brother has lived in Matabeleland for very many years. He believes they might know each other.'

'That's settled it,' Lily said firmly. 'You know how much you enjoy talking about Africa, Ben. You must go.'

Ben was still reluctant, but faced with the insistence of the three women, he eventually capitulated. 'All right,

but I'll try not to be too late or to wake you when I
return . . .'

Ben's hopes of an early night were doomed from the
moment it was discovered that he *had* met Henri's brother.
The Frenchman had passed through Matabeleland with
Cecil Rhodes' Pioneer Column which, in 1890, had set off
to establish British rule in neighbouring Mashonaland.
Later, he had been involved in the uprising when Ben's
father was killed by tribesmen.

Furthermore, the brother had mentioned the Retallick
family more than once in his letters home.

During the course of the evening, Tessa learned that
the Retallicks were the largest landowners in the whole
of the country that was now called Southern Rhodesia.
According to Henri's brother, they wielded more power
there than the man who governed the land on behalf of
the British government.

As more and more links were discovered between
the families of Ben and Henri, word went out to the
numerous Paris members of the Frenchman's family.
They flocked to the café to meet with a man who had
met the exiled member of their clan more recently than
had they, and who bore a name known to them through
the writings of their far-distant relative.

Each new arrival prompted a fresh round of toasts.
To the absent relative . . . to Ben . . . to Rhodesia . . .
to France. Many times too during the course of the
celebrations Henri, beaming happily through his per-
spiration, would repeat to all and sundry that he had
known from their very first meeting that Ben was a man
of great distinction.

Not until the early hours of the morning was Ben able

to overcome their protests and insist it was time for him to leave.

He was further delayed by much hugging, cheek kissing and handshaking before he was able to stumble outside and into a horse carriage with Tessa.

Behind them, the whole of Henri's extremely large family spilled from the café to the pavement to wave farewell to Henri's guest.

Tonight, Ben insisted that the taxi should drop Tessa off at her home before continuing on its journey to the Hotel Crillon.

Tessa's protest was purely nominal and the vehicle eventually came to a halt in a narrow, quiet and ill-lit street.

Tessa pointed to a window on the first floor and said, 'That's my home while I'm in Paris.'

After a moment's hesitation, she added, 'Would you care to come up for a coffee? It might sober you up a little before you return to your hotel.'

Ben too hesitated, but he doubted if it was for the same reason. He had enjoyed the evening more than any other he could remember in recent years.

He had also enjoyed Tessa's company. She was intelligent, quick-witted and fun to be with. Despite the fact that she was very much her own woman, he suspected she was also extremely vulnerable.

What was more, he found her very attractive – and he had a strong suspicion she was equally attracted to him. It was a highly dangerous state of affairs.

'I don't think that would be very wise, do you?'

She shrugged with apparent nonchalance. 'If I relied on wisdom to guide my life I would never have become a suffragette.'

Ben was aware that her statement contained an invitation. He also realised he had drunk enough to weaken his resolve. Then he thought of Lily . . .

'I really must get back to the hotel. We have an early start.'

'Of course.'

She was climbing from the taxi when Ben said, 'We're in Paris now. I didn't think that friends here just said "Goodbye" and walked away.'

Tessa gave him a wry smile. 'I would have thought you'd been kissed quite enough for one night, Ben Retallick. But "Goodnight" anyway.' Standing on the pavement outside the taxi, she leaned inside with the apparent intention of kissing him upon the cheek. Whether it was a misjudgement because of the darkness or a deliberate movement on the part of one of them, Ben could not remember afterwards. Whatever the cause, Tessa's kiss found his mouth – and they both allowed it to last a little too long.

Standing back from the vehicle, Tessa said, softly, 'Goodnight, Ben.'

'Goodnight, Tessa . . . You'll come to the hotel in the morning to see us on our way?'

'Of course!'

They were both aware their relationship had just taken an indefinable pace beyond friendship. They also knew that if Tessa did not come to the hotel to see them on their way there would be a great deal of speculation about the reason.

'I'll see you tomorrow.'

Ben waited until Tessa pushed open the door of the house where she was living before calling for the taxi driver to move off.

But she did not enter the house immediately. She waited until she had seen the taxi turn the corner at the end of the road and pass from view.

Those who had come to rely on her firm management of the Dalston Lane office would have found it difficult to believe the turmoil of tangled emotions she felt right now.

She had been aware from their first meeting that she found Ben Retallick attractive, yet she had allowed herself to be drawn into a situation – an impossible situation. She had fallen in love with him.

What was more, it was entirely her own fault. It was something that even the most naïve of girls should have anticipated.

In the hotel suite, Lily heard Ben open the door and make his quiet way to the bedroom next to her own. She had lain awake for the past three hours wondering where he was and what he and Tessa were doing together.

She resisted the urge to look at the clock on the bedside table and check the time. She did not want to know. If Ben lied to her in the morning about the hour he had returned to the hotel she did not want to be aware it was a lie.

She loved Ben very much, yet she liked Tessa too. Lily had deliberately thrown them together and she must now suffer the consequences of her own actions.

Lily believed that if the clinic in Switzerland was unable to provide a cure for her lung disease – and she feared it would not – Ben would need the support of someone possessed with great inner strength.

She was convinced Tessa was just such a person. A

very exceptional type of woman. Ben's type of woman.
She was strong enough to sustain Ben through what
was likely to be one of the most unhappy situations
life would ever throw his way. At the end of it, she
believed Tessa would be able to help him to put the
pieces of his life together again.

Tessa would be able to give him all the things that
she, as his wife, had been unable to give him – and the
children she knew he wanted.

It was a plan that had been in Lily's mind for some
time. Paris had enabled her to bring it closer to frui-
tion.

However, her plan had been conceived in the cold
light of day, when common sense and rationale came
more easily.

Now it was night, and Lily was alone in a hotel
bedroom in a foreign city. In such a situation, logic
stood aside to make way for the dreams of what might
have been.

Turning on her side, Lily buried her face in the pillow
and wept for all that was slipping away from her.

27

❧

The Swiss clinic was the cleanest place Emma had ever seen. It was also one of the most impersonal. The walls were painted with gleaming, white gloss paint, as was the woodwork surrounding the doors and the window frames.

The floors of Italian marble along the long, wide corridors shone as though they were wet. Walking on them, Emma felt with each step she took that she might slip and fall. She was even more concerned for Lily and maintained a firm grip on her arm until they arrived at the room Lily was to occupy.

The clinic was situated high in the mountains. From a balcony outside the room, a valley dropped away with breathtaking steepness to a river that fed a small lake, which was almost hidden by trees. On either side and as far as could be seen in the distance were jagged mountain peaks. All were adorned with a mantle of snow that appeared as fresh and unblemished as the interior of the clinic itself.

Arrangements had been made for Emma to occupy a room adjoining that of Lily and sharing the same balcony and view. However, the doctor who met them and guided them to their rooms stressed that she would not be allowed unlimited access to Lily. A strict routine would need to be adhered to if they were to effect a cure. Visiting by Emma would be restricted to half an hour in the morning and an hour each evening.

When Ben protested that this seemed unnecessarily strict, the doctor said such a policy was essential, both to protect the patient's companion from risk of infection and in order that his own course of treatment should not be disrupted in any way.

When Lily was showing some improvement in her condition, the doctor said with supreme confidence, they would consider extending the visiting period.

In order that Emma should not become bored, arrangements had been made for her to have French lessons. Should she so wish, she might also take instruction in nursing.

When Emma agreed that both of these were likely to prove useful, it was arranged that she should have French lessons each morning and nursing instruction every afternoon. Nursing, in particular, was something in which Emma had always had an interest. It was always possible she might one day follow it up in England.

Despite the optimism of the senior doctor and the clean and efficient nature of the clinic, Ben left Switzerland a week later with a very heavy heart.

The doctor had been unable to give him any time-scale for Lily's hoped-for recovery. He would say only that treatment was not a short-term matter. Indeed, although he had achieved better results than any other specialist in the treatment of lung disease, a cure could not be guaranteed.

If one was achieved, it would, perhaps, not be for a year – or even longer!

Ben did not tell Lily all that the doctor had said to him, but he had no need to point out that the clinic could not work miracles.

On the day before Ben left for England, a patient had died in a room close to Lily's. The distress of her French family, who were at her bedside when she passed away, was both noisy and prolonged.

This added to the unhappiness the couple felt during their last evening together.

When it was time for Ben to go the following day, the doctor allowed Lily to leave her bed and wave to her husband from the balcony of her room as he drove away down the long, winding drive that led to the road below the hospital.

When he had gone, Emma left Lily alone for a while before going to her room. The doctor had said she might stay with Lily for much of that day to play cards and some of the board games they had brought with them.

It was just before bedtime that evening when Lily suddenly put down her cards and said plaintively, 'I wonder whether Ben has arrived in Paris yet?'

Emma glanced at the clock on Lily's bedtime table. It showed six o'clock.

'I don't know. He said he would be there sometime this evening.'

'Is Tessa still in Paris?'

The question was asked in a casual manner, but something in her voice made Emma look up at her sharply. 'I'm not certain. When we left she was expecting to return to London before too long.'

'I hope she *is* there and that Ben meets up with her again.'

'Why?' Emma was startled. Tessa had never tried very hard to keep her attraction for Ben a secret, even from Lily. Emma could not understand why Lily would want to throw the two together.

'She's good for him. Lively. Intelligent. Full of energy. She can make him laugh too. In fact, she does all the things I no longer can.'

'You'll do all these things again Lily – and Ben *loves* you.' Emma was alarmed at Lily's bout of depression, but she had been half expecting it.

'Yes, Ben loves me. I've never doubted that, Emma. But he's a man – and still a young man. I also know that he would love to have children, although he's said nothing to me about it lately. If anything happens to me he'll be able to marry again, fulfil his wish for children, and one day pass Ruddlemoor on to a son.'

Despite her matter-of-fact way of speaking, a tear escaped from the corner of one of Lily's eyes as she screwed up her face in an attempt to hold in her unhappiness. Emma became alarmed.

'You mustn't talk like this, Lily. Ben would be very unhappy if he knew.'

'I know he would, but I know how ill I am and I'm facing facts, Emma. If he marries again I'd like it to be to someone like Tessa. She'd marry Ben because she loved him, not because he's rich and could offer her an easy life.'

When another tear followed the first, Emma said firmly, 'Lily, I refuse to listen to such nonsense. You're going to get well. When you do, Tessa will be as pleased as everyone else. She's very fond of you. She's said so to me, more than once.'

'I believe you, but I rather fancy – and I sincerely hope I'm right – that she's even fonder of Ben.'

28

When Ben arrived at the Paris railway station, the
weather in the world's most romantic city seemed as
depressive as his mood. It was unseasonably cold and
grey, with a drizzle heavy enough to cause people to
walk with their gaze cast down at the pavement and
not at each other.

His mood brightened temporarily when he was greeted
by the effusive manager of the Hotel Crillon. The
Frenchman bubbled over with optimism, assuring Ben
that Lily would return to him 'a new woman' in 'no
time at all. No time at all.'

The manager's cheeriness brightened Ben, but not
for very long. He had booked a single room for his
brief stay and he found it small and claustrophobic
after the suite he and the others had occupied on his
previous visit.

On the journey from Switzerland, he had decided it
would, perhaps be wiser not to meet with Tessa during

this visit to Paris. After spending two hours sitting alone in the hotel room, he changed his mind.

When he left the hotel the rain had stopped temporarily, but there was a cold wind blowing. Nevertheless, he decided to walk rather than catch a taxi.

He headed for Henri's café, believing Tessa would probably be there. He hoped she would. The café would be lively and noisy and would probably help to shake him out of his mood of depression.

No tables or chairs were in place outside the many cafés and restaurants tonight, but inside they seemed as noisy as ever. Sound leaped out at him as he passed the open doors.

The cafés seemed to be filled with couples, all laughing and happy to be together. But he realised this impression might have had something to do with his feeling of loneliness.

When he entered Henri's café he was treated as though he was a long-absent member of the proprietor's family. Henri, his wife and two daughters all hugged and kissed him – but Tessa was not here.

Henri said she had not called on them for a couple of nights. On her last visit she had spoken of returning to England. He thought she must have already gone.

But Ben was in Paris! Henri insisted he must remain at the café and drink with his friends!

Staying in the café only long enough to down a couple of Henri's extremely large measures of good Cognac, Ben escaped by saying he intended to check whether Tessa had, in fact, returned to England.

He left the café half promising Henri he would return later. He doubted whether he would. In truth, without

Tessa to translate much of what was being said, he had
not understood a great deal of the conversation. The
visit to the café had succeeded only in accentuating the
feeling that he was an outsider. Even more alone than
before.

He found the narrow street where Tessa lived without
too much difficulty and his spirits lifted when he saw a
light burning behind the drawn curtains of her first-floor
room. He tried not to build his hopes too high. The
chances were that the room would have been re-let
promptly after she had gone. She had told him such
rooms were popular with French students, because of
their low rent.

Pushing open the street door, he passed into a hallway
that smelled of garlic – and cabbage. To this was added
the aroma of French cigarette tobacco.

As he went up the stairs he met a girl coming down.
She appeared thin and gaunt in the yellow light from
gas-lamps that burned in the hallway and on each
landing, but there was sufficient light for him to see
her face was heavily made-up.

When they both reached the same stair she stopped
and spoke to him in French.

Although he knew very little of the language, he
understood enough to know she was asking if he had
come looking for her. Smiling, he shook his head and
she shrugged, apparently only mildly disappointed and
continued on her way.

On the first floor there were only two doors. He
knocked gently on the one he believed to be Tessa's,
still unsure whether he should be here at all.

'Quel est?'

Ben's spirits soared. It was a woman's voice. Although

he could not be absolutely certain, he believed it was Tessa's.

'It's me. Ben.'

There was the sound of quick footsteps, a bolt was drawn inside the door and when it opened, Tessa was standing in the doorway.

'Ben! What a wonderful surprise.'

In such a state of excitement it was the most natural thing in the world for her to greet him with a kiss. Suddenly, her expression changed to one of concern. 'Is . . . is everything all right?'

'Yes. I'm on my way back to Cornwall and staying in Paris overnight. I found it a bit lonely at the hotel, so I went to Henri's, hoping to find you there. He said he hadn't seen you for a couple of nights and thought you might have gone back to London. I decided to come and find out for myself.'

He smiled at her. 'Now I'm here why don't I take you back to Henri's for a meal?'

'Like this?' Her gesture moved from her hair, hanging loose about her shoulders, to the somewhat thread-bare housecoat which seemed to be all she was wearing.

Taking his hand, she drew him inside the room. 'As you can see, I've packed everything except the clothes I'll be wearing tomorrow. You see, I'm travelling to England in the morning too. It must be on the same train as you.'

Suddenly, she snapped her fingers and said excitedly, 'Look, I still have a lot of food left. There's more than enough for two. I was going to cook it all up and throw away what I couldn't eat. While I start cooking, why don't you go to the shop on the corner and buy a bottle of wine – two, if you think you can manage one by yourself. I'm sure I could.'

'That sounds a wonderful idea! I must admit I don't really feel I could face Henri's friends and relatives again tonight. I'll buy the wine and we can have our own private party.'

Ben returned to the house with two bottles of wine – and a bottle of Cognac.

When he entered the room, a delicious smell was drifting from the pan Tessa was stirring over the gas cooker.

'I'm having a fry-up,' she explained. 'We'll have mushrooms, bacon and various other scraps. I'm sorry there's no soup, and I can't guarantee it will be the best-cooked meal you've ever had, but there's some delicious cheese to end with.'

Ben opened both bottles of wine and they drank and chatted as Tessa cooked.

When he told her of his encounter with the French woman on the stairs, she laughed, merrily.

'That was Suzanne. You were lucky to escape her clutches, Ben. She's a "lady of the night" who lives upstairs. She's the reason I find it necessary to keep my door bolted. Occasionally her clients come here looking for her. If they've had too much to drink – as they usually have – their navigation is liable to be erratic. I had a man open the door and walk in one night. He quickly realised he'd come to the wrong room, but he assured me I would be a quite acceptable substitute!'

Ben was appalled. 'What did you do?'

'He was so drunk I was able to lead him back out through the door in the mistaken belief that I was taking him to a bedroom. All I had to do then was give him a push, turn off the landing light and dash back in here and bolt the door. He knocked a few times, thought he must be knocking at the wrong door and went to the one across the landing. The couple who live there both work in the fish market and I don't know which of them is the stronger of the two. She certainly has the best command of basic French. I think the unwanted visitor was happy to beat an ignominious retreat before she carried out the more lurid of her threats.'

Although Ben was able to see the humour in the particular incident she was relating, he was concerned that she should be living in such a place. He asked her why she put up with such conditions.

Warm from stirring the contents of the frying pan, Tessa pushed back a recalcitrant lock of her hair before replying. 'Because it's cheap. Besides, whatever the drawbacks, I'm living among *real* people – and they're basically *good* people. It's through them I've come to love Paris . . . but, here, your dinner is served – sir.'

Sharing the contents of the frying pan between two large plates, she put one on the table before him.

It smelled and tasted good. The wine too was a great success. By the time they moved on to the Cognac, they had both relaxed to an extent Ben would not have thought possible a few hours before.

He was not drunk – the food had been sufficient to soak up much of the alcohol – but he felt utterly at ease in Tessa's company. Even a deep discussion on suffragism and its future was carried on in a reasoned and affable manner that would have amazed some of her critics.

Eventually, when they had both drunk a few glasses

of Cognac, Ben declared he should think about returning to his hotel.

Rising to her feet with only the slightest hint of unsteadiness, Tessa said, 'I don't think you've chosen your moment very well, Ben.'

He was puzzled by her words until she went to the window and drew back one of the curtains. In the light from the room he could see rain against the panes.

Opening the window briefly, she said, 'It's absolutely *bucketing* down.'

'Oh! Then perhaps I should get a taxi,' he suggested hopefully.

Tessa smiled at him apologetically. 'I'm afraid this isn't the Hotel Crillon, Ben. You'll find no taxi rank here and there's too little business for them to cruise these streets. You'd better have another Cognac and I'll put on some more coffee. By the time you've drunk it the rain might have eased off a little.'

An hour or so later, the contents of the Cognac bottle had been depleted still further, they were on the third pot of coffee – but there was still no let up in the rain.

Standing together at the window, in the light of the gas street-lamp they could see rivulets of water flowing over the cobblestones of the street outside, fighting for precedence when they encountered others at a barred iron drain.

A curtain of rain, tinted by the flickering gas-lights, fed the rivulets and spurred them on.

'You can't go out in this,' Tessa declared firmly.

'I must if I'm to get back to the hotel,' he replied.

'You could always stay here. It might have stopped by morning.'

Ben looked at her questioningly. There was only one

bed in the room. Of single width and disguised with
a multi-coloured crocheted cover and a scattering of
brightly coloured cushions, it still remained the most
dominant piece of furniture in the room.

'Where would I sleep if I did?'

It was a foolish question and the arching of Tessa's
eyebrows confirmed the fact even before she replied,
'Do you really need me to answer such a question,
Ben?'

'But . . . ?' he floundered foolishly.

'I know. You're married and Lily is a lovely person.
She's also ill, Ben. She's been ill for a long time – much
as we both wish it was otherwise. She's not going to
be well for a very long time. What will you do, Ben?
Pretend you don't know what other men and women
are doing in beds all over the world? Or will you pay for
a few brief minutes of pleasure that might cause you to
one day pass on to Lily a disease even more distressing
than the one she has now? You wouldn't be the only
one to do that, you know. Thousands of men do it all
the time, with far less reason than you have.'

Ben had never heard such talk from a woman before,
but Tessa was speaking with no apparent embarrassment. Neither was she making any attempt to avoid
his gaze. Indeed, she seemed to be daring him to
look away.

'I'm not asking for any commitment from you, Ben.
Neither will I make any to you. What's more, anything
that happens here tonight is between you and I only –
and I would prefer it to stay that way.'

Ben found his heart was beating much faster than
normal. Trying to make a weak joke, he said, 'You make
it sound like the secret of Henri's café.'

She smiled too, although he thought there was sadness in it. 'No, it won't be at all like the secret of Henri's café – unless it's because they are both equally happy memories.'

When he did not reply, Tessa asked, 'Have I embarrassed you, Ben? I suppose I should apologise – but I'm not going to. You see, for me suffragism is far more than getting the vote. It means enjoying full equality with men, even when it means taking the initiative in matters that most men – and women too, I fear – would no doubt find quite shocking.'

Ben still remained silent and Tessa, not quite so self-assured now, said, 'I've shocked you, haven't I? That's a pity. Somehow, I thought . . . No, it doesn't matter what I thought.'

Breaking the suddenly hesitant flow of her conversation, Ben said, 'Has anyone ever told you that you talk too much, Tessa Wren?'

Her eyes widened for just a moment, then she said, 'Frequently, but no one has ever accused me of not carrying out any of my promises.'

'Then I suggest we have another drop of that Cognac, and, for tonight, at least, shut out the rest of the world with the rain . . .'

29

❧

Later that night, Ben lay awake in the narrow bed, one arm trapped beneath Tessa's naked body. He knew he should be feeling guilty about what he had done. Guilty about deceiving Lily in this way.

He winced at the thought of the wife he had left in the Swiss clinic. He *did* feel guilty, and yet . . . He had a disconcerting feeling that Lily had known this would happen. Had the thought not been just too preposterous, he could even have convinced himself she had *connived* at such a situation.

He thought of how eager she had been for him to accompany Tessa on late-evening excursions from the hotel during their stay in the city. She had also been insistent that he should check whether Tessa was in Paris on his return to the city.

He dismissed the idea. In a moment of self-truth he decided he was merely trying to salve his conscience.

As he wrestled with his thoughts he heard footsteps

on the stairs leading to the first-floor landing. Someone appeared to stumble on the top stair.

As he held his breath in anticipation of a knock on the door of Tessa's room he heard two people laugh. It was a man and a woman talking in French. Most probably it was the prostitute from upstairs returning home with a client.

'Can't you sleep, Ben?' From beside him, Tessa sleepily asked him the question.

'I'm not sure I want to. I'm quite happy lying here. I think I just heard your upstairs neighbour come in. She wasn't alone.'

'She rarely is.' Suddenly sitting up, she asked, 'Do you mind if I have a cigarette?'

'Of course not.' He flexed his fingers. His arm had become numb as a result of having Tessa lying upon it.

As he exercised his fingers he was looking at Tessa. Light from the gas-lamps outside in the street percolated through the thin curtains and outlined her body.

He had an urge to reach out and touch her, but desisted. He was not certain she would approve.

When she struck a match and held it to the tip of the cigarette, the silhouette took form. She had a slim, firm body and looking at it roused him again.

'Do you want a cigarette?' She turned towards him as she extinguished the match with a shake of her hand.

'That isn't exactly what I have in mind.'

'Anything else will need to wait until I've smoked this.' Lying back against the pillow, she adjusted her body so it was more comfortable on his arm.

'You're not sorry we're doing this, Ben?'

'Not right now, no.'

'Good! No doubt we'll both have a battle with our consciences when daylight comes, but I don't want you to regret what we're doing just yet.'

She was smoking a French cigarette and the aroma of the smoke was strong in the small room. He was not a smoker, but he did not find it unpleasant.

'Is there no one in particular in your life, Tessa?' It was a question he had hesitated about asking her before.

'Not any more.'

'Do you want to tell me about him?'

'No. Why should I?'

The reply came quickly. Fiercely.

Tessa had not meant it to sound quite so emphatic. 'I'm sorry, Ben, that wasn't necessary.'

'It doesn't matter. Besides, you're quite right. It *is* none of my business.'

They lay beside each other in silence until half the cigarette had become ash. Extending her arm to drop the ash in an ashtray on the bedside cabinet, she relaxed once more before speaking.

'He was a Member of Parliament. A married man too. Our affair lasted for almost three years before his wife found out. She threatened to make it public and bring his career to an end. We had no option but to stop seeing each other.'

'Is he still an MP?'

'Yes. If his party ever comes to power he'll be a minister – and deservedly so. He's a hard-working and clever politician. If we're fortunate he'll throw his weight behind suffragism, although I suspect that will depend upon what happens to be politically expedient at the time.'

'Do you find that hurtful?'

'Why should I? For him, politics is everything. All else must take second place. That's the way I feel about suffragism. We understand each other. At least, we did.'

The red glow sped along the cigarette as she drew hard upon it.

Feeling it wise to change the subject, Ben said, 'I'll return to the Hotel Crillon early in the morning. When I've shaved and packed I'll come back here in a taxi to take you to the station.'

'That will be a help, thank you.'

'We'll need to get to the station early too, so that I can upgrade your ticket to first class.'

He felt her body stiffen beside him. 'You don't have to buy any such luxuries for me, Ben Retallick. If you intend paying for "favours" you should have gone upstairs with Suzanne. She's the one who makes love on a commercial basis.'

Glad the darkness hid his amusement, Ben said, 'I never really thought of it as paying for your "favours", as you like to call it. I was being selfish. I have a first-class ticket and I want you to travel with me. It's as simple as that.'

'You could always travel third class with me,' she countered, but with less conviction than before.

'I could – and I *will*, if you insist, but I can see no reason to turn a railway journey into a social statement. I prefer to travel in as much comfort as is available – and we would enjoy far more privacy.'

Turning on her side towards him, she laid an arm across his body, still holding the cigarette between her fingers. 'I'm sorry, Ben. I'm being a pain, aren't I? All right, we'll travel first class.'

'You're quite sure your East London friends won't mind you travelling in such luxury.' He was teasing her, but he held his breath in case she took it the wrong way and rounded on him again.

'I can't think of anyone who's likely to tell them. Anyway, the thought of having some privacy is enough to sell me on the idea. Thank you.'

Rolling away from him once more, she stubbed out the cigarette in the ashtray. When it was extinguished to her satisfaction, she turned towards him again . . .

30

With the memory of the night they had spent together still fresh in both their minds, Ben feared the long journey from Paris to London might prove embarrassing to both him and Tessa.

To his great relief, their relationship was as easy as ever. Neither said anything about what had occurred. It was almost as though nothing untoward had happened. As though they had not shared the same narrow bed in a small Paris room only hours before.

They reached London after dark that same evening and took a motor taxi-cab to Dalston Lane. Shortly before reaching London, Tessa had suggested that, if he had not already booked into a hotel, he might like to stay in the small flat above the office.

The offer was made without any innuendo. Ben had accepted in as casual a manner as that in which the offer had been made.

The office staff had gone home some time before. In

the street outside, a few costermongers remained amidst the debris from that day's market trading.

There was little to eat or drink in the flat, but Tessa went out to buy something. She returned after about a quarter of an hour with food and drink purchased from the remaining stalls that would stay on the street until there were no more customers, drunk or sober.

Ben did not feel quite as at ease here, in the flat. He was aware this was also Emma's home – and Emma was with Lily, in Switzerland.

Nevertheless, when the meal was over and it was time for bed, there was never any suggestion that he and Tessa should occupy separate rooms.

Despite the matter-of-fact attitude they had both tacitly agreed to adopt towards what they were doing, there were moments when Ben felt a deep sense of tenderness towards Tessa.

When he woke early in the morning she was still asleep. He lay without moving for some time, with Tessa curled up beside him, wondering what the future had in store for her. He would have liked to feel that whatever it was, he would have some small place in it, at least. But he knew it could not be.

'What are you thinking about, Ben?'

Deep in thought, he had not noticed that her eyes had opened. Sleepily, she added, 'Are you wishing you could go back forty-eight hours and change all that has happened?'

'No. I had something very different in mind – and thinking how unfair I am being to everybody.'

She propped herself up on one elbow and looked down at him. 'As I remember, this was my idea, Ben. All right, so you didn't run away.'

She cut short his protest. 'I said in Paris there would
be no commitment – from either of us. Remember?'

'I remember. It sounded a wonderful idea at the time.
But that was then. After two nights with you I'm not
sure I'll be able to keep to my side of the bargain.'

'You must, Ben – for Lily's sake. She needs you in a
way I hope I will never need any man. You mustn't hurt
her. She must never learn what's happened between us.
Emma too would be deeply shocked, though I suspect
she wouldn't be too surprised.'

Tessa raised herself to a sitting position, unperturbed
by her nakedness. 'Now, if you're going to get home to
Cornwall today, we'd better make a move – before the
office staff start arriving.'

She swung herself out of bed and pulled a flimsy
wrap about her. When she reached the bedroom door,
she paused and looked back.

'In spite of what I've just said, these couple of days
and nights have been memorable for me too. If you come
here to see me when you're next in London, I promise I
won't turn you away.'

Tessa telephoned for a taxi for Ben, using the office
telephone. None of the staff had yet arrived for work
– but they were present when he left.

They had not been aware that Tessa had returned to
London and there were squeals of delight when she
opened the door at the bottom of the stairs and entered
the office.

The sound died away to be replaced by a confused
silence when Ben followed, carrying his suitcases.

It was broken by Tessa. With no trace of embarrassment, she said, 'I think most of you know Ben Retallick?

He's a relative of Emma and has just returned from Switzerland. We travelled from Paris together yesterday. He's on his way home to Cornwall now.'

The women began talking again now, the sound more subdued than it had been when Tessa had first put in her unexpected appearance.

Those women who had not met Ben on his earlier visit knew about him through Emma. They were aware he was married and had just left a sick wife in Switzerland.

A few of the women also knew of Tessa's long-lasting affair with the married Member of Parliament and wondered whether Ben had taken his place.

Ahead of the times in their tolerance of behaviour considered by others as being unacceptable, suffragettes were often accused by their opponents of having low morals. This was not so. A number of the women in the office were happily married. They were as censorious of those who did not conform to the code of conduct implicit in the marriage ceremony as were their critics.

They made Ben aware of their disapproval by averting their gaze as he walked between them on his way to the door to the street.

He mentioned this to Tessa when they arrived at the waiting taxi.

'Well, what did you expect? The married women are bound to disapprove of you having spent the night in the flat with me. Some of them will argue that we probably did nothing anyway, while those who are convinced we *did* can't prove anything. Mind you, they'll have a stronger case when you kiss me "Goodbye" – and you *are* going to kiss me, I hope.'

'Of course, but perhaps we should move to the side of the taxi farthest from the office.'

Hidden from the view of those in the office by the stalls, shoppers and the taxi itself, they said a warm farewell and Tessa resisted a strong urge to cling to him.

When he was safely ensconced in the vehicle, she said as evenly as she could, 'I'll keep my promise to you, Ben. What has happened between us began in Paris and ends right here. But I'll be very hurt if I learn you've passed through London without at least telephoning me.'

'If I come to London I will want to see you,' Ben declared. 'And I have a feeling I'll be coming here more often than before. In the meantime, I'd like to telephone you from Cornwall occasionally. I hope you'll call me too.'

'I'd like that. Goodbye, Ben.'

'Goodbye, Tessa.'

He called out the words as the taxi lurched into motion. Looking back as the vehicle made its way along Dalston Lane, he saw Tessa standing where they had parted.

She remained there until the taxi was lost to view amidst the shoppers and traffic of the busy East London street.

BOOK THREE

1

Ben's travels to London, Paris and Switzerland had convinced him the time had come to bring Ruddlemoor into the twentieth century.

The Retallick-owned clay works had always been looked upon as one of the most up-to-date workings in clay country. Yet during his travels Ben had been made aware that many aspects of industry were advancing at a rate that was leaving Cornish industries behind.

This was particularly apparent in the field of transport. The clay industry still relied to a large extent upon horse wagons to convey its clay to the small ports around St Austell Bay.

Some clay works, and Ruddlemoor was one, had rail links with the small port of Pentewan, farther along the valley from Tregarrick. But this small port was having problems with sand silting up the channel that joined sea and harbour. It was so serious there was a strong possibility the port would have to close.

In all the places he had recently visited, Ben had been aware of the increasing use of motor vehicles for the carrying of people and freight. It had convinced him that this was without doubt the transport of the future.

He had decided he would buy a fleet of lorries to transport China clay between Ruddlemoor and Charlestown harbour, the port from which he intended to ship his clay in the future.

However, such an undertaking required a transport manager. A man able to grasp the potential of modern means of transport. A young man. After discussing his ideas at some length with Captain Jim Bray, Ben sent for Jacob.

Standing before Ben and the clay works captain in the Ruddlemoor office, Jacob was asked if he would accept the post of transport manager and revolutionise the means of moving China clay.

The offer came as a complete surprise to Jacob. As he listened to Ben, his expression covered the range from disbelief to delight, apprehension – and back again.

'Are . . . are you sure you feel I can do it?'

'I'm quite certain, Jacob. Captain Bray agrees with me.'

This was only partly true. Captain Bray had expressed doubts about the whole venture, but Ben had finally convinced him that they were entering a mechanised age. One day, and it was not too far away, the horse would disappear from the roads of the land.

'Do you feel you can take on the task?'

Jacob nodded eagerly. 'I think it's a wonderful opportunity – for me and for Ruddlemoor. It'll put us streets ahead of the other clay works. When do you want me to begin?'

Ben smiled at Jacob's eagerness. 'Right away. There are a lot of things you'll need to discuss with Captain Bray. Where the garage is going to be situated; what we'll need there. Then you'll have to look at details of all the different types of vehicle that are available and find men who can be trained to drive them. You'll need to learn to drive yourself, of course. You can make a start by coming to Tregarrick and having my chauffeur give you driving lessons. You'll also need to find mechanics; stock a store with spares. You'll find a hundred and one things to do. In fact, I think you'll probably be the busiest man at Ruddlemoor for a while.'

'I don't mind.' Jacob was filled with enthusiasm for his new appointment. 'Perhaps I can make a start by going to talk with Mr Trethewey down at St Blazey. He's just bought two lorries. I doubt if he'd have gone out and bought the first ones he saw. Talking to him might save a bit of time. Of course, what I should *really* do is go to London and speak to the men who've been operating a fleet of lorries for a year or two. That way we might avoid many of the mistakes we might otherwise make . . .'

Ben looked at Captain Bray and they both grinned. 'Well, if your enthusiasm is any guide, I think I've chosen the right man. Work on any ideas you come up with, Jacob, and don't be afraid of discussing them with Captain Bray before putting them to me. If going to London – or to anywhere else come to that – is likely to help, there's no reason why you shouldn't go. For now I suggest you chat to Captain Bray about the amount of clay we're currently moving, and how much it's costing us. He'll also tell you what we expect to be shifting in the next year, or so.'

Standing up to go, he rested a hand on Jacob's shoulder. 'You know, I am quite excited about this myself. I envy you, Jacob. It takes me back to my own younger days . . .'

That evening, Eve Pengelly could not stop talking about Jacob's unexpected promotion to such a high position at Ruddlemoor. There was awe in her voice when she said, yet again, 'Fancy, a son of ours being given such an important job, Absalom! Why, he'll be the most important man at Ruddlemoor after Jim Bray. And him little more than twenty years old!'

'Ben Retallick was running Ruddlemoor when he was no more than our Jacob's age,' Absalom reminded her. 'And a good job he made of it. Besides, he's always thought highly of our Jacob.'

With a mischievous twinkle, he added, 'Mind you, it could have a lot to do with that young Emma. If our Jacob marries her then he'll be related to Ben Retallick. A man in his position wouldn't want people pointing out that he's related to an engine man.'

As Absalom had anticipated, his wife rose to the bait immediately.

'No one's said anything about our Jacob having to marry *her* to get the job. Is that what he said to you, Jacob?'

'He didn't need to, Ma. I'd marry Emma if I had to pay *him* to do it.'

'Well, then it's a good job she's in Switzerland with poor Mrs Retallick and you're here,' Eve Pengelly said with a disapproving sniff. She had never been able to come to terms with the fact that Emma had left her

family, Cornwall and Jacob to go off to London and
join up with a group of women whose stated aim was
to oppose authority.

News of Emma's term of imprisonment had been
the final ignominy. She was not the most forgiving
of women and the mere mention of Emma's name
was sufficient to conjure up silent but tight-lipped
disapproval.

The news of Jacob's promotion was well received by
Miriam when Ben told her about it at lunch that day.

'You won't regret it,' she prophesied. 'That young
man's got a good head on his shoulders. He'll be running the whole of Ruddlemoor for you one day, you
mark my words. Emma should have snapped him up
while she had the chance. There'll be a few mothers
pushing their daughters in his direction now, you see
if there's not.'

'Emma's still the one for him,' Ben said confidently.
'He won't look at anyone else.'

'I hope you're right, but it's not a good thing for two
people who think a lot of each other to be apart for too
long. Temptation is likely to put in an appearance when
it's least expected.'

Her statement and the look that accompanied it
made Ben feel uncomfortable. His grandmother had
an uncanny knack of hitting a man where his conscience
hurt most.

'Well, Manny and Jane aren't having that problem.'

Jane was yet another of Emma's unmarried sisters.
She had been brought to Tregarrick as a help and
companion for Miriam after Cissy had left to marry
the Glamorgan policeman. Through the window of

Miriam's room, Ben had spotted Jane and Manny walking from the house towards the St Austell road.

Coming to stand beside her grandson, Miriam too watched the couple as Jane took Manny's hand.

'I'd never in a million years have paired those two off,' she said, shaking her head. 'They haven't got the brain of a twelve-year-old between the two of them. Mind you, there's not a ha'porth of harm in them, either – and she'll never find a man who's more protective of her.'

'He's a useful man to have around the house,' Ben said. 'And more than willing to turn his hand to do anything that needs attention.'

'He doesn't mind pushing me to St Austell in that wretched bathchair, either,' Miriam agreed. 'But I do wish he didn't feel he needs to get me everywhere as fast as he can. He'll rattle every remaining tooth out of my head on that road. It's high time something was done about it . . .'

2

Lily had been a patient in the Swiss clinic for six weeks when Ben received a telephone call from Dr Bertauld, the physician in charge of the clinic. The doctor expressed concern about her condition; she was not responding to treatment. He believed it was more to do with her mental attitude than anything else.

He felt that if Ben returned to Switzerland for a while they could discuss the problem in detail and, hopefully, arrive at a solution. Then Ben could spend a few days convincing Lily she needed to adopt a more positive approach towards her treatment.

The Swiss doctor stressed that unless there was a rapid change in her attitude, he could not hope to effect a cure for her condition.

Alarmed, Ben agreed to travel to Switzerland as soon as the necessary travel arrangements could be made. He would certainly set off within the next forty-eight hours. He further agreed that the doctor should tell Lily he would be paying her a visit, in the hope it would raise her spirits.

Ben had realised even before the doctor's telephone call that all was not well with Lily. The letters sent to Tregarrick by Emma, and by Lily herself, had given him some indication of Lily's state of mind. But they had not been as specific as had the Swiss doctor.

He would have preferred to keep news of Lily's condition from Miriam, but there was little that went on, in and about Tregarrick, that escaped her attention.

When he had tea with her as usual that afternoon, she asked, 'Did you have a telephone call from Lily today?'

'No.'

Ben hoped he would not need to amplify his terse reply, but he should have known better. Miriam would not leave the matter hanging in the air.

'Well, who was it from, Emma? I know the telephone call came from Switzerland, I've heard it from the servants. Why aren't you saying anything about it? Was it bad news?'

'It's not good, Grandmother – but I suppose it could be a whole lot worse.' Accepting that he had no choice but to tell her, he repeated his conversation with the doctor and told her what he intended doing.

'If I were younger I'd come there with you,' Miriam declared. 'When do you intend leaving?'

'I should be able to get away the day after tomorrow.'

'That will give me time to write a letter to Lily. You can take it with you when you go. She's got an opportunity to get well that wasn't available to her poor brother. She should be thankful for it.'

'Now, Grandmother, I don't want you upsetting her. I'm going there to try to cheer her up . . .'

'You needn't worry about that, Ben. I'm far too fond of the girl to want to upset her, especially at a time like this. But if you're worried I'll let you read the letter before I seal it. I just want to remind her that she comes from Trago stock – and we are not in the habit of giving up easily.'

Jacob came to see Ben that night to discuss the new motor transport section at Ruddlemoor.

He felt it would be better if the transport depot was established away from Ruddlemoor itself. There was a number of reasons for this, not least of which was the need for huge underground fuel tanks, which would not be entirely practicable at Ruddlemoor.

He proposed that they build the depot on land acquired by Ben some years before, closer to the port of Charlestown. At the time it had been Ben's intention to store China clay there, in readiness for shipping, but it had proved unnecessary.

Now the land could be put to good use. Jacob pointed out that a weigh-bay might also be installed, for weighing the loads of clay en route to the port. This might also be used – for a fee – by other clay producers at some future date.

After a lengthy discussion, Ben agreed the idea was sound. He gave his approval.

'What about the lorries themselves? Have you decided on any particular make?' he asked Jacob.

'I'm giving it a great deal of thought. It's a very complicated issue. First of all, there are two totally different types of vehicle in use at the moment and they both have a lot to recommend them. Steam-driven lorries are very powerful, but they need two men to man them and they have maintenance problems too.' Jacob hesitated, not wanting to sound too pedantic at this stage. 'I believe that lorries with petrol engines are where the future lies.'

'So? Why don't you decide to buy petrol lorries?'

'It isn't quite as simple as it sounds. There are so many makes! There's an American lorry I'm very impressed with – at least, it sounds good from all I've read about it. There's also a very good Swiss lorry that sounds tempting.'

He looked apologetically at his employer. 'I don't want to rush into it. I want to get the very best possible for Ruddlemoor.'

'You will, Jacob. I have every faith in you and want you to be certain before you commit us . . .'

He had a sudden thought and paused before saying, 'You mention a Swiss lorry. How good do you think it might be?'

'The Saurer? I've read some very good reports about it. The French army have tried it out and seem very impressed by what it can do and by its reliability.'

'Well, it so happens that I'm going to Switzerland the day after tomorrow to stay with Lily for a few days.'

Observing Jacob's concerned expression, he said, 'Yes, I had a telephone call from her doctor today. He's worried about her. Look, why don't you come along too? Emma will be delighted to see you. It can't be much fun for her there right now. I'll possibly stay for as long as a week. That will give you time to go to the factory where they make these lorries and assess their capabilities.'

The thought of seeing Emma again excited Jacob even

more than the thought of finding a vehicle that would comprise Ruddlemoor's transport fleet.

'It sounds a wonderful idea!'

Remembering that Ben was employing him to run a transport section and not in order that he could spend time with Emma, he said, hurriedly, 'On the way back perhaps I could stop in London. There's a haulier there who has recently bought a couple of American Macks. I promise that by the time we return to Cornwall I'll be able to tell you exactly what lorries Ruddlemoor should have.'

3

Ben and Jacob did not spend a night in London en route to Switzerland on this occasion. Catching an early train from St Austell, they were able to make it to Newhaven in time to catch an overnight boat train to France. They reached Paris mid-afternoon the following day and arrived in the Swiss clinic after spending two nights and almost three whole days travelling.

When Ben entered Lily's room she appeared to be sleeping. Lying in the hospital bed she looked thin and frail, her face frighteningly pale.

Thinking she was asleep, Ben was about to tiptoe out of the room when she opened her eyes wearily. When she saw him her eyes opened wide and she called out his name. Then she held out her arms to him and burst into tears.

He held her until she had recovered sufficiently to talk. In a muffled voice, she spoke with her face held to his chest. 'I'm so glad you're here, Ben. I believed I would never see you again.'

'Yes, so Doctor Bertauld said.'

'I'm so sorry, Ben. I know you have so many other things to do in Cornwall. You could do without a wife who is making life difficult for you.'

'You are more important than Ruddlemoor, Lily. I want to see you well again, and Doctor Bertauld is convinced he can make you well – but only if you co-operate with him.'

'So he's told me, but I watched my brother grow gradually worse with the same disease until he became a burden to those he loved most. I don't want that to happen to me.'

'It won't. Medicine has taken great steps forward since then, Lily – and we've got you the best doctor in the world. He's going to make you better. But you don't have to take my word for it. I have a letter from Miriam here. She says the same – and neither you nor anyone else can argue with what *she* says.'

Lily produced a fair imitation of a laugh. 'How is she? How is everyone – at home.'

'They're all fine. All send their love to you and look forward to seeing you home fit and well again. Oh, and I've brought Jacob with me. He wants to look at some lorries that are made here, with a view to buying them for Ruddlemoor. Although I suspect the thought of seeing Emma again was an even greater incentive. He's certainly talked more about her than of lorries on the journey here.'

'I'm glad, for Emma's sake. I've given her a hard time these last few weeks.'

'Well, you can give *me* a hard time now. I'll be here

for at least a week. By the time I leave I expect you to
be brimming over with confidence about getting well
again – and you *are* going to get well.'

Ben had his own confidence in Lily's eventual recovery
dented when he had a meeting with Doctor Bertauld
later that day.

The Swiss specialist told him that when Lily had been
admitted to the clinic, her illness had reached a critical
stage. In his opinion she had been brought to him when
the illness was far more advanced than he would have
liked. Nevertheless, he had taken her on as a patient
and had done his best for her.

Now, due entirely to her lack of faith in the clinic, she
had a twenty per cent less chance of survival than when
she was admitted. He said quite frankly that he was no
longer entirely convinced that he *could* cure her.

Pressed by Ben, Doctor Bertauld promised not to give
up on Lily. He had never, he informed Ben, somewhat
majestically, he had *never* given up trying to cure a
patient. But he expressed the firm opinion that his task
would be made very much easier if Ben could convince
Lily of the need to co-operate with him. If she would
only *believe* in his ability to make her better.

Ben left the office after giving the Swiss doctor an
assurance of his own co-operation, then returned to
have a long talk with Lily.

His task was going to be made a little easier because
of the letter Miriam had sent to Lily. In it she had
expressed many of the views held by the doctor. Lily
must have faith in Dr Bertauld if she was to be cured
of her illness.

The only thing that Lily might have difficulty in

accepting was his suggestion that Emma should return to England with Ben.

Doctor Bertauld assured Ben it was nothing to do with the way Emma had behaved during her time in Switzerland. On the contrary, had she not been related to Lily, he would have had no hesitation in offering her work at the clinic. Emma had proved quick at learning French, and she had shown an aptitude for nursing. She would have been most helpful in attending to his English patients.

However, Dr Bertauld felt that while Emma remained at the clinic she was a constant reminder to Lily of all she had left behind in England. He believed Lily needed to make a complete break and devote herself wholeheartedly to a routine that had proven successful with so many patients in the past.

When Ben had asked Dr Bertauld for a frank assessment of Lily's chances of a full recovery, the Swiss doctor's reply had given him great encouragement.

Leaning back in his chair and spreading his arms wide in an expansive gesture, he had said, in sharp contrast to his earlier pessimism, 'M'sieur Retallick, I have gained a reputation for *curing* my patients. Would I put such a reputation at risk by treating someone I did not think might be cured? Take heart, M'sieur. In spite of the setback we have had, Madame Retallick can be made better – but only if she truly believes. If she does not . . . ?' The doctor shrugged. 'If she does not, then it would be better if she returned home with you and Emma – to die.'

4

On his arrival at the clinic, Jacob had been taken to a large house which housed the nurses. It was here Emma had been given a small room to herself.

The move from the main clinic building had been made ostensibly so that she might associate with nurses during her off-duty hours. By so doing she would learn more about nursing and also gain familiarity with the French language.

In truth, Doctor Bertauld had ordered the move in order to distance her from Lily.

Lily had been in the habit of banging on the wall that separated her from Emma whenever she needed something, or if she merely felt the need of some company.

If Emma was not in her room when Lily needed her, she would panic and work herself up to such a state of agitation that it was often necessary for the doctor to be called to give her a calming injection.

Such incidents had ceased once Emma was moved, but Lily would still become extremely agitated if her younger relative failed to put in an appearance when she was expecting her.

This was one of the reasons why Doctor Bertauld felt it would make his treatment of Lily more effective if Emma were to return to England.

The young Swiss nursing orderly who had taken Jacob to the nurses' quarters would not allow him inside Emma's room. Instead, she left him outside the door, in the corridor, after assuring him, in a charming accent, that Emma would soon be returning from the main building.

'Would you like me to tell her you are here, waiting for her?' she asked.

'No. She isn't expecting me. I would like it to be a surprise.'

'Ah, a *romantic* surprise!'

'That's right,' he smiled at her obvious delight. 'A romantic surprise.'

The nurse went away, happy to have a part in the innocent little conspiracy.

Jacob waited for twenty minutes before Emma came into view. He saw her first through the window situated at the end of the passageway. Crisp and neat in a white hospital uniform, she was coming along the path towards the nurses' quarters.

He felt an incredible surge of excitement as she reached the building and disappeared from his view beneath the windowsill. He could feel his heart beating faster and his chest felt as though he had been holding his breath for a very long time.

A few moments later she pushed open the door at the end of the corridor and came towards him. Head down, she appeared to be deep in thought.

Not until she was no more than half a dozen paces

away did she realise there was someone standing by the door of her room.

Looking up for the first time, she saw Jacob.

An expression of utter disbelief came to her face. Her eyes opened wide and the blood drained from her cheeks. For one frightening moment, Jacob thought she might faint.

'Hello, Emma. There's no need for me to ask if I've surprised you . . .'

'Jacob! It really *is* you!'

She threw herself at him with such force it would have bowled him over had he not had the wall at his back.

Kissing him repeatedly, she said, half laughing, half crying, 'For a moment I thought I was having hallucinations! But, how . . . ? What are you doing here? When did you arrive? Is Ben with you?'

'Yes, Ben's with me. We got here no more than half an hour ago. The doctor telephoned him at Tregarrick because he was concerned about Lily. Ben came right away, bringing me with him.'

Suddenly serious, Emma said, 'I'm glad Ben's here. Lily doesn't seem to believe Doctor Bertauld will be able to cure her. We are all very worried about her.'

Standing back from him, she looked at him with renewed delight. 'But Lily will be a lot better now Ben has come to see her and it's just so absolutely *wonderful* to see you again. But why are we standing out here in the passageway. Come into my room.'

Releasing her hold on him, she pulled a key from her pocket, opened the door to her room and they went in together.

It was very pleasant inside, neat and clean. When Emma pulled open the curtains at the window, a small balcony with white wooden rails was revealed, with the same spectacular view of the valley enjoyed by Lily from the clinic.

Turning back from the window, Emma kissed Jacob again, with even more passion. Suddenly she drew back, a puzzled expression on her face. 'I know why Ben's here, but why did he bring you with him? Surely it wasn't just so you could see me?'

'Not entirely, although that *did* have a great deal to do with it.'

Sitting down at the small table while Emma put a kettle on a small oil stove with the intention of making a cup of tea, Jacob told her of his unexpected promotion to the new post of Ruddlemoor transport manager and the reason for the trip.

Looking at him with proprietary pride, Emma said, 'And to think that no more than a year ago you were working in Ruddlemoor dry. The greatest opportunity to come your way then was the chance to take an innocent young servant girl up among the clay tips where no one could see what you were hoping to get up to!'

'That's right,' Jacob grinned at her. 'Now here I am with a top job and earning enough money to comfortably support a wife and family.'

Looking at him sharply, Emma asked, 'Are you trying to tell me in a roundabout way that you've found someone you want to settle down with?'

'There's no "roundabout way" about it. I found someone I want to settle down with a long time ago. You!'

Emma showed relief which was closely followed by sadness. 'I'm still not ready for that, Jacob.'

Disappointed, but not surprised, he asked, 'Why, Emma? The suffragettes have managed without you for all the time you've been here, they'll get along all right if you come back to Cornwall. You've played your part and gone to prison for your beliefs too. Can't you call it a day and marry me? You could still remain a supporter in Cornwall.'

'It wouldn't work, Jacob. Besides, I can't even think about it right now. Not while Lily needs me here.'

'That's something I believe Ben will be talking to you about. Apparently the doctor has said that although you're a great asset to his clinic, he feels your presence here is unsettling for Lily. He believes she needs to cut all her ties with home and devote herself entirely towards getting well.'

'Doctor Bertauld actually said that to Ben?' Her expression suddenly softened. 'I'm not really surprised. It's something I've thought myself, more than once. She's been inclined to rely on me instead of putting her trust in Doctor Bertauld. All the same, I shall be sorry to leave. I feel I've been doing something useful during my time here. I've learned a lot, too. I know quite a bit about nursing now and can make myself understood, at least, in French.'

Emma placed a mug of tea on the small table in front of Jacob. The only other chair in the room was an armchair. Ignoring it, Emma carried her own tea across the room and sat on the edge of the bed.

As Jacob sipped his tea, Emma asked, 'How is Manny enjoying Cornwall?'

'It took him a while to settle, but he's been enjoying it more since he and Jane began walking out together.'

Emma looked incredulous. 'You mean – my Jane? My sister?'

'That's right. I spoke to Miriam just before Ben and

I came away. She says she's beginning to think that Tregarrick is a marriage market for the Cotton family. She also says that the couple who should have been the first to wed are dragging their feet far more than she would like.'

'She was talking of us, I suppose.'

'That's right. She said I was to tell you she can't afford to wait too long, even if you can.'

'Well, I'm afraid she's going to have to wait for a while longer.'

Reaching out, Emma put her cup on the table with half the contents still remaining and gave Jacob a look he could not quite fathom.

'What's the matter, is something wrong?'

'No. I was just thinking, that's all.'

'What about?' he asked cautiously.

'About the last time we were together. In the flat above the Dalston Lane office. Do you remember?'

'It's not something I'm ever likely to forget. I think about it often.'

'So do I. I think that was probably the happiest time in my life.'

Immersed in their thoughts for a while, it was Emma who eventually broke the silence.

'Jacob?'

'Yes?'

'I've told you I won't marry you yet, but that doesn't mean I don't love you and want you just as much as I did then.'

Jacob's throat went suddenly dry, but Emma had not finished talking.

'There's no one likely to disturb us here. If you wanted to we could go to bed together now.'

'Are you quite sure that's what you want?'

'Yes – if you still feel the same way about me as you did then.'

'That question doesn't deserve an answer.' He stood up, clumsy in his eagerness, but Emma spoke once again.

'You haven't said it, Jacob.'

'Said what?'

'Told me how you feel about me now.'

'I've just told you, I want you to come home and marry me . . .' He saw her expression change and added quickly, 'All right, so that isn't enough.' Reaching out, he drew her to him. 'I love you, Emma Cotton. I have from the day we first met. Now what?'

He posed the question as she slipped from his grasp.

'Now you can slip the catch on the door – and don't turn around until I tell you. Then you can come to bed too.'

5

❧

The visit of Ben and Jacob to the Swiss clinic lasted for a full week. Ben would have been content to extend his visit, but the doctor insisted it was time for him to get on with the task of curing Lily.

While Ben was spending his days with Lily, Jacob had travelled to the shores of Lake Constance, to the works of the Saurer motor company. Here he spent three days and two nights, during which time he saw the lorries being produced and was allowed to take one on a test drive around the surrounding roads.

Jacob was accompanied by Emma, Ben having booked them separate rooms in a hotel in the town where the works was situated. Whether Ben was aware that one of the rooms would not be used did not really matter. They were both very happy to be in each other's company, away from all those who knew them.

Jacob was very impressed with the vehicles he had come here to test, but he was informed there would be a delay in delivery if he wanted to buy them. The whole of Europe was becoming jittery as a result of the posturings of the Austro-German alliance and countries were building up their armed forces. It seemed that large vehicles were high on their list of purchases.

However, on his return to the clinic, Jacob gave Ben a report on his findings. As it was apparent that Ben's mind was on other matters, Jacob promised he would make out a full report for him on their return.

Now, as the three travellers returned to England on the train, Jacob said he would like to remain in London for a couple of days before returning to Ruddlemoor.

'Any special reason?' Ben asked.

'To visit the haulage company I told you about, the one that operates some of the American lorries I'm particularly interested in. They're based in the East End and I'd like to have a look at their lorries before finally deciding what we should go for at Ruddlemoor.'

For a brief moment, Ben's glance flicked to Emma. 'Where will you stay in London?'

Emma was aware of Ben's glance and realised what he was probably thinking. Almost defiantly, she said, 'I've told Jacob that if he doesn't return to Cornwall right away, he can stay at the flat in Dalston Lane.'

'Won't Tessa mind?'

Emma looked at him in surprise, then, visibly upset, said, 'I telephoned the office yesterday evening to tell Tessa I was returning. She wasn't there. One of the women in the office told me she's just been sentenced to another month in prison, for smashing windows in a police station. It seems there's been a campaign throughout London with women slashing important pictures in the galleries. The police arrested one of the Dalston Lane women for damaging a particularly famous painting and Tessa and some of the others demonstrated outside the police station where she was being held. When the police tried to move them on they began throwing half-bricks at the windows. I didn't say anything to you before because I know you have enough to think about right now.'

'I wouldn't argue with that,' Ben said wearily.

What Emma had said was perfectly true. Lily had been particularly upset as the time approached for him to leave her once again. He had thought his efforts to help her come to terms with remaining behind in the clinic had met with success. She had promised to put her full trust in Doctor Bertauld and work with him to help her own recovery, but at the last minute she had dissolved in tears, desperately unhappy.

Ben thought he ought to stay on for a further few days, but Doctor Bertauld insisted he must leave. He assured Ben that once he had gone, Lily would settle down and he could resume the task of effecting a cure for her illness.

Ben had not been entirely convinced that Lily *would* do as he said, but he possessed a great deal of faith in the Swiss doctor.

Bringing himself back to the present, he said, 'If Tessa's not there, why not return to Cornwall until she comes out of prison? Your mother would be pleased to see you.'

'I doubt that,' Emma retorted. 'She'd spend the whole time I was there telling me I should be looking for a husband and not gallivanting around London with a crowd of women who are in prison as often as they're out. I know it's so because that's exactly what she wrote in one of her letters to me.'

Ben gave a faint, weary smile. 'What do you think she would say if I told her I'd left you and Jacob to share a London flat for a couple of nights with no one else in the place?'

'Will you tell her?'

Ben shook his head. 'I have enough trouble on my hands as it is. I have no intention of making more.'

Turning to Jacob, he said, 'Stay in London until you've got things sorted out to your satisfaction – but don't stay too long. Otherwise I'll need to answer to your parents too.'

'I'll be away only for as long as it takes me to check on the lorries used by this transport company. When I come back I'll tell you which lorries I think we should have – and why.'

For some time no further conversation was carried on as each of the three travellers in the carriage was immersed in his or her own thoughts.

Suddenly, Emma asked Ben, 'Did Doctor Bertauld tell you how long Lily might have to remain in his clinic?'

'No. All he said was that it would not be a quick cure and might take many months.'

'There's a German lady who's been in the clinic for a full year,' Emma said. 'Mind you, the nurses told me that she wasn't expected to live when she was admitted. I suppose being alive at all is a bonus for her.'

'Doctor Bertauld told me that Lily's condition is also very serious. That's why he sent for me. He's very concerned indeed about her.'

Aware that she might have been less than tactful, Emma said, hurriedly, 'Yes, but the doctor is confident he can cure her once she truly believes she is going to get well. He told me so himself.'

'He said the same to me. Until last night I believed him. I'd managed to convince Lily she was going to get well. Witnessing the way she was this morning, I'm just not sure of anything any more.'

'You mustn't lose faith, Ben. Lily was very upset because you were leaving. That's quite understandable. The nurses are used to that. They'll be fussing around her right now as though she's the only patient in the clinic, asking her what she's most looking forward to doing when she's fit and well once more. I've watched them doing it with four or five patients during the time I've been here. The German lady I told you about might have been there a year, but I've also seen patients leave after only six months, or thereabouts. So, you see, it's by no means certain that Lily will be away from Cornwall for as long as you think.'

'I hope you're right, Emma,' Ben said wearily. 'I'm not at all happy with the political situation in Europe. Before I left I was talking to a Cornishman whose brother is a military attaché in our embassy in Vienna. He says that the Austro-German alliance is building up its forces at an alarming rate. It already had the largest army in Europe. If it carries on building warships at the present rate, it will probably have a navy as large as Britain by this time next year. The only consolation is that Britain is unlikely to be drawn into any conflict – and Switzerland has a long-standing neutrality agreement.'

Jacob understood nothing of European politics and he said so.

Ben smiled understandingly at him. 'I think you're far better off knowing nothing, Jacob. When you know too much you worry about it, even though it will most likely come to nothing anyway.'

Ben lapsed into silence for only a few moments before the matter uppermost in his mind came to the fore once more. Speaking to no one in particular, he contemplated sadly, 'I wonder what Lily is doing right now?'

6

Ben showed that he was concerned about Tessa's welfare too. Before saying goodbye to Emma at the station he amazed her by giving her the very generous sum of twenty pounds, with the instruction that she should use it to buy especially tempting foods to help Tessa regain her strength and health when she was released from prison.

'Why do you think he did that?' Emma asked Jacob when Ben left them and they began their journey to Dalston Lane.

'Because he feels sorry for her, I expect,' Jacob replied innocently. 'I told him how weak *you* were when *you* came out of Holloway after your hunger strike.'

'As long as that's all it is,' Emma mused.

'What do you mean? What more could there be to it than that? It's Ben's way of showing his gratitude to her, that's all. She was a great help to all of us when we were in Paris. Besides, I think he quite likes her.'

Aware of Tessa's expressed feelings for Ben, it gave Emma much food for thought during the remainder of the journey to Dalston Lane.

Jacob enjoyed his all-too-brief stay in London. His evenings and nights were the happiest times of all, spent in the company of Emma.

During the day he was not far away from her either. The garage of E.W. Rudd was also in London's East End, in nearby Stratford.

He found the lorries owned by the haulage company a fascinating mixture of vehicles. In addition to two American-manufactured Mack lorries, they also had a steam vehicle, a Thorneycroft, four Leylands and a number of lesser-known makes. The owner of the company proved remarkably helpful, giving Jacob access to the company's record books, which showed the performance and relative economy of each lorry.

It took Jacob two days to reach his decision. If Ben agreed, Ruddlemoor would have eight petrol-engined Mack lorries. The London company's records had convinced him they would be the most suitable for work in clay country. Besides, the London haulier had an impressive stock of spare parts, which he said Jacob could call on if his own stock proved insufficient for Ruddlemoor's needs.

On the first evening of their return from France, Jacob and Emma went out together to the street market to stock up the food cupboards in the flat above the suffragettes' office.

As they shopped, Jacob was surprised at how many costermongers recognised Emma. They expressed pleasure at having her back with them.

All of them asked after Tessa too. They had learned of her latest hunger-strike and seemed genuinely worried about the effect it would have on her health.

Although they were surrounded by friendly faces, Jacob was nervous whenever they passed by an alleyway. There was no Manny to take his part if the youthful gang of criminals decided to seek revenge for their earlier humiliation.

But the time in London passed peacefully – and far too quickly. Jacob had hoped their renewed happiness in each other's company might weaken Emma's resolve to remain in London. However, she had not changed her mind. Just as his days were filled with matters that were important to his life as the transport manager for the Ruddlemoor China clay works, so Emma's days were spent totally immersed in the affairs of the Federation to which she belonged.

Had either of them been less committed to what they were doing, there might have been some hope of their relationship moving forward in the manner Jacob wished. As it was, both were equally convinced that what they were doing was of vital importance to the things they believed in most. Because of this, and because they were genuinely in love, their evenings and nights were especially precious to them.

On their last night, when they were in bed together, Jacob made one final effort to persuade Emma to return to Cornwall with him.

Reduced to tears by his pleas, Emma still reiterated her intention to remain in London and fight for the cause of suffragism.

Contrite at having upset her on this, their last night together in London, Jacob held her in his arms until her sobbing ceased. Eventually, she whispered, 'Even if I *did* come back, it wouldn't be like this, Jacob. I would need to return to my home on Bodmin Moor and we'd see no more of each other than we do now.'

Sensing a glimmer of hope, Jacob said eagerly, 'There would be no need for you to return home. If we told Ben that we were to be married as soon as it could be arranged, he would let you stay at Tregarrick until the wedding. We could still see each other every day.'

Her next words dashed his hopes once more. 'I'm not ready for marriage, Jacob – although when we're together like this I know it's still what I want one day – and with you.'

Jacob made no reply. Being with Emma only served to increase the awareness of how much he loved her and wanted to be with her always. He accepted her commitment to the suffragette movement as a just and worthwhile cause, yet he resented the fact that it came between them.

Jacob was a liberal-minded man when judged by the standards of the time. Even so, he had been brought up in an environment where the needs of *men*, not women, were paramount. It was not easy to eradicate completely such universally accepted attitudes.

There was little sleep for either of them that night. When they were not making love, they were clinging tightly to each other and, more than once, Jacob felt her warm tears on his chest. Both were desperately unhappy at the thought of the parting the morning would bring, yet neither was able to compromise.

It would need the intervention of fate to bring their diverging paths together – and fate was about to strike a blow that would change the destiny of the whole world.

7

⁂

The summer of 1914 saw a violent upsurge in suffragette activity. More paintings were slashed, houses owned by opponents of the movement were burned to the ground and windows were broken on a scale not witnessed before.

There was also another determined attempt to acquaint King George V with their grievances at Buckingham Palace, this time by the followers of Emmeline Pankhurst. It became the scene of considerable violence and resulted in more than sixty suffragettes being arrested by the police and chaos in the magistrates court the following morning.

At this time, Tessa was released from Holloway Prison when it was announced publicly that if she remained in prison she intended fasting to the death.

No sooner was Tessa free than Emma was arrested yet again. This time for refusing to pay a fine incurred whilst driving the Dalston Lane Sunbeam.

The policeman who stopped her had recognised the vehicle and he accused her of 'driving furiously'. It was a charge she rigorously denied, but to no avail.

The magistrate fined her the sum of forty shillings. When she announced firmly that she would not pay the fine, she was sent to prison for seven days instead.

On this occasion Emma did not refuse to eat, but none of her companions thought any less of her for it. She had suffered enough during her earlier imprisonment.

While Emma was serving her prison sentence in Holloway, a drama that was seemingly quite remote from life in England was being enacted more than a thousand miles away in Sarajevo, capital of the turbulent provinces of Bosnia-Herzegovina.

A cavalcade of motor cars, travelling through the city, took a wrong turn. In one of the vehicles was Archduke Franz Ferdinand, heir apparent to the Hapsburg empire, and his wife, the Duchess of Hohenburg, who were on a state visit. In the ensuing confusion, their motor car came to a halt alongside Gavrilo Princip, a young Bosnian student. A member of a revolutionary organisation, he had been supplied with a handgun by a militant Serbian terrorist group which was violently opposed to the Habsburg empire.

Taking full advantage of this unexpected opportunity – that many thought more than mere coincidence – Princip pulled out the gun and pointed it towards the royal couple.

A minute later the Duchess was dead, the Archduke lay dying – and the world would never be the same again.

Had Emma even been aware of the incident it would

have meant nothing to her. At the exact moment of Archduke Franz Ferdinand's demise she was anticipating release from her Holloway cell.

The assassination meant little to Jacob, either. He heard about it, but quickly dismissed it from his mind. News of Emma's imprisonment would have affected him far more, but he did not learn of this until long after she had been freed.

The assassinations in Sarajevo provoked no more than a passing shockwave of horror in the remainder of Great Britain. Such an incident was considered to be far too remote to affect the lives of anyone not immediately involved. Britain's island status meant the nation had always been able to remain aloof from happenings on the Continent, if it so chose. Most Britons believed it would always remain so.

With the safety of Lily in mind, Ben had more concern for the uncertainty of the situation. A regular reader of the national newspapers, he had long been aware of the enmities simmering just beneath the surface of European politics. Yet, even to him, the tragic events of 28 June were too remote to personally affect either him or Lily.

He was even more reassured after telephoning Doctor Bertauld. Lily was at last beginning to respond to his treatment. As for the assassination . . . The doctor reminded him that Switzerland was a neutral country. It had always remained aloof of European intrigues and would do so now.

When Ben asked him whether Lily was concerned about the situation, the doctor assured him that although allowed to read magazines, she would not have seen any English-language newspapers. She was probably not aware of what had happened and it would not be an event of sufficient interest for the nurses to gossip about.

For a few weeks, it seemed the optimism that Doctor Bertauld shared with the governments of most of the European powers was justified. Then Austria-Hungary issued a humiliating ten-point ultimatum to Serbia, on whom it laid the blame for the assassination of the heir to the Hapsburg empire.

In a surprisingly humble reply, Serbia agreed to implement all except one of the demands. Other European governments thought Serbia's reply extremely reasonable and placatory.

Germany, Austria-Hungary's closest ally thought so too, but the German government chose not to air its views publicly and so risk embarrassing its friend and neighbour.

Austria-Hungary decided it was not enough for Serbia to humble itself. It needed to be taught a severe lesson. At eleven a.m. on 28 July, Austria-Hungary informed Serbia by telegram that their two countries were now at war.

This unique means of declaring war was followed immediately by the bombardment of Belgrade, the Serbian capital, by the big guns of the Austro-Hungarian army.

Even now the remainder of the world was not particularly perturbed. Such disputes were not entirely uncommon in Europe. The general consensus of opinion was that after the bombardment, the forces of Austria-Hungary would occupy Belgrade and hold it in pledge until satisfactory negotiations had been completed.

This, it was believed, would be sufficient to hold in check Russia, Serbia's patron.

It was not. Over the next few days, events moved in an inexorable manner that left the remainder of Europe floundering in disbelief. Seemingly unable to extricate themselves, other nations were sucked into the maelstrom of a war that would leave the countries of Europe mourning a whole lost generation of their young men.

Russia reacted more speedily than anticipated in support of its ally and hinted it would commence mobilisation unless the army of Austria-Hungary returned within its own borders.

Germany, close ally of Austria-Hungary, warned the Russian government that mobilisation would provoke action on Germany's part and inevitably lead to war.

Despite this stern warning, the Tsar signed an order for Russian mobilisation. This in turn resulted in yet another German ultimatum. Halt all mobilisation immediately or face the consequences.

In truth, Germany was not averse to involvement in such a dispute with its neighbours. Its rulers had long been planning for a war against Russia and, more particularly, against France, Russia's ally.

Not surprisingly, Russia ignored Germany's arrogant ultimatum. Twenty-four hours later, Germany declared war on the great Eastern power.

Germany's long-laid plans swung into action immediately. In a deliberate display of arrogant provocation, the German government demanded that France declare its neutrality in the face of the escalating conflict.

Even before the dignified reply, 'France will act according to her interests', was received in Berlin, hundreds of crowded troop trains were heading eastwards along the highly efficient German rail network.

Their destination was the French border – and beyond.

In a cynical attempt to justify what they believed would be a brief but profitable war, the German High Command had one of its own aircraft drop small bombs on Nuremberg. They then set up a howl of protest, declaring the marauding aircraft to be French.

On 3 August, Germany officially declared war upon France.

Despite the war clouds that were now lowering over the skies of Europe, the British government still refused to believe that full-scale war was inevitable.

Great Britain was a signatory to the pact that guaranteed Belgium's neutrality. Now, when Germany demanded that its troops be allowed free passage through this small and neutral country, which was ill-prepared for war, Britain issued a sharp warning.

Both France and Germany were informed that violation of Belgium's neutrality would compel Great Britain to 'take action'.

Such a warning had sufficed to avert war many years before. The government in London believed it would do so now.

It did not.

On 4 August, German troops began to overrun Belgium, en route to France.

Belatedly, and seemingly in a state of shock, the British government awoke to the full seriousness of the situation.

Germany was informed that if it did not agree by midnight to respect Belgium's neutrality, Great Britain would declare war.

At seven o'clock that evening, the German chancellor scorned the possibility of Great Britain going to war 'just for a scrap of paper'. He had seriously miscalculated the mood of the British government. At five minutes past eleven that night (five minutes past midnight in Berlin), the German ambassador in London was handed Great Britain's declaration of war.

None of the countries could possibly have imagined the consequences of their coldly polite formalities.

Peace would not return to Europe until a huge price had been paid by the participants. Nine million fighting men and tens of thousands of civilians would die in the shell-torn fields of Europe.

The seeds sown by Gavrilo Princip in Sarajevo would yield a grim harvest.

The war would also swiftly lay a finger upon the lives of Ben, Jacob, Tessa and Emma.

8

❧

Even though Ben had been following the situation in Europe, the speed of events took him by surprise.

During the final dramatic days he was in a remote area of Bodmin Moor with a team of geologists, exploring the potential of a new China clay find. When he returned to Ruddlemoor, he learned that Germany had declared war on France, invaded neutral Belgium and that Great Britain had been at war for thirty-six hours.

Ben's immediate concern was for Lily. It was unlikely that Switzerland's neutrality would be violated, but if Lily had learned of the conflict she was bound to be worried about what might be happening in England.

He was also worried about the possibility of France being overrun. Would Germany then turn on Switzerland?

Hurrying home to Tregarrick, Ben learned that in his absence Miriam had been quick to react to the European situation.

More agitated than Ben had ever seen her, she told

him, 'I've tried every few hours to telephone the clinic, but the operator tells me it's impossible to get through. It seems as though all telephone lines in Europe have been reserved for military purposes.'

'We can't leave it at that,' Ben declared. 'We *have* to get through.'

'I knew you'd feel that way. You'll try, of course. You must. But I doubt if you'll be any more successful than I've been. It's as though we've been cast adrift by the rest of the world. Mind you, some folk seem to know what's going on. Colonel Tonks, owner of the Wheal Clements works, for one. He was up here earlier today, looking for you. His son is a captain with the Duke of Cornwall Light Infantry and came home on leave from Ireland only last week. He was recalled yesterday. Your chauffeur was also told to report to his regiment yesterday. Did you know he was an army reservist?'

'He probably told me when I took him on,' Ben replied. 'I'd forgotten. But you were telling me what Colonel Tonks was saying to you . . .'

'That's right, he believes the Cornish regiment is off to France. He should know, I suppose, although I don't see why our soldiers should be involved. This war is none of our business. But according to the newspapers, the army chiefs are saying it will be over by Christmas, so I suppose they're out to make the most of an opportunity for a brief moment of glory.'

'Why did Tonks come here?' Ben's immediate thought was that the colonel's visit must have something to do with the matter that was uppermost in his own mind – the well-being of Lily.

When common sense took over the realised it was

a most improbable explanation. Miriam's next words confirmed it.

'He wants to call an emergency meeting of the Clay Works Owners Association. To discuss the effect the war is likely to have on the industry.'

Ben realised the war was likely to have a profound impact on the China clay industry. Much of its output was shipped abroad, to customers in countries that were now at war with Britain.

Even for those customers in lands friendly towards Britain there would be difficulties. Shipping space would be at a premium. Priority would be given to cargoes of materials vital to the war effort. Those ships that did put to sea carrying China clay ran a very real risk of falling prey to the impressive might of the German navy.

Yet discussion of such matters was not a priority for Ben at this moment. 'There'll need to be a meeting, of course, but Cap'n Bray can stand in for me. The most important thing right now is to bring Lily back home to Cornwall.'

'You mean . . . bring her through Europe?' Miriam looked at her grandson in alarm. 'It's in turmoil! Lily's better off staying where she is. After all, Switzerland is a neutral country.'

'So was Belgium,' Ben pointed out grimly. 'It hasn't stopped the Germans from overrunning the country.'

'You only have to look at a map to see why the Germans invaded Belgium,' Miriam retorted, displaying a surprising knowledge of the geography of Europe. 'It's the back door into France. They have no reason at all to invade Switzerland.'

'Perhaps not,' Ben agreed uncertainly. 'All the same, I won't rest until Lily is safely back home in Tregarrick.

Let's make a start by trying once again to get through to the clinic on the telephone. If we haven't succeeded by this evening, I'll pay a call on Colonel Tonks. His son might be keeping him in touch with what's happening.'

Colonel Tonks was reluctant to give Ben any information about the movements of the First Battalion of the Duke of Cornwall Light Infantry – or even to speak of what he knew about the progress of the war in Europe.

When Ben told him of the difficulty he was having contacting Lily in Switzerland, the colonel said patronisingly, 'Don't worry, my boy, everything is under control. Just have patience . . .'

Ben's temper flared unreasonably. 'Patience is a luxury I can't afford, Colonel. My wife is in a clinic in Switzerland. As far as I can ascertain, war is erupting all around her. If Italy enters the war on Germany's side – as well she might, Switzerland will be cut off from the rest of the world and her neutrality will count for nothing. I came here because I thought you might have some idea of what's happening – not to be fobbed off with platitudes. I intend travelling to Switzerland to bring Lily back. I want to avoid trouble along the way, if I can. I mistakenly thought you might be in a position to help.'

Colonel Tonks was genuinely alarmed. 'You must not attempt to go through France at this time, dear boy. The whole country is in chaos. Besides . . .' Although there was no one else in the room, Colonel Tonks leaned forward and dropped his voice to a confidential whisper. 'I shouldn't be telling you this, but I know you will keep it to yourself. My son and the First Battalion of the Duke of Cornwall Light Infantry are at this very moment embarking in Ireland to join a British Expeditionary Force in France. Within a matter of days there will be a hundred and fifty thousand British soldiers in France. Quite enough to add a much-needed touch of ginger to the French army.'

He made a gesture that was meant to be reassuring. 'Give it a month and the Germans will be pushed back to their own borders – and beyond. They'll be begging for an armistice. Ready to accept whatever terms our government is willing to offer them.'

Colonel Tonks smiled confidently at Ben. 'Bide your time, Benjamin. Nothing will happen to your wife. She is quite safe where she is.'

'That's what the Belgian people thought about their country,' said Ben, repeating what he had said to Miriam. 'We all know what happened there.'

'That is quite different. The Belgians have allowed their army to go to rack-and-ruin. They were ripe to be overrun. Switzerland is very different. They maintain a strong standing army. Indeed, every man in the land is a trained soldier. No government in its right mind would attempt to violate her neutrality – certainly not Germany. They are already fighting on two fronts. They won't want to become involved on a third – and they have no reason to invade Switzerland. Your wife is as safe there as she would be in Cornwall.'

'Thank you, Colonel Tonks, but I can't afford to leave matters to chance. I intend going to Switzerland as soon as I can make the necessary arrangements.'

'I do assure you that it is totally unnecessary, my boy. Our troops will throw the Germans back and the war will be over in a couple of months. By Christmas, certainly. But you must do whatever you think is best. The only thing you must bear in mind is the transport situation in France. They have a great many troops to move to the front – French and English. I doubt if there will be a single scheduled train running for a month or two.'

9

Ben would remember Colonel Tonks' parting words time and time again during the days that followed. It seemed the train and telephone systems in Europe had been handed over to the military and were in utter chaos. It was impossible to put through a telephone call to Switzerland.

Ben realised he was going to have to try to cross the Channel and hope he could make his way to Switzerland. However, before he could plan his next move he was presented with a problem much closer to home. This time by Manny.

Aware of the giant cockney's love of wrestling, Jacob had taken him to watch an exhibition of Cornish wrestling soon after his arrival at Tregarrick. Manny had been enthusiastic about this ancient form of his art and Jacob had arranged for him to be taught the rules.

The big Londoner learned quickly. Within a matter of weeks he had beaten every opponent the clay country could provide.

It was natural that when a local team was chosen to take on the Cornwall constabulary wrestling team, Manny was included.

He emerged from the contest unbeaten, but an alert constable thought there was something about him that was familiar.

Returning to the St Austell police station, Constable Martin leafed through many back copies of the *Police Gazette* before he found what he was seeking. The entry read: 'Wanted by the Metropolitan Police for assault on a police inspector, occasioning actual bodily harm. Emmanuel Hirsch, known as "Manny". Hirsch is a champion wrestler and care should be exercised when effecting an arrest.'

Constable Martin showed the *Police Gazette* to his sergeant, who took constable and gazette to the inspector.

The inspector was a cautious man who was marking time until his pension was due in a few months' time. He pointed out that the *Police Gazette* was many months old.

'True, sir,' the constable agreed. 'But Hirsch was already in Cornwall when the *Gazette* was issued. He's been here ever since.'

'Very well,' the inspector sighed, 'we'd better bring him in. However, in view of the offence for which he's wanted, perhaps it would be better if I didn't come along. He might have an aversion to police inspectors.'

Tapping the *Police Gazette* with a forefinger, he added, 'According to this he's a champion wrestler and likely to prove violent. Do you think he'll cause trouble?'

'He'll be a handful if he does,' Constable Martin replied. 'He forced Constable Perry to retire hurt from their contest in less time than it's taken me to tell you about it.'

Constable Perry weighed seventeen stone and was the Cornwall Constabulary's wrestling champion.

'Then you'd better take half a dozen officers with you. Do we know where Hirsch lives?'

'Yes, he's employed by Mr Retallick, owner of the Ruddlemoor China clay works. He has a flat at his home.'

Thoughts of his impending pension rose to the fore once more and the inspector said, 'We can't go *there* to arrest him. Any other ideas?'

'Yes, sir,' Constable Martin said. 'There's a junior wrestling competition taking place at Tywardreath in two nights' time. Hirsch is bound to be there.'

'Very well. Sergeant, send for the warrant. When we have it, take Constable Martin and five others to Tywardreath and bring Hirsch in – but try to do it without violence, you understand? I want no trouble if it can possibly be avoided.'

When the junior wrestling competition took place, Manny, Jane and Jacob were at Tywardreath. They shouted encouragement to a young wrestler, the son of a Ruddlemoor shift captain. Suddenly Jacob became aware of a number of uniformed policemen in the crowd.

Coming from various directions, they were edging their way through the crowd and appeared to be moving in their direction.

It was not unusual to see one policeman at such an event, but looking about him, Jacob counted no fewer than six, plus a sergeant.

He could think of no reason to be alarmed. The abortive police raid on the Dalston Lane suffragette office had happened so long ago Jacob had forgotten it.

However, his unease was justified. Suddenly pushing him aside, the policemen surrounded Manny. Confronting him, the sergeant said, 'Emmanuel Hirsch, I have a warrant for your arrest. I'm taking you to St Austell police station. From there you will be taken to London.'

Manny looked about him for a way of escape. There was none.

A constable took hold of one of his arms, but Manny shook him off violently and the policeman stumbled back in to the crowd.

'Don't start anything, Manny. Go with them. I'll tell Ben Retallick . . .'

Jacob was shaken off as easily as the constable, but now Jane rushed at Manny and flung her arms about him.

'No, Manny! Don't make it worse. Don't fight them.'

She succeeded where Jacob had failed. Chest heaving, Manny stood glaring about him, but he was not fighting now.

'Put the handcuffs on him.' The order came from the sergeant.

'There's no need for that,' Jacob protested. 'He's not going to cause any trouble now.'

'Mind your own business,' the sergeant retorted. 'Otherwise you'll find yourself in trouble too.'

'It's *you* who'll find trouble if you don't listen to what he's saying . . .'

A black-bearded man, only slightly less broad-shouldered than Manny, had come up to stand beside

Jacob. Behind him were more well-muscled men. All were members of the Cornish wrestling fraternity.

The police sergeant was not a stupid man. He had succeeded in arresting Manny. If there was trouble now, he and his men would come off second best and he would receive no support from the inspector for his actions.

'All right, Constable. Put the handcuffs away.'

Pointing a finger at Manny, he added, 'But at the first sign of trouble from you they'll go on, do you understand?'

As Manny was led away to the police vehicle which had been left unnoticed around the corner, Jane turned to Jacob. Close to tears, she asked, 'What are we going to do?'

'We'll speak to Ben Retallick. He'll think of something.'

Although they got a lift for part of the way in the cab of a lorry belonging to another clay works, it was almost dark by the time they reached Tregarrick.

In Ben's study, the clay works owner listened to the story told to him by Jacob and the tearful Jane.

He had spent another frustrating day trying to alternately telephone Switzerland and obtain information about train times in France. He had not been successful with either.

It was almost a relief to have something else to do. He first telephoned the police station at St Austell, where Manny was being held. The inspector in charge of the station stated that nothing could be done at such a late hour. In the morning he intended contacting London for an escort to take Manny there.

Ben could have left it at this, instead, he tried to telephone the solicitor who had represented Emma at her first London trial. But he was frustrated once again that day. There was no reply from the solicitor.

Still not content to leave matters, Ben put in a call to Commander Trethewey. Explaining the situation, Ben pointed out that Manny was now a trusted and well-liked employee.

Although it was quite late, the London policeman said he would make some enquiries. However, he warned Ben not to expect to hear from him until the next morning.

Putting down the telephone, Ben repeated what Commander Trethewey had told him.

Jane was upset that Manny would be kept in a police cell overnight before being returned to London the next day. 'When will I see him again?'

'I'm afraid I can't answer that, Jane. It depends very much on the court.'

Ben did not tell her what Commander Trethewey had told him when he explained that Manny had been arrested on a charge of causing actual bodily harm to the police inspector. The policeman had warned that Manny faced up to five years in prison if found guilty.

'I think you'd both better have a drink,' he said.

'You and Jacob have one,' Jane said. 'I'm going to my room.'

Jacob had been told earlier by Jane how worried Ben was about Lily. When she had left the room, he asked Ben if there had been any news of her.

'None,' Ben said, bitterly. 'I've never felt so frustrated in all my life. I just can't get through to Switzerland. The only solution seems to be to go there myself to find out what's happening, but I can get no information about the French railways. All the railway company in London will say is that services in France are disrupted due to the current situation.'

'Why don't you forget all about the railways and take your car?'

'I'd never get it across the Channel. That's another thing the railway company has told me. All cross-channel services have been temporarily suspended by order of the government.' He made a gesture of helplessness. 'The whole world seems to have disintegrated into utter chaos.'

'You're a clay owner. You needn't be reliant upon the cross-channel ferries. We have a French boat coming in to Charlestown next week. She'll be loading for two days, then sailing for Brest. I'm sure the captain would be willing to take your car as deck cargo. It would mean you'd have further to drive than if you took the normal route, but how you got to Switzerland would be in your own hands.'

Ben looked startled. 'That's a very clever idea, Jacob. I should have thought of it myself. The only problem is, I've lost my chauffeur – and I'm not the world's best driver.'

'You don't have to be. I'll come with you if you'd like me to. We could share the driving and get there much quicker . . .'

Before Ben could reply, the telephone rang. He picked it up hurriedly.

'Speaking . . .' There was a long silence and then Ben said, 'I'm sorry to hear that . . . But it's a great relief to me, but . . . Oh! So what happens now? You will . . . ? When?'

Listening to the one-sided conversation and observing Ben's obvious relief, Jacob thought the call must be from Switzerland, giving news of Lily.

'I just can't thank you enough – and I'm grateful to you for ringing me back tonight. It will relieve all our minds.'

When Ben hung up the telephone receiver, Jacob asked eagerly, 'Is it news of Lily? Is she all right?'

Ben's expression of relief faded. 'No. But it's good news about Manny. The inspector he is supposed to have assaulted died of a heart attack a fortnight ago. The warrant for Manny's arrest should have been withdrawn, but it must have got overlooked. Commander Trethewey is telephoning St Austell police station, telling them to release Manny. I'll go and tell Jane. No doubt she'll want to go and meet him. At least it means she'll be able to sleep tonight.'

'I'll go with her to the police station and then carry on home. I've had enough excitement for one night.'

'I'm sure you have,' Ben said. 'But I'm glad we've got this mess cleared up, at least.' He paused in the doorway. 'Did you mean what you said about travelling to Switzerland with me?'

'Of course!'

'Thank you, Jacob. We'll discuss it again tomorrow, and you can tell me more about this.'

10

For days, English newspapers had been carrying reports of fierce fighting in the Province of Alsace, close to the Swiss border. It was less than a hundred miles from the clinic where Lily was a patient.

It was such newspaper reports that convinced Ben the course of action suggested by Jacob was the right one.

The railway companies were still unable to give any information about trains on the Continent other than, 'All scheduled services have been suspended.'

He told Miriam he was leaving for Switzerland, only the evening before he was due to sail on the clay-carrying ship.

'How will you get to France? You've said yourself that all journeys across the Channel have been stopped for the time being by the government.'

Ben had made his announcement over the evening meal at Tregarrick. Miriam was sceptical about his ability to get to France, let alone plan to cross that beleaguered country in order to reach Switzerland.

'They might prevent cross-channel travellers, but ships are still sailing from Cornwall to French ports. It was Jacob who gave me the idea. He told me we're loading one right now, at Charlestown.'

'A clay boat? How will you get through France once you arrive there? You've said yourself the French railways are in a state of chaos.'

'I won't rely on the railways. I've arranged with the captain of the clay ship to take the Hotchkiss on board. When we get there I'll drive through France.'

His statement filled Miriam with dismay. If the newspapers were to be believed, the situation in France was one of utter and dangerous confusion. They reported that the French army had been heavily defeated on the Belgian border and had been repulsed in Alsace and Lorraine. The latest news was that the French government was preparing to evacuate Paris, leaving the capital city to be occupied by the Germans.

Yet despite such grim news, Ben had just announced that he intended driving from one end of the country to the other in a motor car!

Miriam expressed her thoughts in a characteristically forceful fashion. 'It's a ridiculous idea, Ben! Especially as the chauffeur has been called up by the army. You don't drive very well. You've told me so yourself, many times.'

'I've spoken to Jacob. He's coming with me. He's a very competent driver now.'

'You can't ask him to put his life at risk on your behalf. You pay him well – but not *that* well.'

'I'm not forcing him to come. It's his own idea. Anyway, we're not going to France to fight a war. I'll avoid all the dangerous areas – it shouldn't be too difficult.'

'You don't know what's happening there any more than I do. There's bound to be a breakdown of law and order in such a situation.'

She saw that her words had done nothing to change his mind and shrugged in resignation. 'I might as well have saved my breath. You'll do whatever it is you've set your mind on doing, the same as all the other Retallick men I've known. But if you're hell-bent on running yourself into trouble, then take Manny with you. He's the next best thing to having your own private army.'

'That, at least is a good idea,' Ben agreed. 'He owes me a very large favour – although I doubt if I'll need to remind him of it.'

The journey to Brest took fourteen hours. When the three passengers from Cornwall arrived at the busy French port, Jacob supervised the unloading of the Hotchkiss. It was swung ashore on a sling, suspended from a giant dockside crane.

There were a few times when Jacob thought the motor car would be swung against a pile of cargo from another ship waiting to be taken away. Fortunately for Anglo-French relations, his shouted warnings were as unintelligible to the crane driver as were the Frenchman's comments to Jacob.

Once outside the port, Ben expected them to encounter a scene of panic and chaos in Brittany's largest city. Instead, everything was as calm as in any of the towns and cities they had left behind on the English side of the Channel.

It was the same story in every part of the country they drove through en route for the Swiss border. Jacob had brought along a plentiful supply of petrol, but it proved unnecessary. They were able to purchase all they required along the way.

Because Ben and Jacob were sharing the driving, they needed to make only two night stops along the way. The only danger they encountered were animals straying on to the indifferent French roads during the hours of darkness.

Ben felt decidedly foolish at having brought Jacob and Manny on a journey that now seemed to have been quite unnecessary. However, Lily was delighted to see him. It was also apparent from her surprise that she had not even considered the possibility that she might be caught up in the war raging just across the Swiss border.

'We have a patient here whose husband is a German general,' she explained. 'He's spoken to Doctor Bertauld and assured him there is no question of Germany not honouring Switzerland's neutrality. The doctor has been wonderful, by the way. He comes around every day and assures us that we have no cause for concern.'

She reached out and squeezed his hand. 'But it's wonderful to know you care so much – and to see you again. I'm able to give you some marvellous news, too, Ben. Doctor Bertauld says I have turned a very important corner and am beginning to get better – and he's right too! I can see it myself whenever I look in a mirror and I *feel* better. It's so exciting, Ben! Can you see a difference?'

Ben could, and he said so.

Lily was well on the road to recovery – but she still had a long way to go. After Ben had been in her room, chatting to her for an hour, a nurse came to say it was time for Lily to rest.

Ben left Lily's room with the promise that he would remain at the clinic for a few days and would spend as much time with her as the staff would allow.

Outside, in the corridor, the nurse told him that Doctor Bertauld wished to speak to him.

In the doctor's office, which was as neat and clean as the remainder of the clinic, he asked Ben why he had arrived so unexpectedly and without giving him prior notice.

Ben explained about the alarm in Britain at news received there of setbacks being suffered by the French in the war in Europe.

'I have tried for more than a week to put through a telephone call to you, here at the clinic. It is impossible. It all added to the impression we have of utter chaos in France.'

'You have driven through France, I understand. Did you find the confusion you had anticipated?'

Ben shook his head. 'No. There seemed to be far fewer young men around than usual, but otherwise all appears normal.'

'And so it is. At least, in the east of the country. To the west and north of Paris . . . ?' Hands and shoulders expressed a gesture of despair. 'Nobody knows.'

'I thought there was heavy fighting closer to the Swiss border. In Alsace?'

'That is correct, there *was*. The French army attacked German-held positions and were repulsed. There is little fighting there now. I can, of course, appreciate your concern for your wife, but what was your *purpose* in coming here?'

'I came to take Lily home, to England.'

'Is this still your intention?'

'I'm not sure now,' Ben admitted uncertainly. 'I'd be far happier if she were at home in Cornwall.'

Placing his palms flat on the desk in front of him, Doctor Bertauld leaned closer to Ben. 'If you take your wife from here now, she will be dead before the end of a year. Leave her here and you will be able to take home a well woman within half that time.'

Straightening up, the Swiss doctor leaned back in his chair. 'Your wife has taken the first step along the road to recovery. It is a very important step, but it is a long road. Will you allow her to continue on her way? Or will you make her retrace that single step? The choice is yours, Mr Retallick – but think hard about it. You are choosing between life and death.'

11

Ben and his two companions remained at the Swiss clinic for nine days. This was long enough for Ben to recognise for himself the improvement that Doctor Bertauld had wrought in Lily.

Although she was desperately lacking in stamina and still painfully thin, there were moments when Ben caught glimpses of the zest for life that Lily had lost as her illness became progressively worse.

For the first time since bringing Lily to the Swiss clinic, Ben really began to believe that Doctor Bertauld *was* effecting a cure. In his more honest moments, he admitted to himself that he had brought Lily to Switzerland as a last resort, more in desperation than in any real hope she would be cured.

Now, at last, he allowed himself to believe she would one day be a well woman again.

He knew he could not take her away from the clinic. During his days in Switzerland, Ben had also been able to build up a much clearer picture of what was happening in Europe. Not that anyone seemed to know *exactly* what was happening to the progress of the war.

All that was known for certain was that Germany was fighting a bloody war on two main fronts. Against Russia in the east and France in the west.

However, fighting in the vicinity of Switzerland's borders had died down for the time being. Both sides seemed content to pull back and lick their wounds.

By all accounts, the fighting had been fierce with casualties on both sides being horrifically heavy. But Swiss territory had never been seriously threatened.

It seemed the reassurance given by the high-ranking husband of Doctor Bertauld's German patient was fully justified.

Another of Ben's misgivings had also been resolved. It was certain that Italy's neutrality would hold for the time being. Indeed, it was rumoured that if Italy *did* join the war, it would be on the side of Britain and France. Should this happen, it would be advantageous to both sides to have a neutral, buffer country on their borders. Lily should be perfectly safe.

When his visit came to an end, Ben did not find it difficult to convince Lily that she must stay and allow Doctor Bertauld to continue his treatment. She was quite willing to make sacrifices if they would contribute to her long-term recovery.

As a concession to her improved state of health, Lily was allowed to sit out on the balcony and wave farewell to her husband and the others as they drove away along the long, winding drive.

Jacob was driving for the first leg of the journey, with Ben seated in the passenger seat alongside him.

When the clinic had passed from view and the immediate emotion of parting had passed, Ben turned to speak to Manny.

'Well, how did you enjoy Switzerland?'

'It's just great. Everywhere is so beautiful.'

Manny was enthusiastic in his praise of the country they were just leaving. He had spent much of the time there taking long walks in the surrounding country-side.

'I've heard all about mountains, of course, but I never thought they'd be so *high*! It's a pity that no one outside the clinic spoke English, though.'

Jacob smiled. He had accompanied Manny on a few of his walks and seen the looks some of the local Swiss girls had given the giant Londoner. He thought that had Jane known, she would have enjoyed greater peace of mind knowing about the language barrier that existed between Manny and the Swiss girls.

'Are we going back the same way?' Manny asked a few minutes later.

'No.' Ben had discussed the return route with Jacob the previous evening. 'If we returned to Brest we'd have to take a chance finding a ship travelling to England – and one with a captain who'd be willing to carry the car on board. I've talked it over with Jacob and we've decided to go through Paris and head for one of the Channel ports. Once there we can be pretty certain of getting the car taken across to England.'

Manny was alarmed. 'What about the fighting close to Paris?'

'I doubt whether it's anything like as serious as we

believed it to be when we left England,' Jacob replied. 'If you remember, we thought the whole of France was going to be chaotic, yet we saw no sign of it when we drove down from Brest.'

'The way things are in Switzerland would appear to confirm that,' Ben agreed. 'I thought the people here would feel threatened by Germany. Instead, everyone seems to be ignoring the war. To be honest, I feel rather foolish that I made such a fuss about coming here. I believe we'll probably find things in Paris much the same when we get there. Colonel Tonks was probably right. The war will be over well before Christmas. Things will go back to normal again and we'll look back on this as nothing more than a happy little jaunt.'

12

❦

Ben's confidence that the talk of war had been exaggerated was shaken somewhat when the trio from Cornwall stopped for the night in the village of Sauvigny, on the banks of the River Rhoin.

Just north of Beaune, the city at the heart of Burgundy wine-producing country, vineyards stretched for miles in all directions. There were many workers to be seen among the vines – but all were either women or children.

Ben and his companions found accommodation at a village café, where a lame proprietor did what was required of him in a surly manner – until they came up with one of the few French words they spoke between them. '*Anglais.*'

It was as though they had suddenly discovered a password. There was considerable excitement too among the customers at the café, all of whom were men of advanced years.

For some inexplicable reason they all clamoured around, wanting to shake hands with the three Englishmen. Meanwhile, drinks appeared in front of them, for which the café owner would accept no money.

None of the Frenchmen spoke English. After a frustrating few minutes of trying to converse, a young servant girl was summoned from the kitchen and sent off on an errand. Before she left the café, she dropped a shy curtsy as she passed by the bewildered *Anglais*.

Some minutes later the servant girl returned, accompanied by a pretty young woman in her mid-twenties. She was the village schoolteacher and had been summoned because of her knowledge of English.

Her command of the language was perhaps not as comprehensive as she would have the villagers believe, but her great charm more than compensated for her limited vocabulary.

Introducing herself as 'Denise', she was able to explain that everyone in France was appreciative that Britain alone among the nations of the world had sent her army to stand alongside French soldiers to repel the German invaders.

The old men also wished to know what the three Englishmen were doing in their small village.

Ben's reply caused problems to the translator, but when a gust of sympathy swept through the room it was evident she had grasped the situation and passed on the information.

Ben then commented on the absence of young men at the inn, and said he had seen none working in the fields.

This caused tears to spring to the eyes of the young

schoolteacher and it was a while before she regained sufficient control to speak.

'The young men . . . all have gone to war. Many will not return. Already . . .' She counted on her fingers and held up six of them to emphasise what she was saying. 'Already six men have been killed or hurt. My own brother, he is . . .'

She struggled unsuccessfully to find the word she wanted and said instead, 'My brother, he cannot be seen.'

'He's missing,' Ben said. 'I am very sorry.'

She made an unhappy gesture. 'We did not want this war.'

One of the men in the room put a question to them and the young schoolteacher translated. 'They would like to know where you go from here?'

'To Paris, and then England.'

The translation into French provoked a babble of voices in which the word 'Paris' was repeated several times. When Jacob asked her what they were saying, the schoolteacher said, 'The Germans too would like to be in Paris, but every man in France, no matter young or old, will die first.'

Ben asked her about the situation in Paris and Denise passed on the question.

It was apparent, even before the vague translation, that they knew no more than he had learned in Switzerland.

Then a question came from one of the old men, asking where in England they lived.

When Ben said 'Cornwall', there was another surge of excitement and more drinks were placed in front of the bewildered trio.

Then one of the men produced a letter from his pocket

and brought it to the schoolteacher, all the while talking excitedly and repeatedly jabbing at the letter with a forefinger.

The schoolteacher scanned the letter then said, 'The letter is from this man's daughter. She is a . . . a nurse? She is at a hospital in Paris and many soldiers from Cornwall are in her hospital. She says they are from the . . . the Duke of Cornwall Light Infantry.'

'Yes, that's our regiment,' Ben said. 'I heard they were on their way to France. It sounds as though they have been heavily involved in the fighting.'

'This is a sad letter, M'sieur. She speaks of one soldier. So young. He . . . died.'

The sad news affected the schoolteacher. Tears rolled down her cheeks.

Catching the café owner's eye, Jacob indicated the glass in front of him, then pointed to the young woman.

The Frenchman lifted a bottle from the shelf behind the bar counter, half filled a tumbler with what appeared to be Cognac. He handed it to the schoolteacher with an order that she drink it and she took a very large swig.

The sight of Jacob pummelling her back as she fought to regain her breath managed to dispel the gloom that had settled over the room. Now all the men began talking again at the same time.

The Frenchmen proved deeply appreciative of the fact that British soldiers had crossed the Channel to fight alongside their own men in defence of the French homeland.

During the course of the evening, other elderly men from the village came to the café to gravely shake the hands of the three Englishmen.

The welcoming did not cease even when they sat down to a meal, shared with Denise.

It was very late before they were able to plead an early start in the morning and take leave of their warm and generous host and his friends.

Now they were forced to submit to an embarrassingly warm farewell from the emotional and slightly drunk young schoolteacher before making their way to their rooms.

Even this was not the end of their reign as village celebrities. When they resumed their journey the next morning, the entire population of the village – old men, women, children, and the schoolteacher – turned out to wave them on their way.

Sadly, the warm glow that Ben, Jacob and Manny felt as they left Sauvigny behind would be extinguished before they reached Paris.

13

They began meeting French civilians fleeing south and westward when they were still many miles from Paris. There were families on foot and others travelling in every conceivable type of vehicle. All were burdened with their most precious possessions.

As Paris drew nearer, so more and more refugees were encountered. It seemed people were not only fleeing from those rural areas being overrun by the Germans – many were from Paris itself.

Then, when Jacob estimated they were no more than thirty miles from the French capital, they began to encounter French troops. Heading northwards in large numbers, they brought all other traffic to a halt as they passed.

At one crossroads the Hotchkiss was at a standstill, its occupants waiting for yet another straggling column of soldiers to cross the road in front of them. Suddenly, to their astonishment, they saw a company of British soldiers heading in the same direction as their French counterparts.

Men of the West Surrey Regiment, they were marching along, singing as they went, looking as smart as if they had come straight from the parade ground.

When Ben hailed them in English, their captain brought the company to a halt. Coming across to the Hotchkiss, he enquired what three English civilians were doing so close to a battle area.

After explaining his reason for being in France, Ben said, 'We haven't been able to find out anything at all about the war. The village where we stayed last night is mourning the loss of a number of its young men killed in action, but they didn't have any idea where the fighting is taking place.'

'That's hardly surprising,' the captain informed him. 'The Germans have been advancing through France at an alarming rate. They've covered something like seventy-five miles in ten days, pushing us and the French back almost to the gates of Paris.'

Calling out an order for his company to fall out for a few minutes, he turned back to Ben. 'But this is as far as they are going to get. My company is on its way to reinforce the battalion and there are more of us on the way. The French too are building up their army about Paris. No one has dared talk yet of taking the offensive against the Germans, but that's what's going to happen – and soon. When it does, we'll push them all the way back to Germany.'

'But what if they get to Paris before you're ready to begin this offensive?' Ben was alarmed at news of the speed of the German advance.

He also found it difficult to comprehend the casual

manner of the English officer who spoke of 'driving the Germans back'. It was quite apparent the armies of France and Britain had been unable to prevent them advancing this far.

'They won't,' the captain replied cheerfully. 'You'll understand why not when you see the build-up of the French army around Paris. There are thousands of our own troops arriving in France every day now, too. The Germans are going to wish they'd never started this war.'

Ben was not convinced, even when he watched the company march on their way with a definite swagger in their step. He felt the British officer was being unduly optimistic.

This view was reinforced when the Hotchkiss and its occupants entered Paris. The streets of the city that was reputed to be the most exciting in the world were unnaturally quiet. Many of the houses and most of the shops were closed and shuttered.

When they drove past one of Paris's many railways stations, they saw a sight Ben hoped the British army captain would never witness.

A train carrying wounded soldiers from the battlefield had just arrived. Hundreds of men with shattered bodies were being off-loaded.

The Hotchkiss was brought to a halt by the raised arm of a *gendarme* as a number of vehicles conveying wounded soldiers left the station.

Very few of the vehicles were actual ambulances. There were cars, vans – even flat-bed open lorries. All were crammed with as many wounded men as could be carried.

In addition, there were many walking wounded.

Men with bandaged heads, arms and legs. Too badly wounded to fight on, but able to walk and so need not take up valuable space at the expense of more seriously wounded men.

It was a pitiful sight and one that seemed to particularly move Manny. 'What will happen to them now?' he asked, as the *gendarme* waved the Hotchkiss on and they overtook a group of heavily bandaged and dejected French soldiers.

'Those who are too badly wounded to fight again will return home,' Ben replied. 'The ones who recover will be sent back to the front.'

'I don't think I'd like to be a soldier,' Manny declared unhappily. 'I don't know which would be worse, doing *that* to someone or having them do it to you.' He nodded his head in the direction of a man who waved to them as they passed. The man's bandaged hand was clearly devoid of fingers.

Jacob thought it strange that a man who had earned his living as a wrestler should be so sensitive, but he was not particularly surprised. Emma had said more than once that Manny was a big softy at heart.

For the next few minutes, Jacob's thoughts were far removed from the war in France as he remembered happier moments spent with Emma.

When the trio reached the Hotel Crillon, they discovered it was being run by a much-reduced staff and was almost empty of guests.

However, the effusive manager was still in charge and swiftly made it clear *why* he was manager of one of Paris's top hotels. He recognised Ben immediately and asked after Lily.

He apologised profusely for having no porters available

to carry their suitcases, but promised he would perform the task himself, once he had shown them to their rooms.

'That's all right, you don't have to do that,' Manny said. 'I'll take 'em up. It's no trouble.' So saying, he gathered up all the luggage, tucking a heavy suitcase under each arm and beamed at the dapper Frenchman.

'Magnificent!' the manager said admiringly. 'What would I not give to have two such men working here. Instead . . .'

He gave a gesture of despair as a man whose age must have totalled more than the combined ages of the three Englishman passed through the foyer.

Dressed in a uniform that had been tailored for a larger body, he carried a tray, upon which a number of cups and saucers rattled alarmingly.

Suddenly, drawing himself up to his full height, which was on a level with Manny's second rib, the manager declared, 'I must not complain. If our armies – those of Britain and France – can turn the Germans back from Paris, no sacrifice will have been too much. Not even life itself.'

It soon transpired that a shortage of staff was not the only problem facing the hotel. Food too was at a premium. An aged waiter explained the dull menu by informing them there were armies to be fed.

When the meagre meal was over, Ben said he thought he knew where they might find reasonable food and a more cheerful atmosphere.

With so little traffic on the roads he had no difficulty finding the alleyway where Henri's café was situated – but it was closed and shuttered, with no sign of life anywhere in the building.

As they drove away from the café, disappointed, they reached the entrance to a narrow street which Ben recognised as the one where Tessa had once lived.

This was a seedy area, but livelier than the centre of Paris. It was probable that the occupants owned little of value so had less fear of losing their possessions to an army of occupation. Besides, where would they go?

Ben stopped the motor car opposite the house. Pointing to the first floor, he said, 'You see that window up there? That's where Tessa lived.'

If Jacob was surprised that Ben should know of Tessa's room in this run-down part of Paris, he did not show it.

However, although much of Paris life was temporarily disrupted, there were some aspects of it that were not.

A curtain on the second floor of the house had twitched when the unfamiliar sound of a motor-car engine filled the narrow street. While the three men were still talking a woman appeared at the door.

It was the woman who had once passed Ben on the stairs and who lived in a room on the floor above the one where Tessa had lived.

Swinging her hips in an exaggerated manner, she walked across to the vehicle and began talking to them in French.

Ben smiled and replied in English, 'I'm sorry, but you're wasting your time. We don't speak French.'

Far from being discouraged by Ben's words, the Frenchwoman clapped her hands in delight. 'You are English! My favourite men are from England. For you, I have a special price. Come up to my room and have a drink with me, first.'

Still smiling, Ben shook his head. 'Sorry, we are not stopping. I just came this way because a friend used to live in the same house as you.'

The woman peered more closely at Ben. 'But of course! We once met on the stairs! Ah, she does not live here any more – but she came to see me only yesterday.'

Shaking his head, Ben said, 'I don't think we can be talking about the same person . . .'

'Yes! Tessa. We had a drink together and talked of when she lived here.'

'Tessa was in Paris?' Ben still believed the prostitute was mistaken. 'What was she doing here?'

'Not *was*, but *is*. She is very brave, that one. She is driving an ambulance, bringing wounded soldiers from the fighting to a hospital, here in Paris. Sometimes the Germans shoot at her too, I believe.'

'Which hospital does she bring the wounded men to? Is there any particular one?'

'It is one that has been opened by people from England. Everyone who is still in Paris is talking of it. All the surgeons are women!'

'Where is this hospital?'

As he asked the question, Ben was aware of the quizzical look Jacob was giving him. Ben knew he was taking far too keen an interest in Tessa's presence in Paris.

He told himself he was only concerned for the well-being of a friend.

'It is at the Hotel Claridge, M'sieur. In the Champs Elysées.'

14

The hospital situated in the Hotel Claridge had been open only a few days. When the doctors and nurses arrived from England, workmen were still busy carrying out the alterations necessary to convert the magnificent salons into hospital wards.

To add to the problems of the incoming hospital staff, the upper storeys of the hospital–hotel were occupied by Belgian refugees who had fled from their German-occupied homeland.

However, after almost superhuman work by doctors, nurses and orderlies – assisted by the Belgians – the still-grand Paris hotel was now a fully functioning hospital.

Every part of the hotel had been adapted for the staff's needs. The luxurious ladies' cloakroom, with its useful facilities, including hot water, had been converted into a highly efficient operating theatre, which was in use day and night.

The whole building was a scene of bustle – and human suffering.

When Ben drove the Hotchkiss with its two passengers up to the front door, three ambulances, driven by American volunteers had just arrived.

Stretchers were being unloaded from the over-crowded vehicles and left, with their wounded occupants, on the pavement, while more serious casualties were rushed directly to the operating theatre.

The wounded soldiers were all British. It shocked Ben and the others to see the state they were in. Bloody bandages were much in evidence and the khaki uniforms worn by the men were muddy and torn.

One man on a stretcher pleaded with Jacob to light a cigarette for him. Both his arms were bandaged from shoulders to fingertips. Jacob obliged, and as he held the cigarette to the wounded man's lips, he said, 'I recognise your accent, friend. Where in Cornwall are you from?'

'Mevagissey,' the delighted man said. 'You're from Cornwall too?'

Jacob nodded, observing that one of the soldier's feet was wrapped in a heavy, bloody bandage too. 'I work at Ruddlemoor, just outside St Austell.'

'I know it well. My wife comes from there!'

Suddenly the horrors of war fell away. For a few brief moments the soldier was no longer an anonymous, khaki-clad casualty caught up in the game of war being played by the generals of the warring countries. He was once more a *man*. Loved by his immediate family and respected by his neighbours.

Then, uninvited, memories of the incident that had resulted in his wounds flooded back; he was the sole survivor of his platoon. The young man began to shake

with shock and fear – a luxury soldiers could not afford
to indulge in when caught up in the full fury of battle.

Alarmed, Jacob said, 'I'll be returning to Cornwall in a
day or two. Can I pass on a message to your family?'

With a visible effort, the soldier regained his composure and gave Jacob a name and address before he
was carried inside the hospital by two women orderlies.

Meanwhile, Ben had made his way inside the hospital. Here he asked a receptionist if she knew where he
might find Tessa Wren.

'I don't think I know her,' the receptionist replied.
'Does she work here?'

'I've just met someone who told me she's driving an
ambulance that brings wounded soldiers here.

The receptionist said immediately, 'Yes, of course.
The suffragette! She set off for the battle area first
thing this morning. She hasn't come back yet. We're
beginning to worry about her. Our own soldiers have
been involved in some very heavy fighting. There are a
great many casualties, with not a fraction of the number
of ambulances needed to bring them here to us.'

She paused to reply to a query, spoken in French by a
woman bearing a number of bags loaded with supplies,
a gift from a Paris women's group. After directing the
woman to the hospital kitchens, the receptionist turned
back to Ben.

'The French idea is to gather all the wounded in and
around railway stations. When a train comes through
they load them all on board and take them to any part
of the country to which the train might be going, in the
hope there will be a hospital to take them. If there isn't,
they wait for another train to take them somewhere else.
It's an appalling state of affairs.'

Ben expressed agreement with the receptionist's assessment of the situation, then asked, 'Where exactly is the fighting taking place?'

The English receptionist frowned. 'I don't know, but it's somewhere to the east of Paris – and getting closer. If you listen on a still night you can hear the guns. I believe some of the suburbs have been shelled, but I can't give you an exact spot. I doubt if the military can either.'

Ben returned to the others and told them of his conversation with the receptionist. As they drove away from the hospital, Jacob asked, 'What are we going to do now?'

'I don't know. We'll go back to the hotel and think about it. I would like to speak to Tessa. To ask what she's doing, and what's going on here.'

The men travelled in silence for a few minutes, and as they approached the Hotel Crillon Ben said, 'I know it sounds foolish and there's very little I can do if I remain here, yet by leaving I feel I'm running away from something.'

He halted the car outside the main entrance of the hotel and remained in the driving seat for a few minutes more. 'If I return to Cornwall right away I'll feel I'm turning my back on all the horrors that are taking place here. Acting as though nothing is happening. As though I'm somehow failing those men we saw back there, who've been terribly maimed. It would be failing myself too. It's difficult to explain.'

'I *do* understand,' Jacob agreed. 'It's something I feel too, but short of joining the army ourselves, what can we do?'

It was a question that was answered, for Ben at least,

when they entered the hotel. The manager was in the foyer, talking to a uniformed *gendarme*.

The manager hurried to meet them, followed more slowly by the *gendarme*. 'M'sieur Retallick, this officer is here with an impossible request . . .'

The *gendarme*, with a brief nod of his head in Ben's direction, interrupted the manager's outburst. In impeccable English, he said, 'M'sieur, the German army is no more than twenty-five miles away – and advancing. But General Gallieni, the military governor of Paris, believes they have over-extended themselves and the time is right to strike them – and to strike hard. Every available soldier is being rushed to the battle-front. It is necessary to use all means of transport. All the Paris taxi-cabs and every motor car I have been able to find are now on their way to the front, carrying soldiers. Your country and mine are allies. We will win or lose this war together – and you have a motor car . . .' His gesture suggested no further explanation was necessary.

'It is at your disposal,' Ben said, immediately. 'How do I collect the soldiers, and where do I take them?'

'Thank you.' The *gendarme* executed a shallow bow. 'I will take you to the soldiers. As for your destination, you will not lose your way. Every vehicle leaving Paris is heading for the battle-front.'

'Is there anything we can do while you're away?'

Jacob asked the question of Ben, but it was Manny who provided an answer.

'I'd like to go back to the hospital. I could help with carrying wounded soldiers in, and things.'

'That's a very good idea,' Jacob agreed. To Ben, he said, 'Good luck. You'll know where to find us when you return.'

15

The outbreak of the war made an immediate impact on the activities of the suffragette movement. It also caused a rift in their ranks that would never be healed.

Immediately war was declared, Emmeline Pankhurst abandoned the suffragette campaign waged by the Women's Social and Political Union. She called on all suffragettes to use their talents in support of the war effort.

In response to this 'responsible attitude', the Home Secretary ordered the immediate release of all women being held in prison for suffragette activities.

Not all suffragettes were in agreement with Emmeline Pankhurst's patriotic call to her followers. One in bitter opposition was her daughter Sylvia, leader of the East London Federation of Suffragettes. Proclaiming a pacifist stance, Sylvia urged her supporters to oppose the war vigorously, in thought and in deed.

Not all her followers followed her call. Tessa was one dissenter. Emma another.

Breaking allegiance to Sylvia Pankhurst did not come easily to Tessa. The two women had been friends for many years. Tessa had been particularly supportive when Sylvia had opposed her mother on the occasion that had resulted in the East London Federation of Suffragettes breaking away from the larger organisation.

However, on this issue, Tessa told Sylvia she could not put their cause before the interests of the country, and she resigned from the movement. Emma agreed with the stand her friend was making. She too left the East London Federation of Suffragettes.

The parting between Tessa and Sylvia was more sorrowful than acrimonious. The Dalston Lane premises were rented in Sylvia's name, but she told Tessa that she and Emma could remain in the flat until they could make other arrangements for their future.

Exactly what the future held for them was discussed by Tessa and Emma a few days after the declaration of war, when they were seated in the small flat.

'Will you go back to Cornwall?' Tessa asked.

'Not until I have to,' Emma replied ambiguously. 'How about you? What will you do?'

'I'll probably go to France,' Tessa replied unexpectedly.

'France . . . ? What will you do *there*?'

'I've been talking to Louisa Garrett Anderson. She's a doctor, and also a suffragette. She's hoping to open a hospital in Paris to treat wounded soldiers. She's recruiting all sorts of staff: doctors, nurses, orderlies. I'm not much use at nursing, but I've already approached a great many people and have raised the money to buy an ambulance. I intend taking it to France and driving it for them there. She said she would be delighted to have me working with her staff.'

'How about me?' Emma asked indignantly. 'Couldn't I come too? I can drive – and I learned a whole lot about nursing when I was in Switzerland. Not only that, I can understand and make myself understood in French.'

Tessa smiled. 'You would be absolutely invaluable, Emma. As a matter of fact, I've already mentioned you to Doctor Garrett Anderson. She begged me to persuade you to come to France too.'

'Tessa! You deliberately led me to believe you were going to France without me! I *hate* you!'

'No you don't, any more than I hate you. But it's likely to prove dangerous. I didn't want to commit you until you'd reached your own decision. I'm glad you'll be there with me, Emma, but I think Paris is going to be very different to the city we both remember.'

Tessa and Emma were kitted out with very smart uniforms of a distinctive greenish-grey material by the doctor's organisation. However, a departure date for the staff who would be working in the Paris hospital proved to be tantalisingly elusive.

Tessa had the ambulance fitted out in readiness for service in France and she was impatient to take it across the Channel and begin the work for which she had volunteered.

Eventually, Tessa and Emma decided they would wait no longer. Informing the Women's Hospital Corps – as the new organisation was to be called – they would meet them in France, the two women set off to make their own way to Paris, driving their new ambulance.

They chose to take the route from Dover to Boulogne, the quickest means of crossing the Channel. But when they arrived at Dover, there was such chaos at the English port they began to wonder whether they had made the right choice.

Soldiers and a wide variety of military equipment were everywhere. Civilian would-be passengers were being turned back by police and port officials acting, as they repeated time after time, 'On the orders of Earl Kitchener, Secretary of State for War.'

The arrival of an ambulance, painted in military colours with two uniformed *women* as drivers, posed the authorities with a new problem. They had no authorisation for allowing such a vehicle to proceed to France, and their instructions were 'no authorisation – no embarkation'.

Tessa had some experience of dealing with officialdom. She rose to the occasion now, explaining that the ambulance was needed urgently in Paris to convey wounded British soldiers from the battle-front to hospital. The remainder of their party would be travelling to France via Newhaven to open a new hospital for wounded British soldiers. She explained how, with Emma, she had chosen to cross the Channel from Dover, believing they would reach Paris more quickly and so be able to begin their work straight away.

There were bound to be problems that would need solving before the main party reached Paris. Tessa hoped to have them sorted out by the time the others arrived, so allowing them to begin the task of treating wounded British soldiers immediately.

So, if the port officials would kindly assist and not hinder, Tessa said, she and Emma would get on their way to France to save the lives of British soldiers, instead of bandying words with men who would never know what it was to lie wounded and unattended in a foreign land.

Half an hour later, Tessa, Emma and the ambulance were on a ship that was carrying supplies destined for the British army headquarters in France.

16

The interest Tessa and Emma and their unusual uniforms created on board the cross-channel vessel meant that they secured a half-dozen extra blankets for the ambulance from the friendly driver of an army lorry packed with supplies.

The driver assured them there was so much confusion at the army's French headquarters that they could have taken the whole load, together with the lorry, and no one would have been any wiser.

The two women would find the interest they created repeated time and time again while they were in France, and it invariably worked to their advantage.

The ship docked after dark in Dieppe, having been diverted from Boulogne for a reason no one seemed to know. Once ashore, the two women parked the ambulance and slept on stretchers in the back of the vehicle for the remainder of the night.

With nowhere to stay and no idea of what they would

do when they arrived in Paris, they both felt it would be better to reach the French capital during daylight hours.

Finding a useful niche for themselves did not prove as difficult as they had anticipated. Driving across Paris, heading in the general direction of the Champs Elysées, where the building that would house the hospital was situated, Emma suddenly exclaimed, 'Look! There's an army ambulance – and it's being driven by a woman. Follow it and see where it's going.'

Tessa did an immediate U-turn on the wide, Paris boulevard. Emma closed her eyes as the screeching of brakes and blare of car horns accompanied the near misses as drivers were taken by surprise by the sudden and unexpected manoeuvre.

The other ambulance was travelling at speed and Tessa was hard put to catch up with it.

Eventually, it turned into the forecourt of a building that had quite obviously been constructed as a school. The ambulances parked nearby and the nurses passing through the doors were evidence that it was now a hospital.

When the other ambulance stopped outside the hospital entrance, Tessa drove past and parked clear of the entrance.

As orderlies hurried from the hospital to stretcher the occupants from the ambulance, the driver of the pursued ambulance climbed from her cab and walked over to the driver's side of the British vehicle.

Freckle-faced and ginger haired, the young woman was about the same age as Tessa.

'Hi! I'm Cecily. I saw you chasing me through the streets. I haven't seen you before. Who are you with?' She spoke with a broad American accent.

Cecily listened with great interest as Tessa explained their circumstances, adding, 'We won't be able to do anything for our own hospital until they arrive to set things up, but we decided to come anyway, in case there was something useful we might do.'

'Useful? We Americans living in Paris have opened up a military hospital here. If we had a hundred ambulances it still wouldn't be enough. You'll be welcomed here with open arms. Do you have somewhere to stay in Paris?'

'Not yet. We only landed in France during the night. We'd just arrived in Paris when Emma spotted you.'

Cecily suddenly grinned. 'Your arrival in Paris didn't exactly pass unnoticed. I saw you turn in the road to follow me. I haven't seen such driving since I went to watch the Indianapolis five hundred with my brother! But come inside and meet Doctor Sinclair. He's in charge of the ambulance section. He'll be able to fix you up with somewhere to stay.'

Doctor Sinclair turned out to be a harassed-looking young man with a somewhat abstract manner. Nevertheless, within fifteen minutes of meeting him, Tessa and Emma had rooms in the makeshift hospital and had been issued with identity cards that would enable them to obtain free petrol and food during the time they were working for the American hospital.

'When do we begin work?' Emma asked once the brief formalities had been completed.

'Well . . . if you're not feeling too tired after your journey, you could start work right away. We've just been told a train from the front has passed through Paris and dumped a whole lot of wounded men on the platform of one of the railway stations. Cecily will be going there too. All you'll need to do is follow her.'

With a ready smile that they would learn was so much a part of the Americans, the young doctor added, 'From what Cecily has told me, I'd say you are rather good at that!'

Emma and Tessa worked with the Americans for almost two weeks before the members of the Women's Hospital Corps arrived in Paris to set up their own hospital in the Hotel Claridge.

Both women would have been content to remain with the Americans at their schoolhouse–hospital, but they were persuaded to rejoin their countrywomen by Doctor Sinclair. Altruistically, he pointed out that the experience gained by the two women during their time with the American service would be beneficial to the newcomers.

Tessa and Emma had certainly gained a great deal of experience – much of it extremely harrowing.

Their duties involved collecting wounded men from the railway stations, but recently, as there had been heavy fighting close to the capital, they had taken their ambulances to the battle area to bring back severely wounded soldiers who would otherwise have certainly died while waiting to be transported to a hospital.

This was a dangerous task and one that was to have tragic consequences for the Americans.

Three of their ambulances travelled through the night to pick up yet another batch of badly wounded men from a village some sixty miles from Paris. Unfortunately, as they neared the village they encountered a German patrol that had managed to by-pass the strong-points being held by the French army.

In the darkness, the German soldiers could not see the red crosses painted on the sides of the three vehicles. To them, they were merely enemy vehicles travelling on their way to the battlefield.

They opened fire, killing two of the ambulance drivers and wounding the third. One of the two dead drivers was the red-haired Cecily.

Hers was a death that cast a pall of gloom over the entire hospital.

17

The two English drivers, with their knowledge of the situation in Paris and their experience in transporting wounded soldiers from the battlefield, were invaluable to the dedicated staff of the new British hospital.

The doctors, nurses and orderlies arrived at the Hotel Claridge to find the builders had barely completed their work. Floors were still strewn with debris and no attempt had been made to clean the premises.

Despite this nightmarish scenario, the first wounded men were being admitted only forty-eight hours after the arrival of the hospital staff. Meanwhile, the ladies' cloakroom-cum-operating theatre was being prepared for the first of a continuous series of operations.

At first, American ambulances were used to bring the bulk of the casualties to the hotel, but the hospital now had three vehicles of its own. One was the ambulance Tessa and Emma had brought from England. The others had been purchased for them by a philanthropic French woman.

The fact that the hospital's surgeons, doctors, nurses and orderlies were all women proved a great novelty to the diminishing population of Paris. Anyone who held any official position in the city came to view the activities for themselves.

So too did many high-ranking army and medical officers. When some of these arrived, it was quite evident that they were scornful of the chances of success of an establishment which felt it could function without the aid of men.

However, all left the hospital impressed by what they had seen. Many who had been opposed to suffragism in the past were considerably sobered by contemplation of the future role of women in society.

It was not only officials who came to the hospital. The ordinary people of Paris called in too, and they seldom came empty-handed. Fruit, flowers, cakes, cigarettes and money were all donated to the unique hospital.

If an ambulance carrying wounded men should happen to arrive when able-bodied Frenchmen were passing by, the stretchers were carried inside by willing hands. The citizens of Paris had taken the hospital to their warm hearts.

The hospital had been functioning for only a few days when a crisis descended upon Paris. The sound of gunfire and the flickering fire of big guns might have heralded a fierce and distant storm, but this conflagration was not of God's making. Nevertheless, with the Germans less than twenty-five miles away, it soon became a part of everyday life.

It seemed the fall of the French capital was imminent. The French government was established in Bordeaux and there was nervous talk of evacuating the Hotel Claridge hospital to the comparative safety of one or other of the Channel ports.

But the love of the French for their magnificent capital was such they would not contemplate its occupation by a German army.

The man who had been entrusted with the defence of Paris was a wily old general, Joseph Gallieni. Now sixty-five years of age, a veteran of France's wars in Africa, he maintained that the German army had over-extended itself by its rapid advance upon Paris.

Using sheer force of personality, he persuaded the French and English generals to halt the retreat of their armies and turn on the Germans. To aid them, he promised every available soldier within his jurisdiction – and beyond.

The allied armies about-faced – and took the enemy by surprise. True to his promise, Gallieni comman-deered every available vehicle in his city – Ben's motor car amongst them – and rushed soldiers to the front.

Gallieni was proved correct. The German army, unchecked for so long, suddenly realised the danger it was in and began a fighting retreat, hotly pursued by the French and British armies.

For the citizens of Paris, foreboding was replaced by a fierce and joyful pride. The tide had turned. Paris was saved. The Germans were being pushed back towards their own borders. Surely the war would soon come to an end?

But the price of stemming the German advance was horrifically high. Officials realised that casualties totalled more than a hundred thousand. However, such figures were not for release in the countries of those who had fallen.

In the Hotel Claridge hospital, no one gave a thought to casualty figures. They were far too busy trying to cope with the human flotsam and jetsam of war.

They were dealing not only with British casualties now. The ambulances coming from the front were bringing in French soldiers – and occasionally wounded Germans too.

When a soldier was caked in the mud of the battlefield and swathed in bandages, it was sometimes almost impossible to recognise which army he belonged to.

Tessa and Emma were worked so hard that to Emma it seemed she was permanently on the verge of total exhaustion.

Her duties were not confined to driving. When the hospital was filled to overflowing and could take no more casualties, she was called upon to help in the hospital wards, on the strength of her experience in the Swiss clinic.

At first she was concerned that she did not know enough to help with the more seriously wounded, but she soon discovered that nurses were now being sent to hospitals in France with as little as two weeks' nursing experience!

However, it was always the drive to a battlefield that was the most dangerous part of her duties.

18

The day had begun for Emma as had so many others since her arrival in France. Up at dawn, gulp down a cup of scalding hot coffee and two croissants, with butter and honey. It was all she was able to eat at this time of the morning, even though she knew there might not be another meal until late in the evening.

She was particularly tired this morning. The previous evening she had worked in one of the wards, helping with the many surgical cases that comprised the bulk of the most recent batch of casualties.

Some of the casualties were to be discharged today. None was fit enough to return to military duties. Most never would be. They were to board a hospital train that would carry them to the coast, from where they would be taken by ship to England.

The American hospital had offered their ambulances for this task.

Emma had almost finished her breakfast when Tessa

came in. She too looked tired. Late the evening before she had volunteered to take some urgently required medical supplies to a hard-pressed British army medical unit working close to the frontline.

Seating herself at the table opposite Emma, Tessa said, 'You look tired.'

'I'd say that's a case of the pot calling the kettle black,' Emma retorted. 'Was it a bad drive last night?'

'More than that,' Tessa replied. 'I found it quite distressing.'

It was unusual for Tessa to make such a remark and Emma asked her the reason.

'Do you remember the policeman who arrested me that first night you came to London – the same one who took you off from Buckingham Palace when you were arrested?'

'Of course. Constable Fry. He was rather nice, really. Have you seen him here, in Paris?'

'Not exactly. He was a casualty at the post where I delivered the medical stores last night. It seems he was an army reservist and was called up as soon as war was declared.'

'Is he badly wounded?'

Tessa nodded. Gazing into her coffee cup, she said, 'He's had to have a leg amputated.'

Suddenly, Emma did not feel like finishing her second croissant. She lowered it to her plate. 'The poor man.'

'Yes. I was carrying stores through the church where they'd put the wounded. He recognised me, despite the pain he must have been in. I didn't recognise him at first, but when I did I could have wept for him.'

'Couldn't you have brought him back here with you?'

'I wanted to but the army doctor said he wasn't

ready to travel. Still, you and I are going back there today. We'll make certain he's one of those we collect.'

Emma's spirits sank. She had been hoping that, despite everything, this would be a fairly uneventful day. Driving to an area so close to the fighting could never be that.

Emma's fears were fully justified. The Germans had made a brief stand in order to facilitate the orderly retreat of a unit of their army which was in imminent danger of being cut off and annihilated.

German resistance was fiercest no more than two miles from the village where Tessa had found George Fry. Inevitably, the clash meant a sharp rise in the number of casualties sustained by both sides.

The drive to the village was bad enough in itself. The roads had been churned into ankle deep mud by the passage of vehicles of war. In addition, as the seven vehicles that had been mustered for the journey drew closer to the battlefield, there were shell holes and the wrecks of horse-drawn and mechanical vehicles to be contended with.

Then they began passing soldiers making their way to the rear of the lines for a rest, having been relieved after days of battle. Exhausted, hungry and dirty, they had wounded among them too. Men who called out for help from the drivers of the ambulances.

It was heartbreaking to have to ignore them, but for as long as they were capable of walking, they would need to trust to their own resources. Ahead of the ambulances, there were wounded men in greater need, who could do nothing to help themselves.

The ambulances were eventually signalled to turn

into a churchyard. The wounded men for evacuation were in the church building.

As Emma climbed from the cab of her ambulance, she was distressed by the number of wounded men lying about the churchyard. It was quite evident the seven ambulances would be able to evacuate only a fraction of the wounded soldiers.

The army medical officer in charge of the makeshift hospital recognised Tessa. He told her the ex-policeman was still alive and was among those being evacuated to Paris that day.

He looked as though he too should have been evacuated along with the wounded. Gaunt, unshaven and bloody, he informed Emma he had not slept for three days and two nights.

Emma was aghast. 'That's ridiculous! You can't carry on like this. You *must* sleep.'

Instead of replying, the army doctor beckoned for Emma and Tessa to follow him inside the church.

All the doors of the building stood wide open, but the light breeze that fanned through them could not dispel the stench within.

It was the odour of sepsis, of gangrene – and of death.

Wounded men, wearing tattered and bloody uniforms, lay in profusion on straw strewn on the church floor. Most were still, although a few writhed and moaned in unrelievable agony.

Some had passed, unnoticed, beyond all pain.

Emma estimated there must have been more than three hundred wounded men inside the church building.

Visibly moved, she said, 'We can take only a fraction

of the men here.' She had seen many horrifying sights during the time she had spent in France; even so, she was shocked by such a scene of human misery.

'I know that,' the weary medical officer said. 'If our battleline holds you can come back and take more. Sadly, by the time you do, there will be even more wounded men. You say I must rest – and so I should. Unfortunately, I'm the only doctor left alive in this section of the line. What will happen if I don't tend the wounded?'

He waited for a reply. When neither of the women could think of one, he said wearily. 'Take as many as you can – *please*! Somewhere back in Britain a mother, wife or daughter will offer up her thanks for whatever you are able to do. Unfortunately, I fear many more will know only sorrow . . . All right, I'm coming.'

The overworked doctor responded to the urgent cry from one of his medical orderlies.

'Good luck to you – and bless you on behalf of those men you are able to save.'

The army medical officer moved off, leaving Emma and Tessa to the task of choosing which wounded men would be loaded into the ambulances and given at least an outside chance of survival.

19

❧

The ex-London policeman was embarrassingly grateful that Tessa had returned to include him in those being evacuated to the English hospital in Paris.

He recognised Emma too. In a bid to cheer him a little, she reminded him of the good turn he had once done her by loaning her the money to get back to Dalston Lane from the Cannon Row police station.

'That seems like another world – and so it is.' He put a hand down to the flat blanket where his right leg should have been. 'I'll never know that life again.'

Making a brave attempt to smile at her, he added, 'Having you take me with you now will make that couple of shillings I loaned you the best investment I'll ever make.'

The ex-policeman looked deadly tired and had developed a high temperature since Tessa had seen him the day before. She said, 'Just try to relax now. You'll be the first to be taken out to Emma's ambulance, but I'm warning you, it's not going to be as comfortable as the ride you once took in the Dalston Lane Sunbeam. The roads between here and Paris are a mess.'

'Don't let her worry you,' Emma said with a jocularity she was far from feeling, 'I'm the best ambulance driver in France. If it's possible to float over the potholes, I'm the one to do it.'

As they moved away from him, she spoke to Tessa quietly. 'He looks terrible! Do you think he'll pull through?'

'Even we can't perform miracles,' Tessa said. 'We can only do our best.'

The seven ambulances loaded as many casualties as could possibly be crammed into them. Originally designed to take no more than four stretcher cases, the vehicles had been modified by local French garages when the medical services had realised the unprecedented scale of the task they were required to perform. Adding extra brackets above the top stretcher on either side and cleverly making fittings for two stretchers to be placed laterally in the ambulances, they had increased their stretcher capacity to eight. It meant the men on the top stretchers would bump their heads if they raised them so much as a couple of inches, but they had received no complaints from their patients.

In addition, men were laid on blankets beneath the bottom stretcher and any men able to sit up occupied the vacant floor space. In this way, the drivers were often able to carry as many as fifteen to twenty men.

Emma breathed a sigh of relief when the ambulances

were loaded and they were able to leave the fetid air of the church behind them.

But the horrors of this particular journey were by no means over.

They set off in convoy, with Tessa driving ahead of Emma. At the edge of the village they waved to a group of British soldiers. Moving up to the frontline, the men were astonished to see women driving ambulances so close to the battle area.

Suddenly, without any warning there was a huge explosion, and the window on the passenger side of Emma's ambulance shattered. At the same time the driver's window was plastered in mud and it seemed to Emma a searing blast squeezed all the air from her body.

A large calibre German gun had been brought to bear on the village and this was its opening shot.

Bringing the ambulance to an immediate halt, she threw open the driver's door and stumbled from the cab.

Her first thought was that her ambulance had received a hit, but for Emma it had been a lucky escape. The shell had hit the vehicle ahead of her. Tessa's ambulance.

Unaware that she was screaming, Emma ran to the other ambulance. The soldiers who had only a moment before been waving to the ambulance drivers were there before her.

Among the mangled bodies, two were still alive. One was Tessa – but she was unconscious and badly wounded.

The officer in charge of the marching men sent someone for the army medical officer. He arrived a couple of minutes later. After examining the unconscious woman, he called for dressings.

To Emma, he said, 'She's obviously got shrapnel inside her. I can't do anything here. Her only chance is to get her to hospital – and I can't guarantee that she'll last the journey.'

'But . . . we're all carrying as many men as we can. How can we get her there?'

'You're carrying *soldiers*,' the medical officer said. 'I'll speak to them.'

Hurrying to the rear door of Emma's ambulance, he flung it open and said, 'One of the ambulance drivers has been seriously wounded. She needs urgent hospital treatment. Which of you men will volunteer to wait for the next batch of ambulances to arrive? I promise you'll be the first man loaded then.'

There was silence, then a voice said, 'What's the name of the ambulance driver?' It was George Fry, the ex-London policeman.

The medical officer turned to Emma. Overcoming the emotion she felt, she said, 'It's Tessa. Tessa Wren.'

'Then she'd better take my place,' George Fry said, immediately. 'I'm in no hurry to go anywhere.'

'Good man!' The medical officer signalled for two of the soldiers to remove his stretcher.

Emma knew she should protest. Urge the medical officer to choose someone else. The ex-policeman was a very sick man. It was doubtful he would survive the wait for another ambulance.

But Tessa's survival was in the balance too. She said nothing.

As Tessa was loaded into the ambulance, Emma looked down at George Fry, who had been taken off the stretcher and was on the ground waiting for the orderlies to complete their task and attend to him.

'I'm sorry . . .' Emma was so choked she was unable to say more.

'Don't be. If she can be saved she'll be of more use to the world than I'll ever be, now.'

'You mustn't say that!'

George Fry gave her a tired smile. 'There is something, though. I once gave you a couple of shillings to see you on an unknown journey. Will you give me a kiss to see me on mine?'

Unable to find any words to say, Emma gave him a kiss.

The door of the ambulance was slammed shut and the medical officer said, 'You'd better be on your way as quickly as you can. The Germans have our range. They're likely to fire again very soon – and don't dally along the way. That young lady needs to get to hospital as quickly as you can make it.'

As she climbed into the cab of the ambulance, one of the soldiers finished scraping the mud from the windscreen and another swung the starting handle.

George Fry raised a hand to her as she put the ambulance in gear. She waved to him, then she was on her way.

It was a nightmare journey to Paris. It seemed to Emma every pothole had become deeper and that there was twice as much mud as there had been on the journey from the capital.

There was certainly much more traffic, most of it heading for the frontline.

Eventually, the convoy of ambulances reached Paris. It was easier going here. The Paris drivers, notoriously aggressive, pulled to the side immediately to make way for the mud-spattered convoy, led by Emma's shell-damaged ambulance.

When they reached the hospital, Emma ran to the back door of her vehicle as orderlies hurried from the hospital.

Ambulance drivers and orderlies knew each other and Emma said, 'Quick! Take this stretcher first. It's Tessa. A shell landed on her ambulance.'

Tessa was the first casualty to be carried into the hospital, with Emma hurrying along beside the stretcher of her unconscious friend.

Inside the hospital, she collided with someone as the party hurried across the foyer.

Looking up to apologise, she saw – Jacob!

Jacob opened his mouth to greet her, but the words never came out. Instead, he leaped forward to catch Emma as she slumped to the floor in a dead faint.

20

❦

Emma was carried to a small partitioned room on the ground floor of the hospital and a doctor was sent to examine her.

Jacob wanted to remain with her, but the doctor sent him from the room. When she had completed her examination and left Emma, Jacob, more in control of himself now, asked if he could sit with Emma until she came out of her faint.

Once again, the doctor said, 'No.'

Her explanation was that Emma was thoroughly exhausted and had just undergone the horrifying experience of witnessing her friend being very seriously wounded by a German shell. The doctor also said she had given Emma something to ensure she would sleep for at least twelve hours – probably longer. She suggested Jacob should go away and return in the morning.

In the hospital foyer Jacob found a very distressed Manny talking to Ben.

When he saw Jacob, Ben demanded, 'What's this Manny is telling me about Tessa? How badly is she wounded?'

Suddenly, Jacob felt drained of all energy. He had been thinking only of Emma. Now he said, 'Tessa's been wounded very badly. She's in the operating theatre at this very moment. Emma's been put to bed too.'

Repeating what the doctor had told him, he said, 'It seems they've both been in Paris for some time – driving ambulances. They were up at the front when a shell hit Tessa's ambulance. It was loaded with wounded men. Almost all of them were killed and Tessa was badly hurt. It was Emma who brought Tessa back here. When she saw me she fainted before we could say a word to each other. The doctor says Emma's suffering from exhaustion and has given her something to make her sleep until morning, but she won't let me stay with her.'

Ben rested a hand on Jacob's arm in a gesture of sympathy. There was a choked sound behind him and he turned to see Manny with tears streaming down his face.

'I saw Tessa when they were taking her into the operating theatre, Mr Retallick. She was covered in blood and didn't even know me.'

'She was unconscious,' Jacob explained. 'Try not to upset yourself too much, Manny. I'm sure she's going to be all right. When she recovers she'll have Emma to thank for bringing her back here so quickly.'

'But . . . she didn't know it was me,' Manny repeated.

'She'll know you once she comes round,' Ben said confidently. 'She'll be pleased to see you too, I've no doubt. Look, why don't you two go back to the hotel and get some rest? It's all been very upsetting for you both. Have a couple of drinks, then go to bed. I'll stay here and let you know right away if anything happens before morning. After all, the hotel is only just down the road.'

'Why should *you* stay?' Jacob asked. 'You've just driven for miles. *You're* the one who should go back to the hotel and get some sleep.'

'I'm fine,' Ben replied. 'Besides, I got one of the army doctors to give me something to keep me awake. I doubt if I could go to sleep even if I wanted to. I might just as well be here as anywhere else – and I am related to Emma, remember? Come back in the morning. I'll go off to bed then.'

'Well . . . if you're really sure?' Jacob was still not convinced it was what he should do.

'Of course I'm sure. Off you go, both of you – and have a good night's sleep.'

'All right, Mr Retallick,' Manny agreed, 'but we'll be back early in the morning. You can be sure of that.'

Ben watched the two men walk from the hospital. Then he went in search of a doctor in the hope of learning something new about the two women.

When he did finally corner one of the hotel's doctors, she could only repeat what Jacob had already said about Emma. When he asked about Tessa, the doctor was more vague. She was still being operated on by Doctor Garrett Anderson and could not be in more capable hands.

Ben soon discovered it was impossible to sit in the Hotel Claridge hospital and do nothing. There was far too much going on around him. The casualties at the battle-front were heavier than had been anticipated and the Paris hospitals were being called on to take far more wounded men than ever before.

For the next couple of hours Ben helped to carry wounded men to makeshift beds laid out in the aisles of each of the wards.

As he returned from one of these trips, he met a nurse in one of the corridors and she stopped to speak to him.

'Weren't you asking me about Tessa Wren earlier?'

'That's right. Is her operation over?' He added apprehensively, 'Was it successful?'

'She's a very poorly young woman,' the nurse replied. 'We've just put her in the room partitioned off from that of her friend, downstairs on the ground floor. I doubt if she'll come out of the anaesthetic until the morning.'

'Thank you for telling me. I'll look in on both of them when I go downstairs again.'

'I hope you'll find the time,' the nurse commented. 'From the look of things it's going to be a very busy night.'

Whenever an infrequent lull occurred during the night hours, Ben looked in on Emma and Tessa. Emma appeared to be enjoying a deep sleep of exhaustion, but Tessa's condition gave him far more cause for concern. Her breathing was frighteningly shallow and her cheeks had no more colour in them than the sheet drawn up to her chin.

Once when he was in the room, a nurse came to check on her pulse.

'How is she?' Ben asked hopefully.

'We'll know more about that when the effect of

the anaesthetic wears off,' the nurse replied non-committedly. 'She's undergone a very serious operation.'

Ben's final visit was made soon after dawn.

It had been light for almost an hour, yet there was still no sign of Jacob or Manny. By now, Ben was desperately tired.

Suddenly, looking in on Tessa, he realised her head had shifted position on the pillow since he had looked in on the last occasion.

Tiptoeing to her bedside, he stood looking down at her for a while. Thinking he must have been mistaken, he was about to turn and leave. Then she opened her eyes!

21

For a few moments Tessa looked at Ben with an expression that was a mixture of both pain and disbelief.

She closed her eyes tightly once again for perhaps half a minute before opening them again.

'Ben! Is it really you?' Her voice was thin and as uncertain as the question.

'Yes, it's me.'

'How did you know I was here and had been hurt?'

As she spoke she tried to make herself more comfortable in the hard hospital bed. The move caused her to cry out and her face screwed up in an expression of sheer agony.

'Don't try to move, Tessa. You've been badly hurt, but you're going to be all right now.'

'I'm very thirsty, Ben. Give me a drink of water.'

There was no water on the cabinet beside her bed and he could see none when he looked about the room.

Then he remembered she had undergone major surgery. It was possible she was not allowed to drink yet.

'I'd better speak to a nurse first. I'll go and find one . . .'

'No! No, Ben. Don't leave me just yet. Stay here.'

'Of course.'

He brought a chair from the far side of the room and sat down beside her.

Tessa tried to smile at him, but she was still drowsy from the anaesthetic. Nevertheless, she said, 'Is Emma all right? She was in the ambulance behind me . . .'

Memory brought with it as much pain as the wound she had sustained and it showed in her expression.

'Emma is fine. She brought you here, but she was so upset about you that one of the doctors gave her something to make her sleep. From all I've heard, she shouldn't have *needed* anything. Both of you must have been close to exhaustion. It only took the sight of Jacob to make her fall in a faint.'

'Jacob's here too?'

'That's right – and Manny. He's particularly upset that you've been hurt. We all arrived yesterday – although it feels like we've been here for days.'

Tessa felt unable to cope with an explanation of why Ben, Jacob and Manny were in Paris together. Closing her eyes once more, she said wearily, 'Poor Manny.'

She still had her eyes closed when the nurse who had been on duty throughout the night came to the room once more.

Looking at Tessa, Ben thought she was still asleep and he whispered to the nurse, 'She came around a while ago and wanted a drink of water but I couldn't find any in here.'

'That's just as well,' the nurse said sharply. 'She's to take nothing by mouth, neither food nor drink.'

'Am I *that* badly wounded?' Tessa asked the question without opening her eyes. 'You can tell the doctor that fortunately I'm probably able to last longer without food than most of her patients. I had plenty of practice in Holloway. I'll be all right as long as she doesn't try to force feed me.'

'No one's going to do anything except work very hard to make you better. Now, I think your friend here should leave you and let you sleep.'

'I want him to stay.' Tessa opened her eyes and pleaded with Ben, 'Please stay with me . . .'

Ben looked to the nurse for confirmation and she said, grudgingly, 'All right. He can stay for a while – but he must leave when you go to sleep, or when the doctor comes to see you.' She glanced at Ben. 'Mind you, it looks as though *you're* the one who should be sleeping.'

'I'm all right,' Ben said untruthfully. His head felt as though it might part company with his body at any moment. He could never remember feeling so tired before.

At that moment there was a sound from beyond the frosted glass partition where Emma was in bed. The nurse hurried away to find out what was happening.

Looking decidedly wan, Emma groaned and was putting her feet gingerly to the ground when the nurse entered her room.

'Hello, and how are you this morning? Feeling better?'

'I'm feeling *awful*, but I'll improve. How is Tessa?'

'She's just come round, but the anaesthetic has left her

feeling pretty groggy. We won't know how successful the operation has been for a day or two yet.'

'I'll go and see her in a minute.' Emma swung her legs back to the bed. 'I'll just stay still for a few more minutes.'

The nurse smiled at her understandingly, and Emma said, 'I must have been deadly tired. Before I passed out I could have sworn I saw Jacob . . . but he's in Cornwall.'

'If it's Jacob Pengelly you're talking about, you weren't imagining it. Jacob's in Paris. He was helping here in the hospital for most of yesterday. There are two other men with him. Ben something or another, who's in the next-door room with Tessa, and a great giant of a man named Manny Hirsch.'

Emma sat bolt upright. 'Jacob's *here*? I really *did* see him? Where is he now?' She swung her feet to the ground once again, but as she stood up she swayed and reached out to the bed for support.

Suddenly, she mumbled, 'I'm going to be sick.' Retching noisily, she ran unsteadily for the door, heading in the direction of the toilet.

In the adjacent, partitioned-off room, Ben heard the door slam behind Emma. Then Tessa drew an arm free of the bedclothes and said, 'Will you hold my hand, Ben?'

'Of course.'

She squeezed his fingers affectionately, but Ben was aware there was very little strength in her grip.

He was still holding her hand when Jacob put his head inside the room. It was doubtful whether he was even aware that Ben and Tessa were holding hands. When he spoke he sounded distraught.

'I've just looked in Emma's room. She's not there. Has something happened to her?'

'I don't think so. She's been sleeping well all night. I just heard her door close. She's probably gone off somewhere.'

The expression of relief made Tessa smile, but as Jacob asked her how she was feeling another expression of pain crossed her face. Suddenly she began choking noisily and, without warning, her mouth filled with blood and overflowed, staining the white sheet.

As she continued choking, Ben called to Jacob. 'Quick! Find a nurse. HURRY!'

The nurse who had attended Tessa earlier had been standing only a few paces from the door, talking to Emma. When she heard Ben shout to Jacob, she hurried to the room. Emma was only a couple of paces behind her. The nurse took in the situation immediately.

'Quickly, Emma. Help me turn her on to her side . . . careful now.'

As the two women gently turned Tessa, the nurse called to Ben, 'Go to the reception desk. Tell them to get a doctor here urgently.'

No more than two or three minutes later, a doctor arrived at the room. Seconds later, Emma rushed from the room, only her eyes speaking to Jacob, as he stood with Ben and Manny outside the room.

She returned pushing a wheeled stretcher. With doctor and nurse in attendance, an unconscious Tessa was wheeled from the room and hurried to the operating theatre once more.

When Emma came out, she ran to Jacob and burst into tears.

He held her until she regained some control but,

even now, there was no opportunity to talk. An orderly hurried from the reception desk to say that a telephone call had been received from the Gare de L'Est. A train had just arrived and about fifty badly wounded British soldiers had been deposited on the platform. Most needed immediate attention.

The station authorities were asking that an ambulance be sent to collect them as a matter of urgency. Emma was the only driver available.

Pulling away from Jacob, a red-eyed Emma said, 'All right, I'll go.'

To Jacob, she said, 'Will you come with me? Along the way you can tell me what you're doing here.'

The nurse who had been on duty all night came along in time to hear her. 'Not so fast, young lady. Doctor Parfitt has told me to tell you she wants to see you this morning. She says it's important.'

Emma hesitated for only a moment. 'Tell her, I know what it is she's going to say. It will keep. Those poor soldiers at the station won't.'

Pausing only to tell Ben and Manny she would speak to them later, she hurried away, with Jacob following her.

Left standing with the two men, the nurse made a gesture of despair. 'I was offered a nice quiet post in an asylum before coming here! I don't know where we're going to put any new casualties. But we've got some men going out today, so I suppose we'll find room somewhere.'

To Ben and Manny, she said, 'What are you two doing now?'

'Whatever you want us to do,' Ben offered. 'I'm waiting to see what's happening with Tessa.'

'I want to know too,' Manny said. 'She was always kind to me when we were both in London.'

'Well, we're none of us going to hear anything for a while. In the meantime, it will be far better if you both keep yourselves occupied. If we're to take in more casualties we need to discharge those who are ready to move on. You can help pack their things and carry them down here – though how we're going to transport them, I just don't know.'

'I have a car at the hotel just along the road,' Ben said. 'It can carry five seated passengers, if they squeeze up.'

'They'll squeeze up enough to carry six or seven. Go and fetch your car. Manny can start to pack for them while I arrange the papers to send them on their way home . . .'

22

In the ambulance, Emma gave Jacob a weak but warm smile. 'I haven't yet said how good it is to see you, Jacob. It really is wonderful!'

'There doesn't seem to have been time to say anything. There's been a lot happening. I'm particularly sorry about Tessa. I know how fond you are of her, and how upset you must be. It's a terrible thing to have happened.'

'The most awful thing was being there and seeing it happen,' Emma said, fiercely trying to maintain control. 'Only two of them were left alive out of about twenty . . . and *why*? What good did it do anyone? None of the soldiers would ever have been able to fight the Germans again – and Tessa's done nothing but good since we came to France. She's always helped anyone who needed it, without question. British, French or German, it never mattered to her.'

Tears filled her eyes and Jacob grabbed the steering

wheel in time to steer the ambulance past a plod-
ding horse drawing a cart loaded with second-hand
furniture.

'I'm sorry, Jacob – I'm all right now.'

He took his hand off the steering wheel and she said,
'Poor Tessa.'

'I think Ben must have spent much of the night with
her. He stayed at the hospital when Manny and I went
off to the hotel last night. He was with her when I looked
in her room this morning.'

'Ben?' She looked at Jacob sharply, causing the ambulance to swerve once more, this time narrowly missing
a cyclist.

'He's always admired her for the stand she took for
suffragism, whatever he may have said to the contrary.
And he's filled with admiration for the work you're
both doing here. I think he's probably quite fond of
her, too.'

'Is he?!'

Emma was silent for a while, then she said, 'Tessa has
had a very big thing going for Ben since the first time
she met him at Tregarrick. I'm sure Lily was aware of
it. She took every opportunity to throw them together
when we were all in Paris together.'

'Why would she do that if she thought Tessa had
fallen for him. He's her husband!'

'Lily was convinced she was dying. She felt that if
anything happened to her, Tessa would make him a
very good wife.'

'Well, Lily's not dying now. She's well on the road to
recovery. She's the reason we're in Paris right now. Ben
couldn't get through to the clinic by telephone to find
out what was happening and he was told the French

railways were totally disrupted. He was so worried about her that we brought the car across on a clay boat and Ben and I took turns driving to Switzerland. Ben brought Manny with us in case we ran into trouble. When we got to the clinic, we found that all was well. Not only that, Lily is so obviously on the mend that Ben felt he couldn't disrupt her treatment and bring her away. So he left her there and we drove back to Paris. And here we are.'

'So you didn't come here because you'd had my letters?' She sounded disappointed. 'I suppose I should have known that you wouldn't *all* have come.'

'What letters? I've had nothing at all from you to tell me you were in Paris. Perhaps it's just as well. Had I known what you were doing I wouldn't have been able to sleep at night for worrying about you.'

'Had they reached you, it wouldn't only have been the thought of what I was doing that would have kept you awake, Jacob. It would have been thoughts of what had already been done – by both of us.'

'What do you mean . . . ?' Jacob looked at her in consternation. He did not want to put into words what he *thought* she meant. 'What are you trying to say?'

They had pulled on to the forecourt of the railway station. Emma carefully parked the ambulance outside the entrance before she replied.

'I'm expecting a baby, Jacob. I'm four months pregnant.'

The revelation left Jacob speechless. While he was still trying to put his thoughts together, there came a knock on the window of the driver's door. Then the door was opened to reveal an army medical orderly, standing outside.

'Have you come to pick up our casualties, lady? It's going to need more than one ambulance, but I'm glad you're here, anyway. A couple of the lads are in a bad way. We need to get them to a hospital right away.'

The next twenty minutes were hectic as wounded men on stretchers were carried to the ambulance from inside the station. Jacob, Emma and the orderly were helped by some sympathetic Frenchmen who were passing through the station.

More than once, Emma saw Jacob looking at her almost as though he expected her to stop and give birth at any moment.

She felt a great deal of sympathy for the way in which her sensational news had been given to him. Yet his glances showed his concern for her and this left her with a warm glow inside.

However, right now the plight of the wounded soldiers had to take precedence over their personal affairs.

Jacob bided his time. He and Emma would discuss the situation on the drive back to the hospital.

This too was foiled by the needs of the wounded soldiers.

Emma managed to fit eighteen of the casualties in the back of her ambulance, then the orderly asked Jacob if he would mind remaining at the station. This way, another two men could be squeezed into the cab. One had been blinded by a single bullet from a sniper's gun. The other had somehow managed to put his shoulder in the way of a recoil from an artillery piece he was helping to fire.

When Emma and the ambulance had departed from the station, Jacob tried to find a quiet corner in which to sit and contemplate the implications of the news Emma had so dramatically given to him.

He did not doubt for a moment the baby was his. It must have been conceived when they were in Switzerland together. Or perhaps later, when they were in the flat in Dalston Lane.

But Jacob was not allowed to sit alone and think for very long. The medical orderly accompanying the wounded men seemed eager to talk to someone who spoke his own language and was not associated with the military.

Seating himself beside Jacob, he questioned him for a while before asking, 'What are you doing here if you're nothing to do with the army or the hospital?'

'The wife of my boss is in a clinic in Switzerland. He was worried about her being trapped there by the war. We've just been to see her. I came to help him with the driving.'

'You've driven all the way to Switzerland from England?' The orderly was impressed. 'But what are you doing here, in Paris?'

'We thought it would be quicker coming back this way, but we got caught up with everything that's going on.'

'You wouldn't catch me staying on here if I didn't have to. Mind you, this station is heaven compared with what's going on up at the front.'

The orderly shivered involuntarily. 'I've never known anything like it. Sheer bloody slaughter, that's what it is. I've watched men going over the top with fixed bayonets, only to be mowed down as though they were so many stalks of corn. Then, when they're all lying there dead and dying, some stupid general who's sitting on his backside miles from the fighting, orders another battalion out to have exactly the same thing happen to them, and so it goes on, time and time again. I tell you, it just ain't human.'

The medical orderly shook his head despairingly and repeated, 'No, it just ain't human.'

At that moment some French men and women using the station, who had been eagerly plying the wounded soldiers with food, drinks and cigarettes, called to the orderly, beckoning for him to hurry.

With a weary air of resignation, he climbed to his feet and walked across to learn the reason for their consternation.

Jacob watched dispassionately as the orderly kneeled beside one of the men lying on the ground. He bent low over him. Then, with a word to the French onlookers, he drew a blanket up over the prostrate soldier's head.

The orderly then busied himself among the wounded men for a while, giving Jacob the time he needed to think about himself and Emma.

Jacob was certain of one thing. Emma could not carry on here for very much longer. Indeed, she should not be working as an ambulance driver right now.

Perhaps she would now agree to marry him. He could certainly afford to keep her in far more luxury than when he had first suggested marriage. It was an exciting thought.

Then he thought of Tessa. She had obviously been very badly wounded. Emma might feel she should take her to London and remain with her until she was well again. That might take a very long time.

He was mulling over the various possibilities when the medical orderly returned and resumed his condemnation of British army generals and the manner in which they were misdirecting the war.

The garrulous orderly was still telling Jacob how the war *should* be conducted when the ambulance returned from the Hotel Claridge to collect more British casualties from the station.

Jacob was dismayed to find that Emma was not driving.

When he questioned the new driver, she explained, 'Doctor Garrett Anderson said she was too upset to drive an ambulance across Paris. Her friend, Tessa, died on the operating table.'

23

⤦

The death of Tessa cast a pall of gloom over the hospital. During the time she had spent in Paris, Tessa had become a popular figure among the staff, many of whom had themselves once been active suffragettes.

Ben was particularly upset, but was unable to share his grief with the others. He shut himself away in his room at the Hotel Crillon and did not emerge for two hours. During this time he came to terms with her death.

He would always feel a combination of sorrow and guilt whenever he thought of Tessa, but there would be happy memories too. She had been a very special woman and his life was richer for having known her.

But Lily was special too and she was alive, contrary to all his earlier expectations. He must learn to forget Tessa, for her sake.

Tessa's funeral took place two days later. The occasion attracted the sympathy of the warm-hearted residents of

Paris. They lined the streets between the Hotel Claridge and the cemetery and traffic came to a respectful halt as the cortège passed by.

News of her work and the manner of her death had also filtered through to the British army headquarters and they acted with unusual alacrity.

Tessa was buried in the Paris cemetery with full military honours, the British guard of honour augmented by soldiers of the French army, who had requested that they might be represented.

On her coffin was a wreath, from Emma, of purple and white flowers with added greenery, made up in the shape of a Holloway Badge.

After the ceremony, Ben, Jacob, Emma and Manny returned to the Hotel Crillon. Here, Emma spent the afternoon alone in Jacob's room, sleeping and coming to terms in her own way with the loss of Tessa.

That evening, they all gathered in the hotel lounge to discuss what they would do now.

'I think it's high time you and I returned to Cornwall,' a strained-looking Ben said to Jacob. 'We have work to do. I'm going to be hard-put to keep Ruddlemoor solvent with the loss of so many markets for our clay. Will you stay on here as an ambulance driver, Emma?'

'I can't. Doctor Parfitt has told me I'm not to drive an ambulance for the hospital again.'

'What?! After all you've been through since you've been in Paris. Personally, I'm rather relieved, but what is she thinking of?'

'She says it's in my own interests, Ben. And she's right.'

'What do you mean, in your interests? For what reasons?'

Emma cast a glance at Jacob and he replied for her. 'We were going to put off telling you until the funeral was well behind us, but you should be the first to know. Emma's expecting a baby. I mean, *we're* expecting a baby. She's four months pregnant.'

Both Emma and Jacob were aware that Ben was making rapid mental calculations.

'This must have happened when I left you in London to look at the lorries used by the haulage company?'

Jacob nodded. 'Either there or when we were in Switzerland.'

After a lengthy silence, Ben asked, 'What do you intend doing about it?'

'What I've wanted to do all along. Marry Emma and settle down in Cornwall. Thanks to you I can offer her far more now than when I first asked her to marry me.'

Ben spoke to Emma. 'Is this what you want too?'

Emma nodded. 'I wasn't ready to be a wife when Jacob first asked me. There were so many other things I wanted to do with my life. Well, I've done as much as I want to do now and nothing could ever be the same without Tessa. Besides, there's the baby to think of – and I *do* want to marry Jacob, Ben. I've always known that. Tessa knew it too – and she approved.'

Not wishing to dwell on the subject of Tessa, Ben said, 'I know a lot of people who are going to be delighted. My grandmother and Lily, in particular.'

Turning to the remaining member of the party who had been nursing his own grief for Tessa in silence, Ben asked, 'How about you, Manny? What do you want to do? Now you don't have to worry about being arrested, you could return to London if you wished. Or you can come back to Cornwall. There'll always be a job there for you. But perhaps you'd prefer to remain here in Paris? The hospital will be pleased to keep you on, I'm sure.'

Manny shook his head. 'I couldn't stay here with all you gone and Tessa . . . gone too. No, I'd like to come back to Cornwall. I expect Jane is missing me as much as I'm missing her.'

'Then that's all settled,' Ben said. 'It's been a long and harrowing day. I suggest we find ourselves something to eat and have an early night in bed. Tomorrow I'll make arrangements for our return. We might even be able to leave for home some time later in the day.'

Over the meal, carefully avoiding talking about Tessa, the conversation was of the baby, the future wedding and the impact the news was likely to have upon the families of both Emma and Jacob.

Jacob admitted that his mother's attitude to Emma might pose problems, especially as he and Emma would need to live with his family once they were married. At least until they was able to find and furnish a house of their own.

'I don't think that needs to be a problem,' Ben said, suddenly enthusiastic. 'I think I know just the place for you. My grandmother's home in the Gover valley has been empty since Grandfather died. It's fully furnished too. I'm quite sure she'd be delighted to have you move in there. It would be quite in keeping with your status as my transport manager, Jacob. It's a very happy house too. Lily lived there with my grandparents for a long time. I stayed there too for some years, when I came to England from Africa.'

The mention of Lily conjured up thoughts of so many

things and he said, 'For so long I've not dared to hope I would ever have Lily home again, fit and well. Not until I saw her at the clinic this time. Now I *know* she'll be coming back to Tregarrick again one day. I hope it's soon. I have so much to make up to her for.'

If Emma and Jacob wondered uncomfortably what he might be talking about, they neither of them said anything.

Later, when dinner was over, Jacob left the other men and walked back to the hospital with Emma. She wanted to pack her things in readiness to leave Paris.

At the hospital, she went straight to her room, not wishing to engage in conversation with any of the hospital staff and Jacob took a slow walk back.

He was still a short distance from the Hotel Crillon when, to his surprise, he met up with Ben.

'Hello, Ben, have you decided to take a walk before going to bed?'

Jacob and his employer had been on first-name terms since soon after they had arrived in France. After all they had experienced together, more formal means of addressing each other seemed out of place.

'In a way. Actually, I came to meet you to discuss one or two things with you. Am I right in thinking there's likely to be some unpleasantness between your mother and Emma when you return home and she learns that Emma's pregnant?'

'I *know* there will be. She'll come around eventually, of course, but she's always thought Emma was far too "free thinking" for a girl. This will confirm it as far as she's concerned.'

'That's what I thought. Would it make a big difference if you were already married when you returned to

Cornwall? If you and Emma were able to move into the Gover valley house right away?'

'It would make all the difference in the world – but is it possible for us to be married here?'

'We should know by the morning. After you'd left the hotel to take Emma back to the hospital, I had an idea. The British government had a representative at Tessa's funeral this morning – a Mr Harriss-Gastrell, Consul-General at the British Embassy. The Ambassador has gone to Bordeaux, but the Consul-General remained here. He has the power to marry British subjects. I've just spoken to him on the telephone. He says a notice of an intended marriage should be posted in his office for fourteen days before the wedding, but the Secretary of State has the power to waive such a formality. He's going to ring the Ambassador tonight, who in turn will put a call through to England. We should have a reply in the morning.'

'But . . . why should he do this for me and Emma?'

'It's not so much for you – but it seems that Tessa's death has been widely reported in England. Emma's name has been mentioned too. The Consul-General thinks such a wedding will give wonderful publicity to the work that British women are doing here, for the war effort. He's convinced the Ambassador and the Secretary of State will think so too.'

'I . . . I don't know what to say. Can I run back to the hospital to tell Emma?'

'I can see no reason why not.'

Jacob set off at a run, but he had only gone a few paces when Ben called to him.

'Jacob?'

'Yes.'

'Give my love to the future Mrs Pengelly and tell her
I'll consider it an honour to give her away. I don't know
how you would feel about having Manny as your best
man, but it would make him the proudest man in the
whole of France.'

'I can't think of a better man, Ben. Speak to him when
you get back to the hotel. Tell him I'd rather have him
than anyone.'

24

The marriage of Jacob Pengelly to Emma Victoria Cotton, took place in the office of the British Consul-General. Ben gave away the bride and Manny performed the duties of the best man.

The British Ambassador, Sir Francis Bertie, travelled from Bordeaux to add his substantial prestige to the occasion. Afterwards, he hosted a reception in the Embassy, in a room where kings of England had trod.

Invitations had been sent *en bloc* to the staff of the English hospital, but only one doctor, two nurses and two orderlies were able to attend, such was the pressure of work at the Hotel Claridge.

There were many high-ranking French officials and military men at the wedding. The occasion was being used as an opportunity to lift the spirits of Parisians after the trauma of recent weeks.

After the grand Embassy reception, a much smaller

party took place in the Hotel Crillon, where the resource-
ful manager produced a magnificent wedding cake,
baked by the hotel chef.

There were also six bottles of the finest champagne
from the hotel cellar – which meant it was some of the
finest in the land.

As the British Ambassador had said earlier, the wedding was a small bright light which momentarily less-
ened the darkness of war.

The wedding celebrations over, Emma and Jacob
were escorted to the bridal suite by the manager of
the Crillon, an honour that had been accorded to only
a few newly-wed members of the world's wealthiest
families.

That night, Jacob and Emma began their married life
in more luxury than either of them had ever known
before, or were ever likely to experience again. For this
one night the holocaust that had threatened Paris and
claimed the lives of those who had been close to them
was forgotten.

In Cornwall, Miriam was seated in Ben's study when
she took the call from Paris.

The situation in France now seemed to be under
control and the telephone system was operating with
a fair degree of efficiency once more. The call had
been arranged some hours before and Miriam had been
informed it was coming.

First on the line was Ben, and Miriam immediately
expressed her anxiety. 'Is anything wrong? Has something happened to Lily?'

'No, Grandmother. Lily is fine and she's getting better. *Really* better. She's going to get well.'

'So, where is she now? Are you bringing her back to Tregarrick with you?'

'No, I couldn't bring her away from Switzerland, not after such an improvement in her health. She'll stay there until she's fully cured. Then I'll bring her home. In the meantime, she's in no danger where she is.'

'Then why are you telephoning to me? You could have told me all this when you came home. You *are* on your way home?'

'Yes, but I'm calling you from Paris and there's someone here who wants to speak to you.'

'Who? Who can possibly want to speak to me from Paris?' Miriam asked the question crossly. Why couldn't Ben have explained what his call was about without all this mysterious nonsense?

'Hello! Great Aunt Miriam.'

Miriam recognised the voice, but said, 'Who's that . . . ? Is it Emma? What are you doing in France, girl?'

'I've been driving an ambulance – but I'm calling you to tell you I got married this afternoon.'

'Married?! To whom?'

'To Jacob, of course. Ben said you'd be pleased.'

'Of course I'm pleased. You should have married him months ago, instead of leaving him to mope around Cornwall like some lost soul.'

There was a brief pause, then Miriam asked, 'Why have you married him in France? Why not have the wedding here, in Cornwall? Are you expecting?'

The long silence that followed her question was an answer in itself, but then Emma said, 'Yes, I am.'

'How far gone are you?'

'Four months.'

'Then it's as well you've got married now. You couldn't have left it much longer, girl.'

'Do you wish me well, Great Aunt?'

'Of course I wish you well, and Jacob too. By getting you pregnant he's showed the sort of gumption I expected from him.'

There was a sound from Emma's end of the telephone line that could have been either shock or amusement.

'Well, would you have married him so soon if he hadn't got you pregnant?'

There was another pause before Emma said, 'I don't know. Probably not.'

'Of course you wouldn't. I know it and so did Jacob. It was the only way he could be sure of you. Well, Ben's father was conceived out of wedlock, but Josh and I never loved each other any the less for that. There was a fire in both of us that was never quenched, even in the long evening of our lives. I wish the same for you and Jacob – and for the baby too. I could wish no more for anyone.'

'Thank you, Great Aunt Miriam. I knew you'd understand.'

'I do. But let me speak to Ben again. I'll see if I can't arrange for something more practical than wishes to start you both off in married life . . .'

Miriam agreed that Emma and Jacob could move into her home in the Gover valley. She also promised to give them a handsome sum of money for a wedding present.

When Miriam put down the telephone, she informed Jane of her sister's marriage and told her that Manny would be returning with the others within a couple of days. She then declared she would go into the garden to her favourite seat, to enjoy the autumn evening sun and digest the news she had just received.

When the sun had disappeared behind the hill and the shadows were lengthening, Jane went outside to bring her back to the house.

She found Miriam on the seat. She looked perfectly relaxed. Contented, even. At first, Jane thought she had fallen asleep. It was only when she went to wake her that she realised the truth.

Just as Emma and Jacob had come together in life, so Miriam had gone to join Josh, the man she had fallen in love with almost eighty years before.

It was a beginning and it was an end.

Other bestselling Warner titles available by mail: